6/6/96

To Betty -

Best Wishes,

Mantle Maley

D1508681

ARTISTS DIE BEST IN BLACK

A novel

By Martha Mabey

This novel is a work of fiction. The characters, names, incidents, dialogue, locations and plot are the products of the authors imagination or are used fictitiously. Any resemblance to actual persons or events is purely coincidental.

ISBN: ***0-9638639-4-0***

Book design by Ted Randler, 1614 Claremont St., Richmond, VA 23227.
Cover design by Angel T. August.
Martha Mabey's photo by Jay Paul

To Cindy and Louis,

Friends of the Heart

And with special thanks to Sarah and Loren Williams
for reading so many pages, so many times, so willingly.

I

I could tell Gussie was rolling her eyes even though I couldn't see her face. Her shoulders had that old familiar roll-your-eyes shrug. The two of us were on adjoining treadmills at the Richmond Athletic Club, trying to work up a sweat. In between breaths I was doing my best to explain what was going on at my art gallery that night.

"It's the sort of independent little film Robert Redford funds," I said, "made by a rich little Richmond boy, Lucy Moon's son. I told him he could use the gallery free of charge, that I'd be happy to oblige. Every movie maker starts with his friends."

Gussie turned to look at me. The sweat band across her forehead was soaked. "Not Lucy Moon, Richmond's most reclusive artist?" If I'm lucky, I manage to get at least one special "Gussie Steinhaus look" a day. I was off to a good start.

"'Lucy Moon, all right, though I don't think she likes the fact that he's spending so much money," I nudged the computer down a notch. It was difficult to talk while working out at the speed Superman leapt tall buildings. "...except it doesn't really come out of Lucy's pocket. It's an inheritance from his grandmother, so it's David Moon's to spend as he pleases. Even pretending he's Steven Spielberg. Lucy can only complain so much."

"Sold any of her paintings lately?"

"Not since those last six to Morgan-McDowell. The art business has been slow."

"Fifteen thousand a pop is not what I call slow, Rosemund," Gussie said. "You're hot. Get that through your head. Nobody sells six Lucy Moon paintings to a brokerage firm in Richmond, Virginia, corporate collection or not. I'm always setting people straight who swear you're sleeping with the CEO."

She pushed some buttons to stop her machine. "I'm starved," she said. "Let's get out of here." She mopped the shortest female hair in the gym with the skimpiest white towel in town and headed for the showers.

Gussie Steinhaus is one of my artists. Not that an art dealer ever owns an artist—though certain dealers, whose names will never pass my lips, like to give the impression talent is exclusively theirs to buy and sell. Gussie has been with me since I opened the gallery. She designs furniture. Not sweet little pieces with curlicues, but bold, loud chairs and tables that are all angles and neon colors. "Stuff to make you breathe hard," says my neighbor, Bernard Lewis, the portrait artist. He should know. He owns eight pieces of Gussie's furniture which he stole from me when her prices were immorally low. Bernard likes to say he was only helping her get started. Even with that kind of support Gussie has a ways to go to catch up with Lucy.

"You invite Bernard to be in the movie?" Gussie said, as if reading my mind. She walked naked across the dressing room, her stomach flatter than mine, even when I was nine years old. Some women wrap themselves in towels in the gym, allowing one limb out at a time, like an insect escaping a cocoon. Not Gussie, who looks ten years younger than her thirty-five years and has breasts to die for. She lives in the nightclub district of Shockoe Bottom in an upstairs studio without a bathroom or kitchen. Neighborhood's great, she says, except on weekends when fraternity boys pee in her doorway and knock out street lights.

"I've invited Bernard and a few select others," I said, zipping the new $200 black skirt which took inches off my hips. "Since the scene is being shot in my gallery, David, the movie mogul, says I'm entitled to a few artists and genuine paying clients as extras." I added black tights and boots, a red sweater and huge gold earrings. "...'just as long as everybody doesn't look the same,' David says."

"Everybody in Richmond looks the same," Gussie said as she headed out the door, gym bag over her shoulder. "...and it doesn't even embarrass them." Gussie's gym bag is red and blue, handwoven in Oaxaca, Mexico, the type used by native women for market. Since Gussie wears no makeup and I need all the help I can get, I'm always a few steps behind her. This particular morning my hair was still wet, but the cut had cost the equivalent of a week's groceries so I knew it would look good when it dried. Not that my role in David Moon's movie was more than window dressing. The real star was Lucy Moon's paintings.

"Just show up at eight tonight," I said. "David arrives earlier to install his mother's stuff for the shoot. If somebody buys one, I'll give him a commission. Camera crew's due at seven. The place'll be crowded."

"Your openings are always packed," Gussie said, "whether they're on film or not."

"Oh, yes, and wear black. David thinks artists should always wear black."

Gussie drives a red Chevy pickup she's owned since graduate school. I own a temperamental ten-year old black Jaguar I inherited from the divorce settlement with the Phantom. Although the Beast is in the repair shop as often as it's out, and never runs when it rains, it makes people think I sell Lucy Moon paintings every month. I would never get rid of it. Sometimes it'll even outrun Gussie's pickup. Gunning our engines, we headed for our favorite coffee shop in Carytown, the trendy area where my gallery is located, to see who could claim a fat free muffin first.

II

A Lucy Moon painting is no ordinary work of art. As Lucy would be the first to tell you, she's in a category by herself. Some people, searching for a label, say her work resembles Magritte. "Surrealism", they call it. Lucy, naturally, has created her own term—"adapted illusions"-which is another way of saying that you can see the world any way you like. Since I've been in the business, we've enjoyed an on-going feud over commissions. I claim the gallery should get its usual 45%. Lucy, bless her heart, poor-mouths her way down to 30%. The last batch of adapted illusions I sold to Morgan-McDowell paved Lucy's two mile driveway from the road to the converted tavern where she lives and works in the gentrified farm land of Goochland County.

But even though we've been known to yell at one another, something we're both getting better at, Lucy and I are thick. We go way back. We were friends before I became an art dealer, when I was married to the Phantom and Lucy was married to...but never mind...Lucy's family life has always been a bit odd. And that was the past when we believed we would be poor forever if we were single. Now Lucy Moon's canvases adorn corporate walls from the Chase Manhattan Bank to some Japanese enterprise in Los Angeles whose name I couldn't pronounce even when I held the check in my hand.

"Careful with those paintings," David was saying, as he paced back and forth across the gray carpeted floor of the gallery. He was wearing jeans and a tee shirt, a gold earring and the requisite baseball cap on backwards. His hair curled beneath the cap and down the back of his neck. Standing in the warm light reflected off the white brick walls of the gallery, he could have been fifteen.

"You look like a young Clark Gable," I said.

He squinted. "Who?"

"Don't make me show my age, David. Every morning I work hard just to stay even."

At the opposite end of the gallery a female in combat boots, who looked from the rear like a teenager, was struggling with two paintings. Helping her was a tall young man whose shoulders lunged forward like the wings of a crow. The two paintings were from Lucy's most recent forest series. Each was a rectangle, four feet by six feet, Lucy's trademark shape. Across both canvases, painted to hang in midair, were black plastic streamers. Bunches of wild flowers, more brilliant than life, grew between clusters of heavy-limbed trees. Branches and petals were caught in the plastic in such a way that you wanted to pull them free, even though you knew they were painted on the surface. People waited for years to purchase a painting from Lucy's newest group of trees and black plastic. Her most recent forest series had been a total sellout.

"Hey, David," the woman called, "which one of Lucy's paintings do you want here?" When she turned around I saw she was easily a decade older than David. She was looking at him like a puppy dog. Suddenly I felt very protective. He may resemble a young Clark Gable, I thought, same heart-stopping grin, same short, muscular body, same graceful movements, but that's no guarantee he knows how to deal with older women.

David waved an arm. "The one with the violets and the maple tree," he said. "Hang the daffodils and the weeping willow on the opposite side." He made a pirouette in the center of the gallery just below the curved metal staircase leading to the open balcony above. The upstairs space was considerably smaller than the major downstairs gallery and was often used to introduce Richmond's art community to the work of an unknown artist. Sometimes I managed to pick someone who really took off and a year later would be featured downstairs. "Just be careful, now. That's valuable black plastic you're dragging around." He winked at me. "Ain't that right, Rosemund? Fortune in here tonight."

"Oh, are you Rosemund Wallace?" the woman said. Her voice had that classic *Gone With the Wind* purr. "I'm Barbara Barksdale. It must be a real thrill to have your own gallery. I'd just love to sell art someday." She was speaking to me but the smile was for David.

I went upstairs to my small office situated behind the display space to avoid watching the mistreatment of valuables and the seduction of youth. I had offered the services of my installer, Austin Meyerson, but David had said his crew could manage. 'So you don't have to worry,' he said without a hint of irony. I reminded myself that movie producers had insurance and my job was to help artists earn a living. At any rate, I didn't think Austin would know what to do about Scarlet and Rhett, the labels I gave David and his lady friend.

As I turned the corner of the balcony gallery I heard Scarlett yelling at the tall guy with shoulders like a crow's wings. Peering over the balcony I saw the rest of the film crew arriving, two Asian females in jeans, Korean, perhaps, and an African-American with a beard who was lugging several expensive-looking cameras. Quickly I shut the office door, plopped in one of Gussie's art chairs, closed my eyes and took a few deep breaths. The chair was more interesting than it was comfortable but it was familiar and I knew exactly how to sit in it to get a lot of work done. You've known that boy since he was a baby, I reminded myself. He can handle anything, including the United Nations downstairs.

The phone rang. I grabbed it with my eyes still closed. When my eyes are shut, I can pretend I'm meditating. Somehow that always calms me down.

"It's Arabella," a voice said. "Something's going on at your place."

Arabella Georgiella, cross my heart, hope to die, it's really her name, is the art critic for the RICHMOND TIMES DISPATCH. She never asks questions, but simply declares. In the four years since the gallery opened, I've managed to get her attention three months out of five, "even though you're not main stream, Rosemund", Arabella says.

"A little movie," I said. "One of my artists' sons is filming a scene at the gallery tonight. That's all." I wondered how Arabella had heard.

"And you never called me." Declaration bordering on astonishment. Usually I'm filling her voice mail with reasons she should give a current show the proper coverage.

"Truthfully, Arabella, it's not an art event. It's a film. I'm really doing this as a favor to the artist. It's the kind of little movie that might end up at Sundance." As I talked I traced the design on my Gussie Steinhaus desk with one finger. It was a serpentine pattern that followed the lines of the desk only to circle back on itself in a childlike scribble. Gussie's designs always made me think of children's drawings.

"...and the artist's name is?"

"Lucy Moon," I said, realizing Arabella Georgiella had another story. Lucy was one of the best known artists in the city. She had worked hard to reach the top, put herself through art school without any help from her family, painted for years before she finally started selling. Because of her reputation, not to mention the price of her work, it was a badge of social and financial prestige to own a Lucy Moon painting. Since Lucy was also somewhat of a recluse, everybody wanted to own a piece of her, including art critics.

"I'll be right over," Arabella said.

New voices floated up the stairs and over the balcony. The pitch was louder and female, Barbara Barksdale and the two Asian women. Carefully I stepped out of my boots and lay down on the floor in my good black skirt to stretch my back muscles. Viewed from the heavy wooden beams crisscrossing the entire upstairs ceiling, I was a middle-aged woman with a decent pair of legs and a good haircut, who needed a break. I was also a reasonably competent art dealer who had relinquished control of the gallery to a group of 20 year olds who were rearranging the energy downstairs.

Typically the gallery was quiet and calm, a place to feed the soul as well as the eyes. Even my openings never reached too feverish a pitch, unless I designed them that way; like the month I had the mastectomy photographer from New York, and a thousand people jammed the downstairs. It always surprises me that I manage to have a couple of knockout shows a year. But the photographer's show had been partly for Harry, my partner, whose wife had died of breast cancer two years earlier.

"Rosemund?" Someone was knocking on the office door.

Quoth the Raven, 'Nevermore', I thought. Please don't bother me yet. The hard floor felt good to my back. It was a way to relax following a workout at the gym.

"Some black dude to see you, Rosemund." It was not David. It was his friend with the crow shoulders, calling me by my first name even though I was old enough to be his mother.

"It's probably Tyrone," I said, "wanting to shovel the walk."

"It's not snowing," Crow Shoulders said.

"You don't know Tyrone," I said. "Let me get my shoes. I'll be right down."

"Uh, one more thing—"

"Yes?"

"The guy's carrying a giraffe."

The man standing in the doorway was well over six feet tall, at least 220 pounds of muscle and had a black patch over one eye. He wore gray polyester pants and a striped rugby shirt stretched tightly over arms the size of Gussie's waist. A brightly painted giraffe, which appeared to be mostly neck, was carved from a long thick piece of wood and rested in the crook of one arm.

It definitely was not Tyrone.

"I'm Rosemund Wallace," I said, feeling very small.

"I saw the lights and the people," said the man, "so I figured somebody here could take a look at my animals." His voice was as soft as the September day.

"Well—the gallery's officially closed," I said. "We're getting ready to film a movie." The giraffe stared at me with big soulful eyes. It was beautifully painted, all yellow and black spots, with wild eyes and a mouthful of glistening teeth and a red tongue. It not only had personality, it had an attitude. I reached out to touch it.

The man laughed. "Hard to keep your hands off, isn't it? I got more in my truck, some snakes, a hyena, bunch of fish."

"Hey, you an artist, man?" David had come up behind me and put his hands on the giraffe, too.

"This is David Moon," I said by way of introductions. "He's shooting the movie tonight."

The man in the doorway made a courtly gesture as he shifted his huge bulk so he could shake David's hand. "Nature is the artist," he said, "I'm merely the Lord of the Woods. The animals come floating down the river to me so I can bring them to life."

"But you carved this giraffe?" David persisted.

"No, no, it's driftwood. I find the piece and see the animal. No carving, just paint. What I saw first in this one was the teeth. Then it became a giraffe."

By now the film crew had stopped what they were doing and had gathered around the doorway, like Noah, sniffing for rain.

"Bring in your ark," I said, "so we can see your animals."

I wondered what Harry would say. He had been burned a couple of years ago by some so-called 'folk artists' and refused to trust anyone without a resume an inch thick. We had friendly disagreements about whose work to show and why. But since I put in the hours and he only put up the money, Harry listened to me most of the time. He could hardly run an art gallery and tend to his cardiology patients simultaneously. And Harry wanted to be associated with a gallery. Even a quirky one like mine. In a way, it validated his own extensive collection of contemporary paintings and sculpture.

"Oh—and what's your name?"

"Mayo Johnson." He looked over my head into the gallery, now filled with Lucy's paintings and the portable lights David's crew had set up for the filming. Slowly his unobstructed eye moved from one painting to the next. I wondered what he was thinking. The first time I saw a studio filled with Lucy's paintings I couldn't talk for half an hour.

"I used to box," he said, touching the patch, "state heavyweight champion 'till I lost my eye. Now I got a second vision." He glanced down at me. "You do these pictures? They're really, uh—different."

I shook my head. "I just run the place," I said. "David Moon's mother is the painter." The giraffe looked even better in the bright gallery light. I recognized the old familiar twinge in my chest whenever I stumbled onto something important. It had never failed me. Being an art dealer was a calling. I had to see the other animals Mayo Johnson had in his truck.

"You want to be in a movie, man?"

Mayo Johnson turned to look at David. A slow smile transformed his face.

"The giraffe, too, man," David said. "Your stuff is gonna make you more famous than boxing ever did."

David, who loved to play to an audience, had just expanded it to include the Lord of the Woods. With that kind of power, no wonder he wanted to be producer, director and star.

III

By the time the four actors and all the extras arrived, the giraffe was hanging against the back wall above a Lucy Moon painting featuring a hooded figure dressed in black plastic, standing at the edge of a forest and loosely bound with a red silk cord. Tree branches seemed to tug at the edge of the black plastic, either to free the figure or to console it.

"Nice giraffe," Gussie said as she sipped a glass of wine and stared at the painting and the wooden animal. "Goes well with black plastic." She wore a short black dress, black platform shoes and white socks. She had painted her fingernails black, too.

"New artist," I said, "totally self-taught. A cross between folk art and Art Brute'. Mayo Johnson. David invited him to be in the movie. Maybe I'll do a show for him. He went home to change clothes and get his wife."

Arabella Georgiella stood in one corner, notebook in hand, talking quietly to Lucy. Small boned and slim, Arabella had brown eyes and creamy skin. She was wearing a calf length silk skirt and a black leather motorcycle jacket. Without the jacket she could have passed for the heroine of *Wuthering Heights*, which, of course, was the reason for wearing it.

The star artist of the evening, Lucy Moon, usually wore sweat pants and an old plaid shirt. Tonight she was decked out in a long green dress, an antique jade necklace and a hat with a feather. I almost didn't recognize her. As I watched her take her place in front of her paintings I thought how strikingly handsome she was, especially with the hat flattering her angular features. Too bad she ventured out so seldom. People came to her shows as much to see her as her paintings. I was pleased to see her talking to Arabella with such animation. Both women were about the same height—short—not much taller than five feet.

Good, I thought. A lot of small females here, just like me. I wondered how the tall drink of water who was my red-headed competition across town felt as she towered above her clients. But I guess if you look like you should be on the cover of VOGUE you're supposed to tower.

Peter and Ginny Plagman, two of my favorite clients, were also looking at the plastic draped figure in Lucy's painting. I wondered if they were picturing it in their nearby Fan District row house with the antiques and oriental rugs. They were dressed in black and weren't even artists.

"Too weird for me," Peter said.

"My mother would think we'd really gone off the deep end," said Ginny.

My neighbor, Bernard Lewis, who was standing as close to Peter as propriety would allow, chuckled. Bernard had confided that in his opinion Peter was the most attractive man in the entire city and I found myself examining him in a new light. Bernard was sipping Perrier and had brought his own lime.

"Over the years she's done a lot of these black plastic paintings," Bernard said. "Took her a while to get people to buy them. Now she's got Rosemund, best promoter in town. I've known Lucy for ages; met her when she was still married. Big on angst and entrapment. In this one, though, if you look closely, you can see that the silk cord is untied. The figure is free."

"If it were me," said Peter, "I'd get rid of that black plastic sheet, run through the woods and get the hell out of there."

Five or six other artists were looking at the paintings. Their comments were the typical mix of admiration and cynicism. Lucy was considered one of the most important painters in the area. Didn't hurt, either, that she had been written up in a few critical art journals. People say I'm lucky to be her dealer. I moved away from Peter and Ginny. I didn't want to hear Bernard's response. It was bound to be irreverent. And this was a serious movie.

Harrison Brown, M.D., my business partner, dressed in a gray custom-made silk suit, bolo tie, and burgundy handtooled boots, was having a verbal battle with David's bearded cameraman about the lighting. I made a mental note to ask him where he got the abstract gold pin in his lapel. He had been spending more time on his appearance lately. It was a good sign.

"There's too much glare with those spots," Harry said. "The paintings don't look right. This is a scene in an art gallery. The art has to look good." Harry prided himself on his ability with lighting. I had to admit he was a real professional. 'Comes from years of lighting my own stuff,' he says with the proper degree of modesty. Our shows are always the best lit in town.

"The actors have to look good," the cameraman said. "The art is only background."

Harry glanced in my direction. I shrugged. '"It's not our show, Harry," I said. "We're only two of the extras. Pour yourself a glass of wine. It's better than what we usually serve."

The other six clients I had invited to be in the movie had arrived by this time. Mayo Johnson, too, had returned with an attractive woman in a brightly printed dress and head wrap of kinte cloth. He introduced her as his wife, Billie. Mayo was wearing a loose black silk shirt trimmed in gold over black silk trousers and a black African silk crown with a gold "X". David took them to meet his mother so that Lucy and Mayo could admire each other's work. I wondered how Lucy felt sharing the limelight with a giraffe.

The crowd, the film lights and our lights made the gallery very warm even though the late September evening was brisk. Cooling the place was always a problem when a lot of people were there. If an opening got too crowded and too hot we just propped open the front door and let the art lovers spill out onto the sidewalk, wine glasses in hand. Neighboring merchants loved it. It added to

Carytown's reputation as THE area of Richmond to shop and be seen. In fact, Carytown was on its way to becoming a second Georgetown, minus the parking problems.

"Go upstairs and open the bathroom window, Harry," I said. "We've got to get some more air in here. It's sweltering."

Standing in the back of the gallery I surveyed the crowd. Like special guests at a private party, they were all people I liked. It made me feel good to see them there. An ex-Boston artist, scheduled for a January show, was talking with a twenty-year old painter I had discovered while he was still in school. I was certain both painters were destined for great things. A couple who purchased something almost every month was looking at a price sheet. I wondered if they were practicing for the scene or whether they were seriously interested in Lucy's work. It would be a stretch for them, both in terms of content and price. But that was something the gallery had been able to do since I opened it several years earlier—push people, help them grow, expand their vision. I was modest, but not overly modest. I knew what I was able to accomplish.

"Just your thing, isn't it?" Gussie said in my ear. "You must be sighing with contentment."

Instead of telling her I was feeling more satisfaction than I cared to acknowledge, I indicated the crowd with my wine glass. "You lied when you said everybody in Richmond looks alike," I said. "Nobody would guess this group was partying a few blocks from the home of Robert E. Lee." Of course, Lee did not quite live next door. His house was on Franklin and Grace, not far from St. Paul's Church and the home of the illustrious governor of Virginia. She was right about the contentment, though. Everything was going just the way it should.

"Okay, people, lemme have your attention." David clapped his hands in the center of the gallery. There was a warm glow to the room and the same sense of anticipation I always felt ten minutes before the doors opened to a new show. "When the camera starts rolling I want you to be talking to each other, just like a real opening. The four actors will be standing where they are now and the camera will be on them. Pretend they're folks just like you—come to see some new art. Don't look at the camera. Just act natural."

He glanced around the room. Scarlet and the Crow hovered behind the camera near the front door. Everyone stood a little straighter and smiled a little brighter. The Beard looked at Harry out of the corner of his eye, made just the right amount of noise for Harry to notice him, and then adjusted a spot light one final time.

"Action," David said, "roll 'em."

IV

It was not over until after midnight. Two of the actors stood on the sidewalk outside the gallery, smoking cigarettes and talking with Barbara Barksdale and the Korean women, whose names, I had learned earlier in the evening, were Mee and Connie Lee. Arabella, Lucy and Mayo were sitting on the curved metal stairway that led to the balcony. In between shots, Arabella had been scribbling furiously in her notebook all evening. I wondered what kind of story would emerge. Arabella could take the most disparate elements and create a masterpiece of an article.

"It's late, Rosemund," David said. He looked exhausted. "What if I get a key to the gallery and come back early in the morning to move Lucy's paintings and clean up? The gallery's closed on Sunday."

I was tired, myself. I wrote down the code for the alarm system and told him I'd come by late Sunday afternoon to check on things.

"The place'll be spotless," he said. "I'll have your stuff back on the walls just like it was. You won't even know we've been here."

And, of course, I believed him.

Bernard often worked on Sundays. I tapped on the door to his studio before I unlocked the gallery.

"Great party last night," he said. "Do you think we'll ever see the movie?"

"If David doesn't run out of money," I said. "He told me the gallery scene meant the film was half done. Has he been here this morning?"

"Somebody's car is out back. I don't know what David drives. Could be his. Ask Beverly and Jack. They see everything that goes on in the alley." Beverly and Jack lived on the opposite side of the gallery from Bernard.

In a garage.

Beverly and Jack are our local street people. Beverly has a large abdominal tumor that makes her look perpetually pregnant. Jack is thin and wiry and never without a cigarette. They had currently taken up residency in a rundown garage behind a former beauty shop that had been sold and earmarked as an upscale boutique. Every new store that opened in Carytown drove up the real estate taxes for the rest of us. But nobody complained too loudly. The new shops also brought more people to the area. And more people meant more business for everybody. It also meant the street people were being forced to look for other places to live. Bernard and I wondered when it would be Jack and Beverly's turn.

"I hope it's somebody else's car," I said. "David promised to have everything out of the gallery by now."

"See you in the movies," Bernard said and went back to the portrait he was painting.

As I unlocked the front door I discovered the alarm system was off. There was no sound announcing my entry.

"David? You in here?"

No response. Several of Lucy's paintings had been removed from the walls and were stacked neatly against one side. The gallery looked lonely with only a few paintings in place and no spot lights on them. The partial emptiness of the space seemed to accentuate the nail holes and marks on the white walls. There were also stains on the gray carpet, wine spills or something. I'd have to repaint, and have the floor cleaned.

"Damn," I said. "...David, are you upstairs?"

The gallery was very quiet. He must have gone across the street to McDonald's, I decided, uncertain as to whether to go after him or to attack the ever-present stack of paperwork in the office. I relocked the door and started up the stairs.

Except for fifteen or so paintings on the floor, the balcony gallery looked the same as usual. The space had not been used for the filming, only to temporarily store the paintings from my current show. The light in my office was on, however, and the telephone off the hook. The line was dead. David must have knocked it off, I thought, as I hung up the receiver and looked around. I like my environment neat and organized. Everything in its place, the chair behind the desk, file folders put away, art magazines in the proper basket. It irritated me that David was so slow in putting the gallery back together. Had he not been Lucy's son...

The bathroom door was shut. Probably still a mess, I thought. The actors had used the upstairs bathroom next to my office to put on makeup. As I put my hand on the doorknob to open it, I stopped suddenly.

I was uneasy without knowing why.

Slowly I turned the knob and pushed on the door. It opened a few inches and then refused to budge. Something was in the way.

A pedestal, I thought. Someone has left a pedestal on the other side of the door. I pushed again. It refused to give. It wasn't a pedestal. It was something heavy blocking the door.

Oh God, I thought. And closed my eyes.

When I opened them I was halfway down the stairs. With a shaking hand I unlocked the front door and raced for Bernard's studio. I pounded on his window. The framed portrait peering out at me had blank eyes and a frozen smile.

"What's the matter?" The alarm on Bernard's face as he opened the door must have reflected my own fear.

"I don't know. I hope I'm just imagining things. But you've got to come next door and go upstairs with me. There may be a problem."

Back in the gallery with Bernard close behind, I paused before we climbed the stairs to the balcony. The space beneath the circular stairway was almost claustrophobic. I considered turning on the air-conditioning and then realized I was trying to postpone going upstairs. I swallowed hard and went first. When we reached the balcony I turned and said, "Something's blocking the bathroom door."

Bernard looked at me sharply. I watched him take a deep breath and suck in his lower lip. "And you want me to see what it is?"

I wanted to say, "Yes, open the door by yourself so I don't have to look." Instead, I wiped my now damp hands down the sides of my slacks, prayed that I was being overly dramatic and said, "We'll do it together."

Side by side we shoved on the door.

It didn't give immediately. It was definitely more than a pedestal. Dead weight was the phrase that came to me. Whatever it was seemed to move backwards and then forwards in response to our pressure on the door. Bernard held the door open long enough for us to take a look into the bathroom.

It was David Moon. His body was hanging by the neck from a rope looped over the wooden beam just inside the door. He was still wearing his baseball cap.

V

Get back!" Bernard shouted. "Get out of here! Don't look. My God, don't look!" He gave me a shove, trying to push me out of the doorway. But I had to look. I had held him when he was a baby. I had rocked him to sleep. Fed him ice cream and laughed when he turned the bowl upside down on his head. Oh David...no...not this...I felt my chest go numb. My hands had no feeling even though I was reaching out to touch him. Black plastic. Slick. Something happened to my eyes. I couldn't see very well. The room resembled the highway from inside a car when automobile wipers are struggling to push rain off the windshield.

"Rosemund," Bernard said softly. In actuality, I don't believe Bernard spoke at all—only a whisper. He took me firmly by the shoulders.

"Rosemund, listen to me. Go into your office and call 911. The police, Rosemund, you've got to call the police."

I felt my head shake up and down. Yes, I thought, call someone to help.

"Help." It was my voice speaking into the receiver. It seemed small and very young. "There's been an accident. The Rosemund Wallace Gallery." That's me, I thought. It's here. My place. "In Carytown. No, I don't know the address. I can't remember..."

A man pried the receiver out of my hand. It was difficult to let go. It was Bernard, giving them some numbers. And saying "hurry".

I threw up.

Bernard put his arms around me. I hadn't remembered Bernard was so big. He was also warm. His arms enveloped me, and for a moment I felt safe.

We stood that way for a long time, Bernard holding me close, whispering some words again and again. And then we were downstairs, though I don't recall going down the steps. Two policemen were at the front door. One was black and one white. They weren't smiling. A squad car was sitting in the middle of Cary Street, its blue light flashing in the late afternoon sun.

"She's the gallery owner," Bernard explained, shielding me slightly with his body. "She came back to the gallery this afternoon to check on things. The boy whose body is upstairs shot a scene for a movie here last night."

"Who are you?" one of the policemen said. The other one was looking at Lucy's paintings.

"Bernard Lewis. I'm an artist. I have a studio next door."

"Where's the body?"

Bernard pointed towards the balcony. "Upstairs. The bathroom."

I watched the two men climb the circular stairs, their heavy black shoes loud on the metal steps. They seemed too large for the space, their uniforms incongruous against the white walls still partially covered with Lucy's paintings. They were upstairs for a long time. Bernard held my hand tightly and asked if I wanted some coffee. No, I didn't. Did I want a chair? No, not to sit. Just to stand and then to pace. I glanced towards Lucy's forest paintings. They were some of her best work. The black streamers appeared to flow out into the room. My mind began to stir. Why was black plastic in the bathroom with David?

"Detective Mavredes is on his way," the black policeman said from the balcony. "Don't go anyplace. He'll need to ask you some questions. Police ambulance is on it's way, too."

"Good thing it's Sunday," the white officer said. "Be less of a crowd outside."

Detective Mavredes had blond hair cut close over his ears like Gussie. His shirt was white and crisply starched. He wore a brown tweed sports coat draped perfectly across his shoulders. He smelled clean. He moved quickly throughout the gallery, barely glancing at any of Lucy's paintings until he was in front of the figure in black plastic standing in the woods. He stared at it for a long time. Bernard and I stood a few feet behind him, trying not to watch as the medics struggled with the problem of how to get David's body down the circular stairs. Finally they handed him over the balcony like a piece of furniture to the two policemen waiting below. They had wrapped him up so I didn't have to see his face again. As they placed his body on a stretcher and carried it out the front door, I wondered what they had done with his baseball cap.

Mavredes seemed unconcerned about the entire procedure. Perhaps it was because he had watched it all too often, I thought. "What's the point of this picture?" he said, indicating Lucy's painting. It was impossible to tell whether he liked it, was confused by it, or repulsed.

"Has to do with freedom," I said, "getting loose." This curt response was in sharp contrast to how I was feeling. I couldn't get the image of David out of my mind—particularly, his eyes staring and not seeing. My voice sounded strange to my ears as though I hadn't heard myself speak for a long time. It seemed absurd to be explaining the meaning of an artist's work when her son had died a few hours earlier in the place where that work was displayed.

Mavredes frowned.

"See—" I pointed. "The cord in the painting is untied." I felt ridiculous. Mavredes probably had never set foot in an art gallery in his life. Words I would have used with a collector sounded forced and artificial. I remembered how easily Bernard had explained Lucy's work to Peter and Ginny Plagman the night of the filming.

Turning to me, Mavredes said, "Did you get a good look at the boy when he was upstairs?"

"What kind of a question is that?" Bernard said, frowning.

I tried not to recall how David's face looked, the color of his skin especially. His baseball cap had been perched on top of his head as though he had reached up and adjusted it just as the noose was tightening around his neck. The baseball cap is what I wanted to remember. He had worn one since he was six years old, long before they became de rigueur.

"He was a family friend," Bernard said. "You can understand how hard this is for her." He gestured around the room. "The boy's mother did these paintings. David used them in the movie. Who's going to tell her what happened?"

The detective unbuttoned his jacket and turned his back on Lucy's painting. He was wearing suspenders and a revolver strapped beneath one arm. "The boy was hanging by a red cord—or rope," he said. "Did you see that?"

I shook my head and looked at Bernard. Had the rope really been red? This line of questioning was making me sick. All I could think about was Lucy.

"I noticed," Bernard said. He reached over to squeeze my arm. It was very comforting.

"He was naked," Mavredes continued, "except for the black plastic draped over him like a Roman toga." He pointed towards Lucy's painting. "Coincidence, isn't it?"

"I saw the plastic," I said. "I touched it. I didn't remember how it was—was draped."

"Black plastic and red cord," Mavredes repeated. He pursed his mouth and frowned. "Freedom, huh? How do you know this picture is about freedom? Why isn't it just some sadomasochist tied up in the woods?"

"Art is like life," I said, sounding more confident than I had intended. "Sometimes you have to look beyond the obvious."

Mavredes irritated me. But then, I needed to be irritated at somebody. The red rope and black plastic bothered me, and for reasons I couldn't quite put my finger on. Where had I seen sheets of black plastic?

Mavredes seemed unable to stand still. He shifted his weight back and forth, bouncing slightly on the balls of his feet. I had the sense that he could be out the door in two seconds if somebody moved wrong. "Got any more of this bondage stuff?" he said.

"Lieutenant..."

Then he smiled. It caught me off guard. "Don't get bent out of shape," he said. "I'm not a complete Philistine. I even paint, myself. Nothing like this, of course. And I don't mean black plastic. Her technique is fantastic. I'd swear you could pick those flowers right off the canvas."

I felt myself exhaling in one long, steady stream. It made my body limp. I had been holding myself tense since I ran next door to get Bernard.

Bernard put words to the thought I was unwilling to articulate. "Is it suicide?"

"Hard to tell," Mavredes said. "I don't assume anything until the lab guys are finished." He gave me a sideways glance. "...never assume the obvious." Then he looked around the gallery and shrugged. "Locked building, rope deliberately strung over a beam, clothes piled neatly in a corner—all signs of a plan by somebody—probably the victim. But it's too early to know. The phone off the hook doesn't fit..." He shifted his shoulders again, not quite a shrug this time—more like a question. "The guys upstairs say fingerprints are everywhere."

"Of course they are," I snapped. "Dozens of people were here last night—in the bathroom, in the office, using the telephone. " If the phone was off the hook was David trying to call someone to say goodbye, I wondered, or to phone for help.

"There was a loose key in his pocket," Mavredes said. "We'll check to see if it fits the front door. I need a list of who else might have a key to the gallery, just in case..." He sighed and rebuttoned his jacket. "A suicide is a damn thing," he muttered. "Don't art galleries have chairs? No place to sit in the whole damn building. Come on, let's go across the street and grab some coffee. You can tell me who was here last night." He took one final look at Lucy's forest painting as we headed for the door.

VI

The converted tavern where Lucy lived in Goochland County had been built in the early 1800's and was a tall narrow building with living space on three levels. A living room, dining room and kitchen were on the level reached by steps up to the front porch. Lucy's bedroom, bath and library were on the top floor while her studio occupied the entire lower level of the tavern. Two out buildings had been converted into guest quarters not far from the main house. A creek which flowed across the back of the property was visible from the rear of the house. Windows from Lucy's studio opened out to a broad view of the creek. It was a beautiful, picture-perfect setting for an artist.

Lucy stood in the front door and screamed when Mavredes and I told her.

It seemed to take forever for her to lead us to the kitchen where Mavredes and I placed ourselves across the table and watched her cry for a long time. Eventually I got up to rummage around for the coffee pot while Mavredes talked to her about David. His kindness surprised me.

"I'm sorry," he said. "I'm sorry we have to do this. It's a terrible thing."

"He wasn't unhappy," Lucy said. She had pulled her hair back from her face and kept running her fingers through it like an old lady. Beneath the plaid shirt and sweat pants her body seemed stooped and suddenly crippled. She was not a woman who accepted physical comfort easily. I poured the right amount of cream in her coffee and placed the mug in her hands.

"He was in a good place in his life," she said. "He was willing to do anything to get that movie finished. Why? Oh God, why? Why?"

"Think," Mavredes said. "It will help you focus. Good place or not, he was bound to have his share of problems. Girl friend, maybe? Money? Depression?"

Lucy shook her head. "The usual," she said, "like everybody else. Broke off with a girl—woman, really—Barbara Barksdale, a few months ago. You met her. She was helping with the movie—the woman who wasn't Korean. A few disagreements with John Owen about the film..."

"Who?" Mavredes said.

"John Owen Smith, one of the cameramen. The disagreement didn't depress him, though. David was philosophical about Barbara and money. He never kept anything inside. Like with John Owen—he knew how to get angry and blow it off. " She stared out the window at the creek. We had arrived at the tavern when it was almost dusk. Now it was so dark the water below the house was barely visible from the kitchen.

"David never had any secrets," Lucy said softly. She took a sip of the nearly cold coffee, grimaced and handed me her mug.

As I refilled the cups something niggled at me. That instinct which told me when a piece of art was good also told me when something was not good. Barbara and David hadn't acted like a couple who had just broken up. Everybody has secrets, I thought, even Lucy Moon. What sort of secrets belonged to David?

Over 300 people gathered in the Memorial Garden of the Episcopal Church on Monument Avenue to bid goodbye to David Moon a week later. The trees surrounding the church were golden. Richmond in the fall is a photographer's dream. Gussie and I arrived together. Many of the people I knew. Artists, long-time neighbors of Lucy's from Goochland County, young people David's age.

I had expected the movie crew to stand together as the priest read the service for the burial of the dead from the Prayer Book. But they were scattered throughout the crowd, with their own friends, I decided. And yet it seemed odd to me, almost as though something about David kept them apart instead of drawing them together.

John Owen Smith, otherwise known as the Crow, towered above many of the mourners as he stood on the edge of the crowd, practically in the street. He scowled when I spoke to him, barely acknowledging my greeting. I wondered what he and David had argued about. Barbara Barksdale, the ex-girl friend, wore a dark dress, thrift store variety and clutched the wrought iron fence on the edge of the Memorial Garden, weeping quietly. In grief she appeared younger than she had at the gallery.

At first I was able to find only one of the Korean women from the movie crew—Connie Lee, I thought—and then I spied the second one with an older couple who might have been their parents. The bearded cameraman never appeared. I wondered why. At the filming he had seemed more interested in the movie than any of the others.

David's father was there, his face ashen. I had not seen him in years, and he had aged. He stood beside Lucy but they never touched. If David had needed money to finish the film, I wondered if he had approached his father. After a while, I had to look away. When I did, I saw Mayo Johnson, whom I had mentally added to my stable of artists, with his wife, Billie. He caught my eye and nodded. When the service was over, I made my way in their direction while Gussie talked with a couple of other artists she knew.

"Good of you to come," I said.

"We liked him," said Billie. "We're so sorry. It's such a tragedy."

"The police are calling it suicide," I said. "Have they met with you yet?"

"You talk to her," Billie said, patting Mayo on the arm. "I want to give my condolences to the mother."

Mayo was silent. He rubbed the vacant eye the patch had covered when we first met, pulled a pair of dark glasses out of a pocket and put them on. The glasses made his face impassive.

"Yes," he said, his soft voice barely audible above the quiet buzz of the crowd. "The police met with us, but I didn't tell them everything."

I was suddenly chilled in spite of the warm autumn sunlight showering us beneath the red and orange trees in the church yard.

"No?"

"You welcomed me into your gallery when you didn't even know me," he said. "A young man invited my wife and me to be in his movie when we were strangers..."

I waited.

"There's talk," he said finally.

"Who? Where?"

"Church Hill. Billie and I live in Church Hill. There's talk about David Moon."

Church Hill is the oldest section of Richmond. Very historic. Pre-Civil War. Beautiful restored houses next to slums advertised as developers' dreams. Certain Church Hill neighborhoods are enclaves of gentrification while others are scenes of the city's most violent drug deals and unsolved murders. Middle class blacks share the largest section of the area with an unwieldy mix of intellectuals, artists and welfare recipients of both races. I remembered David also lived in Church Hill, although that fact hadn't seemed important enough to Mavredes for him to mention. Next time I spoke with Lucy I would ask her about it.

"What kind of talk?"

"Some of the people he hung with—" Mayo shrugged and made a gesture with his hand.

"What about them?" I had assumed David's friends were the people who had been helping him make the film.

"Just talk," he said. "The boy was young. He may not have known what he was getting into..."

"Drugs?"

A shadow crossed Mayo's face. He shook his head without speaking, then turned so that it was impossible to see his eyes through the dark glasses.

"We can talk if you'd like," he said. "Maybe you can go down to the river with Billie and me next time I need a new batch of driftwood."

VII

"The police are saying it may be an accident," I told Gussie later that night. We were having a light dinner at Carytown's local Vietnamese restaurant not far from the gallery. "...accidental suicide. Flirt too close with death and you can make a mistake." I wasn't yet ready to talk about what Mayo had said at the church. "They think it might not have been deliberate—that he didn't plan to die. The black plastic and the red cord..."

"Kinky, they mean." Gussie took a bite out of a cold spring roll after first dipping it in sauce.

"Umm humm. Near asphyxiation to bring on orgasm. Terrific sex if you don't kill yourself first."

"Ever tried it?"

"No—my sex life with the Phantom was never that creative. The only rope I ever considered using would have been to strangle him deliberately." I refrained from mentioning a time early in our marriage when he suggested that I strap him to the bed so I could have my way with him—woman to man, reverse missionary position—but then the Phantom never could make up his mind about his position on anything.

Our waiter placed two huge bowls of noodle soup in front of us. Tiny chunks of shrimp and pork nestled coyly among the noodles. The waiter bowed and backed away. Gussie poked at a noodle with her chopsticks.

"David Moon never struck me as the kinky type," she said.

"How can you ever tell?"

"Artistic intuition."

She tried sticking some noodles in her mouth but they slipped through the chopsticks and back into the bowl.

"If you eat soup with chopsticks you'll always be thin," I said. I was nursing a Tsing Tao, the light Chinese beer I favored when we ate Vietnamese food.

"That's the idea," Gussie said, successfully spearing a piece of shrimp.

"What do you know about that kind of stuff?" I said. "—pushing the edge?"

"Near strangulation supposedly heightens orgasm," Gussie said. "Has to do with breathing—or lack thereof. Remember reading about that British guy, House of Lords or something, who was found dead with a plastic bag over his head and naked except for garter belt and stockings."

"Sexual secrets," I said. "We all have them. Take us, for example. As well as we know each other, we never discuss our sex lives. Maybe I'm the kinky type, or maybe I like women—"

Gussie gave me her special look over the noodles.

"You like men, Rosemund," she said. "You just never stop working long enough to—"

"Uh oh, it's starting," I said as a couple came through the door, spied us and headed directly for our table.

"Oh, Rosemund, what an awful experience," the woman said, grabbing my hand as they reached the table. She was dressed in a red skirt and white boiled wool jacket with gold buttons. A black hair band pulled her straight blond hair away from her face, exposing gold rope earrings. Over her shoulder dangled a small quilted purse on a chain strap. A whiff of "White Diamonds" settled over the table. Her husband stood a few steps behind her, his cheeks radiating the slightly ruddy flush exhibited by so many white men in Richmond of a certain age and a certain whiskey capacity.

"Armistead and I saw it on the news the night after it happened," she said. "Everybody's talking about it. I suppose now you'll be forced to close the gallery. And just when you were doing so well."

With great deliberation Gussie put down the chopsticks and picked up her fork. Then she stabbed a cluster of noodles, twisted them round and round on the fork and with a loud slurp slid them into her mouth.

"This is Gussie Steinhaus," I said, "one of my artists."

"Oh," said Mrs. Armistead Foster, looking at the disappearing noodles, "didn't we read about you in the paper? Fabric design or something?"

"Chairs," I said, "and tables. Actually, it's artists like Gussie who depend on me to keep the gallery open. I could never close the gallery—no matter what happens."

Armistead was looking at Gussie's black polished fingernails. Then he looked at her short hair. "Good to see you," he said. He followed his wife to a table in the back of the restaurant and cast what could only be described as furtive glances in Gussie's direction the rest of the evening.

"Let's drive down the alley," I said after dinner, "just to look."

We got into the Jaguar and headed for the gallery a few blocks away.

The gallery had been roped off, both front and rear, until yesterday. Even though I would never have indicated to the Armistead Fosters, I had mixed feelings about reopening it for business. Yet it tugged at me like a neglected animal that needed to be fed. I inched the Jaguar past two interior design shops that had recently opened, past the photographer whose 1950's sign indicated the depth of his roots on Cary Street, past the architect's office and the hair salon.

"'Artists like me', huh?" Gussie said.

I stopped the car behind the gallery and stared at the iron gate which protected the wide rear entrance. It looked lonely and vulnerable without the yellow police tape which had covered it for days.

"'...who depend on you to keep the gallery open...'"

"Let's get out," I said. "I want to look at something."

"Who was that woman, anyway?" Gussie said.

"Junior League. Friend of the competition. In her own way she was trying to be sympathetic."

"Has she been in the gallery? She doesn't look like one of your buyers."

"Of course she's been in. We art dealers have our spies everywhere," I said. "Art is a cutthroat business. Limited market for designer furniture, especially. You know old money in Richmond is never spent in a place like mine. Why do you think the competition shows the work she does?"

"I'll never get used to Richmond if I live here a hundred years," Gussie said. She got out of the car carefully as if we were trespassing. "What are we looking for, Rosemund?"

"Just follow me."

I turned the back corner of the building and took a few steps into the dark space that separated the gallery from Bernard's studio. It was difficult to see in the dim light but I had been up and down the alley so many times I could do it blindfolded. After a few more steps I leaned against Bernard's wall to look up. Gussie stood close to me in the darkness. It didn't take long to grow accustomed to the shadows.

"The upstairs bathroom window," I said. "I asked Harry to open it the night we were filming the movie."

"So?"

"It was still open when Lieutenant Mavredes arrived. He asked some questions about it."

"I don't get it. What's significant about an open window? It would take Spider Man to climb this wall."

Behind us the brick was cold and damp. October was promising to be a month of rain. Since David's death at the end of September it had rained several hours every day. 'Almost as though the sky is crying,' Gussie said.

"The alarm system," I said. "When we left the gallery Saturday night I gave David the key and told him how to turn on the alarm. If the window was still open, the alarm would have gone off."

I could easily touch both Bernard's building and mine at the same time. I estimated the distance between them to be about three feet. The long, narrow passageway from front to rear of both buildings was at least sixty feet. The only window in the gallery was midway in the building in the upstairs bathroom overlooking the spot where Gussie and I were standing. A window in Bernard's building was almost opposite it.

"And?"

"But it didn't. The alarm company would have called me. Which means David never turned on the alarm when he left. Or he never left the gallery at all. Mavredes hasn't told me the time of death yet."

Gussie kept glancing behind her at the alley. Although she didn't urge me to leave, it was not difficult to tell how she was feeling. Her jaw was set. Her shoulders were scrunched forward. Her fists were little balls at the end of her arms. I wanted to tell her to go home and loosen up with a sketch pad, design a new coffee table or something. But more than that, I didn't want to be alone at the gallery today.

What Gussie said was polite and uncharacteristically patient. "...or he shut the window Saturday and left as he said he would, turned on the alarm, and opened the window again Sunday." Perfectly reasonable, only I was certain she was wrong. David would never exert that much effort. Especially without an audience.

"The window is very difficult to open," I said. "It sticks. Harry had to struggle with it and then propped it up with a piece of wood from under the sink. It's a hell of a lot of trouble. And the wood was still there when we found David's body."

"In the same spot?"

"Who knows? Harry just remembers opening the window and sticking the wood under it."

"You're saying David stayed at the gallery all night? That he didn't go home?" She shivered. It had begun to rain again. The closeness of the buildings provided enough shelter so the rain was more like a damp mist settling over us.

"In fact," Gussie said, "why don't we go home, Rosemund. If somebody sees us, they'll think we're nuts skulking around the gallery at night in the rain. The Jag doesn't do well when it rains, anyway. It might not start."

I continued to stare up at the window. "Lucy left before David did," I said. "So did the crew. Everybody Mavredes talked to said they told David goodbye at the gallery. They were all so beat they said they went home and crashed. Why would he hang around? Something doesn't feel right. His friends at the funeral..."

"Rosemund..." Gussie took a few steps closer so that our faces were very near in the darkness. I could see her eyes clearly. "...you've got to come to grips with the fact that David wanted to take his life, or that he was doing something risky and made a mistake. Stop trying to make a conspiracy out of a personal tragedy. Of course he would find an excuse to stay around if he had it all planned out. Isn't that what suicides do, make their plans and then fool people. He certainly wasn't going to announce to the world that he..."

"Shhh," I whispered, grabbing her arm. "Somebody's coming."

We shoved ourselves against the brick wall, hoping that the noise in the alley was someone passing who wouldn't look in our direction, nor even realize we were there. It was no later than ten p.m., but there had been some minor robberies in Carytown and a couple of muggings. People leaving a restaurant, I recalled, holding my purse tighter.

There were definitely footsteps in the unpaved alley that ran behind the stores in our block of Cary Street. We could hear the gravel crunching. It sounded like more than one person. And perhaps a dog. The noise stopped in the rear of the gallery. Examining the Jaguar, I thought, steeling myself for the sound of an object smashing the windshield.

Voices. Someone was talking. A woman's voice. Then I could smell hamburgers. Carytown gourmet dining—McDonald's.

I called out. "Is that you, Beverly?"

Silence.

"It's me, Rosemund Wallace, Beverly. From the art gallery. I'm here beside the building with a friend."

More gravel crunching. Then a high-pitched, squeaky little voice replied. "Yes, it's Beverly. Beverly and Jack. Been across the street for supper. You scared us. We thought maybe you was killed, too."

I made my way to the back of the building with Gussie close behind. In the shadows I could see Beverly's distinctive shape. The tumor caused her stomach to protrude as if she were nine months pregnant. On her head she wore her customary gray knitted cap. Plaid knee socks sagged just below the hem of her blue dress. High top black tennis shoes and a too short black coat completed her outfit. Jack stood behind the Jaguar, the glow from the ever present cigarette the only indication that someone else was there.

"You heard what happened, then?"

"Oh yes," Beverly said, "that young boy—everybody on the street is talking about him. He was murdered, you know. Nobody's safe anymore." She took a bite from the hamburger.

"The police think it's suicide, Beverly."

"Oh, no, they're wrong." Carefully she wrapped the partially eaten hamburger and placed it on the hood of the Jaguar. Then she removed a plastic cup from the McDonald's bag and took a delicate sip of her Pepsi.

I waited silently, hoping simultaneously that she was wrong and that she was right.

"The police just don't want to know the truth."

"And do you know the truth, Beverly?"

She almost snorted. "Of course I do! Anybody with half an ounce of sense knows the truth!" She took another sip of her drink. Again I waited. There was no hurrying Beverly. She followed her own timetable about everything. In the background the glow from the cigarette moved erratically. There was the sound of gravel disturbed as though Jack was shuffling his feet. I wondered if he was uncomfortable about what Beverly was about to tell me. Next to my shoulder I sensed Gussie breathing a little harder.

"He was a picture show maker, that boy, ain't that right?"

"Yes, I guess you could call him that."

Beverly took a few steps closer. There was a slightly musty smell about her mingled with the aroma of onions from the hamburger. The Carytown merchants surmised she bathed in the McDonald's ladies' room.

"Movie makers," she whispered conspiratorially, "the devil's pastime. Too much violence. Nothing fit for families no more. All communists. It's the government's duty to eliminate them."

Gussie could stand it no longer. "The government!"

Beverly jumped. Jack was by her side in an instant, the cigarette weaving in circles like a sparkler on the fourth of July. I put my hand on Gussie's arm.

"You think the government murdered David Moon and made it look like suicide?" I said.

"Come on," Jack mumbled, pulling on the sleeve of Beverly's black coat.

"Yes ma'am," Beverly said. "Government people in big black cars, slinking through the alley, keeping a body awake." By this time Jack had succeeded in coaxing her into the shadows near the garage they called home. She waved the drink cup in the air as if she were proposing a toast.

"Big black cars with a sign telling the world they're number one," she said, "watching the boy." And then they disappeared.

In the darkness I turned to Gussie. "That's why we sell your furniture in places like St. Louis and Dallas," I said.

"What? Because of communists?"

"...because Richmond is filled with two kinds of naysayers and we've encountered both of them tonight."

VIII

If the communists weren't enough, there was Tyrone. He stopped me just as I was parking the Jaguar in the rear of the gallery the next morning. I couldn't have been in a darker mood. Somehow Tyrone always caught me at just the right moment.

"I brought you a pumpkin," he said, holding it out in front of him, "bargain price. Got it from my uncle." Tyrone's thin face always glistened when he had been drinking. But today I was surprised to detect no more than a normal sheen to his skin. Whenever he needed money he stopped by the gallery with something to sell or some service he was certain I needed him to perform. Once it was a rabbit jacket just my size I could have for twenty-five bucks. Usually it was to pull the weeds where I parked the Jaguar. 'So it don't get all scratched,' he says.

Behind him his bicycle leaned against a garbage can. In the slightly bent bicycle basket sat another pumpkin. He followed my glance.

"For Bernard," he said.

"Bernard and I never decorate for Halloween," I said. Especially this year, I thought.

"You should get in the spirit," Tyrone said. "Everybody else on the street decorates. Little ghosts and candy. Stuff like that. What's the matter with you? Jack-o-lantern look good through all that glass in the front of your place. Put a spot on it. Everybody know you ain't scared of nothing."

A large expanse of glass in the front of the gallery reaches upwards two floors creating a dramatic entrance to the building. A brick area inside the door is where I usually put sculpture so it can be lighted and easily seen from the street. Somehow a jack-o-lantern did not fit the bill. A large neon sign saying 'Rosemund Wallace Gallery' hung an appropriate distance from the top of the glass into the sculpture display space, which, since David's death had been empty.

"No," I said, "no pumpkins for Halloween. No watermelons for Watermelon Festival, no Christmas trees for Christmas…"

"How 'bout a turkey for Thanksgiving?"

"Get outta here, Tyrone. These past few days have not been easy."

His grin disappeared. "Yeah," he said. "People coming by, pointing. Stuff like that." He straightened his shoulders and drew himself up taller. He was very thin. "What you need is a bodyguard."

"Why, thank you, Tyrone. I'll consider it."

Tyrone followed me as I made my way from behind the gallery where I parked.

"Hey," he said suddenly as we found ourselves between the two buildings that housed the gallery and Bernard's studio. "Lemme show you something. That window up there. Looks like somebody starting cleaning off the crud and then stopped. Classy place like yours don't need a dirty window." I stopped and looked up.

"What are you talking about?"

Carefully he placed the pumpkin on the sidewalk between the two buildings. Bracing his narrow back against Bernard's wall he began to slide his body upwards, keeping himself steady with his shoulders and arms wedged against the brick. He anchored his feet against the side of my building. I noted only someone with long legs like Tyrone's could straddle the space. I was much too short.

Like a crab scurrying across the sand, he scooted upwards for several feet until he was high above my head.

"You want me to be Santa Claus?" he called, "go down the chimney?"

"Get down here, Tyrone," I said. "You're going to hurt yourself."

But he continued to push upwards until he was just a few feet below the bathroom window. Then with a sharp scraping of his work shoes against the brick, he slid back down to where I was standing, landing with a more dramatic thud than necessary.

"Could of gone higher," he said, panting. "scraped my hands though. Rough going. Was right about the window. Looks like crap." He held his hands in front of him, an expression of exaggerated surprise on his face. "Bleeding," he said, "look at that. You gonna call me a doctor?" Then he wiped his hands down the side of his pants, grinned again and turned towards the street.

"Oh, almost forgot," he said. He picked up the pumpkin from the sidewalk and thrust it at me. "Hey, cut a mean face in this thing and put it in your window. Keep the bogeyman away."

I stood for a few moments holding the pumpkin and looking up at the window. "...somebody started cleaning off the crud," Tyrone had said. Spiderman, Gussie had said.

The pumpkin sat on my desk like an orange Buddha as I took the first telephone call of the day. It was the last person I would have expected, the tall redhead on the other side of the city, my competition in the art world of Richmond, Virginia.

"Rosemund, this is Lila Hunt," said the voice on the other end of the line. She pronounced her last name Richmond style, "Hoo-ont,"as if it had two syllables.

"Hello, Lila." I felt a sharp, unexpected tightness across my shoulders.

"I don't want to beat around the bush, Rosemund," Lila said. "I know you must still be reeling from the shock of David Moon's death."

I could sense something coming. My hands were unexpectedly cold.

"Nothing personal, Lila, but I'm reeling from the number of boorish, insensitive people calling the gallery," I said. "It's difficult to be civil some days."

Although we always smiled and kissed the air the way women do whenever our paths crossed, Lila never called me about anything. Her voice on the line caught me off guard. When that happens, I always talk too much. I heard myself going on and on.

"The questions I've been asked are unbelievable," I said. "Especially about Lucy. People want to look at her paintings. They particularly want to see the paintings in the gallery for the movie. Some people have even offered to buy them. It's the ugliest thing I've ever encountered in my life, and I'm only the art dealer. Lucy must be going through hell. I haven't seen her since David's funeral." I didn't add that Lucy hadn't wanted to see me even though I'd phoned her a dozen times.

"Well, actually, that's why I'm calling."

The tightness in my shoulders was worse. I needed to spend an hour working out at the athletic club. A few sets with the free weights would do it. As I swung them around, I could pretend they were Lila.

"Yes?"

"I just met with Lucy this morning," Lila said, "at the tavern. I drove out to Goochland. She didn't feel up to making the trip to town."

Considerate of you, Lila, I thought.

"We had a little discussion about representation," she said, "particularly about how difficult it would be for her to show her work in the place where David, you know…"

"You offered to help her out. Is that it, Lila? Help her extricate herself from an awkward situation?"

"I just offered to..."

"...to become her art dealer?"

"Well, yes. It seemed the best thing under the circumstances."

"Go to hell, Lila. The poor woman's distraught. Her son is dead. Nobody should be talking to her about business."

"Life goes on," Lila said.

I slammed down the telephone and sat for a long time staring at the bare walls of the gallery. Although I had removed all of Lucy's paintings, no one had arranged to pick them up. And I had canceled the next scheduled show. Both Gussie and Harry had been after me to get back in the loop, but I had no enthusiasm about facing a crowd again.

Lucy's paintings were part of the problem. Until they were out of the gallery I was certain there would be no semblance of normalcy. I decided I had no choice but to call Austin, my installer, and pay him to take the paintings back to Goochland to Lucy's studio. Except for the painting of the standing figure bound with black plastic and red rope they were stacked against a wall in my office. Detective Mavredes had taken that particular painting down town to police headquarters. He had not told me when he would bring it back. For all I knew he had hung it in his office and was studying it every morning.

"...trying to figure out the meaning of freedom," I muttered. I had been muttering to myself a lot the last few days. And now Lila had only made it worse. Every insecurity I had about being an art dealer seemed personified by her phone call.

The phone rang again. Numbly I let the machine get it.

I had lost Lucy Moon.

No, Lucy is my friend, I thought. She would never go with someone else. I've been her dealer forever.

Lucy has lost her son, I reminded myself. I have only lost a friend.

Maybe I should close the gallery, I thought. Maybe no one will come into the place except a bunch of sickies, thinking the scene of a suicide is performance art.

Abruptly I sat back in my chair.

"Performance," I said. The word came out of my throat loudly enough to echo through the empty gallery. David loved performances. That was what was behind the movie. He wanted to direct and act and produce and be a star. What if the black plastic and the red cord were costumes, an act that David was putting on, an act that had a terrible ending. But if it were a performance, I thought, it would need an audience.

By this time my head was really hurting. 'Don't think so much,' Gussie was always telling me, 'just see what comes.'

Yes, I said to myself. Stop thinking. I'm an art dealer. Who am I to be asking these questions. I can't let Harry down. I can't let my other artists down. I've got to get back to work. But the word 'performance' kept running through my head.

IX

One of the messages on my machine was from Lieutenant Mavredes. "We've established the time of death," he said. "Call me." Instead, I went next door to talk with Bernard.

"I see you've got a pumpkin," I said. It was perched on a paint splattered table next to the easel where Bernard was painting.

"It was a good price," Bernard said. "I'll put it on my front porch at home."

I sat down in the worn wing chair across the studio from the easel. It was the best spot in the room to study Bernard's latest painting.

"The hand isn't right," I said. "The fingers are too long."

Bernard stood back and squinted at the canvas. "Think so?"

"Look at it for a while," I said. "Men don't have fingers that long."

"How do you know this man isn't a famous pianist?"

"You would have told me," I said. "I need to ask you something, Bernard."

"If it's how to make pumpkin pie, forget it."

"David Moon worked on some productions with the Fire Station Players, didn't he?"

Bernard put down his brush. He was on the board of the Fire Station Players, an experimental theatrical group negotiating with the city for the rights to a deserted fire station at the end of Cary Street. Gussie and I had been to one of their productions—a gloomy play about a horse trainer who burned down a stable filled with horses and who then strangled the young stablehand who discovered his secret. He strangled him with a piece of red rope.

"Props and costumes," Bernard said.

"I thought it was something like that." I peered at the unfinished portrait. "Those fingers are definitely out of proportion, " I said. "Red rope is not something you find everyday. Suppose there was a lot of it in the prop box, or wherever you store props, not just a small piece used in a play. How easy would it have been for David to get at it?"

Bernard stood very still. I wondered if he always stood to paint. Lucy did, resting one foot on an old stool that had belonged to her mother so there was less strain on her back. There were two folding chairs in Bernard's studio in addition to the wing chair.

Bernard sat down in one of the folding chairs. "I don't know," he said quietly. "I could ask some questions."

"Red rope," I said. "Somebody should know if there was red rope."

"Suppose there was," Bernard said. "What would that prove?"

"Well, at least it might tell us where David, or somebody, got the rope."

"Somebody?"

As we talked, two police cars drove slowly past Bernard's studio. So slowly that the frantic traffic on Cary Street was forced to creep along behind them, the drivers swallowing their irritation at having to slow down. You could hardly give the bird to Richmond's finest. I walked to the window to watch them, wondering if they were checking out the gallery for some reason. A cloud seemed to hang over the place. Every time I heard a siren I expected the worst. The policemen pulled into the loading zone next door to the gallery in front of the hair salon that had recently been sold. Two men and a woman, who appeared to be waiting for the police, were standing in front of the building.

"What's going on?" said Bernard, walking to the window behind me. He had picked up his paint brush again. "Haven't we had enough excitement around here?"

"I don't know. Maybe they're our new neighbors. They're pointing towards the building."

As we watched, the police officers and the three people walked up the steps to the hair salon. One of the men unlocked the door and the group disappeared inside.

"I've heard it's going to be a clothing store," Bernard said.

"Expensive stuff, I hope," I said. "Clothes to wear to an art opening."

Bernard shook his head. "Wrong," he said. "I've seen what people wear to your openings. Look, they're coming back out."

Sure enough, one of the men and the woman came out the door and headed for the gallery.

"Let's go meet them," I said, "welcome them to the neighborhood."

Bernard stuck his brush in a jar of turpentine and joined me outside. The man and woman were looking through my front windows. Since the place where I usually put sculpture was still empty I wondered if they thought the gallery was closed permanently.

"I'm the gallery owner," I said. "Looking for me?"

"Oh," the man said. "Didn't look like anybody was here." He straightened his back and took a few steps towards us. He had that official air about him I had learned to associate with building inspectors.

"The police are getting ready to block the alley," he said. "They have a warrant to clear out the squatters in the garage."

"Squatters?" I looked at Bernard.

"That word went out with Venice Beach," Bernard said under his breath.

"You mean Beverly and Jack?" I said, "Carytown's homeless?"

"Richmond has shelters for the homeless," the man said. "I'm the architect for the building next door. We're going to tear down the garage and push the shop out the rear. It's going to be rather grand. But we've got to do something about the trash in the garage."

"I've never seen so much stuff in my life," the woman said, shaking her head. "I'm Mitzi Emerson. The shop's going to be mine, 'Emerson's Apparel'. She looked me up and down. I was wearing jeans, a black turtle neck sweater and a velvet vest. I must have passed, for Mitzi Emerson smiled slightly.

"I would think you'd be bothered by those people, too," she said. "The city should do something."

"The dump truck's just pulled into the alley," the architect said. "I'll go supervise." He turned to me. "If that's your Jaguar," he said, "you might want to move it. No telling how long the alley'll be blocked off."

He headed toward the rear of the buildings, his footsteps loud on the cement beside the gallery. The two policemen had already driven around back, blue lights flashing. I wondered where Beverly and Jack were. Asleep? At breakfast? Did the architect knock on the door of the garage and say, 'don't mean to disturb you, but you've got to find someplace else to live.'

The new owner of 'Emerson's Apparel' was studying me closely. "It was your gallery, wasn't it?"

I returned her gaze.

"...where that boy killed himself."

Bernard took a couple of steps closer.

The woman shuddered. Her silk jacket rearranged itself across her shoulders. "Gives me the creeps," she said. "I'd be long gone if it happened in my place." And then she was gone, too, her high heels making an even louder echo on the sidewalk than the architect's.

"There goes the neighborhood," Bernard said.

We watched for a while as two men in overalls tossed bag after bag from the garage into the waiting dump truck. The two police cars blocked the alley on either side of the truck. I felt like a voyeur. At the same time I wondered how in the world two homeless people could have accumulated so many things. Where had they kept them before they moved to the garage? There was enough clothing to outfit a Salvation Army Store.

"And I thought Beverly just had one dress," Bernard said.

"Where will they go?" I said.

"That's not our problem," the architect said. "Don't you want Carytown to have a certain ambiance? Isn't that why your gallery is here? Those people are trespassing on private property. It's against the law."

Dying young should be against the law, too, I thought.

I gave the dump truck a parting glance and went inside the gallery to call Mavredes. But before I picked up the phone I took a good look at the empty white walls, the nail holes, the still soiled carpet and Lucy Moon's paintings stacked in a corner. Some ambiance, I thought.

"He died about 3:00 a.m. Sunday morning," Mavredes said, "officially a suicide, questionable whether it was deliberate or not, but we'll never know. David Moon certainly can't tell us whether he was playing games. I've talked to everybody at the gallery that night. Pretty weird crew, some of them, but they seemed genuinely broken up. Lots of innuendo that David was willing to bend the rules to get what he wanted, that he liked to push the edge sometimes. Nothing specific, nothing to pin down, a few gestures and half-baked theories about how the 'artistic temperament' might have given David the idea that he could do things 'normal' people would never think of. Frankly, I get tired of that kind of stuff. You may have a different opinion, being an art dealer, but it seems to me that the same rules apply to everybody. Anyway, it doesn't look like foul play or murder."

"So you're not going to investigate any further?"

"What's to investigate? Kinky sex? Pressure applied a little too long. Poor judgment? Bad timing? He was alone. The door was locked. You said the only other people with keys were your partner, Dr. Brown, and the cleaning service. I think David Moon was just a young man experimenting with something that backfired. Emergency rooms are full of this kind of stuff. Younger they are, the more they believe they're invincible."

When I didn't respond, he said, "You still there?"

I nodded my head though he couldn't see me. "Yes, still here. So that's it? You're not going to talk to everybody again, just in case?" I wanted to ask him why he hadn't questioned Mayo Johnson more closely. Mayo knew more about David than he had told the police.

It was Mavredes turn to be silent. When he spoke, his voice had a slightly different tone to it. "Why?" he said. "You got something new to tell me?"

I thought for a moment about the road not taken, and remembered how Mayo had made a point of singling me out.

"No, " I said, "I don't have anything to tell you."

X

Five or six couples were strolling across the bridge to Brown's Island when Mayo pulled his battered blue truck into the parking area the next day. His wife, Billie, and I were squeezed into the front seat with him. Mayo had told me to wear old clothes and boots. He had on paint stained coveralls which zipped up the front. Neither the black patch nor the dark glasses had reappeared. His blinded eye had only the slightest film across the cornea. When he looked directly at you, it was barely noticeable. Only when he shifted his gaze in another direction was it apparent that something was wrong.

He lifted a plastic grocery cart out of the bed of the truck. "For the wood," he said as the three of us started across the bridge. "Easier than carrying it."

"Folks look at us kind of strange," Billie said, "especially when the pieces are big like the giraffe."

At midpoint the bridge arched high over the James River and then dipped down for the descent onto the island. Several of the city's major corporations graced the edge of the river—one of which had been the driving force behind the renovation of the riverside after waiting in vain for the city officials to forego their turf disputes and bring the city back to life. Since the Civil War, when it had been the site of a munitions manufacturing plant, Brown's Island had been a much discussed and much neglected piece of real estate. But when civic pride raised a wet finger to the wind in the form of business threats to the city's political structure, the island had been cleaned up. With its war ruins and sweeping view of the city and the river it was now both a tourist attraction and the scene for newsworthy monthly events which both the city and the business establishment claimed as their idea.

"We come here because the shore's not so littered with trash," Billie said. "Other spots along the river are terrible. You wouldn't believe what people throw out."

"Wood's got to be strong," Mayo said, "and have just the right twist so there's a head or a tail—or maybe a wing or a leg." He bent down to pull a jumble of driftwood from the roots of a rotten tree partially submerged in the water. Squatting, he separated the pieces, tossed two of them back into the water and stroked a third piece lovingly.

"I don't see anything," I said, peering at the wood.

"The eye," he said, "find the eye." He placed the wood in my hands. I examined it for a few seconds and then my imagination kicked in.

"There. Is that it?"

Mayo grinned. "You got it," he said. "What kind of animal you think it is?"

I returned the piece to him. "I wouldn't touch that one, Mayo. You're the artist."

He laughed and tossed the wood into the shopping cart. We continued walking along the shore for a while, examining and discarding dozens of pieces of driftwood. After about thirty minutes and a partially filled cart, we reached the back side of the island where there were fewer people.

"Let's sit for a minute," Mayo said, dropping heavily onto a gray outcropping of rock. As Billie and I sat down opposite him I realized he had picked a spot where he had a view of the entire island, all the way to the bridge.

"That boy," he said, "David..."

"Yes," Billie said.

I nodded my head.

"What have you found out about him?"

"I thought you had something to tell me."

He sighed. "So you don't know nothing?"

"Well," I said, "it's hard for me to believe he wanted to kill himself. When you're in the middle of something you want to do, you don't usually decide to end it all. And as far as I can tell, he really wanted to make that movie. I plan to ask the camera crew to let me look at the footage." Actually, I planned to try to talk to everybody helping David with the film as soon as I could figure out how to contact them. With Lucy refusing to return my phone calls I had to find some way to locate everybody without letting Mavredes know what I was doing.

"You think maybe that boy was queer?" Mayo said.

I shook my head slowly. "No, no, I don't. I've watched him as a child. I don't think so. He was a creative kid. When males are creative, it doesn't mean they're gay." I gave him a sideways glance. "...does it?"

Billie threw back her head and laughed loudly.

"I always liked to draw," Mayo said deliberately. He was not smiling. "In grade school the teacher said I should be an artist. She didn't throw away my drawings. She put 'um up on the bulletin board for everybody to see..." His voice became even softer. I had to lean forward to hear.

"In high school I played football. I was a big man, you know. Football star. Girls..."

Billie cast her eyes upwards and uttered a mock moan.

"...never did much drawing in high school."

"A lot of black male athletes," I said, "not many black male artists."

He nodded. "Took up boxing in the army. They told me I'd make a lot of money. When I got out I started getting calls from all over the country for fights. Then one day, it was a big fight, I got hit the wrong way. They took me to the hospital and I saw my career flashing before me. I said, 'Oh Lord, please don't take my eye. Please don't take my eye.'"

"They operated and God did the rest," Billie said.

"I see double now. I'm not totally blind in this eye. I can see if someone is throwing a punch, but I can't fine tune. It's like moving that dial on the end of the binoculars. I can't focus."

"But he's still legally blind in that eye," Billie said. "I'm not glad about the eye, but I'm glad he's not boxing anymore."

"One might say the universe intervened," I said.

"I wanted to be successful," Mayo said, reaching into the grocery cart for a piece of driftwood, "but I guess if it's to come to pass, God wants me to do it another way. There's more to life than banging someone across the head."

He stroked the wood gently as if it were alive.

"There's a certain crowd in Church Hill," Billie said easily, as though we had been discussing it all along. "The boy was with them sometimes—partied with them, things like that."

"David."

"Um hum."

"Whites and blacks," Mayo said. "Big parties. Coke. That kind of stuff. Trouble."

"Tell her the rest," Billie said. She placed her hand on Mayo's arm and left it there.

Mayo shifted slightly on the rock and looked over my head towards the bridge. Several yards away, a family, bundled up in sweaters, was spreading out a picnic in the sun. Two children were laughing.

"No women at these parties," Mayo said. "Only men. A certain set of older guys with money. Young guys invited. Creative young guys." He looked at Billie. She nodded her head encouragingly.

"What kind of older men?" I said.

"To each his own," Mayo said. "Not my taste, though." He paused. I couldn't understand his reticence. Gays were no longer people you threw rocks at, even in Richmond, Virginia.

"Tell her everything," Billie said.

"Guy I know was at a party when David Moon was there," Mayo said. "Birds of a feather, maybe..."

"Lots of straights go to parties with people of other persuasions," I said.

"That boy was with a lot of heavy hitters," Mayo said.

I waited. This was about more than sexual orientation.

"Governor of Virginia may be the biggest bird of all."

"The governor? But Clayton Brookfield hates gays. He's gone on record about homosexuals destroying the family life in America. I guess that includes Virginia, too—"

"Governor Brookfield," Mayo repeated, "doesn't visit Church Hill. But somebody on his staff does—somebody who goes around in a big black Lincoln

Towncar with a license plate that says number one."

"Just a coincidence," Gussie said the next morning while we were working out on adjoining step machines at the athletic club.

"Perhaps," I said, "and perhaps not. Beverly may live in a garage but that doesn't mean there's something wrong with her eyesight. Communists or no communists, what if there was a Lincoln with number one on its tags in the alley while David was at the gallery early Sunday morning? What if David had invited someone to come to the gallery all alone? You know it's important to pay attention to coincidences. Look how often a coincidence has led to something big in your life. Your furniture wouldn't be in D.C. if that designer hadn't stopped for coffee at McDonald's and decided to run across the street to take a look at the gallery."

"What did Mayo's friend say about the car? Who was in it?"

"All he told Mayo was that it was a white guy who worked for the governor."

"A lot of white guys work for this governor," Gussie said. "...few blacks, few women and certainly no gays."

"Right," I said. "No homosexuals in Republican politics in Virginia."

"Maybe you could tell Lieutenant Mavredes to talk to Mayo's friend."

"...and let the world know David might have been involved with drugs?"

"David's dead, Rosemund," Gussie said quietly. "It doesn't matter."

I stopped the machine. "Yes, it does matter," I said. "His mother and father are still alive. There's no reason to cause them any more grief."

Gussie concentrated on the step machine for a few moments. The back of her neck glistened. Her short hair was damp around her forehead. Finally she said, "I don't suppose you plan to talk to Mayo's friend."

"He's already set it up," I said. "We're meeting tomorrow night. That gives me two days to locate Beverly and Jack."

XI

But Beverly and Jack were nowhere to be found. Except for a few loose pieces of clothing, the garage behind the beauty salon, soon to be Emerson's Apparel, was empty. The new owners of the building, along with the trash collectors, had done a thorough job. The garage door, which hung open on broken hinges, created a gaping hole into the dirty, dank place which two people had once called home.

I went across the street to McDonald's, hoping that someone behind the counter had seen their two regulars. "Ain't been around lately," a woman told me as I paid for a cup of coffee. "Those two, they usually here every day. Somebody ask about them just the other morning." Then she leaned forward conspiratorially. "Folks say some rich people throwed 'um out of the place they was living."

"What folks?" I said, leaning closer.

"Them people they eat with most everyday. Ain't here now, but you can't miss 'um. Always sit in that corner on the other side of the door. White man in a derby hat, white lady with gray hair sticks out in all directions and a black sister 'bout my age." She jerked her head towards the door. "Some customers don't want to sit next to 'um, but they don't bother nobody." Then she lowered her voice even more. "The manager, he give 'um leftover stuff, you know, burgers been out longer than allowed, stuff like that." She straightened her body. "Could be us, you know, you and me, living off the street." And then I was no longer there for her. She looked through me to the next customer.

"Take your order, sir," she said.

I decided to camp out at the hamburger place as long as I could stand it. They had free newspapers daily. I grabbed one that had been folded inside out and took a small table by the front window where I could watch the street. Every ten minutes or so a woman came to the table, offering a coffee refill, one of the burger chain's latest services.

Jack and Beverly had not appeared by the time the lunch crowd began arriving. I slunk lower in my seat, hoping that no one would notice that I had been there for almost three hours. Throughout the morning I could see people going to the door of the gallery across the street, reading the note I had left announcing that we would reopen soon and then leaving. I wondered when "soon" would be. My sense of detachment from art shows and artists was almost palpable. A boy had died in my gallery. How could I pretend things would ever be the same.

Austin, my installer, had loaded Lucy's paintings in his van the night before and planned to deliver them to her studio that morning. I had left a message on her answering machine to that effect. I assumed she would let him in. There was always the chance that I'd feel better about resuming business now that Lucy's paintings were no longer holding the gallery hostage.

At 1:00 p.m. I broke down and ordered a grilled chicken, "hold the mayo,"sandwich. The multiple cups of coffee were playing havoc with my body and I had to eat. I could almost hear Gussie's voice ringing in my ear: "You ate WHERE?"

About 2:00 p.m., after one more trip to the ladies' room, I saw them.

Not Beverly and Jack. But three people who fit the description of their friends the woman behind the counter gave me; a white man in a battered felt hat with two women, one white, one black. The white woman's hair did stick out in all directions, I thought, as I watched them settle at the table on the other side of the door. The restaurant was nearly deserted in the mid-afternoon, but the three didn't go to the counter to order. They sat and talked with each other for a while. One of the women left the table and went to the ladies' room, brushing me gently as she passed.

I went to the counter, looked over the items which hadn't changed since breakfast, and reluctantly ordered a hot apple pie. The sticky juice in the pie dripped down my chin as I attempted to eat it unobtrusively, newspaper in hand, a few feet from the trio. By now I had read each section three times, including the classifieds. I noticed the cozy threesome still hadn't ordered anything. Maybe this is simply the place where they meet, I thought, to discuss world affairs. Finally the man got up, ambled over to the counter and returned with a tray filled with burgers, fries and drinks. Since I didn't see any exchange of cash at the counter I figured perhaps this outpost of corporate America had more going for it than simply improving the bottom line.

When the trio finished their meal I laid down the newspaper and walked to their table. "Sorry to disturb you," I said, "but I need your help."

The woman with the hair sticking out in all directions flopped back in her seat as if I had hit her. The other woman didn't even look at me. The man removed his hat, smoothed his thinning hair and frowned.

"I'm looking for Beverly and Jack," I said. "I need to ask them some questions."

"Never heard of 'um," the man said. His voice rumbled as if he were speaking from a cave.

"I don't want to hurt them, or get them in trouble," I said. "I own the art gallery across the street." I pointed through the window. "I used to see Jack and Beverly a lot when they, when they lived next door to the gallery. Beverly may have some information that could help me with a problem."

"Let's go," the white woman said, rising from her seat.

The black woman pulled a large shopping bag from under the table and got to her feet, too.

"Please," I said, "if you see them tell them I need to ask about a Lincoln

Towncar."

The man jammed the derby onto his head. "Towncar," he said, rolling his eyes. And then they were gone.

Bernard saw me as I crossed the street headed for the gallery. He was standing in the doorway of his studio. "Where've you been? he said. "I've been looking for you all day."

"Doing research," I said, "on what America eats."

"Well, forget all that," he said. "I wrangled a key to the Fire Station Theater. I thought you might want to go over there with me. We could look around by ourselves."

"Now?"

"Anything better going on? I noticed you haven't reopened the gallery for business yet."

"How could you tell?"

"Since you won't sell them any art, your patrons have been begging me to do their portraits," he said. "I'm booked for the next five years."

"That'll change soon," I said. Bernard always did me a world of good. He reminded me why I had gone into the art business in the first place. In spite of their quirks, or maybe because of them, I liked artists. I liked hanging around with them. I liked seeing their newest work. I liked the joy of discovering somebody whose reputation I might be able to help. But mostly, I liked the fact that with the best ones, you couldn't buy their souls.

"Mayo Johnson has enough work in his house for an exhibition," I said. "Maybe I'll put him in the slot where I canceled a show because of David. After that we'll get back on schedule."

"Glad to hear that," Bernard said. "I was getting a little concerned over all the business you were throwing my way. Come on. We'll take my car. The Jaguar can't be trusted to keep running. Besides, the damn thing's not very comfortable for somebody my size."

"I don't know, Bernard," I said. "I'm sort of...waiting for somebody." If Jack and Beverly appeared, I should be there. It was important that I talk to Beverly before I met Mayo's friend. I wondered if Beverly and Jack's friends would even tell them what I said. They didn't exactly invite me to sit down to discuss current events over a steaming cup of coffee. Since nobody had seen them in a while, maybe Jack and Beverly had moved out of town. The thought of homeless people moving out of town struck me as so typically middle class that I was too embarrassed to hang around waiting the rest of the day.

"Okay, let's do it," I said, "even though my car will never recover from such a vicious attack on its integrity." I took one last look at McDonald's and followed Bernard down the sidewalk between our buildings and climbed into his Volvo.

Although it was nine months old, it still smelled new. The Jaguar always smelled like oil paint.

The abandoned fire station being used by the theater group was only six blocks away. We could have walked. Bernard walked a lot, and jogged several days a week. But he knew that I liked my exercise organized and confined to a temperature controlled building filled with machines and free weights. I leaned back into the Volvo's leather upholstered seats and tried to forget the chicken sandwich and apple pie sitting like a lump in my stomach.

"Bernard," I said. "I don't want to get personal, but Richmond is a small town. What do you hear about parties in Church Hill?"

"What kind of parties? Naked women? Sex? Rock n' Roll?"

"Parties I wouldn't be invited to…"

"Why? Because you're a Democrat? Or because you're an art dealer?"

"You know what I'm talking about," I said.

"I'm the wrong person to ask," Bernard said. "Ever since Barry Lopez painted his swimming pool black and unleashed an orgy in his neighborhood that left me stranded in Shreveport, I don't go to those kinds of parties anymore."

"Shreveport?"

"Don't ask," Bernard said. "Here's the fire station. Look theatrical in case somebody's here."

The outside of the station had a slightly baroque appearance as if the architect didn't really want to design a building so mundane as one that housed fire trucks. With proper renovations, it might have housed a fancy restaurant or law firm. Even the stone trim around the windows and small doorway next to the garage sized doors for the fire engines seemed to be putting on airs. I could picture the firemen of an earlier era sipping sherry around a wood stove.

Once inside, however, the fanciness disappeared. The building was bigger than a two-story barn and was cold and dark, the cement floor cracked and paint peeling off some of the walls. The ceiling was so high it seemed to disappear into the darkness, giving the impression the heavens were not very far away. This created a spaciousness that comfortably enveloped the small wooden stage and folding chairs in the center of the building. At strategic spots were the only remnants of the building's former life, metal fire poles from floor to ceiling. Movable walls had been set up behind the stage for props and costume changes. It was a place that might easily have appealed to David Moon, a place where imagination would be forced to work hard to transform it into a new location every few months.

But that's what art is all about, I thought as I repeated to myself the description of Lucy Moon's work: altered illusions, manipulating images until the viewer sees what you want him to see.

"There's not a lot of storage space," Bernard said as he switched on some lights in the back. "Usually the director only keeps stuff being used in the current play." He yanked at several metal hangers draped with nondescript clothing and poked at a couple of wooden crates. "These are empty," he said. "Not much here."

"What does the props person actually do?" I said.

"Gets all the detail stuff that makes the play authentic. Sometimes it doesn't seem like much but if the script says a hero's stabbed with a butcher knife, a boy scout knife won't do."

"Wonder where you'd buy red rope," I said.

"You're sure the rope in that play you and Gussie saw was red? It didn't make an impression on me. I can't imagine why it was crucial to the story. Rope is rope, seems to me."

"We sat on the second row, Bernard. And I'm an art dealer, remember? I notice color." Whether the rope was red or not didn't seem to matter, I thought. Perhaps it was David's personal touch.

Glancing around once more, I had to agree with Bernard. There was not much there. I pointed to the wooden stairway in the far corner of the building. "What's upstairs?"

"It's where the firemen used to bunk," Bernard said. "The theater group uses it for makeup. There's a small bathroom, not big enough for the city to approve for public use. We've had to set up 'portapotties' in the back of the building during performances."

"Sorry I didn't know that when Gussie and I were here," I said. "Would have been a thrill. Let's take a look."

We climbed the steps and opened the first door off a long, narrow hallway. Inside were two metal beds, a number of folding chairs scattered around the room and several tables with mirrors propped up on top of them. A makeshift string of lights hung above the mirrors like Christmas decorations. The windows were painted shut. But I didn't have time to comment on the decor.

A man was sitting in one of the chairs, his back to the door, his feet propped up on a metal stool.

When we opened the door he almost fell off the chair.

"Holy shit!" he said, staggering to his feet, "scared the hell out of me!"

"Didn't you hear us downstairs?" Bernard said.

"Hell, no," the man said. He waved a handful of papers at us. "Been working on this script. Used to be the quietest place in town…" Then he took a few steps backwards. "Who are you, anyway?" he said. "How'd you get in?"

"I'm on the board," Bernard said. "Bernard Lewis. This is Rosemund Wallace. I was, showing her around."

"Fucking place is Grand Central Station," the man said. He grabbed his coat from the back of one of the folding chairs. "First that other guy, and now you. Thought I could get some work done on this script..." He waved the papers at us.

"I'm the playwright, you know. This is my production next month."

"What other guy?" I said, speaking for the first time.

"I don't know—'Jim'—'James'—something like that. Said he was on the board, too. He went through a bunch of trunks over in the corner, threw stuff everywhere, made a lot of noise like he couldn't find what he was looking for and then left. If you guys had a board meeting scheduled, the least somebody could have done is let me know. The director said I could work over here in privacy. Hell, fucking three ring circus."

"'Jimmy'?" Bernard said. "'Jimmy Travers'?"

"Could of been. I told you I'm the playwright, not the fucking social secretary."

"Who is Jimmy Travers?" I said.

"New board member. Real hot shot. Thinks he can get some state money for the theater project."

"With Brookfield as governor?"

Bernard waved his hand in the air. "That's just it," he said. "Jimmy Travers works for the governor."

XII

Harry was sitting at my desk talking on the telephone, when Bernard and I returned from the fire house. We didn't find any red rope, but I discovered something, or someone, I was certain was more important. The difficulty was in not showing my excitement to Bernard while dragging out of him everything he knew about James, or Jimmy, Travers. Not to mention trying to figure out why Jimmy Travers had been at the fire house ("looking through stuff," the playwright had said). Looking for red rope, perhaps? Bernard had promised to find out whether the script for the play I saw with Gussie required that the rope which strangled the stable boy be red.

"Do we have an art gallery or not?" Harry said after he hung up the phone. "I've taken six calls since I let myself in. Covering for you is not my idea of a fun day off. People want to know when we're reopening."

"I'd forgotten you were coming," I said. "I've had a lot on my mind." Jimmy Travers was one of the governor's aides, Bernard had told me. 'Junior' aide, he had emphasized. Jimmy Travers had not endeared himself to Bernard. Bernard did say that he had no idea whether Jimmy had ever met David Moon. I wondered if a junior aide would have access to the governor's private Lincoln.The whole thing just seemed odd to me. When that happened, I was not able to let something go until the odd aspects either cleared up or became so predictably peculiar that they were understandable.

"You said you wanted to talk about some ideas you had about David's death," Harry said, "but why me? Why not Lieutenant Mavredes, who considers the case closed?"

"How do you know he considers it closed?"

"You're not the only one who cared about David," Harry said, observing me closely. "I called Mavredes myself, to find out what was going on."

The office seemed very empty without Lucy's paintings. I had thought I would be relieved when they were gone. Instead, the emptiness was a reminder that she was gone, too.

"I think David invited somebody to the gallery after the filming was done," I said, "somebody he didn't want at the shoot, somebody special. He waited for him, or her, and then let them in and locked the door afterwards." Maybe someone in a black limousine, I thought, someone like Jimmy Travers who might have access to the automobile used by the governor of Virginia. It would be easy enough to call Mavredes. But what would I say: that two homeless people claim to have seen a black car with number one on the tags in the alley the night David died? And a man I've never met says David attended parties frequented by someone who arrived in a Lincoln that broadcast to the world it was number one. I could imagine Mavredes' response. Especially since Beverly and Jack had disappeared.

Harry was looking at me with an expression not unlike the one Gussie frequently wore. I glanced at his feet to see what he had on today while giving him time to consider what I had just said. He was wearing scuffed black boots—his plain, day-off variety. He had on jeans, a blue chambray shirt and a sports jacket plus the bolo tie. The bolo tie was his trademark. He was never without it. I wondered if he took it off when he went to bed at night.

Harry pressed the palms of his hands together. Then he drummed his fingers lightly on the edge of the desk with the serpentine design. It was a beautiful desk, with an inlaid wood top that curved in a cantilevered fashion over an s-shaped base. The edges of the desk were painted black, silver and burgundy. Nobody but me called the design 'childlike'. It was a bargain at $7,000.

"Suppose he did let somebody in," Harry said at last, "if Mavredes is right that his death was a sexual accident, David and this special somebody were into dangerous games. If somebody was here, and David strangled himself, are you saying this guy got scared when it went too far and checked out? But the door was locked, Rosemund. How would he let himself out of the gallery?"

"Whatever was going on, I can't believe it was an accident," I said, "and I can't believe it was suicide."

Harry leaned back in the desk chair and placed his booted feet on the desk. I knew he did it deliberately to show how easy it was to be comfortable in surroundings that were also works of art. It was Harry's way of proving that art was for everybody, that it wasn't something you locked up in a museum. In a way he was right. He proved it by never breaking anything.

"That leaves murder," he said.

"Yes," I said. "I know. But I also know David knew David Moon. There was not a self-destructive bone in his body. All those bones worked towards his self-enhancement. He was determined to make an award-winning film. So he took chances, all creative people do. But not this kind of chance." I leaned across the desk so that I was not more than a foot away from Harry. I had to make him see that I was serious.

"What if somebody was here with him," I said. "What if they had an argument and knocked over the telephone. Mavredes doesn't have any explanation for that. What if David were putting on a big show for him, maybe even dressed up in that black plastic. What if this guy had one thing in mind and David was only playing games, leading him on. Maybe there was a fight and this guy strangled David and strung him up with the rope and then climbed out the window and scooted down to the ground between the two buildings. He wouldn't have to use a key." I knew better than to say that I got this idea from watching the Carytown handyman climb up my wall to look at a dirty window. "What if—"

With a graceful swing of his legs Harry put his feet back on the floor. He got up from behind the desk, walked around to where I was standing and put both hands on my shoulders. Gently he began to massage the muscles there. I could feel how tight they were as he pressed with his thumbs. Obviously, I needed to increase my work-out time at the gym.

"We've known each other a long time, Rosemund," he said. "Most of your wild ideas turn out to have some sense in them. I trust you. I trust your intuition. You've got a terrific eye for art and for talent. The gallery is an enormous success because of you. But this time, this time, you've lost it. Climb down the walls? That's the craziest idea I ever heard in my life. Bust your head wide open if you fell. Nobody was here with David. There's nothing to indicate he had company. He was all alone. Maybe you don't want to accept the fact that he was playing a dirty little game with himself—but, come on, Rosemund—murder? Your imagination is way out in left field this time. "

Harry put his arm around me and gave me a big squeeze. Whenever he did that I knew it was his way of humoring me, sort of like a pat on the head accompanied by 'now, now, calm down. Let's not be so hasty.' "This thing has affected you more than I thought," he said. "I suggest we close the gallery for three months, you take a long vacation. Get Gussie to go with you to Mexico or someplace. Or, what the hell, go alone and meet some man. But you've got to get hold of yourself."

He dropped his hands to his sides. I could see that his concern was genuine.

"That's all I'm going to say, Rosemund. A lot of people care about you. A lot of people cared about David Moon. But he's gone and you're here. You can't bring him back. We've got to get on with our lives."

That's what my arch competitor, Lila Hunt said.

"All right, Harry," I said, "I'll think about it." I knew he would not like what I was going to do.

By the time Austin returned from delivering Lucy's paintings to Goochland it was almost dark. I had spent the hour since Harry left moving the paintings that had been in the gallery before the movie shoot. They needed to be put in storage bins downstairs. Harry offered to help but I managed to talk him out of it. I wanted to straighten up and put away, to patch and paint the walls and clean the floor myself, a ritual to cleanse the gallery of what had happened. Besides, Austin could be a little intense about art sometimes, and I didn't feel like participating in an art critique. I needed to decide whether I would try to talk to Jimmy Travers myself or call Mavredes. If I could prove the red rope looped around David's neck had come from the fire station, and the driver of the Lincoln cruising the gallery the night of David's death was driven by someone with access to props at the fire station, Mavredes might be willing to question more people after all.

I was on a ladder upstairs in the balcony gallery with a paintbrush in my hand as I heard Austin's key in the lock. I realized I had forgotten to give his name to Mavredes when he asked for a list of those who had access to the gallery.

"Some place Lucy Moon has," Austin said as I came down the metal stairs to greet him. "I've never seen anything like it."

"The tavern?"

He nodded his head. "One person and all that space," he said. "And the view. Place must be worth a fortune. Wonder how long it took her to turn a tavern into a painter's paradise? Have you seen the inside? She's got art everywhere, her own paintings hanging in the downstairs, sculpture by other artists outside the front door, wood carvings in the kitchen, even a sculpture by the swimming pool. I would call her Artist with a capital "A"."

Yes, I thought, I've seen the inside of Lucy's house, drunk coffee and brandy in her kitchen, swum naked in her swimming pool, passed judgment on work in progress in her studio. And what do you know about artists with a capital 'A', Austin Meyerson? You're still wet behind the ears.

But instead of jumping all over him in anger because he had been to Lucy's place instead of me, I said calmly, "How was she? How did she act?"

"Glad to get the paintings, I guess. She still seems kind of dazed. Man, do I admire that woman's work. I'd give anything to own one of her paintings. Maybe someday, oh yeah, she wondered where the plastic was that they were wrapped in before delivery to the gallery."

I was tired. It had been a long day. "Plastic?"

"Yeah, black plastic. She said she likes to recycle the plastic sheets. Expensive, heavy duty stuff, she said." He looked around at the empty space. "I hate it when there's nothing here," he said. "The art makes the place come to life."

I stood very still in the middle of the gallery. Lucy had wrapped her paintings in black plastic, I repeated to myself. That's where I remembered seeing it before the movie shoot. But what happened to it? Where did it go? Who got rid of it, except for the piece that was draped around David.

Austin was at the front door, ready to leave. It irritated me that he looked so young and so strong. He'd probably stay out all night and still be fresh the next morning. "Don't you want to go home, Rosemund?" he said. "You look exhausted."

"Soon," I said, "I'm leaving soon. Gussie's coming by, maybe we'll go to a movie."

"Well, if you're sure you'll be all right..."

He was almost out the door when he stopped, reached into his pocket and waved an envelope in the air. "Almost forgot," he said. "Lucy sent this to you."

I nodded as though it were an everyday occurrence to receive a letter from an artist and old friend who wouldn't return my phone calls. As soon as Austin was gone I tore it open. Inside the envelope was a single piece of paper with a few typed words:

PLEASE TRY TO UNDERSTAND............LUCY

XIII

Gussie, who mistrusts the Jaguar as much as Bernard does, picked me up in her red truck and insisted we see an Italian film that was in town for only three days. It was with sub-titles. But since I was preoccupied with what had happened earlier I couldn't concentrate on the words flashing across the screen and hadn't a clue as to the story line. Something about three anorexic women running around Rome in designer clothes. I was relieved when it was over. It didn't help, either, that Gussie kept casting concerned glances in my direction over the popcorn. After hearing my account of the day's events, and especially the contents of Lucy's note, it was obvious she was now vying with Harry to see who could be the most motherly.

"How 'bout a cup of coffee?" she said as we left the theater. "The new Starbucks is open late."

"Not tonight," I said as we got in the pickup. "Just drop me off at the gallery. I need to go home and get a good night's sleep." I lived in a small house in the Fan District not far from the gallery.

"I still think you should call Lieutenant Mavredes," Gussie said. "He might be more interested in your idea about the fire station and the rope than you give him credit for. He could talk to Jimmy Travers."

"And say what? That a foul-mouthed playwright saw him in the fire house? Bernard says board members have every right to be there. Until somebody reliable links David and Jimmy Travers I could be in big trouble suggesting there was something going on between the two of them."

"You, of course, plan to find that 'somebody'."

"It may not be as hard to locate some of the film crew as I thought," I said. "I looked up Barbara Barksdale in the telephone book. Her answering machine message sounded like it was recorded in a bar, glasses clanking, people laughing. 'Your call is so very important to me,' it said. I hope she means it. If I can get her to talk to me without all the southern syrup I might be able to find out something about David that a man wouldn't even think of, like what his social life was really like. Mavredes didn't have any reason to ask about Jimmy Travers, but wouldn't it be interesting if Barbara knew who he was? Besides, we've got to start somewhere."

"We? What do you mean we?"

"Well, I certainly can't do this by myself," I said, "and Harry's no help. He thinks I should go to Mexico and drink margaritas."

"What about Bernard? He knows Jimmy Travers."

"You're the only one who doesn't think I'm crazy."

"I wouldn't go so far as to say that..."

"When I couldn't reach Barbara, I looked up John Smith in the phonebook. There were sixteen of them, but only two John O. Smith, neither of which answered to John Owen. If Barbara returns my call, I'll get her to tell me how to find him."

"Why him?" Gussie said. "Lucy said they had a disagreement about the film or something. He'll be no help."

"David's relationships may not be what they appeared on the surface," I said. "At the funeral, John Owen was clearly angry about something, and I think it was more than David being dead. So I want to talk to everybody, even if it's going over stuff Mavredes already asked."

"You're contacted the Lee sisters?"

"Do you have any idea how many Lee's with oriental first names are listed? It was worse than John Smith."

By this time we reached Carytown. Gussie pulled the truck into the alley behind the gallery and I climbed out. The Jaguar may be old, but it's always a relief to find it intact and waiting for me.

"Want me to wait around until you get the car started?" Gussie said.

"No, I'm fine. See you in the morning at the gym." But she didn't leave immediately. This overly solicitous behavior was getting to me. With Harry it was no great surprise, but it wasn't like Gussie to hover. I stuck the key in the car door and waved her away. The pickup coughed a little, the gravel spun beneath its tires and then it was gone. As the sound of the truck faded, the alley became very quiet. I had rarely been in Carytown so close to midnight. Even Cary Street seemed devoid of traffic.

"Alone at last," I said, patting the Jag on the hood. Instead of getting in, however, I stared at the iron gate across the gallery's back door. Locked from the inside, front and rear, I thought. The window was the only way out of the gallery that night. But nobody seemed to think it was a possible escape route except me. Maybe Harry's right, I thought. Maybe it is a crazy idea to think that somebody was with David and climbed down the walls between the buildings. Maybe I just don't want to let him go.

I opened the car door to get in. And then I heard something. Ordinarily it would have been enough to make me lock the door immediately. But not this time. Perhaps I was preoccupied. Perhaps I was tired. Whatever the reason, I stood still and listened.

It sounded like "pssst."

Slowly I looked around. Nothing. Only darkness.

There it was again. "Pssst." It was a human sound and it was coming from the shadowy space between my building and Bernard's.

Bracing myself, I backed away from the car and took a few cautious steps in the direction of the sound. Peering into the darkness, at first I could see nothing.

And then a sort of denseness seemed to take on a human form. Someone was definitely there and was trying to get my attention. I was more curious than afraid. But I was not interested in stepping into the darkness all alone. I stood at the edge of the walkway running between the two buildings and called out.

"Looking for me?"

"Who are you?" a raspy voice called back.

This is ridiculous, I thought, wishing now I had asked Gussie to wait.

"It's Rosemund Wallace," I said, wondering if this was some new mugging strategy. First you discover the victim's name, then you rob them. "I own this art gallery," I said, hoping such a power play would scare them off.

"We heard you was looking for us," the raspy voice said.

"Beverly? Is it Beverly?"

"Yes," the voice said. "Why did you want to talk to us? The police told us not to come here no more."

"It's all right," I said. "They won't bother you. I need to ask you a couple of questions. Can we go across the street to McDonald's and talk. It's dark and cold standing here. How 'bout a cup of coffee? My treat."

There was some indistinguishable whispering. Beverly conferring with Jack, I assumed.

"Suits us," Beverly said at last. "Come on. Person catch pneumonia standing out here in the elements."

I was surprised at the number of people in McDonald's. Midnight snackers, I decided, or a portion of Richmond's homeless seeking shelter in all-night spots around the city.

"I'll have a biscuit, too," Beverly said as we stood at the counter together.

"How 'bout you, Jack? Anything besides coffee?"

"Biscuit," he said. It was the first time I had ever heard his voice.

We took a table in the back of the restaurant and munched on our biscuits for a while. Finally I said, "I've been thinking about the black limousine you saw in the alley the night David Moon died."

Between sips of coffee Beverly nodded her head. Jack lit a cigarette.

"Well, did you really see a Lincoln with number one on the plates? Maybe it was just a big car."

"I reckon I'd know a Towncar if I seen one," Beverly said. "It was a Lincoln all right. And I sure as heck can read a 'one' when it's right in front of my nose. Black, shiny car, dark windows, no driver though."

"How did it get there if there were no driver?"

Beverly looked at me as though I had lost my mind. Jack took a drag on the cigarette and coughed. "The man drove hisself, of course," she said. "Tall man, lots taller than you." She laughed at her own joke. "Lots taller than Jack, too." A policeman entered the restaurant. Jack gave Beverly a nudge and gestured with his cigarette. "'Bout as tall as him," Beverly said.

I turned to look. "That policeman? That tall?"

Beverly nodded. She glanced down at the table where the wrapper containing her biscuit was empty except for a few crumbs.

"How 'bout another round of biscuits?" I said. "I'm still hungry."

"Fine," Beverly said. "Suit us fine."

I went to the counter and stood behind the policeman as he ordered a double burger, hold the cheese. He towered over me, easily six two, I decided. Even taller than Tyrone who had no trouble scooting up the walls between the gallery and Bernard's studio. I needed to get a better description of the tall man from Beverly.

But when I turned back to the table where we had been sitting, Jack and Beverly were gone.

It was not a good night. I slept about as well as a religious penitent on a bed of nails. Even my dreams would have run a close second to those of Saint Anthony. Faceless bodies wrapped in black plastic being cradled by Beverly in the center of the McDonald's kitchen while fries sizzled in the background like the fires of hell. It was the midnight biscuits that did it, I decided as I pulled on my black exercise tights and an over-sized tee shirt with a map of Carytown printed on the front. The tee shirt had been one of those ridiculous marketing ideas the local merchants promoted. In reality, what brought people to Carytown was a folksy atmosphere, increasingly rare in America, where individual business owners knew their clients personally. It was a touch of the past which could never be duplicated by the malls.

"I thought you were planning a good night's sleep," Gussie said as we met in the free weight room. "You look terrible."

"So full of compliments," I said as I struggled with two 12 pound bar bells. It was one of those days when even holding in my stomach was an effort. "I thought you were one of my loyal artists."

"Twelve pounds?" she said, "that's all you're doing this morning? What's the matter with you?" I saw she was showing off with 20 pound weights in each hand, straining delicately as she lifted them high above her head. Competition is the staff of life, I thought, that's why I'm an art dealer. I wondered what Austin, my installer, was lifting these days. He was the strongest twenty year old I had ever seen, with muscles so over-developed in his arms and shoulders that his upper body looked like it had been placed on the wrong legs and pelvis.

"Ready to talk to Lieutenant Mavredes now?" Gussie said. She was doing shoulder lifts with the weights, three sets of ten. "Sounds like Beverly could give a good description of the man she saw behind the gallery."

"We don't know that David let him into the gallery," I said. "Beverly didn't say that. Besides, she and Jack have disappeared again. And they're the only witnesses."

"The police have their ways of finding people," Gussie said. She had moved on to deep knee lunges, designed to firm up an already flawless rear end.

"I would never turn the police loose on Jack and Beverly," I said. "They'll find me when they're ready to talk some more. Meanwhile, I'll try to think up some way to meet Jimmy Travers without making him suspicious."

"No wonder you don't reopen the gallery," Gussie said. "First, Beverly and Jack, then Jimmy Travers and Barbara Barksdale. You're too busy having a social life to sell art. And isn't tonight when you're supposed to meet Mayo's friend?" She wiped the sweat off the back of her neck. I was still dry as the proverbial bone. I put down the 12 pounders and fingered a 15 pound bar bell.

"We're having a drink at the Hill Cafe," I said. I rubbed my towel across my shoulders like a real athlete. The Hill Cafe was one of the few watering holes in Church Hill with a genuinely mixed crowd. Its location was part of its appeal. Because it was on the edge of a rough neighborhood, only the bravest West End Richmonders frequented the cafe. It was also far enough away from Shockoe Bottom, the fraternity heaven where Gussie lived, that twenty year olds who were affecting the latest hip hop garb couldn't find it. And it was friendly enough that you could huddle around the bar nursing a beer for a couple of hours and the regulars of both races would think you were one of them. On weekends there was live jazz. It was one of Gussie's and my favorites. Often we went on Sundays for brunch and the WASHINGTON POST.

I hoped Mayo's friend would show up. The prospect of being questioned about partying with a dead man might not appeal to everybody. But I reminded myself that I was only an art dealer. Just how threatening could that be?

"What if Mayo's friend says the limo guy he'd seen at parties was named Jimmy Travers?" Gussie said. She put the weights back on the rack and was looking at me with her hands on her hips. Her stance was multiplied a dozen times in the mirrored wall behind the rack. "...then what do you do?"

"Take your advice and call Mavredes," I said.

"Promise?"

"Promise," I said aloud. But only if I find Jack and Beverly first, I said to myself.

I spent the rest of the day looking out the gallery window to see if they would show their faces. I even went across the street three times for coffee from McDonald's thinking perhaps they had slipped into the restaurant when I wasn't looking. But they didn't appear. Neither did their friends. At one point Bernard stopped in, waving the morning paper, to say he decided the real problem with

Governor Brookfield was not his politics but his speech writer.

"Worse use of the English language I've ever seen," Bernard said. "In print Brookfield's speeches sound even more incoherent than when you see his mouth moving. This blather could only be encouraged by our friend, Jimmy Travers." He folded the newspaper and stuck it under his arm. "By the way," he said. "I located a copy of the play about the guy who burned down the barn filled with horses and then strangled the stable hand who saw him do it."

"Yes? And did the script say the rope needed to be red?"

Bernard shook his head. "Not a word about color. Could have been covered with polka dots for all the stage directions indicated. Just rope, it said—garden variety rope."

We had drawn a blank. I was certain the rope I had seen the night of the play had been red. If it was just my imagination, then Jimmy Travers became a less likely suspect.

"There is one thing, though," Bernard said. "I got hold of the director who told me David was always playing tricks with the props, that he had to get after him a couple of times..."

"What sort of tricks?"

"Oh, he would sometimes write a message on a prop to surprise an actor when he picked it up or fill what was supposed to be a glass of water with wine, that kind of thing."

"Could he have substituted a piece of red rope for ordinary rope during a performance?"

"Could have," Bernard said. "The director told me that one night David was walking around with a can of red paint but nobody ever figured out what he had painted. They thought maybe he'd painted a chair so somebody would get a red rear end if they sat down at the wrong time. There is one thing, though."

"I knew you'd find out something," I said. "What is it?"

"One particular board member was always available to advise David how to behave. I never saw it, but then, I was never there during rehearsals."

"Jimmy Travers," I said, "I knew it. You've got to find a way for me to meet him."

"Jimmy's too tall for you, Rosemund."

"Tall, gay guy, huh?"

"We don't run in the same crowd, if that's what you're asking."

"See if you can find out what crowd he does run in," I said.

Bernard gave me a sharp look. "This is about more than red rope at the fire station, isn't it," he said.

"It's about David's killer," I said, thinking for the first time that maybe I should be careful.

I was slightly nervous as I drove into Church Hill in the early evening, headed for the Hill Cafe. It wasn't the neighborhood. It was what I was afraid I might learn about David. Never having met a drug dealer, at least as far as I knew, I had no idea what to expect from Mayo's friend. But then, I didn't really know for a fact the man I was about to meet was a drug dealer. Except for the one remark about coke, Mayo had been noncommittal when I mentioned drugs. Perhaps Mayo's friend was merely an inveterate party goer or maybe near-sighted like our Virginia U.S. senator who didn't recognize the stuff when it was being snorted six feet from his face.

It was already dark by the time I drove around the block several times to try to calm my feelings of anxiety and my imagination was running overtime. Mayo's friend was certain to be black, I had decided, probably gay, wearing dark glasses and an Armani suit. I parked the Jaguar beneath a street light half a block away in front of Church Hill's only Korean-owned grocery store and headed for the restaurant. If the Beast turned temperamental and refused to start, at least it was in a well-lit spot if I needed to call for help.

The striped awning of the cafe was frayed in a genteel sort of manner that seemed to underscore the shabbiness of my evening's mission. One end dipped slightly above a beveled glass door which opened into an octagonal space lined on one side by a long bar and on the other with green plastic booths. The light was comfortably dim in the cafe. Paintings filled the space along the wall above the booths. I scanned the paintings automatically before I looked down the bar to see if Mayo and his friend had arrived. The paintings featured females rendered in blue enamel with red hearts bursting out of ample breasts. The women were faceless. Because of a series of wavy lines around them, the hearts seemed to be throbbing.

Although I am always open to new artists, this was not one I would sign up for my next show.

Mayo and his friend were nowhere to be seen. Nor were there any familiar faces in the restaurant. Two black men of indeterminant age were slumped at the bar. Three yuppie looking couples were laughing in a back booth. A couple of females who might have been librarians were engaged in earnest conversation over a bottle of wine. Suddenly I felt lonely and wished I had asked Gussie or Bernard to come with me. If I hadn't been so certain that David Moon could never have taken his own life I would have gotten back into my car and gone home to a good book and a bowl of popcorn. But I had come this far. My habit of following something through to the end was too hard to overcome at this stage in my life. Besides, I reminded myself—a coincidence is never just a coincidence. I took a seat at the bar and ordered a glass of chablis.

"Rosemund."

The voice was so soft I didn't hear my name being called until Mayo was at my elbow. I braced myself for my first encounter with a drug dealer and turned to greet Mayo and his friend.

The friend was not wearing dark glasses nor an Armani jacket. Nor was he black. On the contrary, he was a white, almost gaunt, man in his mid-fifties, wearing a bow tie and a wrinkled suit. The floppy tie served to accentuate his angular features. He might have been handsome in a craggy way had he been taller and not so thin. Something about him also seemed oddly familiar. I wondered if I had seen his picture in the newspaper. Or perhaps he had visited the gallery and there was no reason to identify himself.

I stuck out my hand. "Rosemund Wallace," I said, "thanks for coming."

The man took my hand in his. I thought for a moment he might kiss it. The skin around his eyes crinkled as though he were enjoying a good joke. "Walter McGowan," he said. "Mayo's told me a lot about you."

"Doctor Walter McGowan," Mayo said, "the man who saved my eye."

"Let's get a booth," Walter McGowan said, "so we can talk freely."

I sat on one side and the two men on the other. Mayo had white wine and the doctor a whiskey and soda. Mayo explained he and Walter had developed a bond because of the operation on his eye. Walter McGowan had given him back his sight. And in turn, started him on a new career as an artist. It had been Dr. McGowan, Mayo said, who first encouraged him to take up painting. Mayo had given him a small driftwood sculpture of a dog and McGowan had convinced him he had talent.

"But I only agreed to come tonight," Walter said, "because Mayo tells me you don't act like most white women." He and Mayo exchanged a look that was neither sexist nor racist but could have been interpreted as either if someone was in the mood to take offense.

I smiled. What else could I do? If Gussie had been there, she would have laughed.

"I thought maybe you could tell me something about the young man who died at my gallery," I said, "David Moon."

"What's to tell?" the doctor said. "He's dead. It's sad, wasted potential, a very creative person. Charming, really, and very ambitious. I have a particular fondness for young artists. He might have gone far. With a painter like Lucy Moon for his mother, he certainly inherited good genes." He sipped his whiskey and watched me carefully. I had the distinct impression that in spite of his southern manners, if I said the wrong thing he would be gone in an instant.

Of course, I didn't know what the wrong thing might be, and I didn't have a clue as to the right thing to say. There was more to Walter McGowan than anybody was indicating. I wondered about his reference to Lucy. But perhaps it was only because he knew I was her art dealer—or ex-art dealer. He certainly seemed as curious about me as I was about him. I glanced at Mayo, hoping he might help.

His face was expressionless. So, for a change, even though my mind was racing, I didn't say anything. I merely touched the chablis to my lips and nodded as though I knew what was going on.

My silence seemed to make Walter more comfortable. He leaned back into the fake leather booth and signaled for another scotch and soda. "Why don't we get a bite to eat," he said. I decided on shrimp quesadillas. Mayo ordered a hamburger and the doctor a bowl of black bean soup smothered in sour cream and chopped green onions. Mayo talked about his boxing career. Walter talked about being on call when Mayo was brought in after the blow to his eye. The two men were easy with each other, like Gussie and me, I thought.

"So you want to know about David Moon," Walter said as his empty soup bowl was replaced by a frozen slice of Chocolate Decadence.

"I already know his family," I said, "so I don't need to know too much, only about the limousine, and the person you saw with David, the man who arrived at the party in a limousine. Currently I have a special affinity for limousines, especially if they're affiliated with a certain political party."

Mayo got to his feet. "Excuse me," he said. "The men's room calls."

Walter watched him walk to the rear of the restaurant, dabbed his mouth delicately with his napkin, and then said, "Ah yes, the prick who puts words into the mouth of our illustrious governor, the double prick who goes shopping with the governor's wife, the triple prick with access to a limousine because Brookfield keeps one on the grounds of the governor's mansion at all times..."

I caught my breath. It seemed too easy. "Jimmy Travers?" I said.

"Who else?" Walter said, wrapping his tongue around the last bite of Chocolate Decadence. "Biggest prick in Richmond."

"Would you say he and David Moon were...uh, friendly?"

Walter licked a remaining piece of chocolate off his fork. Then he folded his hands in his lap and looked at me. "They knew each other," he said.

The longer I was with Walter McGowan, the more familiar he became. I struggled to figure out where we might have met. I was almost certain it was not in the gallery. "Would you be willing to tell that to the detective investigating David's death?"

"Well, now," he said, "that's another question."

"Please," I said. "It might be important."

"Such a dear girl," Walter said. "Mayo tells me you may be giving him a show at the gallery."

I saw that it was going to be a long evening. "Mayo has a real future," I said. "David didn't have the chance for one." It was driving me a little crazy trying to place him. When he held his head at a certain angle he almost resembled, no, I thought, pushing the notion out of my mind. We had met somewhere. That was why his face was so familiar.

"We all have our futures to consider," Walter said. "If I spoke to your good detective I would have to explain how I happened to be at that particular party. I might be required to name names..." He smiled benignly and for the first time I noticed his hands. I had never seen a man's fingernails so perfectly groomed. "It would be so embarrassing," he said, "having one's dinner partners on the police blotter."

"What if I told Lieutenant Mavredes about our talk," I said. "What if I told him what you said?"

He leaned back in his seat and glanced regretfully at the empty dessert plate. "You mean the evening we met at the Hill Cafe to discuss Mayo Johnson's career as an artist?" he said. "Why would an art dealer discussing an artist's future with his agent be of interest to the police? I can't imagine that your Lieutenant Mavredes would be nearly as excited by an ex-boxer's wood carvings as we are." He got to his feet, straightened his bow tie and took my hand in his as he had done earlier in the evening. As he stood up, I would have sworn he looked just like Lucy Moon. I decided it was the chablis.

"I'm afraid you're on your own, dear girl," he said. "Just keep those lovely eyes focused on art and I have no doubt that you'll continue to be an enormous success." He glanced towards the bar where Mayo was waiting. It occurred to me Mayo was the smartest of the bunch. He didn't want to hear anything that was said about Jimmy Travers. And what was said was mostly innuendo coupled with refusal to repeat even that much to the police.

As the two men walked out the door I realized I'd been left with the bill and hadn't even had the chance to ask Walter if he was a drug dealer .

XIV

I phoned Gussie at 6:30 the next morning to say I'd skip our workout and meet her for coffee. After Chocolate Decadence in Church Hill with an eye surgeon who was willing to lie to the police, the last thing I needed to distract me were trim bodies, animal grunts and cheerful grimaces of pain. And I wanted to think.

I was getting nowhere by myself. Jack and Beverly had disappeared again after saying that the driver of the limousine behind the gallery the night David died was a tall white man. Bernard had confirmed that Jimmy Travers, who worked for the governor, was tall, and that he might have met David through the Fire Station Players. Doctor Walter McGowan, the surgeon who had saved my newest artist's eye following a boxing accident, said Jimmy Travers and David knew each other and appeared to share some sort of social life. However, the actual details of that social life the good doctor wanted kept private.

And there had been a message on my answering machine. Not from Barbara Barksdale, David's girlfriend whose call I had been anticipating. But from the corporate buyer for the Japanese firm in Los Angeles who bought a number of Lucy's paintings earlier in the year. The buyer planned to be in Washington, D.C. later that week and wanted to drive down to Richmond to look at more of Lucy's work.

"Just what you need," Gussie said as she plopped down beside me at the coffee shop, workout bag brimming over with clothing, papers and books. "..another corporate buyer for Lucy's work. You call the guy back and tell him to forget it?"

"I called him. But I sort of beat around the bush."

"Why?" Gussie took a dainty bite out of her bran muffin in an all-too obvious attempt to affect a non-judgmental tone of voice.

"I don't know. He sounded, nice, I guess."

"Oh my God," Gussie said. "Nice. You have that funny look on your face, Rosemund. And it's not just because you forgot your makeup. What else is going on?"

"About David?"

"About David and his mother."

"Well, first of all, I'm not quite sure what to do about this California buyer. His firm spent a ton of money on Lucy. Lucy's income went through the roof that month. But then the gallery didn't suffer either. Michael, his name is Michael DeBord, I told him there was a slight problem and I was no longer Lucy's art dealer."

"'Slight'?" Gussie said. "You do have a way with words."

"He said he wants to come anyway."

Gussie munched on her muffin. It looked as though she was trying to chew each bite thirty times.

"It's for the Japanese, for heaven's sake."

"Michael DeBord doesn't sound very Japanese to me."

"He's from Michigan, he told me. Art history degree from the University of Chicago. Speaks Japanese, which is how he ended up the corporate art buyer for a Japanese firm. Anyway, I told him even though I was no longer her dealer I still had access to one of Lucy's paintings. The figure in black plastic in the woods, the one Mavredes took down to his office. Would be ironic, wouldn't it, if this particular painting of Lucy's was sold by me."

Gussie drained her cup and carefully wiped a couple of drops of coffee off the table. "You plan to give this Michael DeBord Lila Hunt's phone number? Or does he think you sound nice, too?"

"And here I thought you were on my side," I said.

"I am," Gussie said, "that's why I did some research for you." Reaching into her bag, she rummaged through some papers and pulled out a xeroxed copy of a newspaper article.

"I went over to the TIMES DISPATCH," she said, "and asked Arabella to help me look up any stories dealing with the governor's staff. It wasn't hard. He hasn't been in office that long. Arabella may write about art but she knew just what to do. The newspaper has all this stuff on computer disks. It was pretty amazing."

She thrust the paper into my hands. The photograph of two people smiling up at me had the names of a woman and a man printed beneath it. And the caption "Governor Names New Aides". The woman was identified as Brookfield's former campaign manager, which surprised me, considering it was Brookfield, but I was only interested in the man, the 'junior' aide, Bernard had called him, James C. Travers.

"I thought you might be interested in what he looked like," Gussie said. "Maybe you can peer into his eyes and see the face of a murderer."

I studied the photograph carefully. Jimmy Travers was attractive in an angular sort of way. Dark hair, moustache, dark eyes. But the picture offered no hint to his personality nor his proclivity for young film makers.

"Did Arabella ask any questions?" I said.

"Not really, but she doesn't miss much. Said to get in touch if I needed anything else." I looked at the photo again. "I've got to meet this man," I said. "Short of asking him for dinner, there must be some way to do it."

"Maybe you could have a private showing of that painting of Lucy's," Gussie said. "Invite Jimmy Travers plus your California corporate buyer and Mavredes, a cozy threesome. Offer it to the highest bidder."

I took a long sip of coffee. It was hazelnut, my favorite. "Thank you, Gussie," I said, "you've just given me an idea. But first, I want you to call Arabella and see if she can get a copy of David's film. Give her the names of the film crew. If someone like Arabella offers to do a feature article on a young film maker who died tragically, it should be easier to get the film footage than if you and I went after it. Lucy may even have a copy she'd loan to the right person. She and Arabella know each other. Arabella's been praising her work for years. Just tell her I want to see the unedited footage of the movie."

"Why? If David's on the film it'll upset you."

"A hunch maybe. I'm not sure. In between takes, the cameraman kept panning the space that night. Maybe we'll see something important."

"Arabella's going to want more than that."

"Then tell her the truth, that I don't believe David took his own life and we need her help because I'm busy pursuing another lead."

Gussie gave me one of her looks. "And to think," she said, "that I could be in the studio, painting furniture and listening to Vivaldi."

"I thought it was Jimmie Dale Gilmore."

She shrugged. "Whatever..."

"All you have to do," I said to Bernard later that day," is suggest to Jimmy Travers he take a look at Mayo Johnson's work. In particular, an American eagle that's been painted by a black, self-taught artist who's made it on his own without help from the federal government. Brookfield needs the black vote, doesn't he? Supposing his favorite aide introduced him to a local black artist lacking the effete background Brookfield criticizes the NEA for funding. Wouldn't the governor find this man right up his alley? Think of the photo opportunities."

"'Effete background'?" Bernard said. "You mean college?"

"I mean the art establishment. Mayo Johnson and the art establishment are at opposite ends of the spectrum. You can be sure ART FORUM has never heard of him. He's so non-political that even Jesse Helms would love his work. And, as a matter of fact, so do I. Mayo's eagle, not some expensive bronze bird cast by an out-of-state artist, should be in the Virginia governor's mansion."

Bernard rolled his eyes. He was beginning to resemble Gussie. "And you want me to take advantage of my board membership with an elite cultural organization to get a man I dislike to see Mayo's work? We don't even sit on the same side of the table when the Fire Station Players meet."

"Please, Bernard. It's important."

Why Bernard disliked Jimmy Travers was none of my business. Perhaps he instinctively knew the governor's aide was capable of more than a political perspective that Bernard didn't share. What mattered was Bernard's ability to convince Jimmy to look at Mayo's sculptures. I had it all planned. Once Jimmy was in the gallery he would 'accidentally' discover Lucy's painting in my office. I would retrieve the black plastic forest painting from police headquarters, place it on an easel upstairs in the gallery, find some excuse to get Jimmy up there and then watch his reaction. The black plastic and the red cord were bound to have an effect on him. I was certain I would be able to detect something in his response that would tell me whether or not he had been with David the night he died.

Mavredes, however, had his own agenda.

"I'd planned to return the painting to Lucy Moon, myself," he said when I called him. It was the first time we had spoken since he told me he was labeling David's death suicide and closing the case. "There's no reason to have you involved again," he said. "The whole thing has been unpleasant enough for you without seeing the painting one more time. I think it definitely had an effect on the boy. If he was as prone to theatrics as his friends said, he would do something like covering himself with black plastic and using a red rope. And by the way, the rope was red because somebody had dipped it in red paint."

For a moment I couldn't decide what was more important, that David had been seen with a can of red paint or that his friends suggested he was dramatic enough to wrap himself in a plastic toga. I decided to go with the friends. The paint could wait.

"You didn't tell me somebody said he was prone to theatrics. Was it one of the film crew?"

"The black guy, Lawson, Arik Lawson, the cameraman with the beard."

I never knew his name, I thought, quickly writing it down as Mavredes and I talked. Arabella should contact him, too. Since he was operating the camera, he would have a copy of the film.

"Who else? Friends means more than one person."

"The two Korean women. They said David was always dressing up and clowning around their parents' grocery store in Church Hill."

Church Hill. Where I had visited the Hill Cafe. The night I met Mayo and his doctor friend at the cafe I had parked in front of the area's Korean grocery store. I held the receiver tighter. I may not have found Barbara Barksdale or John Owen Smith, but I now knew how to locate Mee and Connie Lee. After Jimmy Travers visited the gallery, I would make a trek back to Church Hill. If only one person who had worked on the movie with David mentioned Jimmy Travers...

My head was pounding. "Just let me borrow Lucy's painting for a few days," I said to Mavredes, "then you can take it out to her place." Now that I knew the rope had been painted red—and probably by David, as part of some game he was playing with the Fire Station Theater props, the painting was crucial to my plan. In fact if I didn't have the painting to confront Jimmy Travers, I had no plan.

Mavredes finally agreed I could have it for three days. That wasn't much time. But if Austin was available to set up Mayo's sculptures and Bernard succeeded in convincing Jimmy Travers to visit the gallery, it would be long enough. And if I still had the painting in my possession when Michael DeBord flew in from the West Coast I could show it to him, too. Otherwise I would have no choice but to introduce him to Lila Hunt since she was the person now selling Lucy's work. It would be like delivering the head of John the Baptist to Salome of the Seven Veils.

Fortunately, Austin was between classes. He was studying sculpture at Virginia Commonwealth University, our local urban college, and had a pretty flexible schedule most of the time. It was one of the reasons I hired him to help with installations in the first place. He was strong, was good with his hands and could help me at odd times during the week. In addition, Austin loved art more than anyone his age I'd ever met. I might even hire him to help me run the gallery when he graduated.

"Man is this ugly!" Austin said, pointing to the eagle we had placed on a pedestal in the center of the gallery.

"Well, you probably couldn't get a degree in driftwood sculpture," I said more defensively that I would have wished. It was clear that I would have to revise my evaluation of Austin's artistic sensibilities. After his enthusiastic outburst about Lucy's paintings I had thought him a natural. "But you've got to admit the eagle's pretty unusual."

"Unusual! It's crude and it's ugly. No sophistication, whatsoever."

"It's not supposed to be sophisticated," I said. "It's precisely the lack of sophistication that makes Mayo's animals so appealing. There's an innocence, a certain charm, to them." Austin was sounding just like my partner, Harry. What if Jimmy Travers felt the same way about self-taught artists and refused to come to the gallery?

"True beauty is never entirely innocent," Austin said. "Take Lucy Moon's paintings, for example. You would never call her work innocent. It's terribly sophisticated and loaded with symbolism. Its beauty is in its lack of innocence."

I wondered what art professor Austin was quoting. "All art is not the same," I said. "There's room for many kinds." Actually, he was right about Lucy. I would never call her work innocent, either, but until that moment I had never equated innocence with lack of perfection.

"I suppose next you'll say there's room for duck prints and hunting dogs?"

"Well," I tried to laugh. I had never seen this side to Austin. But then I had never shown work like Mayo's animals, either.

I decided to change the subject. "I have one of Lucy's paintings here," I said.

"It's upstairs in the office. Take a look at it. It's one you've never seen. David's crew installed it when he did that movie scene at the gallery. It's been at police headquarters until a couple of hours ago."

"Lucy Moon? You have some of her work? I thought I took it all back to her studio." He seemed genuinely confused, as though he had done something wrong.

"Don't worry," I said. "You didn't overlook anything. The detective had the painting. He thinks it might have had some kind of influence on David, that it might have given him some weird ideas. I don't agree. But take a look. See what you think. It's a pretty strong painting."

Austin was upstairs a long time. Much longer than I would have expected. No sound came from the office as I busied myself with Mayo's animals. Some needed to be displayed on pedestals. Others could be hung on the walls. The sculpture would make a full gallery exhibition. Perhaps it would be a way to have a quick show. I debated whether to ask Austin to do the lighting or to call Harry. Either way, it appeared I was in for a lecture for showing the work. But I didn't care. In a few hours the driftwood American eagle would be occupying a prominent space in the middle of the gallery where it would await the one viewer who mattered: Jimmy Travers. I wondered if there were any way I could ask him about David's can of red paint, too.

"Austin, what are you doing upstairs? Are you lost? I need you down here. This stuff is too heavy for me to lug around by myself." Sometimes Austin seemed lost in his own world, but I suppose that was his way of letting me know he was determined to be a real artist.

He came down the metal stairs without answering, more slowly than he usually moved. Perhaps he was still put out with me for showing Mayo's animals. I started to hand him the hammer when I glanced at his face. He was crying.

"I've never seen anything so beautiful," he said. "It's the most beautiful painting I've ever seen in my life. And to think that her son will never be able to look at it again..."

Beautiful is not what I'd call Lucy's painting, I thought, as we arranged Mayo' s animals throughout the downstairs space. Exactly what I would call it, I hadn't decided, *provocative, disturbing, paradoxical,* perhaps, maybe even the impetus for a murder. Austin was forcing me to think harder than I wanted. The painting certainly had an effect on him. I reminded myself the painting seemed to have an effect on everyone who looked at it. I turned my attention to Mayo's pieces. It was important they be right. The lighting, in particular, was crucial. With the proper lighting, the animals would seem to come to life. It would be that quality that would impress whoever walked through the door of the gallery, including

Arabella. What she said about Mayo's work might be important if we were going to get the governor's attention.

Regardless of what Austin thought, the driftwood eagle was an extraordinary piece. Knots on the wood had become its eyes and were painted to look bright and wild. Mayo seemed to have a special gift for animal eyes. I noticed that immediately when I first saw his giraffe. What must have at one time been short branches had become the eagle's wings. They were lifted in such a way to suggest the bird was soaring. The wings were painted so carefully between the cracks and sharp angles in the wood that a viewer might be tempted to ruffle the feathers. I wanted to point that out to Austin, to tell him it was a painterly trait Mayo shared with Lucy. But this was not the time to deliver an art appreciation lecture on self-taught artists. I was certain, however, Mayo had his own vision as truly as Lucy Moon. And I was going to use that vision to catch a killer.

Bernard stopped in to see how we were doing as Austin was adjusting the spot lights. "It's a jungle in here," he said. I smiled. Austin did not.

"Are you a vegetarian, Austin?" Bernard said. "You don't seem very happy with these animals."

"It's not my favorite show," Austin said. "Now, if it was a room filled with Lucy's paintings..."

"Eagle looks good," Bernard said. He walked all the way around the pedestal in the middle of the gallery. "I think you're on to something with Mayo's work. A little publicity, the right people buying, who knows?" He gestured towards the back of the gallery. "I see you've got the giraffe, too. Actually, I think it's the best piece here. Loved it at the movie shoot."

"Arabella said she'd do a story," I said.

"Well, I've done my homework, too," Bernard said. "Jimmy Travers has agreed to take a look at the eagle. He'll come the end of the week."

The end of the week. The end of the three days Lieutenant Mavredes said I could keep Lucy's painting. I prayed he would show up.

"Who's Jimmy Travers?" Austin said, "somebody important?"

Bernard and I just looked at each other.

Heavy rain had been forecast for the rest of the week. But I assumed rain wouldn't prevent Jimmy from paying a visit to the gallery. When Bernard told him the art critic from the newspaper was coming to review the show he seemed even more interested in stopping by, especially after Bernard assured him that it would be all right to arrive at the same time Arabella did.

The day before Jimmy's scheduled visit, Michael DeBord, the art buyer for the Japanese company on the West Coast, called to say he was in Washington and would like to drive down to Richmond to take me to dinner and then look at Lucy's painting. When I mentioned the weather, he reminded me he had grown up in Michigan and wasn't afraid of a little moisture. Dinner with a man might be a nice diversion, I decided. And Michael DeBord sounded interesting over the telephone. Even if he didn't look as good as he sounded, he seemed to love Lucy's work. At least we had that in common. I suggested we go to the new Cuban restaurant which had recently opened across from the old Farmers' Market in Shockoe Bottom and go to the gallery later. If we didn't hit it off, the place was lively enough that we could at least enjoy the atmosphere.

Hitting it off didn't turn out to be a problem. Michael was tall, gray haired and very trim. He told me he swam. I told him about the Richmond Athletic Club and breakfast with Gussie. We laughed a lot and compared arm muscles. He also listened when I talked, leaning across the table in my direction as though everything I said was important. It was a bit like being with Gussie. I felt like I could tell him anything.

"Sometimes you meet a person," I said after we had talked for two hours, "and it seems like you've known them all your life." I fingered my wine glass. "...and then all of a sudden it seems unnecessary to say anything."

The corner where we were sitting was small and private. The restaurant felt warm and safe. It wasn't so much that Michael said anything profound. There was simply an ease between us I hadn't felt with a man since long before the Phantom appeared on the scene. It was almost disconcerting. That kind of comfort between a man and woman ought to take years to develop, I thought. Perhaps it was sexual attraction disguised as something else.

Outside the restaurant the rain was filling the narrow cobble stone street with such torrents that cars were having a difficult time navigating the deep pools of water. I was glad we hadn't brought the Jaguar. It hated rain. Periodically the wind whipped the rain against the windows with a loud crash and conversation in the former warehouse would pause, then lunge forward with even louder intensity. Everybody was getting sloshed, inside as well as out. The rain and the noise, combined with the Old Havana setting made the evening slightly surreal. The wine had been just dry enough, the red bowls filled with black mussels the perfect artistic presentation, the ceiling fans, the faded blue shutters and the old jeep in a corner the right touches.

"Yes," Michael said, leaning towards me. "it seems unnecessary to say anything and yet you want to tell them things you've never told anybody." He was looking at me, not at the rain or the mussels. I had the distinct sensation he wanted to touch me though he made no move in my direction.

"Well," I said. "...well."

All around us people were talking and laughing. Waiters hovered about with fresh coffee and Cuban cigars. It was one restaurant in town where smoking was encouraged. I looked down at my partially eaten dinner and across the table at Michael. He smiled slightly as he pushed his chair back. "Come on," he said in a low voice, "let's do something crazy. Let's go for a walk in the rain."

It wasn't the first time I was attracted to a man since the divorce from the Phantom. But it was the first time I wanted to do more than walk in the rain. I wondered what Gussie would say when I told her. I knew she saw me as a woman who poured all my sexual energy into my art business. Discovering new artists, launching careers for the most talented ones, developing a reputation as the most unusual gallery in the city, most of the time such achievements were as satisfying as orgasm. Most of the time.

Michael had brought a large black umbrella. When he opened it he put his arm around my waist and held me tightly. "If we're going to drown," he said, "we'll go down together. Let's make a run for it."

His rented car was only three blocks away, but by the time we had splashed our way over the cobblestones my good black shoes were soaked and water was pouring down both our faces. Seeing a man as a sodden mass always brings out the best in me. I let him keep his arm around my waist longer than necessary.

"It's a good thing I work out," I said. "Otherwise my little southern body couldn't take all this exertion."

"Why don't you come to California," he said, bending over me so low that the water from his coat dripped onto mine, "so your little southern body can see how it likes the west coast. It never rains in Los Angeles."

"I have an art gallery," I said. "I have artists depending on me. I love what I'm doing. Besides, I don't speak Japanese."

"The Japanese don't own all of Los Angeles," he said. "Gangs own the other half."

I smiled up at him. There were possibly men as attractive as Michael DeBord but since none of them had his arm around my waist in the middle of the Sixth Street Market in a torrential downpour, all paled in comparison. But meeting an attractive man was the last thing I needed at the moment. Lucy Moon's paintings had brought him there. And there was one in particular I wanted him to see.

"I'll consider it a serious invitation," I said as we settled into the dry car, "but first I need to tell you about David Moon."

XV

"So, what did Michael DeBord think of Lucy's painting?" Gussie said the next morning at the athletic club. The mirrored workout room gleamed with new turquoise and chrome equipment designed to incite even the most recalcitrant member to a feverish pitch of activity. Feverish would hardly describe Gussie and me, however. It was our day to work on lower bodies, not our favorite exercise. We adjusted the weights on machines designed to produce Cindy Crawford thighs and settled stoically into our routine.

Gussie and I have few secrets from each other. I pushed hard against the forty pounds of pressure I gave myself on the outer thigh machine and pondered how much I was going to tell her. "Michael's reaction to the painting was not what I had expected," I said.

"Well?"

"He told me to name my price," I said, "that he would be serving his collectors well by buying the painting."

Gussie stopped her machine and looked at me. "No kidding? Any price?"

"He said the Japanese would love it, that it was a cross between tongue-in-cheek surrealism and a Hiyakawa film."

"He talked like that? Hiyakawa?"

"Yep, and that's not all."

"There's more?"

"He said when I had negotiated the sale I should deliver the painting to the West Coast in person. His firm would pay all expenses."

"The two of you waterlogged from all that rain last night?"

"I liked him, Gussie," I said. "I liked him a lot."

Gussie bent over in mock dismay, clasped her head between her knees and moaned loudly. "You are really something," she said. "First of all, Lucy won't talk to you because she can't deal with the fact that David died in your gallery. You have no idea whether she's even interested in selling this painting. Secondly, you're using the painting to try to lure David's murderer into confessing. And now you're falling for a man who speaks Japanese and lives on the other side of the country."

"I didn't say I was falling for him, only that I liked him. Besides, there may be no reason ever to see him again. I know Lucy. I'm certain that she won't part with that painting, no matter what anybody offers. And if she did, it would be Lila Hunt's sale, not mine. So let's finish with these machines before I decide all this pressure is a metaphor for my life."

But I couldn't say for sure that I knew Lucy anymore. Now that David was dead, everything in her life was bound to be different, even her attitude toward her work. Perhaps she would sell the painting. In fact, maybe she would want to get rid of it. Having it around might be a constant reminder of David's death. "Please understand," her note to me had said. But understand what? That she didn't want to talk to me because of David? That she didn't want to talk to me now, but would later? Or was there something else I was supposed to understand?

"Tell Lucy to name her price," Michael had said. "It's an extraordinary painting. If it's in the right collection, it can make her famous." I remembered David had told Mayo his giraffe would make him famous, too. Now David was dead. And both the giraffe and the painting were on a section of film that nobody had seen. Only for the briefest moment did I contemplate how much money Michael's corporate collectors might be willing to pay for a picture that was ostensibly about getting loose and which, in reality, was about dying.

But there was little time to be philosophical. Both Arabella and Jimmy Travers were due at the gallery and I had to set the scene properly. I let go of the pleasant, but sodden, recollection of the night before with a man who had kissed me lightly on the forehead as he headed up highway 95 for Washington, D.C. "I'll call you," he had said. I wondered if I cared.

As soon as I unlocked the gallery I thought about David's penchant for the theatrical. I'll match him drama for drama, I decided as I set up the metal easel in the center of my office. Lucy's painting stood in a corner with the painted surface facing the wall. Before I turned it around an image of something else shoved against my memory, not quite coming into focus. What was it? Something odd about the gallery the night of the filming. Something that had to do with Mayo's giraffe. But it kept eluding me. I closed my eyes and tried to picture the gallery as David had arranged it for the filming. Mentally I went round the room, taking in first one painting and then the next. I could visualize the forest paintings especially.

Next I pictured the giraffe. Who had hung it on the wall above the plastic covered figure in the woods? Had it been David's girlfriend, Barbara Barksdale? Or perhaps John Owen Smith? At one point I was vaguely aware that Barbara and John Owen seemed to disagree about something. No, perhaps it was David and John Owen. Lucy had told Mavredes and me that David had quarreled with John Owen over the film.

I squeezed my eyes tighter. It was neither Barbara nor John Owen who had installed the giraffe. It was, the figure was blurry. A lot was going on at the time. Neither the face nor the person involved would take shape. Out of frustration I grabbed Lucy's painting away from the wall, yanked it around so I could see the front, and yelled at it as though it were alive.

"Who are you, damn it? Who are you under all that plastic?" It had never occurred to me until that moment to question the identity of the figure. I looked closer to see if I could tell whether it were a man or a woman. But there was nothing to give it away.

And then a face came into focus. Connie Lee. One of the two Korean sisters. Connie Lee had carried the giraffe across the gallery while David was giving directions about the placement of Lucy's paintings. Connie Lee had hung the giraffe above the picture of the draped figure in the woods. The placement in the gallery had been her choice. I could even hear David's voice saying, "The giraffe can go anywhere, Connie. You like animals. Use your judgment."

"This painting," Connie had said. "I want the giraffe above this painting." It was all coming back to me. It had been Connie Lee, too, who unwrapped Lucy's painting. But then the image faded again. All I could recall was the plastic wrapping being tossed into a corner. At least I knew now that Connie Lee had been responsible for at least one piece of the black plastic. Had it been the piece draped over David's body?

I shifted my attention back to Lucy's painting. "Here we go," I said, lifting it onto the easel. Then I backed up to the doorway to test the viewing angle. I moved the easel several times before I was satisfied that it was in the right spot. It couldn't be immediately accessible. The viewer would have to step into the room before seeing it. Finally I was ready to adjust the lights. I had debated calling Harry to do the lighting but quickly discarded that idea. He would only give me a lecture and increase his insistence that I take a vacation. As I climbed on a stool to focus several spot lights on the painting I wondered what Harry would say if I told him I might take a brief trip to Los Angeles. There was a message from Michael on my answering machine asking if I had spoken to Lucy about selling the painting.

When I finished in the office I decided I had time for a cup of coffee and was locking the door to the gallery to head across the street to McDonald's when someone called my name.

"Miz Wallace?"

I turned quickly to see Beverly standing in the narrow space between Bernard's building and mine. Behind her in the shadows as usual was Jack.

"Oh, Beverly, I've been wondering where you and Jack had gone. I'm so glad to see you. Please promise you won't disappear again. I need you."

"Jack and me are moving," Beverly said. "That's what we come to tell you."

"Moving? Where? Out of town?"

Jack laughed softly.

"No," said Beverly. "The social worker wants to put us in a house over on Grace Street."

"Is that all right with you?" I wondered when Beverly and Jack had last lived in a house.

"Suits us," Beverly said. Behind her, Jack cleared his throat. She turned her head slowly to exchange a glance with him. Then she nodded imperceptibly and said, "that man, you still looking for him?"

Oh Beverly, God bless you, I thought. "He's coming to the gallery today," I said. I tried to keep my voice calm. Beverly and Jack had disappeared before. They could vanish again. But this was my opportunity. "I want you both to do something for me," I said. "I want you to sit across the street at the restaurant and watch out the window when a man comes to my place in the next half hour. I want you to tell me if it's the same man you saw in the limousine the night David died."

"Won't be no police, will there?" Beverly said.

"No police, a woman, maybe. But she's with the newspaper, not the police. Besides, nobody can see you across the street. Nobody will know what you're doing."

Beverly stared at the restaurant. "Your treat?" she said.

"You bet," I said, reaching into my purse for a twenty. "Anything you want."

I glanced at my watch. Arabella was due in ten minutes. I decided to forego the coffee. As I watched Beverly and Jack dodge the traffic on Cary Street I wondered if I was doing the right thing. Harry would have called Mavredes long ago. Gussie had warned me to be careful. I went back inside the gallery to check Mayo's animals one last time. At my direction Austin had hung the giraffe in the same spot where it had been the night of the movie shoot. His only comment had been how heavy the wood was.

The telephone was ringing. As I reached for it, I prayed that it was not Jimmy Travers saying he couldn't make it, after all.

"Hello?"

The softly accented voice on the other end seemed to take several deep breaths before announcing her name. "This is Barbara Barksdale," the voice said. "I believe you called me a while ago. I'm so sorry it's taken this long to get back to you."

Barbara Barksdale, David's girlfriend. Everything was happening at once.

"Yes," I said. "I wondered if I could ask you a couple of questions about David." I hoped Jimmy and Bernard would not appear while I was on the phone.

There was another long interval of soft breathing. "I suppose so," she said. "It couldn't hurt, could it?"

"Do you have a copy of the film shot at the gallery?" I said.

Abruptly the gentle voice changed. "That's all you want? The film? I thought you wanted to know something about David." The soft accent vanished.

"David and I were together for a long time," she said, the indignation rising in her voice. "I probably know more about David Moon than anybody in the world. Why the hell don't you ask what kind of person he was? He wasn't just the creative young artist on the way up, you know. David used everybody like he used me. He was willing to do anything to get that movie finished. And that screwed up family of his, Lucy painting her weird nightmares, his father, the perfect businessman except when it came to helping his son, an uncle nobody talks to, all those tears shed at the funeral. Bunch of shit. Nobody cares he's dead. So why the fuck do you want the film?"

"I care that he's dead," I said. "And I'm sorry you're so upset. You probably care, too. I'd like to get together with you to talk. I've got one of his mother's paintings at the gallery now, the one with the figure covered with black plastic, standing at the edge of the forest. Maybe you could stop by to take a look at it again and we could talk about the night you did the movie shoot."

On the other end of the line Barbara Barksdale began to sob. "I don't care about the damn painting. I hate that painting! It wasn't even supposed to be in the movie, but Lucy insisted. David and Connie Lee had a thing about that picture. Maybe I'll tell her to come look at it. It'll give her a big charge." She was crying in earnest by this time.

"I'm sorry—I'm truly sorry." I waited for what I hoped was the appropriate amount of time. "Did David ever mention a man named Jimmy Travers?"

The sobs stopped abruptly. "Look," she said. "I don't have a copy of the film. Maybe Arik does. Call him. The painting never bothered him. He always considered it as big a joke as David's family. He works part-time for Park Place Video."

"Not Arik," I said, "nor David's family." I was getting tired of hearing about the peculiarities of David's relatives. I knew Lucy, she was no stranger than the rest of us. "Jimmy Travers. Please, did you ever hear David ever say anything about him?"

Outside I saw Bernard walking up the sidewalk, headed straight for the gallery with a tall man with dark hair and a moustache. The receiver was still in my hand. But it didn't matter. The line was dead. Barbara had hung up.

I was frustrated as I went to the door. Barbara Barksdale had been no help other than to stir up my curiosity about Lucy's painting. But there was no time for artistic or psychological analysis. This was my moment with Jimmy Travers. My chance to confront the man who may have killed David. Could I pull it off? I opened the door and smiled, not too much, just enough.

"Hello, Bernard," I said. I stuck out my hand towards the man with him. "And you must be Jimmy Travers. I'm Rosemund Wallace. I've been looking forward to meeting you. Thank you for coming."

Jimmy Travers was almost as tall as Michael DeBord. But that was the only characteristic they had in common. Although he looked at me, I had the distinct sensation that he didn't really see me. His handshake, too, was perfunctory. I've done this a hundred times, he seemed to be saying, let's get it over with in a hurry. I could understand why Brookfield had hired him. It was his style, too. Bernard's face was expressionless, a sure giveaway he would rather have been anywhere but there.

But once inside the door, Bernard whistled softly. "The place looks terrific," he said, as if seeing it for the first time. "Lord of the Woods, indeed."

Jimmy looked at Bernard. "What?"

"Lord of the Woods," I said. "It's how Mayo Johnson refers to himself. He gives these sticks and branches life through his art." I was watching Jimmy carefully. At first he didn't seem to know what to do. Then he took a few tentative steps in the direction of the eagle.

"This the piece?"

"Yes," I said. "The American eagle. The one I believe the governor might like."

Jimmy walked around the pedestal which displayed the bird. He frowned. His eyes were dark and unreadable. "He carve this stuff?"

"No," I said, "that's what's so special about Mayo's work. He finds the driftwood and sees an animal in the wood. Then he paints what he sees. That giraffe on the wall in the corner is the first piece he brought to the gallery." I paused, "...we used the giraffe in a movie that was filmed here. It got lots of attention."

Jimmy looked at me with no expression on his face. "I didn't come here to see a giraffe," he said. "I came to see this eagle." Then he grinned and his angular features softened. "Let's not mix our metaphors," he said. "Governor Brookfield isn't going wild game hunting. He's just trying to create a Republican atmosphere in the mansion." He turned to Bernard and laughed. Bernard's mouth twitched in a manner that might have passed for a smile.

"You got here at just the right time," I said, looking past both men. In front of the gallery I could see Arabella getting out of her jeep. "Now we can hear an expert's opinion of this work."

"So that's Richmond's noted art critic," Jimmy said, almost to himself. "Looks like she couldn't find her way out of a shopping mall." Arabella was wearing slacks and her leather jacket. Her hair was pulled back in a pony tail. She looked even younger than she did at the movie shoot. I wondered if she would recognize Jimmy from the photograph she had given Gussie.

"Good to meet you gentlemen," Arabella said, after introductions, "though I'm afraid you'll have to play second fiddle to these animals. Rosemund was very insistent that I see them. Every once in a while she picks a winner." With a wave of her notebook she dismissed us and began a sweep of the gallery. It was the perfect time to lead Jimmy to the bait.

"While Arabella's looking at Mayo's work I'll show you the rest of the gallery," I said, touching him on the arm. "I have another exhibition space in the balcony area upstairs."

Jimmy looked at Arabella. Then at the eagle.

"Don't pay any attention to me," Arabella said over her shoulder. "After I've taken a look, I'll tell you what I think, if you're interested."

Jimmy had no choice but to follow me up the metal stairs. I wondered what he was thinking, especially if he had been there before. I forced myself to act casual. Bernard remained downstairs with Arabella, responding with a quick laugh to a remark she'd made which I couldn't catch. I had installed several new paintings in the balcony space so I would have something to discuss with Jimmy as we made our way upstairs. Pointing to the first one, I commented on the artist's technique and said something innocuous about his background.

As we neared the door to my office I could feel my heart pounding. I didn't even glance towards the bathroom, partly because Jimmy was with me and I didn't want to act too obvious, and partly because it was the room where someone I cared about had died. I stepped in front of Jimmy and entered the office first so that I could take a position behind Lucy's painting. In that way I would be able to see his face the exact moment he first encountered the painting. I learned if you watched carefully, it was possible to read the subtleties in a person's expression when you caught them with their emotional pants down. As I concentrated on Jimmy I heard my voice chattering away as if my vocal chords were on automatic.

What happened next was almost too fast to note. Jimmy entered the office, his expression polite and almost bored. Then he stopped abruptly and stared at the painting. His eyes didn't exactly pop but his pupils dilated slightly. I had situated the lights exactly right to reflect off the black plastic in the picture, creating a three dimensional effect that I knew would be particularly unnerving, especially combined with the light reflected on the branches of the trees. It was a dramatic work of art to begin with; occupying the center of the room with several spot lights trained on it gave it an unsettling intensity that was impossible to ignore. Even the mysterious standing figure covered with plastic took on a new, and almost ominous meaning. It could have been male or female. Most importantly, if you were preoccupied with David Moon, it could have been David himself.

"My God!" Jimmy said in a hoarse voice. "What's this doing here!"

"You recognize it, then," I said quickly.

"Yes, I mean, no" He looked up from the painting, his eyes narrowing in a manner that made me glad I was not alone in the gallery with him. He was strong enough to lift me with one hand. I thought about how strong you would have to be to choke David and then hang his body from the rafters. I sensed Jimmy poised to move in my direction and then something seemed to warn him to stay where he was. Arabella and Bernard, I thought, thank God they're downstairs.

"What's going on?" Jimmy said. "What are you trying to do?" His eyes were colder than the eyes Mayo painted on his driftwood animals.

"I want to understand why a young man died," I said, sounding much more confident than I felt. "Perhaps you could help me."

"You're fucking with my mind," he said. "The last time I saw this painting it was hanging in David Moon's apartment. What's it doing here?"

"So you knew David?"

"Sure I did." He made an off-handed gesture, as though to say 'so what?' His hands were huge, twice as big as mine. I remembered that David was not very tall. A man as large as Jimmy Travers could lift him easily. "We saw each other a couple of times socially. David hung around the Fire Station Playhouse a lot. He liked actors, the theater, that kind of stuff. You know how it goes."

I decided to take a chance. Opportunity was slipping through my fingers. If Jimmy could change the subject to the Fire Station that easily I would lose whatever momentum I had going with the painting. Drawing my five feet, two inches up as tall as possible, I placed both hands on the back of the easel and took a deep breath.

"This painting was never at David's," I said, hoping that my voice didn't break. I had no idea whether it was in David's apartment or not, but it seemed the right thing to say. "It was in Lucy's studio until she brought it to the gallery to shoot a movie scene." I clutched the easel tighter. "If you've seen this picture before, it was either at Lucy's or here at the gallery...and I would bet money it was here."

Like two children playing double dare, Jimmy and I stared at each other. I waited for him to do something to give himself away, to prove he was in the gallery the night David died—hoped he would do something, because I had run out of things to say.

His eyes dilated again. I had never seen a grown man's eyes dilate so easily. I didn't know whether it was out of fear or anger, but I had definitely hit a chord somewhere. I tried to imagine what kind of relationship he might have had with David. It made me shudder.

"Bitch," he said, turning to walk out of the office.

"You blinked first," I said. But he was already on the metal stairs so fast I couldn't tell whether he heard me or not. He clattered down the steps and must have rushed past Bernard and Arabella without a word. I heard the front door open and close and then he was gone. I didn't care. At last I believed I had a reason to call Detective Mavredes.

"Does this mean he didn't want the eagle?" Bernard said as I made my way down the stairs after giving Lucy's painting a parting pat of approval.

"It means he knew David Moon," I said, "and he's seen the painting before this afternoon."

"What painting?" Arabella said, "will somebody tell me what's going on? I thought we were trying to make friends with the state's power structure. What did you say to him upstairs, Rosemund? Friendship was the last thing on that guy's mind. He was mad as hell."

I rubbed the driftwood eagle on its bald head. "The governor just missed a wonderful opportunity to own a piece of art that will only increase in value," I said. "Too bad he doesn't have folks with a better eye working for him ." I pointed out the front door at McDonald's. "Across the street are two, ah, unusual witnesses who may be able to tell us whether Jimmy Travers is the man they saw at the gallery the night David died," I said. "If we're lucky, they got a good look at him. We need to get over there now. On the way across the street I'll explain about the painting."

"Right," Bernard said. "The couple in question have a bad habit of disappearing."

"So we need to move fast," I said, "and talk to them before they're gone again. We've got to treat them with kid gloves, too, not scare them away. They're rather...well, shy."

"Act casual, is that what you're saying?" Arabella said. Then she stuck her fists in the pockets of her leather jacket and assumed a swaggering stance. "Hey, youse guys, you do a stake out? Huh? Huh? Squeal or we'll lock youse up."

"And my realtor told me Carytown would never be very exciting," Bernard said, as the three of us hurried across the street, dodging traffic with an intensity that in an earlier era might have characterized a lynching party.

XVI

I was worried for nothing. Beverly and Jack were waiting for us. And instead of clamming up in the presence of a newspaper reporter, they beamed. They grinned. As soon as they visualized themselves in the headlines, they could have been signed up as guests on a national talk show. I couldn't believe the transformation. Instead of being intimidated by the three of us or what they might have witnessed, Carytown's most retiring couple wouldn't shut up. Once she learned that Arabella was a reporter, Beverly was animated and talkative, spilling her life story while Jack exchanged guarded glances with Bernard, actually preening at times, as though he were sitting for his portrait.

"Yes, ma'am," Beverly said, "Jack and me was born in this city, went to Thomas Jefferson High School back when it had the winning football team, not that Jack was big enough to play on the team. It was a white school then, nobody knew no better. Coloreds got a right to schooling just like the rest of us. I tell you. That's why the country's in so much trouble, keeping people from having the opportunity to amount to something..."

"Shy," Arabella said under her breath.

I busied myself with my coffee, thankful at least that Arabella had the decency not to look at me as she scribbled in her notebook.

I kept quiet as long as I could stand it, and finally said to Beverly, "Could we talk about the man who was in the gallery half an hour ago? The tall guy who left right before we joined you."

Jack lit a cigarette. Beverly looked at Arabella.

"Nobody will hurt you," Arabella said. "The newspaper will help you. We're on your side."

"He was dressed different," Beverly said in a whisper, "but we could see him clear across the street, better even than that night."

"Well," I said, taking a deep breath. This is it, I thought. With Arabella and Bernard as witnesses, I can call Mavredes and have him invite Jimmy Travers downtown for questioning. Maybe there's enough evidence to hold him for murder. Maybe Jimmy would even confess when confronted by two people who saw him at the gallery the night David died. My old sense of assurance had returned. If I could prove David didn't kill himself but was murdered and I found the man who killed him, the break between Lucy and me might be healed. Maybe she'd even let me sell her painting to Michael DeBord's Japanese company and I would take it to Los Angeles. I could see Michael again and...

I smiled with great confidence and sat up a little straighter in the restaurant booth. In my mind Jimmy Travers was already in jail. Lucy's grief might be relieved a bit to realize her son hadn't wanted to end his own life. The governor might even call her to offer his condolences and express his dismay that one of his staff committed such a terrible crime. I could get back to running an art gallery. "Sooo," I said, drawing out the word slowly and dramatically, "you saw that same man go into the gallery the night David died?"

Beverly leaned forward across the booth. "Why, no, honey," she said. "He didn't go in no where. The boy, he come out of your place and got in that black TownCar with him and they drove off."

"It doesn't mean Jimmy didn't take him back to the gallery and do him in later that night," Gussie said that evening when we met for dinner at the Vietnamese restaurant. "At least your Lieutenant Mavredes agreed to ask him some questions. You've accomplished that much."

"Sure, he agreed to question him," I said, "but he wasn't very happy about it. And I feel like a fool. 'Two homeless people fingering a man who works for the governor,' he said. 'What kind of odds can we give this one?'" I rolled a bottle of my favorite Chinese beer between both hands. I had no appetite for dinner. My plate of shrimp broiled on stalks of sugar cane sat untouched. "I'm in trouble, Gussie," I said. '"Jimmy Travers knows I'm behind this. I as much as accused him of doing away with David. If he's publicly embarrassed, you can bet he won't let me off the hook. I may be finished as an art dealer."

"What could he possibly do?" Gussie said. "Come on, Rosemund, lighten up. Eat your shrimp or I'll eat it."

I took a few bites. My mind was filled with images that seemed to be struggling with each other. Connie Lee removing black plastic from around Lucy's painting was one image. Connie Lee exclaiming over something in the picture, something that must have been familiar, or upsetting to her. It was a similar reaction to Jimmy Traver's when he saw the painting in my office. I remembered his eyes had gone to one spot on the canvas. Where? What part of the picture had caused such a strong response on his part? And what could it possibly have to do with Connie Lee?

I dropped the chopsticks holding a piece of shrimp.

"The rope!" I said, "he was looking at the rope."

"What are you talking about?"

"Something odd about the red rope that both Jimmy and Connie Lee saw in that painting of Lucy's. It wasn't the figure in black plastic—it was the rope. All this time I've been thinking the draped figure was the most important thing in the painting." I pushed my chair back from the table and stood up. "Come on," I said. We've got to go back to the gallery and take another look at that picture before Mavredes picks it up in the morning."

It took less than ten minutes to pay the bill and drive up the street to the gallery. Gussie kept quiet as I parked the Jaguar in front of the building, although she did shake her head a couple of times. At night the gallery always looked particularly dramatic with the broad, two-story expanse of glass. The neon sign hanging from the rafters just over the brick sculpture area flashed "Wallace Gallery" in brilliant pink and turquoise. I had spent more money than necessary to have the name scripted in lights with the kind of flourish I liked. Sometimes I would drive down Cary Street by myself late at night to look at the neon. In the darkness it provided a warm invitation into the gallery—especially when there were pieces of contemporary sculpture glowing beneath it.

"Why is the gallery so dark?" Gussie said as she got out of the car. "Your sign's off."

"It can't be," I said. "I never unplug the neon."

"See for yourself." She pointed towards the front door. The gallery was totally black. No pink and blue neon, no spot lights, not even the tiny red light visible on the wall through the glass front door indicating that the alarm system was activated.

I felt a knot forming in the pit of my stomach—a cold knot that was nothing less than fear. All the electricity was off in the gallery, including the backup for the alarm. Otherwise, it would have been ringing and the police would have been there. To the right of the gallery a portrait of a middle aged woman with soft wavy hair was framed in the window in Bernard's studio, and flooded with light reflecting warmly off the rose-colored walls in the entrance to his building. To our left "Emerson's Apparel" was also lit from the inside even though the boutique's new owners had only begun their renovation. Behind us McDonald's was doing its usual bustling evening business, its own neon signs inviting customers to try a 99 cent special.

The gallery was the only dark building on the block.

I wondered if my emotions were similar to those of a person who comes home to find her house has burned down.

"The electrical box is on the side of the building," I said in a surprisingly calm voice. "I'll check it out."

As I stepped into the shadows between my building and Bernard's I could see in the darkness the door to the electrical box was ajar. Cut wires were sticking out in all directions like a tossed salad. Slowly I looked upwards toward the bathroom window on the side of the building. Even from where I stood it was obvious the window was open. This time it was propped up with a piece of metal sculpture that had been on my desk. For one odd moment I remembered Tyrone's comment about how it looked like somebody had taken a few swipes across the dirty window. This time there were more than a few swipes. I was convinced now someone had climbed out the window the night David died.

The silence in the gallery as I unlocked the front door could only be described as cold. With the neon out of commission all the warmth in the place had vanished. I had never been in the building when it was completely dark. Mayo's animal sculptures stood like blind witnesses to the darkness. I almost bumped into the pedestal holding the American eagle as I groped for the metal stairway. Gussie and I climbed it in silence. Once we reached the balcony exhibition space we felt our way across the floor to the bathroom. The streetlight cast a silver sliver of illumination through the open window. From where we stood in the doorway, there was enough light to see that the metal sculpture which held up the window was dented across the top as though it had been jammed beneath the edge of the window with a great deal of effort.

Neither of us showed any inclination to enter the bathroom although we could tell immediately it was empty. It was small enough to see the entire interior, with a sink and counter along one side, a toilet on the wall which held the window and a closet in the spot which once was a shower. I cast a quick glance upwards at the beams across the ceiling and shivered. Unless someone was in the closet there was no place to hide.

"You're not going to check out the closet?" Gussie's fears were clearly the same as mine.

"Be my guest," I said. "It's filled with rolls of bubble wrap. If someone's in there, they would have a hard time breathing." Though I didn't think the closet was large enough for both a person and the packing material, the truth was I had no intention of being the one who discovered another body wrapped in plastic.

"Come out with your hands up!" Gussie cried as she gave the closet door a good yank. The bubble wrap gave off a funny, almost clean odor. Harry had gotten hundreds of yards of it free from one of his medical suppliers. It was the sort of thing he did for the gallery; no glamour, but it saved a few bucks here and there. Just as I had hoped, only the bubble wrap filled the space. I was more interested in the office anyway. The door was closed, though I remembered leaving it ajar after Jimmy Travers had stomped out of the room. My heart was beating fast as I turned the door knob.

The last time I pushed open an upstairs door something terrible awaited me on the other side. This was the gallery I had loved for the past four years. Now it was fast becoming a place where I dreaded what was behind every closed door and open window. Only this time the horror was Lucy's painting. Or rather the absence of the painting. For it was gone. Only an empty easel was waiting on the other side of the door. The emptiness was as frightening as actually seeing someone cutting the electrical wire and climbing up the side of the building.

Gussie had to put it into words, almost as though stating it aloud gave us a reason for standing in the empty room.

"The painting," she said, sounding like a child who had lost her favorite toy, "someone stole Lucy's painting."

I slumped down in the chair beside the desk and picked up the telephone, forgetting for a moment that it, too, was useless. When I turned around to say something to Gussie, she was no longer in the room.

"I'm trying to see how they got the picture out the window without damaging it," she called from the bathroom. The hurt, childlike astonishment in her voice was gone. She was the old, independent Gussie again.

"Don't touch anything," I said. "The police will want to fingerprint the window sill and the thing wedged under the window.

"Rosemund," she said. "Come here, quick."

XVII

With the window open, a brace of cold air filled the room. It was almost refreshing. I was feeling sick to my stomach. But it was more from relief than from fear. We hadn't found another body. Someone had simply gone to a lot of trouble to steal a picture. They could have slashed it to pieces still on the easel, or covered it with spray paint—or worse. Since it was gone, perhaps whoever wanted it would keep it for them self. Or maybe they stole it because of something in the painting they didn't want seen—something that had to do with the red cord, I was certain. By this time Lucy's painting had taken on almost monumental importance to me and my imagination was really working overtime.

"What is it?" I said to Gussie as I entered the bathroom. "What's the matter?"

She was standing by the window with her back to me. I thought she had seen something on the sidewalk below and wanted to show me. I wedged myself in beside her and looked out the window. It was a tight squeeze but she refused to budge from the spot where she had called me.

"Look," she said, "look closely." Instead of something out the window, she was pointing to the bent piece of sculpture jammed into the window frame.

I squinted in the darkness, trying to see better.

"Right there," she said, "around the base of the sculpture. Look."

I leaned so close that my face was almost touching the metal. Then I saw that there were some strands of fabric or something like fabric caught in the sharp edges of the base of the piece.

"...string or something," I said, frowning. "I don't understand what's so important about—"

"Rosemund!" She almost shouted my name. "Are you blind? It's red, for God's sake. It's strands of red silk!"

This time I was sick in earnest. I leaned back against the sink, struggling with waves of nausea. "What's going on?" I said finally. "What are we overlooking?"

"Mavredes," Gussie said, taking me firmly by the arm. "I'm calling him myself. Come on, there's a pay phone across the street by McDonald's. I don't care where he is tonight, he's coming to the gallery."

The nausea disappeared as soon as I hit the cold night air. I took half a dozen deep breaths and felt like myself once more. "Mavredes can wait one more minute," I said. "The contractor redoing the shop next door had a couple of ladders here for his crew. Let's take a look in back. Maybe our thief used a ladder this time."

"This time," Gussie repeated under her breath. "Nobody but you thinks somebody murdered David and crawled down between the buildings the first time." I was aware she sounded a little less certain than usual. The better part of wisdom told me not to comment. Gussie would come around. Reluctantly she followed me into the alley.

By now I was so angry I was no longer afraid of anything. Lucy had lost her son in my gallery. Somebody had violated my space twice, the second time, to take a painting somehow connected with the first violation, David's death. It was as though a shootout had been staged at my house and I was the last to know about it.

Sure enough two metal ladders were sprawled against the back of the building destined to be Emerson's Fine Apparel. I wondered why the construction crew had left them so exposed until I noticed a tarp carelessly tossed over a stack of scrap lumber.

"The tarp probably covered them," I said, "...but not very well. The work crew obviously doesn't know this block. They're lucky the ladders are still here." I was surprised the architect didn't warn them about the neighborhood, what with homeless people living in garages and young men hanging themselves in art galleries. My bad mood was intensifying.

I turned towards Gussie and said more gruffly than necessary. "Now we can call the police."

She was not looking at the ladders.

"Rosemund," she said in a harsh whisper. "There's someone lying in the alley over there near Bernard's garbage cans. And he doesn't look drunk. He looks...dead."

Even from where we stood in the shadows behind the gallery I could see it was Tyrone.

He was sprawled on his back in the gravel with one arm flung across his chest. Blood seeped down his neck from some unseen wound. As we knelt beside him I thought about all the turkeys, watermelons, pumpkins, flowers and fur jackets he had tried to sell me. I remembered the weeds in the space where I parked the Jaguar needed pulling and the windows in front of the gallery needed washing. I had been too preoccupied lately to do anything but say "no" to all of Tyrone's requests for money. And now he was dead. I was filled with remorse.

"He's still alive," Gussie said. "I can feel his heart beating."

I placed my hand on his body. Sure enough there was a steady rise and fall of his chest. Carefully I touched his face. It was warm. If this is a trick, Tyrone, I said to myself, you'll never pull another weed in this town again.

"I'll stay with him," I said to Gussie. "Call an ambulance before phoning Mavredes."

Half an hour later Tyrone, who had regained partial consciousness and was moaning in a particularly pitiful manner, was on his way to the hospital. Two police cars were also parked in the alley and Lieutenant Mavredes stood in front of the still-darkened gallery with Gussie and me. He was not a happy man.

"I let you have that painting against my better judgment," he said. "I should have kept the damn thing until I delivered it personally to Lucy Moon. You and that picture are nothing but trouble. It's already brought the governor's wrath down on the department. Brookfield called you a loose cannon. Implied you should be sued for defamation of character."

"The person who stole it might have killed Tyrone," I said. "A man's life is as important as Governor Brookfield's wrath."

"There you go again," Mavredes said, "assuming a conspiracy. The guy we scooped up out of the alley reeked of alcohol. He may have fallen and knocked himself out."

"Even Tyrone wouldn't hit himself on the back of the head," I said with an unexpected surge of motherly concern. "I know Tyrone. He sort of, well, looks after the gallery. He probably saw somebody suspicious hanging around and got beat up for his troubles. When will the hospital let you talk to him?"

"Suspicious! How could anyone look more suspicious than Tyrone," Mavredes said. "He may have stolen the painting himself to try to sell it."

"Personally, I never thought Tyrone had much of an eye for art," Gussie said. "Besides, he didn't know the painting was in the gallery."

Mavredes sighed deeply. Until that point he had more or less ignored Gussie. It struck me at that moment that he and Gussie could easily patronize the same hair stylist. The same sharp cut over the ears, a similar lock of hair across the forehead. Maybe Mavredes was not married. I could fix him up with Gussie. They would make a knock-out couple.

"But other people knew?" Mavredes said. "Is that what you're implying?"

His question yanked me out of my matchmaker mode. "Besides you and me?" I said. "Yes, several people knew about the painting. Jimmy Travers, for one."

By this time the policemen who were examining the back alley had joined us in the front of the gallery. Across the street several people who had noticed the squad cars had come out of McDonald's and were standing in the parking lot talking and pointing.

"Found this in the alley, Lieutenant," one of the policemen said. He was holding a plastic bag containing what appeared to be a piece of wood, painted wood which struck me as oddly familiar. "Blood all over it. Looks like it could be the assault weapon."

Gussie rolled her eyes. Good thinking, she mouthed.

I reached for the bag to get a better look. The policeman snatched it back until Mavredes frowned and nodded his okay for me to examine it. I carried the bag to the front of Bernard's studio where the bright light from his window confirmed what I had feared. The piece of wood was yellow with black marks on it. One end was jagged as though it had been broken off from a bigger piece. The sick place in the pit of my stomach had become an actual ache.

"I think it's a piece of Mayo's giraffe," I said.

"What?" said the policeman, "giraffe?"

Gussie and Mavredes were by my side in two seconds. Mavredes mumbled something under his breath and then jerked his head back towards the alley where we had discovered Tyrone. "Look in the garbage cans," he said to the policeman, "see if you can find anything more that resembles this…this…"

"...animal," Gussie said. "It's an animal, a painted giraffe."

The policeman tried unsuccessfully to keep a straight face.

"Don't just stand there," Mavredes said, "get going. The woman said giraffe." He started for the front of the gallery. "I suppose your prints are all over the door," he said to me over his shoulder. "Might as well open it again and we'll take a look inside."

Instead of following him with the gallery key I looked back down the darkened passageway between Bernard's building and mine. "Whoever stole the painting probably got the giraffe the same way," I said, "out the bathroom window, not the front door. But the giraffe was heavy. Maybe they dropped it on the cement. Why don't you get a flashlight and look below the window? See if something is there."

"First a fucking picture and now a giraffe," Mavredes said. "Why couldn't the boy have died in a bar." But he seemed to decide that maybe my suggestion was not so bad. "Hey, Wayne," he called to the second policeman who had joined the first policeman looking for remains of Mayo's sculpture.

Wayne appeared quickly from around the corner of the gallery. "Yes, Lieutenant?"

"Get a flashlight," Mavredes said. "Look up and down the walk between these two buildings. Don't touch anything. Just see what you can find."

"Pieces of a giraffe," Gussie said, "that's what you're looking for." Leave it to Gussie to retain her sense of fun.

Mavredes glared at her. "Open the gallery," he said to me. "Let's make sure the thing is really gone."

"It's gone," I said. "You can see through the glass that it's not there. Gussie and I never noticed the giraffe was missing when we went in the first time. The place was dark and we were thinking about Lucy's painting."

"Just unlock the door," Mavredes said, "so we can file a report. When we're finished here you can leave. But I want to see you in my office at 8:00 a.m...both of you."

"Cute," Gussie said as we watched him walk angrily to his car for his notebook.

"I thought you might say that," I said.

Fifteen minutes later I was on my way home.

The lights in my house were on a timer so I never had to come home to a dark house if I worked late or was out for an evening meeting. The Fan District where I lived, with its tree lined streets fanning out from Monroe Park, had become a little more dangerous than I liked. Not as dangerous as Washington D.C.'s Georgetown, though the Fan's turn-of-the-century row-houses were often compared to that high rent district. Sometimes I was even out late for social reasons though those occasions were few and far between. Mostly I was involved with the gallery and the business of selling art.

Take Gussie's furniture for example. We were on the verge of going national with a line of her painted furniture. Only a week before David's death I had put together a press package to send to a dozen national design magazines. A brochure with the Gussie Steinhaus Furniture Line exclusive through the Rosemund Wallace Gallery was also in the works. I pushed aside the unpleasant prospect of being sued by the governor's office and closing the gallery.

"You'll be famous," Bernard had told Gussie. And promptly raised his insurance coverage on the pieces of her furniture which he owned. Another promise of fame, I thought. Will it go the way of Mayo's giraffe? Or his American eagle?

Reassured by the blazing lights, I parked the Jaguar in front of my house with its neatly trimmed boxwoods and wrought iron fence, and wondered how many people in my life had recently been told they were headed for fame and fortune. Certainly David Moon expected to be famous. He had big plans for the movie. I hoped Arabella would be able to get a copy of the raw footage. I was eager to see it for all sorts of reasons. For one thing it now seemed important to discover what the movie was about. I had never bothered to ask David the plot.

David's first words to Mayo Johnson, too, were that his painted animals would bring him fame. And Michael DeBord had told me that Lucy's painting, the one that was now missing, would make her famous. But David was dead. Mayo's potential foray into Republican politics via the American eagle and Governor Brookfield had been aborted. Lucy's painting had been stolen. "To hell with fame," I muttered as I locked the car door.

My house was small, but it was filled with art, paintings and sculpture which I had been collecting for years. I even got some of the good stuff when I divorced the Phantom. Fortunately, his taste and mine were dissimilar. "Dissimilar in everything," I thought. In the living room, in a central spot over the fireplace, hung an early Lucy Moon painting. It was of an open field, one of her favorite subjects. Pine trees lined the edge of the field. In the distance someone was walking. The figure was painted from the rear so it was difficult to tell whether it was a man or a woman. That had never bothered me before tonight. Now I stood in the bright living room, staring at the painting and wondering why Lucy never clearly identified the figures in her paintings.

"What is she trying to say?" I dropped my purse on the sofa and walked closer to the painting. "Or what is she trying to hide?"

It was late. I was tired. But I wasn't ready for bed. The light was flashing on my answering machine which was connected to the kitchen telephone. I rummaged through the refrigerator for a Tsing Tao before rewinding the tape to listen to my messages. Fortunately a couple of bottles were cooling on a rear shelf. I should entertain more, I thought as I looked around the kitchen. For one fleeting moment I pictured Michael DeBord leaning against the sink watching me saute some exotic dish on top of my barely used stove.

"Humm," I said, then kicked off my shoes and listened to the voice on the machine. It was Arabella.

"I'm working on this story about David Moon," she said. "The angle I'm taking concerns the gallery, artists connected with the gallery, that sort of stuff. It's kind of a package, Lucy, Mayo Johnson, I did some research on both of them..." On the machine her voice hesitated. I sat my beer on the counter and leaned closer to the machine. "...discovered something...odd," she said. "Something I need to talk to you about. Are you certain Lucy and Mayo never met until the night of David's movie?" She paused again as though expecting an answer from me. In the empty kitchen I shrugged, wondering at the same time what she was getting at.

Then she dropped a bomb.

"Rosemund," she said, "did you know that the doctor who operated on Mayo Johnson's eye is Lucy's brother?"

I didn't bother checking for additional messages but replayed Arabella's words twice and clicked off the machine and walked barefoot back to the living room where I plopped on the sofa, beer in hand, to stare at Lucy's painting and think about Walter McGowan, Lucy's brother. No wonder the man seemed familiar when I met him at the Hill Cafe. In spite of his gaunt appearance he resembled Lucy. Yet in all the years we had known each other Lucy never mentioned a brother named Walter. Actually, she rarely mentioned her parents—only that her family had moved to Virginia from North Carolina when she was young. Since there was never a reason to discuss her maiden name, I had no reason to know she was related to anyone named "McGowan".

But if her brother lived in Richmond, why had there never been the first comment about him? Even a slip of the tongue? Instead, as far as Lucy was concerned, it was as though Walter McGowan didn't exist. I thought back to the night of the filming at the gallery. I was certain it was a first meeting between Lucy and

Mayo. There was probably never even a mention of the doctor who saved Mayo's eye. Or was there?

I also remembered the odd feeling I had at David's funeral, the sensation that something about David kept people apart instead of bringing them together. And then Barbara Barksdale's outburst about my not knowing the "real" David Moon. Although I had paid little attention to her ramblings about David's family I recalled a comment about an uncle that everyone avoided, undoubtedly Walter McGowan. I took a long cold swallow of the Chinese beer. Who is the real Lucy Moon? I asked myself.

Her painting hanging on the wall in front of me suddenly seemed strange. It had always been a comfortable part of my environment, not exactly an "old shoe", but a connection between Lucy and me. And now as I examined the perfectly painted scene I felt decidedly uncomfortable. There was no denying that Lucy favored a number of idiosyncratic images that appeared and reappeared in her work. As her art dealer I was very familiar with them. They helped identify her work. It was part of her appeal. If you visited someone's home or some corporate collection, you knew instantly if you were viewing a Lucy Moon. But that was nothing new in the art world. Images that repeated themselves again and again were a reflection of something important in the artist's unconscious.

So what about Lucy? The unknown figure in the picture I owned was wearing some sort of draped garment, certainly not black plastic, but not conventional clothing, either. Its hands were by its sides as though the figure were walking slowly, deep in thought. I placed the beer on the coffee table and moved directly in front of the painting. I had had it for years, but now I examined it as if for the first time. Where was it walking? Why did it seem so thoughtful? One hand of the figure seemed to be drawn up into a tight fist. The other hand had open fingers. Something was in the fist, something so minute I had never noticed it before.

It was a tiny piece of cord, red silk cord, clutched tightly as though the figure would never let it go.

XVIII

I didn't know whether I was in a bad mood because meeting Mavredes at his office so early made it impossible to have my morning workout or whether I was still angry because two pieces of art had been stolen from my gallery. Or maybe the red cord I discovered in Lucy's painting at my house was making me edgy. And Arabella's information about Walter McGowan had only made a bad situation worse. I had tried her number several times and got her voice mail. Perhaps she knew why Lucy kept her own brother's existence a secret. But if David had a close relationship with him, Lucy's silence was even more peculiar, unless she didn't know David was seeing him. In which case, the family secrets were mounting. If only I could call Lucy and ask her directly what was going on.

Instead, I would have to work through Arabella. In addition to being on good terms with Lucy, Arabella had contacts and access to information that I would never have. Actually it felt like everybody but me was on good terms with Lucy Moon. When I telephoned Arabella before I left for Mavredes' office, her recorded message at the newspaper said she wouldn't be available until later that afternoon.

There was so much on my mind that I forgot I had told Gussie I would pick her up, but when she arrived twenty minutes later at police headquarters all she did was smile benevolently and say, "I didn't want to ride in the Jag, anyway."

I flashed her a grateful look.

I looked at her again. There was something funny about her face. It dawned on me she was wearing makeup, not much, a little blush and eye-shadow, maybe even some lip gloss. This was definitely a first: Gussie Steinhaus, doing her face at eight in the morning. But if Mavredes noticed, he didn't act any different. He did appear rested and refreshed, like some salesman who had had a good week, not somebody who investigated suicides and picked up drunks who had been knocked unconscious in an alley. I was jealous. Both Mavredes and Gussie looked better than I did, and certainly better than I felt.

"As usual in your place," he said, "it was impossible to get a definitive set of prints from the window sill, but we did find splinters of wood on the concrete beneath your bathroom window and the remains of the giraffe in a trash can behind a photographer's shop up the block."

"Why would anybody go to all the trouble to lower the giraffe out the window, or drop it out the window, and then throw it away?" I said. I was only slightly chagrined to realize that I felt as bad about Mayo's giraffe being destroyed as I did about Tyrone being knocked over the head.

"You tell me," he said. Then he leaned back in his chair, crossed his arms over his chest and waited as if I were holding out on him. The question served the purpose of making me feel better. By concentrating on the giraffe I could temporarily forget about Lucy and my growing concern about what might be called coincidence hanging over her family like a foul-smelling fog.

After several moments of silence Gussie shifted in the chair where she was sitting opposite Mavredes. She crossed and uncrossed her legs a couple of times. Beneath a short brown skirt she was wearing striped tights the color of her tan sweater. Thick brown socks peeked over the tops of her work boots. It was definitely the "Gussie look". I wondered if Mavredes had ever encountered anyone like her. He was looking at her quizzically. Although it was obvious to me that she was dying to say something, Mavredes didn't seem to realize it.

"I'm not a detective," she said finally, "but the giraffe must have been in the film. It was installed above Lucy's missing painting and I know the camera was aimed in that direction during the movie shoot. The actors delivered most of their lines in that corner of the gallery. Maybe that's why it was stolen, maybe there was something special about it and whatever it was is right there in living color, captured on film."

Mavredes and I exchanged looks as if to say, 'this Gussie Steinhaus is really something'. He leaned forward across the desk and smiled at Gussie with an expression of growing appreciation. "Could be," he said. "We only found half the giraffe's body in the trash. Its head was missing. I thought probably the whole thing was used to knock out your neighborhood handyman and a piece broke off. That was the bloodied hunk of wood one of the officers found. I figured the head would turn up somewhere, but maybe the thief took the head with him for some reason."

"Or her," I said. "We don't know the thief was a man."

Mavredes tried not to look smug. "I thought you were convinced Jimmy Travers was the culprit."

"Lieutenant," I said, "this morning I don't know what to think." I then proceeded to tell both him and Gussie about the piece of red cord in Lucy's painting hanging in my living room and that David had been seen at the Fire Station with a can of red paint. Last of all, I told them about Walter McGowan. When I had finished, Mavredes tapped the top of his desk thoughtfully.

"Why didn't you tell me about your meeting with this doctor and the folk artist in the first place? You could have gotten yourself in a lot of trouble."

"Because McGowan said he'd deny knowing David, or socializing with him. He said he'd claim he met me at the cafe to discuss Mayo Johnson's future as an artist. Dr. McGowan seems as close-mouthed about the family as Lucy."

"And the man was David's uncle," Gussie said. "It doesn't make any sense. Surely he knew you couldn't keep a family relationship secret forever."

"Lucy did," I said, "and Walter McGowan was in no hurry to tell. When we were talking about David at the cafe he had every opportunity to say he was David's uncle. The most he said was that David was determined to make the movie."

"I'll call her," Mavredes said, "but don't let this go to your head. I'm still not personally convinced that David Moon's death was anything other than 'accidental suicide'. His mother probably has some explanation for never mentioning her brother, maybe some old family feud. Everybody has them. But there's enough peculiar stuff going on to ask a few more questions. And if Lucy's got a copy of the unedited movie, we'll have a little preview here in the office."

Gussie and I discretely excused ourselves while Mavredes dialed Lucy's number. It didn't seem appropriate to eavesdrop. And he made no effort to urge us to stay. We found a coffee machine down the hall from his office and leaned against the wall in silence sipping the weak flavored hot water that came from the machine. I was trying to think clearly. Walter's silence about his relationship to David bothered me as much as Lucy's silence. Less than ten minutes later Mavredes joined us in the hall. His face was flushed. Even the tops of his ears were red beneath his carefully trimmed hair.

"She swore at me," he said. "A sensitive woman like that. Couldn't have been more gracious when we were at her place earlier. I never would have expected it. Said she'd do anything she could to help us, except talk about the film or her brother."

"Artists swear all the time," I said, "especially since Christopher Brookfield moved into the governor's mansion." Lucy never swore unless she had been drinking, I thought, but recently she had good reason to drink. At least she acknowledged she has a brother. That was a step in the right direction.

"She also told me where I might find a copy of the damn thing," Mavredes said, "after telling me where I could stick my ass..."

"I'll bet it was Arik Lawson," I said, "one of the camera guys. David's ex-girlfriend, Barbara Barksdale, said Arik probably had a copy of the film. For what it's worth, Barbara also knew I had Lucy's painting at the gallery."

"Why? She have a crystal ball?"

"I told her."

"My God," Mavredes said. "Why didn't you hang a sign outside the gallery saying steal this painting?"

I pretended he said nothing and calmly repeated Barbara's remark that Connie Lee had a "thing" about the painting, but that the picture had never bothered Arik. He considered it a joke, she said.

"So it's both the painting and the film that pushes people's buttons," Mavredes said.

"Looks that way," I said. "I assume you told Lucy the painting had been stolen"

Mavredes' face turned red again. He slapped the side of his head with his hand. "Damn," he said, "a little thing like that." Then he glowered at me. "Of course I told her," he said. "Her only comment was that painting is like a bad penny. Now what do you suppose she meant?"

Perhaps it was the painting that made Mavredes invite Gussie and me to go with him to the video production company where Arik Lawson worked. Or maybe it was something about Gussie, herself. Whatever the reason, the two of us found ourselves in Mavredes' car, Gussie in front and me in the rear. As it turned out, that may have created a traffic hazard, for Mavredes addressed every comment to me in the back seat, twisting around slightly each time he said something. It didn't seem to bother Gussie, however. She rambled on about Mayo's missing giraffe head as if it was a piece of her own art that was stolen and used as an assault weapon.

She was stopped in mid-sentence by a call to Mavredes on his car transmitter. Tyrone was fully awake in the hospital, the caller said, and talking non-stop.

"The assault victim seems to be hallucinating, however," the voice said. "He's convinced he was attacked by an animal."

"It was an animal," Gussie said sweetly.

"A wooden giraffe," Mavredes said into the receiver. "But assure our victim that the giraffe was not in the alley on his own legs. A two-legged perpetrator used a hunk of the damned thing to knock him unconscious."

"Lieutenant?" The voice on the other end sounded tentative.

"Yeah?"

"The victim claims it was a girl giraffe..."

Behind Mavredes' back Gussie and I exchanged a quick glance.

"Girl? How'd he know it was a girl?"

"She laughed, he says, and I quote, 'laughed like a fucking bitch.'"

XIX

Arik Lawson was not particularly overjoyed to see us although I did my best to counteract Mavredes' scowling demeanor as we were ushered into a small viewing room. Arik insisted on showing us the footage in person instead of letting Mavredes take the film back to his office. The least we could do, I thought, was to act appreciative. There was also the possibility Arik might reveal something unexpected if he were there with us.

"I don't know what you want to see the movie for," Arik said. "It should be destroyed, if you ask me. Man's dead. What's the point of stirring up the dead?"

"But you've kept it," I said. "You and David must have been close."

Arik shrugged. "We were in school together," he said. He was watching Mavredes out of the corner of his eye. The detective had situated himself in one of the viewing chairs, folded his arms across his chest and propped his feet on the chair in front of him. Gussie seemed more interested in the equipment and monitors, walking around the room nodding like an expert.

"You agreed to work on the movie with him," I said, "so you must have spent a lot of time together. What was he like?"

"Like a lot of rich white guys," Arik said. "Money to throw around, women to impress." He glanced at Mavredes as if to say, why is this woman asking all these questions? But Mavredes had leaned his head back in the chair and closed his eyes like he had all the time in the world and didn't care who was doing the questioning.

"Did he ever say anything personal?"

Arik laughed. "...about who he was screwing?"

"...or parties?" I said, "who he partied with?"

"I told you," Arik said. "Man had money to spend. He could afford to party."

"What about his mother?" I said. "Did he ever discuss his mother?"

With a loud noise, Mavredes put his feet on the floor and said, "Let's look at the film." Immediately Gussie took the chair next to him. I sat beside Gussie while Arik disappeared into the adjoining room to start the movie. So much for revealing conversation with the cameraman. The lights dimmed where we were sitting.

"All we need is popcorn," Gussie said. Mavredes loosened his tie and looked straight ahead.

As the first images came on the screen it was something of a shock to see the inside of the gallery in front of us. I knew every square inch of the area and yet it appeared very different framed like a picture on the small screen. Ironically, the space actually appeared bigger. And classy. I was impressed. It could have been a New York gallery—not one in Richmond, Virginia. Even the extras looked Big

City. There were the artists I had invited, as well as Gussie and Bernard. The two of them looked particularly good on film although Gussie mugged once for the camera. There were a few jerky movements as though whoever was doing the filming almost dropped the camera. We were definitely seeing an unedited version. A quick sweep of Mayo's giraffe also took in the plastic draped figure in the woods. I felt a momentary twinge of sadness, thinking about the giraffe broken into half a dozen pieces and without its head. How was I going to tell Mayo? Then the camera did a slow pan of the space, focusing on the rest of Lucy's paintings, before moving in closer to the actors.

The strong colors Lucy used on all her canvases were striking on film—particularly the reds. The flowers and trees which were part of so many paintings looked real—perfectly real. And yet, there was something unsettling about so many of Lucy's personal images in one space. Looking at them on film seemed to provide a distance or detachment that was impossible standing in the gallery a few inches from a painting. Perhaps they were too perfect, too much perfection in a space not big enough to contain perfection. A single painting over my mantle at home was one thing. A dozen powerful representations of Lucy's view of altered illusions was something else. Ambiguous figures walking or sitting beside a tree, plastic streamers caught by some unseen source of wind, flowers without roots, and the ubiquitous red cord—all images important enough to Lucy to be painted to perfection again and again until they were bigger than life.

I saw in that instant what Michael DeBord meant when he compared her work to that of Hiyakawa. Hiyakawa's films also portrayed a reality that was larger than life, bigger than the experiences of the characters who struggled and fought and loved in his moving pictures. The difference was that Hiyakawa's was a flawed reality.

I was jerked out of my reflections by words coming from the people on the screen. Two young women and two young men were talking in front of Lucy's forest painting. The actors I had met the night of the movie shoot had suddenly become someone else.

"Life holds no thrills for me, anymore," one of the women was saying in a bored voice which made her sound much older than she was. "There's nothing left to try."

"Why don't you go to graduate school," one of the men said. "Get a Ph.D. in something."

"I don't believe in degrees," the woman said. "Ph.D stands for 'Fooled you, Dummy'. I only believe in having fun."

"My astrologer told me the planets were entering a new configuration," the second woman said. "If you have Saturn rising like I do, you're in for an emotional roller-coaster ride."

"So what's new?" the first woman said. "That's the story of my life."

Beside me, Gussie groaned and slid down lower in her chair.

On the film the second man began to stroke the first woman's shoulder. I heard David Moon's voice say, 'cut, do another take, more sympathy this time.' I wished David's face had been caught on the film and not simply his voice. The actors reshot the scene. When the first actress repeated the line, 'that's the story of my life', Gussie said to the screen, "Good grief, David, can't you do better than that?"

Then the camera angle shifted slightly and Lucy's painting and Mayo's giraffe came into greater focus. I leaned forward in my chair. There was something about the giraffe that caught my attention.

"Arik! Stop the film a minute."

The lights came on. Arik stepped into the room, frowning.

I pointed to the screen. "Go back a few frames. Stop when the camera is directly on the giraffe. There's something I want to see."

Mavredes moved his chair back a few inches so it was even with mine. Arik dimmed the lights again, but this time he left the door open between the two rooms.

The film jerked ahead in slow motion, frame by frame, past the actor with his hand on the young woman's shoulder, until it froze on the giraffe.

"That's it," I said. "Can you enlarge the image?":

"I can understand why you don't want to listen to that female again," Gussie said, "but aren't you being a little sentimental about the giraffe?"

"It might have been the light," I said, "but it might not. I think I saw something." Sometimes my visual memory records things that I'm not aware of until later. Bernard says that's what happens when you're painting a portrait. Your mind sees things your eyes don't register consciously. Then something comes out in a portrait and everybody's surprised.

"Are you gonna talk or look?" Arik said. "They don't pay me to show movies to the police."

I expected a sharp retort from Mavredes. Instead he said quietly, "We appreciate anything you can do to help us, Arik."

Gussie gave Mavredes one of her million dollar looks. Had he recognized its value, he might have asked Arik to dance.

As the giraffe's head grew larger on the screen its eyes took on a wild expression. 'It's a girl giraffe', I heard Tyrone saying. A girl, I repeated to myself. Could a woman have climbed up the ladder and stolen both Lucy's painting and Mayo's giraffe? And if so, which woman? Barbara Barksdale? Connie Lee? The giraffe was heavy. Was either of those women strong enough to hit Tyrone on the back of the head and knock him out?

The giraffe seemed to be grinning at us with its full mouth of white teeth. I looked harder, wondering why I couldn't see its red tongue. Maybe the angle at which it was hanging on the wall shaded its tongue. No, there was something different about the animal's mouth and it wasn't the way it was installed.

"The giraffe has something in its mouth," I said.

"Teeth," said Mavredes. "All animals have them."

"In between the teeth," I said, "covering the tongue. I'm certain something white is stuffed in its mouth."

Arik was framed in the doorway, listening carefully.

"Anything you can tell us?" Mavredes said. He was looking at the giraffe on the screen but we all knew he was speaking to Arik.

Arik shifted his weight from one foot to the other. Mavredes continued to stare at the screen as though such a subtle gesture would convince Arik that he didn't really care what he said. But Gussie and I were not subtle. Filled with anticipation, we looked directly at Arik.

Finally he spoke. "David had an uncle," he said. "Man lived in Church Hill. Nobody in the family gave a shit about him except David." Arik looked at me. "You asked about David's mother. She hated the uncle, probably because he was always telling David how to make it big. He had done it, David said—made it to the top a couple of times. Told David he could do it, too..." Arik's voice trailed off as though he had said more than he had planned to say.

When Mavredes spoke his voice was so quiet he was almost mouthing the words. "What else?" he said. "What are you not telling us, Arik?"

Arik rubbed his beard. Then he pulled on his ear. I saw that his earlobe was pierced to hold a small gold earring. "Lot of shit going on in that family," he said.

"Like what?"

Arik frowned. "I look like one of their relatives?"

Mavredes flicked an imaginary speck off his perfectly tailored jacket. "Talk to the uncle, is that what you're telling us?"

"Whatever makes you happy, man," Arik said. "You want to see the rest of the film, and let me get back to work?"

I forced myself to concentrate on the film all the way to the end. At least to the conclusion of the footage that Arik showed us. The movie seemed to stop abruptly after another snatch of angst-filled conversation between the four actors. But the evening of the filming there had been a scene in the gallery where the actors had waltzed through the crowd and out the front door. Though all the extras moaned in protest, David had been insistent that we were to waltz. I remembered clearly because Mayo, who had been standing near me, said, "You ever see a black man waltz?" There was even waltz music provided by Barbara Barksdale on a tape player. Gussie had waltzed with Bernard. My partner had been Harry. The camera had followed the four actors through the crowd and out onto the street. I couldn't recall whether Arik had been the cameraman during that shot.

"What about the waltz scene?" I said. I recalled that when asked about the dancing, David had quipped, "metaphor, all metaphor." It occurred to me that perhaps it hadn't been a quip at all. And Lucy Moon hated her brother. What metaphor did she use in her paintings to illustrate that hatred?

"What waltz scene?" Arik said. "This is all I got. I'm not holding anything back."

"I was there," Gussie said. "There was definitely a waltz, Strauss, I believe. Bernard was humming 'The Merry Widow' in my ear. And I'm certain the cameras were running."

Mavredes stood up and straightened his tie. "I can see that I've got to attend one of your openings," he said. He gestured for the lights. "Fun and games are over." He turned to Arik. "If you find the rest of the footage you know where to reach me."

Arik looked like he had swallowed something sour.

"I still can't figure out the plot," said Gussie.

An expression resembling a smile crossed Arik's face. "It's about the meaning of life," he said. "White people are always trying to figure out the meaning of life."

"And you?" she said.

He flashed her a real smile. Gussie was like that. No one could resist her. "Black people already know the meaning of life," he said.

XX

When we left the video studio we headed directly to the hospital to see Tyrone. I was aware that Mavredes seemed in no hurry to get rid of Gussie and me, and, in fact, began to address remarks to her as we headed up Broad Street bound for the Medical College of Virginia Hospital, MCV, for short. I flattered myself that Gussie and I were allowed to keep company with the Law because Mavredes sensed I could get more out of Tyrone than he could. I only hoped Tyrone didn't blame me for almost being taken out of this world by an art object from my gallery.

MCV hospital was located at the edge of one of the seven hills that had spawned Richmond several generations earlier. If you went down that hill you found yourself in Gussie's neighborhood, Shockoe Bottom. Historic Church Hill, where I had dined with Mayo Johnson and Walter McGowan at the Hill Cafe, sat on the top of the opposite hill. Since the largest percentage of the city's crimes occurred in Church Hill, it was no surprise that most murder victims, or would-be victims, were taken to nearby MCV hospital. I wondered if that's where David's body had gone. The few times I had had reason to visit MCV I was struck by the constant scream of sirens. Today was no exception.

"So you design furniture?" Mavredes was saying to Gussie. "What's it look like?"

"It's really just high brow Tex-Mex stuff," Gussie said. Riding in a police car was making her uncharacteristically modest. "I grew up on a farm near the Texas-Mexican border. Listened to mariachi bands in the cradle..."

"...wet-nursed on tequila," I said from the backseat.

I watched Mavredes' back stiffen slightly. Then he laughed and his shoulders relaxed. "Hang around artists long enough," he said, "a little culture's bound to rub off."

He bantered with Gussie while I grew restless in the back seat. The Medical College hospital parking deck was just one block away and Mavredes had yet to mention Walter McGowan. I wondered if he had forgotten or whether he didn't consider it important enough to mention again.

I couldn't stand it any longer. I leaned across the front seat and said, "When do you plan to see David's uncle?"

"Eventually." Mavredes pulled up to the ticket booth and showed his I.D. to the parking attendant. "Don't be so impatient."

"But David's dead," I said.

"That's my point," Mavredes said. He looked over at Gussie, but she had already opened the door on her side of the car and was halfway out.

I kept my mouth closed until we reached the room where Tyrone was holding court behind a door protected by a uniformed guard. If Tyrone was difficult before, I thought, as we entered the room to see two nurses and another policeman on either side of the bed, when he gets back to Carytown, he'll be impossible.

The biggest surprise, however, was Arabella.

She was so small at first I didn't see her. But she was seated in a green vinyl chair near the window, the ever-present notebook in her lap, her leather jacket draped neatly over the back of the chair. She was wearing an embroidered peasant blouse with form-fitting jeans. Her hair was pulled back on one side in a simple and very youthful style. How she managed to get past the guard amazed me. But a disarming appearance had gotten her more than one award-winning story.

"Hiya," she said. "When the police report came in that a guy had been whacked over the head with a giraffe, I knew there was only one giraffe in town so I hustled on down to the hospital to get an interview."

"I been telling her about the gallery," Tyrone said, nodding in Arabella's direction. "...hottest place in Carytown." Tyrone's voice was weak but he looked as though he had been cleanly shaved. The blood was gone. A pristine bandage covered one side of his head. Since he was also hooked up to an I.V. I decided he had been hurt worse than I had thought. The two nurses hovered at the foot of the bed, seemingly unsure as to whether to stay and be in the way or leave and miss all the excitement.

"How you feeling, Tyrone?" Gussie said. "You looked terrible last time we saw you."

"You the one saved my life?" he said, gingerly shifting his body in her direction.

Gussie blushed and smiled demurely.

"The doctors say he lost so much blood he might have died if you hadn't found him," Arabella said.

Tyrone moaned slightly and closed his eyes. "Tyrone's too tough to die," I said. As I had predicted, my lack of sympathy brought him back to life. His eyes snapped open. Mavredes moved in closer.

"Feel like answering a few questions?"

Tyrone narrowed his eyes, pushed his head back into the pillow, and again pretended to fade out of consciousness.

"He talked to me," Arabella said, "told me how he helped out at the gallery."

Tyrone rolled his head to one side and tapped the bandage gently. "Feels like a hole all the way through to my brain," he said. "Hard to remember what happened."

"You said you heard a female voice," Mavredes said. "You see anybody?"

"I was walking along the alley, minding my own business," Tyrone said, "when all at once this animal he sticks his head out between them two buildings and next thing I know, I'm in an ambulance with folks sticking needles in my arm."

"The voice," Mavredes repeated patiently. "Can you tell me about the female voice?"

Tyrone squeezed his eyes tightly and grimaced as though thinking hurt. "They laughed," he said at last. "The giraffe lunged at me and then they laughed."

Mavredes' expression did not change. "They?"

This time when Tyrone opened his eyes his gaze was perfectly clear and guileless. "Yeah," he whispered, "now that I think about it, it was two voices, laughing and saying, 'we got it.'"

Arabella was writing as he talked. "What do you suppose they meant by, *it*?" she said without looking up from her notebook.

Mavredes opened his mouth to say something and just as quickly closed it.

"Could be the giraffe or the painting," Gussie said. "Both were taken."

This time Arabella put down her pen. "What painting?" She looked directly at me. "One of Lucy Moon's?"

"Yes," I said, "the one I told you about when you were at the gallery with Bernard. The painting I put upstairs in my office to get a reaction from Jimmy Travers. Remember? I described it to you when we went to McDonald's to meet Jack and Beverly. Somebody stole it."

"A figure covered with black plastic, standing in the woods?"

"That's the one. It's gone."

Mavredes nodded in agreement. "It's gone, all right," he said. "I was at the gallery with these two and the picture wasn't there."

"It was in the movie shoot, too, wasn't it, hanging in the corner beneath the giraffe?" Arabella said. I couldn't understand why she kept talking about the painting. "I remember discussing it with Lucy before the filming started that night."

"What did she say about it?" said Gussie. "Lucy was never one to explain her work."

"'She told me there was a story behind that painting, one that concerned her brother," Arabella said. "I didn't think anything of it when she said brother until I started doing some digging and discovered her brother was the eye surgeon who had worked on Mayo Johnson..."

"So," Gussie said, "what's the story?"

Arabella folded her hands in her lap across the notebook. The expression on her face reminded me of a prim school teacher who has just caught her students cheating. She pursed her lips into a thin line. "David started filming and she never told me. I forgot about it—until just now..."

I had known Arabella since I opened the gallery. We talked a lot about art.

But we also discussed ways of seeing what was not always apparent on the surface. I knew by the tone of her voice that there was more. The hospital room felt crowded, the air stuffy. If the window hadn't been sealed permanently I would have opened it to let in some fresh autumn air. Just like we did at the gallery the night David died. I shivered in the warm room and waited.

Arabella looked straight at me. "Have you known Lucy to paint the same picture twice?"

I shook my head. "She uses some of the same images over and over," I said, "but each painting is different."

"That's what I thought," Arabella said. "I was at her house, the old tavern, in Goochland earlier today. I drove out there to interview her. I've given her shows enough favorable reviews that she trusts me. She's in a hard place right now, but she was willing to talk when I told her I was doing a sympathetic story about young artists and wanted to feature David. What I didn't tell her was that I was helping you investigate his death."

Arabella had no way of knowing she had just gotten me in big trouble. Mavredes shifted his weight and glared at me. He had the good judgment to keep his mouth closed until we were alone. The room was silent. Even Tyrone seemed to sense that something important was coming.

"If we're talking about the same painting," Arabella said, "a hooded figure covered with black plastic, standing on the edge of some trees and tied with a red cord, it can't be missing. I'm certain it was hanging in the front hall at Lucy's house."

It surprised me that the person I wanted most to tell what was going on was Michael DeBord. Perhaps he was far enough from Richmond not to be affected by all the craziness surrounding Lucy Moon and the stolen painting which appeared not to be stolen at all. Michael also knew no one but me, not Tyrone, not Arabella, not Lieutenant Mavredes, not Walter McGowan, not even Lucy. He only knew her paintings. That fact might give him an edge in helping me understand what her work was really about. Though Gussie and Bernard knew Lucy, they were too close to be objective. Questions kept tumbling through my mind. Why had Lucy not told Mavredes the forest painting was at her house? And who, for God's sake, was responsible for putting it in her hands? At this point, that person, or persons, appeared to be thieves who had broken into the gallery, stolen both the painting and Mayo's giraffe and almost killed Tyrone.

"It could have been two separate thefts," Mavredes said as he dropped Gussie and me off at police headquarters to retrieve the Jaguar and the pickup, following the trek to MCV. "Maybe Lucy stole her own painting from the gallery."

"Please," I said. "Artists are odd, but not that odd."

"I'll ride out to Lucy's place," Mavredes said. "Hopefully, she won't lie to me in person about the painting. I'll also ask her why she's so close-mouthed about her brother, the doctor." He shook his head. "Why didn't she just tell me over the phone the damn thing was back home? Most secretive woman I've ever met."

His questions were getting on my nerves. Maybe because I was asking the same ones myself, and was no better at figuring out answers than he was. It was the secrets, especially, that troubled me. David's friends had implied he had secrets. Why would he and his uncle keep their relationship a secret? Not even Mayo knew they were related. Or, if he did, he certainly fooled me.

Gussie, who knew me well enough to recognize when I wanted to be alone, made no comment as I lowered myself into the Jaguar and pulled away from the station. The Beast only coughed a couple of times and then sped around the corner headed for Carytown. I didn't even wait to see if Mavredes told Gussie goodbye.

I telephoned Michael from the gallery only to reach his secretary who told me he was in a meeting, but Michael himself called back within five minutes.

"Nice surprise," he said, "I've been thinking about you."

"Must be raining in Los Angeles."

"There were other pleasantries I recall in addition to the rain."

I smiled to myself. Yes, there were, I thought.

"What's up?" he said, "got a painting to sell?"

I proceeded to tell him everything; from Governor Brookfield and Jimmy Travers to the mysterious return of the painting and the fact that Lucy's brother had operated on Mayo Johnson's eye.

"Well," he said, after I had run out of steam. "You art dealers certainly lead exciting lives." Then he was quiet for a few moments. I could almost hear his brain working on the other end of the line. When he spoke again he was all business. "Can you get me a complete set of slides of Lucy's work?" he said. "...and not simply the most recent stuff. I'd like to see images she's been doing for the past twenty years."

"I've got a thick file on her. I'll put something together as soon as I can." I tried unsuccessfully to imagine what he might be thinking. He had met artists from all over the world but that didn't guarantee he'd be able to figure out Lucy.

"What are you going to do, Michael? How can the slides help?"

"A hunch," he said. "I seem to remember that a certain Richmond art dealer believes in hunches."

"Yes," I said. And at that moment I had my own hunch about something. It concerned Mee and Connie Lee. Mavredes had interviewed them at police headquarters following David's death, along with everyone else at the movie shoot.

But since there had been no mention of their parents' grocery store in Church Hill I hoped that meant he didn't know about it. If I was right, I would have some time there by myself. If only Mr. and Mrs. Lee spoke good enough English to talk with me. While I wouldn't exactly accuse their daughters of breaking into the gallery to steal the painting and the giraffe, I would ask some leading questions.

As soon as I hung up the telephone with Michael I dug through my office files for Lucy's slides. At one point in our business relationship she had given me a complete set of slides from the past twenty years. I had hoped to put together a retrospective of her work. It would have been the show of the year in Richmond. But before I had organized the first few dozen slides to begin plans for the retrospective, David had asked to use the gallery for the movie shoot. Everything since then had come to a halt.

I spread the slides out to examine them before slipping them into plastic sheets to send to Michael and wondered if Lila Hunt would be the one having the retrospective. I had not heard from her since she telephoned to inform me that she was now Lucy's art dealer. I had a feeling I'd be the first to know if she had something big in the works. It occurred to me she might even request Lucy's slides. I would need to hurry to put something together to send to the West Coast.

After about an hour of sifting through hundreds of slides to make certain there were no duplicates and that all the images I mailed to California were dated and labeled, I addressed a large envelope with Michael's name, drove a few blocks to the post office and sent the package by overnight mail. Only then did I realize how tense my shoulders were. The stiffness seemed to follow my spinal cord all the way down to my lower back. My whole body was screaming for a good workout. It was not the time of day I usually went to the gym, but I drove home quickly and pulled on a pair of black tights, an oversized T-shirt and a pair of comfortable Reebocks. I made a point of not looking at Lucy's painting in the living room as I left for the athletic club. At least nobody had broken into my house to steal it.

XXI

An hour and a half later, when I left the club headed for Church Hill, I felt much better. Thirty minutes on the bicycle and thirty minutes with the free weights had done wonders for the stiffness in both my legs and my shoulders. Since Gussie hadn't been there to bounce ideas off, I'd been forced to do my strategizing in private. Actually, it might have been just as well that I was alone. Gussie would have disapproved of what I planned to do. While Gussie was the genuine thing, a real artist, a true non-conformist, she was constantly chiding me for thinking too much. She was also one of the most creative people I knew. Her authenticity came from the fact that she wasn't self-conscious about either her creative ideas or her lifestyle. In fact, she was usually surprised when anyone commented on either. But having said all that, I knew that Gussie thought I was trying to read more into David's death than was there. Perhaps that was the major difference between us: Gussie accepted things the way they appeared to be and I was always trying to see around corners.

One particular corner was literal. It housed the Church Hill Grocery owned by Mee and Connie Lee's parents. A parking place accommodated the Jaguar easily a few doors down from the store. As I locked the car door I wondered if I should have dressed more formally to talk to Mr. and Mrs. Lee. I was wearing my casual art dealer-away-from-the-gallery outfit of jeans, black turtle neck and vest and my hair was still damp from a long shower at the gym. I needn't have worried. The middle-aged Korean man standing near the cash register when I entered was dressed in jeans and a plaid shirt.

He was busy with two customers and didn't see me at first. The aisles were so narrow and crowded with cans, bottles and boxes that I wondered how he was able to keep track of anyone who entered the store. I made my way past a woman with a grocery cart taking up most of the width of one aisle and pretended to examine the produce while I really examined the proprietor. He looked vaguely familiar. I assumed it was because he was the man I saw at David's funeral with Mee and Connie. When he was finished with the people at the checkout counter I walked over to talk to him.

"Mr. Lee?"

"Yes?" His face wore the slightly anxious expression of the overworked, understaffed retailer whose customers always wanted more than he was able or willing to provide.

I stuck out my hand. "I'm Rosemund Wallace, Mr. Lee, the director of the art gallery in Carytown where your daughters helped film the movie for David Moon."

Only his eyes changed "Ah yes," he said, dipping his head slightly. "How do you do, Mrs. Wallace."

I had not been addressed as "Mrs." for a long time. It was a bit disconcerting. The Phantom sometimes called me "Mrs.", particularly as our marriage began to unravel. Funny, I thought, I never called him "Mr." Wallace. He was always the Phantom.

"May I ask you a few questions, Mr. Lee?" He didn't respond, but continued to look at me. I hoped the woman with the grocery cart took a long time with her shopping.

"Your daughters said David Moon came to the store. Did he come often? Did you know him very well?"

"David Moon. Yes, very fine young man. But, no, did not know him very well." Mr. Lee placed both hands on the counter top, almost as though he was steadying himself.

"But your daughters," I said, "they were close friends with David. They must have told you something about him. Especially after his death." I hesitated, then said, "I saw you and your family at his funeral."

Mr. Lee's head moved. He was looking at something or someone over my shoulder. Turning slightly, I saw a woman. I assumed it was his customer who was ready to have him ring up her groceries. But when she spoke it was in a language that must have been Korean. He answered in the same language. It was probably Mee and Connie's mother, she looked familiar. There was a quick exchange between the two of them, which, from the glances Mr. Lee cast in my direction, I was certain concerned me. The woman disappeared just as quickly as she had appeared without a word passing between us.

"Yes, we were at funeral," Mr. Lee said. "Was proper to pay respects." By this time he was visibly nervous. Whatever his wife had said to him had been unsettling. He moved from behind the counter and situated himself at an angle requiring me to move, too. It seemed odd, like he wanted me to be facing away from the front door so I couldn't look out the window to see the sidewalk or the street. For a few seconds I obliged him and turned so we were again looking at each other. It was difficult to talk to an empty space.

"Connie and Mee learned film making from David Moon," he said. "He taught them much. Their mother and I, we are very grateful to David Moon."

Something was wrong. Mr. Lee kept shifting his body in one direction while his eyes looked out towards the front window. I took a few steps toward the door and he almost grabbed my arm. As I jerked back he reached for my hand.

"Please," he said, squeezing my hand tightly, "please, Mrs. Wallace. My daughters are good girls. They very sad David Moon is gone."

But I wasn't listening. I was looking out the window as someone came running around the corner of the store. His head was covered with a cap and he was moving fast, but his tall, angular shape gave him away. It was the other cameraman at the movie shoot, the one I had privately labeled "The Crow," John Owen

Smith.

I twisted free of Mr. Lee's grasp and ran out the door. John Owen was already half way up the block. I yelled his name as loudly as I could. He turned briefly to glance back. But when he saw me he pulled his shoulders up higher around his ears like the wings of a bird and continued running. His name is appropriate, I thought. If only he doesn't fly away before I can ask him why he was at the store and why he wanted to avoid being seen by me.

By the time I reached the Jaguar it had begun to rain. Fortunately the Beast started the moment I turned the key in the ignition. Hardly believing my good fortune, I pulled away from the curb, only to barely miss another car I hadn't noticed in my rear view mirror. The driver of the other car honked loudly. I hated to think what he was saying about me. The blast of the horn caused John Owen to look around again. He tripped on something, probably a break in the sidewalk. The trees in Church Hill were so old and their roots so large and grotesque that many sections of sidewalk had buckled and cracked, creating a real pedestrian hazard.

But it was enough to slow John Owen down. I'll catch him, I thought. I'll find out what's going on between him and the Lees. I figured he had probably slipped out the back door and Mrs. Lee told her husband to distract me so I wouldn't see him leave. I pushed harder on the gas pedal and then something happened. The Jaguar coughed, jerked twice, uttered a strange noise resembling a death rattle and died. Frantically I tried the starter, pumped the gas, even pounded in desperation on the horn. Nothing happened. I tried again. This time the engine turned over.

"Good girl," I said, "let's go!" But instead of going anywhere, black smoke began to pour from under the hood. I jumped out and looked at the dark stuff bellowing from the front end of the car. I prayed it didn't blow up.

"Damned Beast." The insult did no good. John Owen had disappeared.

I was soaked by the time I walked to the Hill Cafe to use the telephone. I had no intentions of calling Mavredes from the Lee's grocery store. For one thing, he would yell at me for going there all alone. And secondly, I was a little scared. There was no telling what was going on between the Lees and John Owen Smith.

When Mavredes answered the phone and learned where I was and why I needed him, he was unexpectedly calm. This was the third or fourth time he had surprised me with a patient and almost consoling response when I would have predicted a blow up. Maybe he could tell by my tone of voice how I felt. My car had exploded, I was drenched and cold, and I had lost the one person connected with David Moon who acted guilty of something.

It was only mid-afternoon but I took a seat at the bar and ordered a Scotch, something I never drank. Someone had told me that Scotch would warm you up fast and I definitely needed warming up. Even the insides of my boots were soaked. The bartender, who knew me because I came in often on Sundays with Gussie, poured me "a double", adding, "It'll make you feel much better." I appreciated the fact that he didn't comment on my appearance.

Mavredes arrived an hour later, but by then I didn't care.

"Put this on," he said, draping a sweater around my shoulders. It smelled like perfume but I didn't ask where it came from. He must have paid my bar tab, I have no recollection of opening my purse for money. I vaguely recall after seeing Tyrone at MCV he was planning to drive out to Goochland to question Lucy. I wondered if that was the reason it took him so long to meet me at the cafe.

"I called a towing service for your car," he said as he ushered me into his own warm, dry vehicle. "Now tell me everything that happened at the grocery, including what you said to the two Lee girls' parents."

As best I could in my worsening condition, I recited my encounter with Mr. Lee, his brief but anxious conversation in Korean with his wife, his attempt to maneuver me into a position where I couldn't see the street and then the chase after John Owen Smith. Mavredes took notes as I talked, patting me on the shoulder a couple of times to keep me going. It reminded me of Harry. "Are you attempting to calm me down?" I said. "My partner always pats me on the shoulder when he thinks I'm talking crazy."

"Talking is the least of your problems," Mavredes said. "You're lucky I was on duty when you called."

The "why?" that came out of my mouth sounded to me like "bly", but Mavredes seemed to understand. At least he didn't pat me on the shoulder again.

"I was still in the office because I never made it to Lucy's," he said. "The governor's office called and I was on the line for a while." I couldn't understand why he would prefer the governor over Lucy Moon, but then understanding was not my strong suit at the moment.

"Blookfish," I said, leaning back into the comfort of the car seat. Maybe if I closed my eyes I would feel better.

"Brookfield."

",,,at's what I said, Lieutenant. Guvner Blookfish. Why he call?" I could feel myself sinking lower into the seat. It was very cozy. The perfume from the borrowed sweater seemed to coat the inside of my nostrils. My head was spinning. The whole experience was most pleasant.

"How much did you have to drink, Rosemund?"

"'nough." It was definitely getting cozier. An attractive man was calling me by my first name. I couldn't quite remember whether it was Michael or someone else.

"It seems a package was delivered to the governor's office," the male voice continued. No, it couldn't be Michael DeBord, I decided. He wasn't into politics.

I folded my arms together and leaned against the window of the police car. My arms made a comfortable pillow.

"Was it a Christmas present?" I heard myself ask.

Just as I drifted into unconsciousness I thought I heard him say, "No, Rosemund. It was the head of a giraffe."

When I came to, I wondered how many art dealers had slept it off in the front seat of a homicide detective's automobile. Maybe Mavredes had even broken some law by locking me in the car unconscious while he questioned the proprietors of the grocery store. The headache that threatened to split my skull in two prevented me from caring too much, however. I had no idea how long I had been asleep. Mavredes must have finished talking to the Lees just as I was coming out of it. The rain had almost stopped and although it was dusk by this time, I could see him heading for the car tapping his notebook against the palm of one hand. He was frowning, seemingly deep in thought.

"I should charge you hotel rates," he said as he slid behind the steering wheel.

"Don't shout." I pulled the sweater up over my head to keep out the loud noise.

"Either you scared those two people out of their wits," he said, "or they're graduates of Seoul's School of Dramatic Arts. What did you tell them?"

"Mr. and Mrs. Lee?"

"Yeah, the Korean connection."

"Nothing, I didn't tell them anything. I only asked about David Moon." This rigorous line of questioning required an expenditure of energy I didn't possess. "Coffee," I said. "What I need is a pot of strong coffee."

"Well, I'm not taking you any place where I'd be recognized," Mavredes said. "Have you taken a look at yourself recently?"

I pulled down the visor on my side of the car and peered into the mirror. It wasn't a pretty picture. "Walking away from a smoking Jaguar in the middle of the rain will do that to a girl," I said. Actually, I didn't think I looked as bad as he was implying.

"McDonald's," I said. "We're welcome there day or night. They don't care what I look like. Hell—they don't care what anybody looks like. And then we can keep an eye on the gallery in case somebody's trying to burn it down. At this point, there's no telling who's over there."

"I'm glad to see you're feeling better," he said. "While we head for Carytown I'll fill you in on the Lees of Church Hill and the governor of Virginia. I have a hunch they're connected—but not like the history books would have you think."

Mrs. Lee, it seems, was visiting with John Owen Smith, who, she said, had paid a strictly social call on her daughters, when I walked into the store. Although they were in the rear of the building awaiting Mee's and Connie's arrival, they overheard me asking about David and the two girls' relationship with him. John Owen was so broken up over David's death that he didn't want to run the risk that I'd see him and ask him about David, too. That was the reason, according to Mrs. Lee, that he had taken off from behind the building and run up the sidewalk.

"'Too broken up,'" I said.

"Practically on the verge of tears, according to Mrs. Lee."

"Yes, and I supported Richard Nixon," I said.

"If you learned to hold your liquor better, you'd make a good detective," said Mavredes. "It was obvious even to my occidental brain that she was stretching the truth."

"Anytime you want, we'll trade jobs."

"Only if you look at my paintings first," he said.

I was beginning to consider McDonald's my home-away-from-home. By now some of the help recognized me and almost smiled as Mavredes and I placed our order. Mine was for a large coffee and a large orange juice. Mavredes ordered two apple pies and a coke. I wondered if Gussie could go for a guy who ate all that sugar. We plopped in a corner booth in the non-smoking section where I could see the gallery out the window. Or at least I plopped; Mavredes slid into the seat with the gracefulness that characterized a man in his profession. Across the street the gallery was still woefully dark. The necessary electrical work to restore power to the building was on hold until the police had completed their investigation of the break-in. The note I had put on the gallery door several days earlier announcing that we would reopen soon was still there, albeit a little soggy from the rain and peeling from one corner.

"Now that we have achieved perfect understanding as to why John Owen didn't want to talk to me," I said, "we can move on to the governor." I was alternating the coffee with the orange juice, a sure-fire hangover remedy Bernard had put me on to.

"We'll get back to John Owen and the Lees in a minute," Mavredes said. "A box wrapped in brown paper arrived today at the governor's mansion addressed to Brookfield. The usual precautions were taken to make sure it wasn't a bomb. When one of his staff opened it, there was the giraffe's head, its mouth wide open, and empty." Mavredes took a large bite out of one of the apple pies and grinned. "I gotta tell you," he said, "scared the hell out of Brookfield, according to one witness."

"Probably thought it was a repeat of that scene in "The Godfather"," I said, "where the guy wakes up to find the head of his prize race horse in bed with him."

Mavredes laughed so hard I decided he must be a Democrat. Republicans would not find the giraffe or the horse story very funny.

I turned towards the counter to look for the woman with the coffee refills. Instead, I found myself looking directly into the face of Beverly. I lifted my hand to wave but she shook her head so emphatically that I stopped. She gestured in the direction of the Ladies Room, then placed a warning finger in front of her lips. It all happened so fast, I was certain Mavredes hadn't seen anything.

"I'll be right back," I said, getting to my feet. "If the refill lady comes by, I'll take another full cup."

Beverly was standing in the corner of the bathroom when I pushed open the swinging door. It was odd to see her by herself without Jack, almost as though she were missing a necessary appendage. In a way, I suppose she was. They were always together. You never saw one without the other. I wondered what she would do if something happened to him. I started to speak but she pointed to one of the stalls and said, "shhhh." I looked under the door to see a pair of feet. I went to the sink to busy myself and made the mistake of looking in a mirror under a bright light. My eyes were puffy, my hair plastered to the sides of my head. Any semblance of makeup I had worn earlier was gone. I splashed my face with cold water since it seemed the proper gesture under the circumstances. By this time the woman in the stall had come out, glanced first at Beverly and then at me, and left without washing her hands.

"What's up, Beverly?" I said, trying to smile. The effort made my face hurt.

"That colored man who's always around," she said in a whisper. "Is he dead, too?"

At first I didn't know who she meant. The trip to the Medical College Hospital seemed a long time ago. "You mean Tyrone?"

"Tall, skinny fellow, long legs? Rides a bicycle?"

I nodded. It was easier than talking.

"Is he dead?"

"No, no, Tyrone's alive. He just got banged over the…" I paused and looked at her more carefully. "How did you know he was hurt?"

She bent down to peer beneath the doors of the empty stalls. "Ain't nobody here but us. Right?"

I nodded once more.

She folded her arms over her enlarged belly. One of her socks had fallen down over the top of her tennis shoe. The bare leg was thin and bony. It made her appear very vulnerable.

"Jack and me, we was walking up the alley behind your place the other night on our way to supper..."

"Yes?"

"Sometimes we go by the garage, you know, old time's sake. It was real dark that night. No moon, no stars, probably been raining. The colored man…"

"Tyrone."

"Tyrone, he was messing around that building where the garage was. Jack and me thought he might be looking for something to steal. Anyways, he looked like he heard a noise in that walkway beside your place and kinda sidled over there to see what was going on."

I hadn't considered Tyrone so brave.

Beverly waved her hands in the air dramatically. "All of a sudden," she said, "this thing that looks like a animal swoops out of nowhere and rams right into—into…"

"Tyrone."

"Yeah, Tyrone, he yells like he's hurt real bad. Jack and me ducked behind the garage and watched. I tell you, we was some kind of scared."

I formed my words carefully, at the same time praying that no one would come through the swinging door and interrupt us. "Did you see anyone, Beverly? Did anyone come out from between the buildings after you saw the giraffe hit Tyrone."

She pursed her lips into a tight little grimace. "Yes, ma'am," she said. "Certainly did. They was two foreign looking girls, all laughing and carrying on. One of them acted like she was going to kick the colored, kick Tyrone, until the man with them stopped her."

I grabbed the sink with both hands. I was feeling unexpectedly dizzy. "Man? What did this man look like? Did you get a good glimpse of him?"

"Kinda funny shaped," she said. "His shoulders were all hunched over. Made me think of a bird."

XXII

"Stay in here a few minutes, Beverly," I said. "A homicide detective is out there with me. He's investigating David's death. I want to tell him what you said, but I don't want you to come out until he guarantees protection for you and Jack. As soon as he tells me what he'll do I'll come back to get you."

Beverly stared down at her protruding stomach. "Somebody might hurt us, that what you saying?" Her squeaky voice took on a shriller tone.

"If certain people know you saw them, you might be in danger," I said as gently as possible. "That's why I'll arrange police protection for you. But I don't want anybody to see you talking to us. So you're safe if you stay in the Ladies Room until we figure out how to get you out of McDonald's."

"Jack," she said. "What about Jack? He's out there."

"Where? I didn't see him in the restaurant."

"Out in the parking lot. We seen you when we was passing by. He said he'd wait outside while I tried to get your attention." She began to run her hands up and down over her belly. The front of her dress was covered in stains.

"We'll figure out what to do about Jack, too," I said, patting her on the arm. "Just stay here five minutes. I'll be right back. Everything will be okay."

As I hurried back to the booth where I had left Mavredes with his hot apple pie I was torn. I knew it was risky to leave Beverly alone. She was liable to disappear again and there was no predicting when she'd reappear, especially now that I told her somebody might be looking for her. But I couldn't lead her out into the public light of McDonald's dining room where anybody who drove down Cary Street might see her talking with Mavredes and me. And the Lee sisters or John Owen Smith, or somebody else, could be watching the gallery and might have seen me enter the burger place with Mavredes. By this time all the people involved with David Moon's film knew who the detective was and would be wary if they saw the two of us together. They also knew I was asking a lot of questions.

"We've got a witness," I said as soon as I rejoined Mavredes in the booth.

"What are you talking about? A witness to what?"

"Someone who saw who attacked Tyrone, she's in the Ladies' Room waiting for me."

He took a long sip of his coke. "The attacker or the witness?"

"It was the Lee girls and the cameraman," I said. "Connie and Mee Lee and John Owen Smith. They hit him with the giraffe. They must have stolen Lucy's painting, too."

"I thought the coffee would have sobered you up," he said. "And I take back what I said earlier, you are crazy."

I reached across the table to grab his arm. "This is serious," I said. "Beverly saw everything that happened—Beverly and Jack. You've got to get protection for them. Somebody might want to kill them, too."

He leaned back into the booth and looked at me sympathetically as though I were six years old and had just skinned my knee. "It's called paranoia," he said. "I hadn't realized art dealers were so susceptible."

"She's here," I said, jerking my head towards the back of the restaurant. "...in the ladies room, waiting for me. If I don't get back there soon she'll vanish again."

"Bring her out," he said. "I'll talk to her, get a statement. Beyond that I can't promise anything."

"No protection, you mean."

"For God's sake, Rosemund. She's a street person. She was living in a garage. What am I going to do? Assign an officer to sleep on the adjoining park bench to watch her?"

I folded my arms across my chest. I couldn't believe I had actually thought the man was attractive enough to match him up with Gussie. David's death had affected me more than I realized.

"Then she can just stay in the Ladies' Room," I said. "I won't bring her out to expose her to danger. She's already vulnerable. She saw David leave the gallery with Jimmy Travers, remember, even though you haven't managed to question her about that, either."

Mavredes shook his empty coke container, rattling the ice noisily. He scrunched it into a ball with one hand. Ice water dripped out onto the table. "Someone's playing games with the governor, " he said, "sending him animal heads, and you want me to provide protection for a street person. My God!"

"Tyrone, too," I said. "When Tyrone gets out of the hospital I want somebody watching him."

Mavredes' face turned several shades of red. He was not a man who hid his emotions. He got to his feet. "I'm stuck with taking you home because you don't have a car," he said. "Call your lady friend out of the john or we're getting out of here. We both need a good night's sleep."

Gussie tells me I can be stubborn when pushed to the wall. I decided to see if it was true. I crossed my arms tighter, squinted my eyes and balled my fists into tight little knots. Mavredes didn't seem to notice. "No," I said. "I won't call her out until you promise to protect her."

"Suit yourself," he said. "I'll have the manager get her out. When I hear what she has to say then I'll make a decision." He turned on his heel and with bureaucratic efficiency strode to the service counter.

It was my only chance. I pulled a card imprinted with the gallery phone number from my purse, raced across the restaurant and yanked open the door to the ladies room. Beverly was cowering in a corner. When she saw me rush in, her eyes got bigger. By this time I was getting pretty good at recognizing fear in someone's face.

"Get out of here," I said as I grabbed her arm. "Run, Beverly, run. He doesn't know what you look like. I'll protect you the best I can. Call me at the number on this card." I jammed the card into her hand while holding the the door open and pushed her out. It was only a few feet to the side door of the restaurant which opened onto the parking lot. I hoped Jack was waiting for her.

Barely one minute later there was a loud pounding on the door. "Management!" a male voice called. "Coming in!"

I dashed into one of the booths, locked the door and sat down on the toilet.

"Police!" another voice said. I didn't have to peek through the door to know it was Mavredes.

"Privacy!" I cried in a shrill voice, mimicking Beverly as much as possible. "You men are breaking the law!"

"Cut the crap, Rosemund," Mavredes said. "Come on out with your witness. You can't hide her in there."

I flushed the toilet on general principle, opened the door several inches and batted my eyes at the man with Mavredes. His expression didn't change. I remembered that I was not at my best.

"And I thought this was a family restaurant," I said, easing myself out the door and glancing over my shoulder as though someone were behind me.

"Come on, come on," Mavredes said. "We're not going to hurt the lady. Tell her to come out."

"All right," I said. "If you insist."

Carefully I opened the door to the stall. "Come out, Beverly. The big man with the big gun is really just a pussy cat."

When nothing happened I peered back into the stall. "Well, my goodness...it looks like she's not here. She must have left when I wasn't looking."

Mavredes yanked open the door, glared at the lonely toilet, then slammed the door hard enough to rattle the walls of the stall. All this violence was obviously upsetting to the manager for his mouth began to twitch. I wondered if he was the person responsible for feeding Beverly's and Jack's friends the leftover burgers. If so, he clearly wasn't cut out for stalking homeless women in the rest room. He took a step forward in an attempt to assert himself.

"Lieutenant..."

Mavredes ignored him and slammed the door again. A metal screw fell out of the door hinge and rolled across the floor. A woman poked her head into the room, saw Mavredes, the manager and me in our menage a trois around the toilet, and quickly vanished.

"Rosemund," Mavredes said. "You are pushing me to the limits of gentlemanly behavior. For all I know you have made up the whole thing. There may be no street people. There may be no witnesses except in your imagination. There may be nothing but a suicide that you're determined to blow into a full-fledged conspiracy. You've managed to terrorize a Korean couple trying to make a living in a dangerous neighborhood, you've accused a state employee of murder, you've angered the governor of Virginia—for all I know, you sent him that giraffe head, and now you've got me cornered in a woman's fucking rest room with a bunch of women needing to pee pounding on the door."

All that yelling was hurting my head. The coffee/orange juice remedy had only dulled the hangover. I took a few steps past both men and called over my shoulder as I pushed open the door. "Don't bother to drive me home," I said. "I'll phone for a cab." I almost bumped into five women fuming on the other side of the door.

"Go on in, ladies," I said, "the guys won't look."

I had my hand on the door to the parking lot headed for the outside pay phone when I heard Mavredes yelling from the entrance to the Ladies' Room. "You know you can't get a taxi in Richmond this time of night," he said. "Call your buddy with the boy's haircut. You can tell her what a bastard I am."

"Gussie was right," I yelled back. "You are cute."

As it turned out, calling Gussie was a good suggestion. She was in her studio painting furniture when I phoned, and was easily convinced to take a break. Ten minutes later her red pickup pulled into the restaurant parking lot. Since Mavredes hadn't followed me to the phone booth I assumed he was gone. We didn't hang around to find out.

"You look like hell," Gussie said as I slid across the front seat. "What happened to you?"

As we drove to my house I told her about the Lees, John Owen, the Beast that blew up, Mavredes and Beverly. The only thing I omitted was the afternoon refreshments at the Hill Cafe. As close as Gussie and I were, she didn't need to know all my weaknesses.

"If you've alienated the Richmond police force," Gussie said as she dropped me off in front of my house, "what do you plan to do next?"

"I'm not sure," I said, "but I think I have to find a way to talk to Lucy. Maybe Arabella can help."

The pickup pulled away from the curb. For a change Gussie didn't wait around to see that I made it safely into the house. It surprised me that I was a little uncomfortable on the street alone. Maybe I am becoming paranoid. I rummaged around in my still damp purse for my house key. I was eager to stand in the shower for a long time, letting the hot water drain the stains of the day off both body and soul.

The man who was crouched in the boxwoods lining the front porch of my house was up the steps behind me before I had a chance to shut the front door. In that brief interval when I realized he was there I tried to slam it but it was too late. He shoved me against the wall in the foyer, knocking the painting that was hanging inside the door to one side. For one absurd instant I was more concerned about the picture than I was myself and swung my arm across the canvas to protect it. It wasn't so much that it was a valuable piece of art like Lucy's work, but it was mine and someone was trying to damage it.

It didn't matter. The man knocked me across the side of the head as I turned toward the painting and then shoved me against the piece of furniture under the picture. I lost my balance and grabbed for the painting. It fell forward off the wall, hitting me on the shoulder and startling the intruder. He jumped back a a few steps, then hit me again—more in surprise, I thought, as I tried to catch my balance, than in anger. In fact, although I was frightened, something in me sensed that he had followed me into the house for reasons other than murder and mayhem.

Mayhem is what I got, though. This time he hit me in the stomach. Bad manners, I thought as I slid onto the floor against the table in the hallway. Very bad manners—hitting a lady who is much smaller than you are. I kicked out at him with all my strength. The first kick connected and he yelled. Working out at the gym had its rewards. I got to my knees and grabbed at his legs. They were long and skinny. He was so tall that it was hard to see his face from my kneeling position. His head was covered with a hat pulled low over his forehead. I pulled hard on his pants. As he stomped to get free he gave me another whack as though I were a bothersome mosquito.

Passing out is not as painful as I would have thought. You do manage to bruise parts of your body that you would prefer to preserve intact. I wondered what people at the gym would say about the black and blue spots. But, what the hell—that was the least of my problems at the moment. He raised his arm to hit me again and I didn't care anymore. As I lost consciousness I had the sensation of him spinning round and round above me—almost as though something or somebody had thrown him off balance. And then I blacked out.

"Rosemund—Rosemund—drink this—just take it easy now." Someone was holding me up and trying to pour water down my throat. Someone whose arms were very strong and whose skin was very dark. At first I gagged and coughed and then eagerly gulped down the water. Tasted better than a Tsing Tao. I ached all over and could barely focus on anything in the foyer. However, there seemed to be a body stretched out a few feet away. His hat was gone—his long limbs akimbo.

It was John Owen Smith.

I looked up at the black face peering down at me.

"Mayo! What are you doing here?"

"You all right?"

I tried to stand up and then fell back against him. "Lots better," I mumbled.

Mayo put his arm around my waist and lifted me easily to my feet. "Just take it slow," he said, "very slow. That's what you do in boxing, get up slow and careful. Put on a good face for the crowd so nobody knows how bad you're hurt."

"There's no crowd but you," I said. "...and I hurt a lot."

He half carried me to a chair in the living room. As he eased me into it, he noticed Lucy's painting hanging over the mantle.

"Lucy Moon," he said. "I'd recognize her work anywhere." He walked a few steps closer to the painting. "This is an early one, isn't it? The pictures at the gallery the night of the movie are a little, a little different."

"Mayo," I said, "this is no time to discuss art. I could be dying. What are you doing here, anyway? Not that I'm ungrateful..." With a healthy shudder, I glanced back out into the hallway where I could see John Owen's feet. "...just how hard did you hit him?"

Laughing, Mayo turned from the painting. "Oh, he'll recover," he said. "I just gave him a little tap." Then he looked very serious. "Good thing I was hanging around the gallery, keeping an eye on my animals. I saw you and the detective go into the burger place. The man could of killed you."

"But how did you know to follow me home?"

"I wasn't the only one keeping an eye on the gallery," he said. "That guy…" He gestured towards the foyer. "—he was there, too, parked around back. Didn't seem right. Just sitting in a dark car, watching, unless he was an artist, too."

"Oh my God!" I said. "He was waiting for me to come back to the gallery from Church Hill. I had followed him down the street from the grocery store and he must have assumed I would go to the gallery."

"No power in the gallery," Mayo said. "You couldn't have phoned for help."

I let that discomforting remark pass without comment. "If he was parked in back, how did John Owen know we were at the restaurant?"

"At one point he got out of his car and walked up the alley between your building and the portrait painter's place. The windows are all lit up at McDonald's. You and the policeman stood out. Anybody could of seen you. Then you and the Lieutenant split and you went to that phone booth. A few minutes later your friend picked you up in her truck. The guy in your front hall followed you and I followed him."

I looked at the Lord of the Woods and smiled. Protecting his animals, indeed.

"Well, Mayo, I need you to do one more favor for me tonight. Call

Lieutenant Mavredes and have him pick up our intruder. If he hears my voice on the line he's liable to hang up."

XXIII

If stones could sleep they would have had nothing over me that night even though I was alone in the house after the police left. Mayo had offered to sleep on the sofa, "just in case." Mavredes grudgingly offered to send over a cop. I guess since I wasn't a street person he could spare one. But I was too tired to be afraid or even angry at Mavredes anymore so I declined both offers. But, as usual, my curiosity had been piqued. A sullen John Owen Smith had been hauled away in a squad car, muttering that he had nothing to say. Of course, he would eventually have to say something. You don't push your way into an art dealer's house and beat her over the side of the head for nothing. Even the most disgruntled artist rarely does that. The most we knew for certain was that John Owen had helped steal Mayo's giraffe and presumably had knocked out Tyrone with the giraffe. Or, at least, that was what Beverly said. The major question was whether attacking me meant John Owen had replaced Jimmy Travers as the major suspect in David's death.

It had been a very long day. I pulled off my dirty, wrinkled clothes, dropped them on the floor and climbed under the covers naked.

Yes, he replaces Jimmy, I thought as I drifted into sleep, he killed David Moon for some reason we don't yet understand. But my final thought was that it might be a bit more complicated than that.

I was awakened the next morning by the telephone. I grabbed it with as much eagerness as possible given the early hour, 10:00 a.m. I almost said, "Wallace Gallery" and caught myself just in time. Emotionally I was not ready to go back to work anytime soon.

"This is Barbara Barksdale," the voice said. It was less brimming with sweetness and light than usual.

Immediately I sat up in bed, glanced at the pile of clothes on the floor and tried hard to reconstruct the night before. "Hello," I said, "I think this is Rosemund Wallace."

"I don't want to be an obstructionist of justice," she said, "so I decided to let you see a copy of the film we shot at your gallery that night. I wasn't, wasn't telling the whole truth when I said I didn't have it."

'Obstructionist'? I wondered if Barbara had studied under the same professor of the muffled metaphor at Virginia Commonwealth University as Austin. I hadn't thought about Austin for several days, not since his emotional reaction to Lucy's missing painting which no longer appeared to be missing. He was probably wondering when we were going to use him to install the next show. Or if we were ever going to have a next show.

"Thanks," I said. "That'll be very helpful." I didn't mention that Arik Lawson had already let us view the copy he had. It was possible that Barbara had more footage than Arik. And in spite of her angry outburst about him earlier, she probably knew David better than anybody else. If I played my cards right, there was bound to be more she could tell me. "When can we get together?"

Instead of naming a time and place, she said, "I really did love David, you know."

I leaned back into the comfort of the pillows. The sheets were still warm and soft. Sleeping naked is not so bad, I thought. An image of Michael DeBord flashed through my mind, also naked, which was even better. It had been a long time since I had pictured a naked man in bed with me. And even longer that a man had actually been there.

"If you loved him, then you'll want to help as much as possible," I said.

"Yeah, I guess..."

Something she said when we talked the first time came back. I sat up a little straighter in bed. "You told me David's mother was always painting her weird nightmares. Do you remember?"

There was a long silence on the other end. "That's what I said, huh?"

It was my turn to wait.

When she spoke again, her voice showed genuine concern. It was the first time I felt like she was showing her real side. "You really believe somebody killed David? That he didn't do away with himself?"

"No, I don't think David killed himself, Barbara. That's why I want to see the entire unedited version of the film, all the way to the end, including the waltz scene. It could help us find out who did kill him…now, what about his mother's nightmares?"

I could almost sense Barbara's discomfort through the phone line. She took a deep breath and then blurted "bondage."

At first I didn't think I heard right. But she continued. "Lucy had all these dreams about being tied up," she said. "David said she tried to laugh them off, but they came a lot. That's why he didn't want that painting in the movie. It made him uncomfortable. The other paintings had flowers and trees. But you know how artists are, their personal stuff always comes out in their work someplace or another."

Yes, I thought, I'm an art dealer, I know how artists are. But if Barbara was telling the truth, I had missed the boat on Lucy. Bernard had said she was big on "angst and entrapment" and Mavredes had labeled the missing painting "this bondage stuff". Since Bernard was always joking, I hadn't taken his comment seriously. And I had dismissed Mavredes' remark as coming from one of the uninformed. Maybe I should look at the Lieutenant's paintings after all, I thought. Perhaps his eye was better than I gave him credit for.

But most of all, I needed to take a look at myself. I had known Lucy for years and I hadn't wanted to see "entrapment" in her work. I loved and admired her genius. There was nothing in her life that I knew about that should make her feel trapped. Certainly not her marriage, she had been divorced even longer than I had. She was far too creative to let anything or anybody trap her. I felt honored to show and sell her work. She was one of the most sought after painters I represented. No wonder Lila Hunt wanted to get her hands on her. Lucy was practically perfect.

In a business where too many would-be artists slapped paint on canvas and expected accolades and big bucks, Lucy's perfectionism was one of her most appealing qualities. The trees, the flowers, the enigmatic figures, even the black plastic and red cord. Lucy was able to lay paint on canvas like nobody I had ever known. It was Lucy who had gotten me started in the art business in the first place. 'Bondage' was not a word I wanted to hear.

I remembered Mavredes' initial assessment of David's death, "near asphyxiation to bring on orgasm." If you pushed too close to the edge sometimes you didn't make it back. Now the edge was pushing me and I didn't like it.

After I made a date to meet Barbara I reluctantly eased my aching body out of bed, climbed stiffly down the stairs still naked and stood in front of Lucy's painting for a long time. The figure on the beach seemed lonelier and more enigmatic than ever. The tiny piece of red cord now appeared to dominate the picture. At least there was no black plastic anywhere. And then I remembered the slides I had assembled for Michael. Black plastic had begun to appear somewhere in the sequence of images I had put together. I had not paid attention at the time, at least not consciously.

Dear God, I thought. What does it all mean?

The phone rang several times while I was in the shower. Since I was in no mood to talk with anybody, I let the machine take all the messages. I knew Mavredes would be one of the callers if he had something to tell me about John Owen. If John Owen had confessed to knocking out Tyrone and attacking me, Mavredes would not have to provide protection for Beverly and Jack. John Owen would be behind bars, maybe even on trial for the murder of David Moon. But there still seemed to be no motive for murder. Except that there had been a disagreement about something, according to Lucy, something that David had gotten over. Whatever it was, maybe John Owen didn't get over it.

But I couldn't dismiss Jimmy Travers so easily. David had gone somewhere in a black Lincoln Town Car with Jimmy the night he died. Beverly and Jack had seen the two of them leaving together. Where had they gone? Mavredes had promised to interrogate Jimmy until the governor intervened. Perhaps Jack and Beverly were still in danger.

And then there was the giraffe head. It made no sense for John Owen or the two Lee girls to send it to the governor. Even if the three of them knew Jimmy

Travers, why involve the leader of the Commonwealth of Virginia? What did the giraffe head represent? Mavredes indicated that Brookfield seemed as puzzled as everyone else. I stood in the shower with the steamy water pouring over my head until the water began to turn cold. Reluctantly, I got out. The real world was not very appealing at that moment. Instead of contemplating my next show I was trying to figure out why the governor of Virginia had received a giraffe head as a present.

In spite of the long shower, my body was so stiff it was difficult to get dressed. My most comfortable jeans still lay in a heap beside the bed, so I pulled them on and yanked a clean turtleneck out of a drawer. For a change I had little desire to put much effort into my appearance. I decided to check my phone messages. There were two calls from my partner, Harry, wondering if I had fallen off the face of the earth and insisting we pick a date for the next show at the gallery. I wondered how much sympathy I'd get from him when he learned I'd been beaten up in my own house by a twenty-year old who had followed me home after my car blew up in Church Hill.

The third call was from Mavredes saying John Owen claimed to have come to my house to try to talk with me about David and I had not only attacked him but had my black bodyguard beat him up. At least Mavredes had the decency to laugh.

"The Rosemund Wallace mythology is getting better every day," he said. "After threatening the governor you've attacked someone twice your size and half your age. Come on down to the station when you get out of bed so I can take your full statement about the incident. Maybe just seeing you will reduce the accused to a trembling mass of jelly."

Knowing John Owen would stay put for a while allowed me the leisure of seeing someone else first. Barbara Barksdale had invited me to her apartment to look at the version of David's movie she had in her possession and I was eager to get over there before something else happened.

She smiled almost demurely as she opened the door. She was wearing the same combat boots I had seen the first time I met her. They clattered loudly as I followed her across the floor into a room designed to be a living room and was now set up as a photographer's studio with black and white photos clipped to lines hanging across one wall. Enlargements of several photographs were tacked above a long table strewn with still more pictures. Several of the large photos were of David. A couple of shots were of him grinning like I remembered. One with his baseball cap turned backwards was particularly upsetting, however. The cap was perched at almost exactly the same angle when Bernard and I found him in the bathroom at the gallery. I turned away quickly.

A portion of the room was closed off by a make-shift partition with a black curtain draping the entrance. It reminded me of the stifling experience I had as a child entering one of the sideshows through a thick black cloth at the state fair. I must have shivered as I recalled the unpleasant sensation; Barbara gave the cloth a quick yank and pointed inside.

"My darkroom," she said. "David built it for me. Equipped it, too." She shrugged and let the black drape fall. "David had money, you know. His grandmother was rich. So was his mother, richer than most artists in this town. David was always trying to get out from under her shadow. That's why he liked film. As an art form, it was quicker, he said."

I was glad to be distracted from the cubicle with the black cloth. "Quicker than what?"

Barbara picked up a handful of photographs and began shuffling them as though dealing a deck of cards. "Oh, you know, creating illusions, that kind of stuff. It was a game with him. 'I'll out-illusion Lucy,' he used to say."

That David wanted to get out from under his mother's shadow was not my impression. He was very proud of her success. When he asked if he could use the gallery to film some scenes for his movie he insisted that we install her paintings for the shoot. I was certain he wanted them for more than background. I took another look at the photographs that were strung up around the room.

"You do these?" I said.

Barbara nodded and held up one of the photographs in her hand. "These, too," she said. "David thought I was pretty good. That's how we got hooked up in the first place. We were in a photography class together at V.C.U. That guy that installs shows for you at the gallery was in the class, too."

"Austin?"

"Yeah, Austin somebody. He was always bragging about how he worked at a real gallery while the rest of us were still trying to break into the art world. He was a real pain sometimes, so sure he was right about what constituted 'real' art."

Yes, I thought, Austin could be that way. He tried to see 'real' art every time he turned around. At least he always showed up on time and did his job most of the time without complaining, even when I changed my mind and had him rehang half a dozen paintings.

"Did Austin know David was Lucy Moon's son?"

"I suppose so. Everybody else did. David was not exactly modest about things like that." She gestured towards an open door leading from the living room. "Hey, can I get you a drink?" Though the doorway I could see a stove and refrigerator and counter stacked with dirty dishes.

"No, thanks," I said. My shoulder was beginning to ache where I had hit it when John Owen pushed me under the table. Had Barbara waved a Tsing Tao in my face, however, I might have relented. "You said we could look at David's movie."

"I've not seen it since he...he died," she said. "Arik gave me a video copy and told me to keep it, just in case."

"Just in case, why?" I said.

"Beats me. You never can tell with Arik. He's hard to read." She disappeared behind the black curtain of her dark room and returned with a video tape. "This is it," she said. "Want the lights off?"

"Sure." I settled back in the chair she offered and reflected on her comment that Arik was hard to read. It was an obvious lie. Arik was very easy to read. He hadn't liked Mavredes and me, and he certainly disliked having to show us David's film. In addition, he knew exactly what I was talking about when I mentioned the missing waltz scene. The one thing that could be said in his favor was that he liked Gussie.

As the unedited film played on the television screen in front of us I relived the night at the gallery for the second time. Barbara's copy was not as good as the one Arik showed us in the studio, but perhaps it was her lack of sophisticated equipment. So far, nothing on the film was any different from the action I had seen with Gussie and Mavredes. Actually, I might have missed the fact that something white was stuffed in the giraffe's mouth had I only seen the footage in Barbara's apartment. I was grateful that we had already seen that portion at Arik's.

I paid little attention to the dialogue. It had been boring the first time. I was more interested in the segments between the scenes when the camera was still running for a few seconds. Even though I watched carefully there were no surprises, just a number of jerky movements, voices laughing in the background, a few shots of the expanse of glass in the front of the gallery as though the camera person had aimed the camera towards the street.

And then I heard David's voice off camera saying, "Everybody get ready for the waltz scene." The scene Arik had not shown us. The scene he said he didn't remember. The camera focused on David for a fragment of a second. Seeing his image flash across the screen caused my breath to catch in my throat. His face was very intense, more serious than usual. Then the camera did a slow, almost deliberate, sweep of the gallery, producing a panoramic view of actors, extras, and art. There was Gussie in her black dress next to Bernard, her waltz partner. They were both smiling. There was even a glimpse of Harry and me, looking like art dealers, or something. Mayo and his wife were behind us. The gold "X" on Mayo's black silk crown glistened, making him seem even taller than usual. He was staring over everyone's heads, looking towards the rear of the gallery.

At what?

But before I could guess what had grabbed his attention the camera seemed to find what it was seeking—the corner featuring Lucy's painting of the seated figure in black plastic which looked like it was guarded by Mayo's grinning giraffe.

Grinning?

I could see its red tongue. Which meant its mouth was now empty. In the interval between the scene earlier in the evening and the waltz scene, someone had removed whatever had been stuffed into the animal's mouth. The camera, or whoever was operating the camera, appeared to realize that something was wrong. It froze on the giraffe for several seconds too long, capturing the grinning set of teeth and red tongue, then zoomed in closer as if not believing the mouth was empty.

I turned to ask Barbara who was operating the camera for that scene when she began to cough. "Sorry," she said, "something in my throat. I need a glass of water. Sure you don't want something to drink?"

David's voice cut through the coughing as if he were in the darkened room with us. "Places, everyone. Let's get it right the first time."

I followed Barbara into the kitchen and put my hand firmly on her shoulder. "Okay," I said, "what's going on?"

XXIV

What do you mean?" She wouldn't look at me, but stared into the glass of water as though mesmerized by something only she could see.

"Mayo's giraffe. There was something in its mouth earlier that night and it was gone when we started the waltz scene. Something white, a wad of cloth or a bag, something soft and malleable enough to stuff in the space between its teeth and tongue."

Barbara raised her eyes slowly and looked at me over the rim of the glass. It was hard to tell whether her expression was one of admiration, anger or simply fear. "How did you know?" she said. "How did you figure it out?"

"If you're in the art business long enough," I said, "you become pretty good at seeing things. A nuance of color, just the right angle, a shadow, a distortion that makes the difference between something wonderful and something ordinary. Unconsciously, you train yourself not to miss much. I held that giraffe in my hands when Mayo first brought it into the gallery. The teeth got my attention, the red tongue, especially the tongue. When I looked at the film at the place where Arik works, the tongue seemed to be missing. It was because something had been stuffed in its mouth."

Barbara took a long swallow from the glass, then leaned against the cluttered kitchen counter. "So you'd already seen the film? You tricked me."

"I hadn't seen the waltz scene. For some reason it wasn't on the footage Arik showed me. But I knew it had been shot. I was in the movie, remember? I was there that night. I danced out the front door with everybody else."

"Arik was into protecting David," she said. "...not that it did much good. He kept telling David he was getting in over his head. Arik thinks David got scared, that that's why he, he hanged himself." She stomped the floor angrily with one of her heavy boots. "Oh, what the hell difference does it make anymore? He's gone." Her eyes teared up and her nose began to drip. She wiped it with her sleeve and let the tears seep down her cheeks. There were dark smudges where she had rubbed her eye makeup. I decided the tears were genuine, though it was impossible to tell who they were being shed for.

"Yes," I said, "he's gone, but I..."

Barbara waved her hand impatiently as though brushing off an annoying insect. "I know, I know, you don't think he did away with himself..." She exhaled one deep breath that seemed to stop the flow of tears, filled her glass again with water from the tap and looked at me with eyes which had been made a bit ludicrous by the smeared mascara.

"Okay, Rosemund Wallace of the Wallace Gallery, if David didn't kill himself, who did it?"

"Let's go back in the living room," I said, "and look at the waltz scene again. In slow motion this time or frame by frame. If Arik was really trying to protect David, maybe that's the reason he didn't show us this scene. Maybe there's something in it he thinks would hurt David—or compromise him. Let's rewind and start with the part where David comes on camera for a minute to tell everybody to get ready."

I took a seat and waited while Barbara fiddled with the VCR. Then she sat down close to me with an attitude resembling cooperation. I didn't say that when you're dead, you're already compromised.

With both action and sound slowed down, David's voice was gravely, almost a growl as he intoned, "Pla—ces—ev—ery—bo—dy—Le—ts—get—it—rig—ht—the—fir—st—ti—me." And then the waltz music began, also in a slow, draggy tempo that accentuated every gesture of the dancers captured on film. One camera was shooting from the balcony that overlooked the downstairs gallery. The angle was interesting. I hadn't recalled anyone going upstairs with a camera. It could have been John Owen or one of the Lee girls or Barbara Barksdale, herself. As we danced in slow motion we resembled a Chagal painting with twirling figures captured forever in space. Gussie and Bernard looked particularly good in each other's arms. For some reason it made me think of Michael De Bord with his arm around my waist as we raced for the car in the rain. I wondered if he had received the package containing Lucy's slides.

Lucy's slides.

One in particular exploded in living color in my mind. It was of a window with a curtain or drape pulled to one side by a cord of red silk. In the painting a child was staring out the window beside the drape. Neither its hair or body shape or clothing identified the child as male or female. Like the figure on the beach wrapped in black plastic, it was androgynous. The date written on the slide in Lucy's handwriting was also imprinted in my mind: twenty years ago. I remembered because it was one of her earliest paintings. Twenty years ago when she began painting in earnest the red cord was present—and already tying something. In this case, it was tying a curtain, not a figure. Over the years the cord had come off the drape. The curtain had come down.

But who was the child?

I forced myself to watch the scene unfolding on the t.v. screen. I would deal with the slides later. Perhaps Michael had already seen something else I had not allowed myself to see in Lucy's work. On the film we were dancing with smiles on our faces. I remembered how I felt as Harry and I waltzed to David's directions. Harry would never have been dancing in a movie had he limited himself to his cardiology practice. I was glad he was there. Suddenly I missed him and the gallery and the monthly shows and Arabella's critiques. I hadn't seen Lucy or Arabella in the movie. Where were they? Instead of being in the film, had they gone off somewhere to talk that evening?

I recalled how hot the gallery had been. There was a closeup of Mayo's face with sweat beading his forehead. He was frowning as he glanced toward the back of the gallery where he had been looking earlier in the scene. And then the camera skimmed the tops of our heads to stop at the front door of the gallery. At David's directions the door had been propped open so the waltzers could dance their way out into the night while the music played.

The second camera positioned downstairs took over. Two of the actors in the movie were dancing out the front door in slow motion as the camera followed them. There was a close up of their faces. I steeled myself for more cliche-ridden dialogue when my attention was diverted from the actors to the automobile parked at the curb in front of the gallery.

It was a black Lincoln parked at such an angle that I could see the "1" on the license plate.

"Hey!" I jumped out of my chair so fast that Barbara gasped. "Stop the film—no, back it up. I need to see that car."

Instead of doing what I asked, Barbara turned on the lights in the room. Her skin was ashen in the unexpected glare. She blinked. Her pupils were dilated. "It was the car," she said, "the limo—that Arik didn't want you to see. I didn't know it was on the film, but Arik did." She stuck her fist in her mouth like a child trying to keep from crying.

"Jimmy Travers," I said. "It's the governor's car that Jimmy Travers drives around, isn't it?"

She nodded her head. Her eyes had filled with tears again. By now her mascara was so smeared that she resembled a raccoon.

"So you knew him after all," I said quietly.

She sobbed, then stuck her fist back in her mouth.

I put my hand on her arm and held it there until she pulled her fist away from her face.

"There was a deal going down," she said between sobs. "I wasn't sure who was supposed to collect. David was hush-hush on that. But when I saw Jimmy that night cruising Carytown I figured he was the one. I swear I didn't know he was in the film, though. He was a fool to park in front of the gallery while we were shooting. It was supposed to happen later."

"The pick-up?"

"Yeah," she said. "The giraffe was a terrific idea. Nobody would look there. The drugs would be put in the giraffe's mouth, the right person would make the exchange and everybody would be clean."

I felt the tension drain from my body as though I had spent an hour working out hard at the gym. Mayo had been right about the people David Moon partied with. And I had been right about the drugs. The bag in the giraffe's mouth must have contained some heavy duty stuff, probably worth a small fortune. Whether Jimmy Travers was the pick-up man or not, maybe Lucy hated her brother because he was involved. But something obviously had gone terribly wrong. In my mind the governor's junior speech writer was back in the picture as the person most likely to have murdered David.

"So David and Jimmy Travers had some sort of drug deal going on," I said.

Barbara looked puzzled. She frowned and shook her head. "No," she said, "not David. John Owen. It was John Owen and somebody David knew. Only he wouldn't let on who it was—not even to me. Maybe it was Jimmy—maybe it was somebody else. I tried to get it out of him but he wouldn't tell. David and John Owen got in a big fight about it. It was John Owen's stash—he could do what he wanted with it, David said. David had more important things on his mind than running drugs out of Church Hill. He wanted Jimmy's help with something else—not drugs. He was scared John Owen was going to screw everything up. And somebody sure screwed it up. The drugs were supposed to be in the giraffe's mouth so John Owen could sneak the giraffe out of the gallery..." She stopped talking. It must have been the expression on my face.

"What did I say wrong?"

"Nothing," I said. "John Owen did steal the giraffe, but if there was no stash, why did he bother? We could both see from the film that the stuff was already gone before the movie was finished. The bag had been taken out of the giraffe's mouth sometime between the last scene and the waltz scene."

Barbara looked as bewildered as I felt.

"What do you mean John Owen 'stole' the giraffe?"

"He and the Lee sisters put a ladder up to the side of the gallery, climbed through the bathroom window and took Mayo's giraffe," I said. I didn't mention that they probably took Lucy's painting, too. "Then he pushed his way into my house and knocked me around. Maybe he thought I had the drugs. Lucky for me, Mayo followed him to..."

Abruptly I stopped. Mayo had been looking at something going on in the rear of the gallery while everybody else was engrossed in the waltz scene. Perhaps he saw someone tampering with his giraffe. Maybe that was why he went back to the gallery last night, to protect his animals, all right, but not for the reasons he said. Maybe he went back to the gallery because he was the point man. Maybe his introduction of Walter McGowan had been a total ruse. Rosemund Wallace, the gullible art dealer, would be a good cover for a drug deal. An art gallery in Carytown would never be suspect, a street corner in Church Hill, maybe, but not the spot where high culture showed its newest face monthly to the local aesthetic elite.

"Barbara," I said. "You've got to tell me the whole truth. Had you ever seen Mayo Johnson before the night we filmed the movie?" I prayed that the answer would be no, that none of us had ever met Mayo Johnson until he appeared at the gallery with his driftwood menagerie. Until that moment I was certain Mayo was on my side, that he was as concerned about finding out why David died as I was. He was lucky enough not to have struck out, he should have been on the side of someone who hadn't been so fortunate. But if he and John Owen had planned a deal which included tricking both David and me then I couldn't trust anybody. The thought that Mayo's unexpected appearance with the giraffe had been a setup to get him into the gallery the night of the filming cast a shadow across every artist I knew.

"Well, I don't know," Barbara said. Her nose was running again. She was looking more and more unattractive. "I didn't pay that much attention to him. I had other things on my mind that night. I was trying to get back with David and all he cared about was making his damn movie and being famous. Besides, the giraffe made me nervous. He looked like he was laughing at me." She rubbed her eyes with her sleeve and I was afraid she would start crying again.

"Think hard," I said. "A man like Mayo Johnson doesn't come along every day. Had you ever seen him before? With David, with John Owen, with anybody connected with the movie?"

"Is this going to get me in trouble?"

"You're already in trouble," I said, trying to think of the words Mavredes might use. "Withholding evidence, that kind of thing..."

She walked to the table covered with photographs and ran her hands over the images as though seeking comfort from something she recognized. "He looked familiar," she said in a whisper. "I've seen him before."

My hands were cold. I could hardly speak. "With David?"

Barbara's eyes were bright, almost too bright. "I honestly don't know," she said slowly, "and I swear that's the truth." I had no trouble at all in telling it was a lie.

I took Barbara's copy of the film with me and headed downtown to see Mavredes. Barbara seemed almost relieved to let it go, like saying 'goodbye' to a bad house guest who had overstayed his welcome. I was armed with footage of the governor's automobile parked in front of the gallery. That, coupled with Beverly's testimony that she saw what was undoubtedly the same Lincoln in back of the gallery and that David left with Jimmy Travers in the same black car after we shot the movie, was enough to bring Jimmy in for serious questioning. Perhaps it was even enough to charge him with David's murder.

Except...

Except for an explanation of the so-called drug deal planned between John Owen and somebody. Was it Jimmy? Mayo? Or someone else? And what about Mayo's behavior in the film and his appearance at my house? Plus the fact that

Barbara said she recognized him from somewhere. And the Lee sisters? Were they involved? Both Tyrone and Beverly described them as two of the people who took the giraffe and attacked Tyrone in the alley. And who had stolen Lucy's painting and how did it end up at her house in Goochland County?

On a whim I pulled into a 7-Eleven with an outside phone booth near the gasoline pumps. I stuck a quarter in the slot and called Arabella's number at the TIMES DISPATCH. As expected, I got her voice mail.

"It's Rosemund," I said to her machine. "See if you can find anything in the paper's archives about a boxer, or ex-boxer, named Mayo Johnson. He may have had an accident in the ring, lost his eyesight or something. Anything you can locate will be great. I'm on my way to the homicide detective's office to talk to him about...about..." I considered the message I was leaving and the fact that anybody could check Arabella's voice mail. "...about a giraffe," I said. "I'll try to track you down later."

After hanging up I stood in the 7-Eleven parking lot for a moment, then reentered the phone booth, stuck another coin in the slot and dialed Harry's work number.

His receptionist answered, her Richmond accent as pronounced as ever. It was one of the reasons Harry hired her, makes the locals feel comfortable, he says. 'If I'm going to fool with their hearts they need to know I'm one of them.'

"Doctor Brown's office."

"Hi, Louise, it's Rosemund Wallace."

"Harry's in surgery, Rosemund," she said. "Anything I can do for you?"

"Just one question."

"Shoot."

"I'm trying to find out something about another surgeon, an eye specialist named Walter McGowan. See if Harry knows him."

"Is he an artist? A doctor who paints? There are more and more of them who do. I read an article the other day about..."

"This is important, Louise," I said. "Tell Harry it's a matter of life and death." As I hung up, I thought about Lucy's painting, altered illusions, it was a business we all seemed to be in.

I had started out with seventy-five cents in my purse. After spending two quarters I had enough left for a third call. It was my own number this time to check my voice mail. Arabella and Harry were not the only ones who received messages. There were four calls waiting for me but only one that mattered: Michael DeBord saying he had discovered something very interesting about Lucy's slides, urging me to phone him, joking that I could spend my nickel this time. Didn't he know phone rates had gone up?

XXV

I was all set to confront John Owen Smith with what I learned from Barbara. The film would be my ace. I would show him the entire footage and we'd have him. I had to admit that I was a little unclear as to exactly what we'd have him on, but it would be serious and it would implicate Jimmy Travers. I was still smarting from being attacked in my own house and angry that I didn't know the real reason for the attack, only that John Owen had jumped me and Mayo Johnson had come to my rescue. To tell the truth, being rescued by Mayo only muddied the waters because his motivation was as unclear as John Owen's.

The longer I thought about it as I drove up Broad Street in the Jaguar's temporary replacement, past the boarded-up department stores to the government building housing the Homicide Division of the General Criminal District, the angrier I got. And it wasn't simply because I couldn't find a parking place and would be forced to park in one of the city's over-priced lots. I was convinced that David might still be alive had there been no drug deal. And John Owen, and maybe Mayo, was certainly a player in that deal.

At that moment I hated the police for not cleaning out the drug dealers in Church Hill, hated the city for allowing Beverly and Jack to live in a garage, hated whatever Walter McGowan had done, which probably was drug-related and had alienated his own sister, hated the governor for cutting art subsidies in the state, hated...

Abruptly I caught myself and began to backtrack. The one area of artistic endeavor that Governor Brookfield had not cut was the burgeoning film industry in Virginia. Beginning in Charlottesville, moving up and down the coast and focusing on Richmond as a stand-in for major cities like Washington, D.C., the Virginia Film Office enticed big bucks to the area in the form of major production companies seeking new markets. That meant jobs, plus wealthy outsiders spending their salaries at our restaurants, hotels, stores and, as I recalled the last Hollywood face to appear on my Carytown doorstep, even art galleries. Every time Brookfield slashed another dollar from the arts budget in Virginia he cited the film industry as an art form that paid its own way, generated funds for the Commonwealth, and never asked for a government handout.

Jimmy Travers worked for that very same governor. Brookfield had made it clear that he did not appreciate anyone suggesting inappropriate behavior on the part of one of his employees, which made it a little awkward for me since I was suggesting a lot of inappropriateness. Yet there was something David Moon had wanted from Jimmy. Bernard said Jimmy as good as promised state money to the Fire Station Players; maybe he promised the same to David. But what was David supposed to do to get it? Whatever it was may have cost him his life.

After driving around the block in my rented car half a dozen times seeking a parking place near the Criminal Building, I gave up and pulled into a parking deck on 9th Street closer to the Medical College of Virginia than to Mavredes' office. Both the government and the hospital generated more business and more traffic than any part of the city except Carytown. Everybody I knew tried with equal fervor to avoid the court buildings and MCV. A traffic violation or a midnight shooting generated the same sort of dread; hunting for a place to park.

Shockoe Bottom, the restaurant district where Michael and I ate dinner, which was also the place Gussie called home, ran a close second in terms of parking problems. But nobody except Gussie complained too loudly about the traffic in the Bottom. All those drivers prowling the streets in search of parking filled the city coffers nicely. The rest of downtown Richmond resembled most urban areas throughout the country. Discount shops with iron grates stood next to deserted storefronts whose sidewalks had been taken over by colorful pushcart vendors. Except for impersonal marble and cement buildings like the one housing Lieutenant Mavredes' office, downtown Richmond was rotting at the core.

Lately, the investigation into David Moon's death seemed to be doing the same.

"Your friendly intruder is still in the holding block," Mavredes said as he greeted me at the door. In spite of our ups and downs, I was glad to see him. His dress-for-success appearance was reassuring. Today he was wearing a navy blazer, a red and blue Rep tie and gray wool slacks with a crease as sharp as a razor blade. I couldn't figure out how a man in his profession always managed to look so put together. Perhaps he had his shirts done with extra starch or shaved twice a day. "I thought you would have been here earlier," he said. "I was getting ready to send him over to the lock up."

"I was busy," I said, "working on the case."

Mavredes was a graceful man. Unlike me, he never plopped onto a piece of furniture. He let himself down easy on the edge of his desk and straightened the crease in his gray slacks.

"I can hardly wait to hear," he said.

Usually I took a great deal of care with my appearance. Having someone like Gussie as my friend inspires me to take care of myself, if for no other reason than to keep up. Today, however, I felt like a slob. No makeup, no color coordinated clothes, no jewelry. I was certain Mavredes recognized the dirty jeans I had worn the previous day when he rescued me from the Hill Cafe. At least he wasn't throwing me out. Must be because I had combed my hair.

"A little earlier today I saw Barbara Barksdale, one of the women filming the movie with David," I said.

"I won't even ask where," Mavredes said.

I ignored his remark and focused instead on his immaculate tassel loafers. He had crossed one leg over his knee and I could see the sole of the shoe. There was not even a worn spot. "Barbara told me John Owen was involved in some sort of drug deal," I said, "with somebody who had arranged a pickup at the gallery. The stuff was stuck in the giraffe's mouth as we suspected. My guess is that John Owen never got his money and that when he stole the giraffe and found neither stash nor cash he went looking for his bag of goodies at my house." I rubbed my arm which still ached from being tackled in the front hall. "We've got him now," I said.

"Not quite," Mavredes said. "No tickie, no laundry." He stretched slightly, just enough to cause a momentary gap in his jacket, but long enough for me to see a chipped button on his shirt. He was not perfect, after all. "The Holy Mother of God can accuse him of crimes against humanity, but without evidence we've got nothing but a photo of a giraffe with a mouth full of teeth. Besides, David Moon's ex-girl friend doesn't make the most reliable witness. Lucy filled me in on a few details about Ms. Barksdale. She's got a little drug history, herself."

That revelation didn't surprise me, but I was more interested in hearing what he had learned from Lucy. "So you went out to the tavern?"

He nodded. "It was a nice drive. Goochland county is beautiful this time of year. She was a little chattier, too. Had a friend there with her. Maybe that had something to do with it, good looking woman."

"Lucy?" I would not have picked Lucy as Mavredes' type, or maybe I was hoping he would hold out for Gussie.

"The friend. Tall redhead in brown suede with high heeled leather boots."

"It's all in the details," I said. I felt a sinking sensation in the pit of my stomach. The most visible tall redheaded fashion plate in the city was Lila Hunt, my arch competitor.

Mavredes got to his feet, brushed off his trousers and buttoned his jacket. Maybe he realized I had spotted the chipped button. "It's my business to notice everything," he said, "just like you. What I noticed primarily was the missing painting hanging in the hallway just as your reporter friend said."

"Well?" I hadn't doubted Arabella, but it was a shock hearing from Mavredes that it was actually there.

"She found it on the doorstep."

"That's what she told you? That's it? No other explanation?" I pictured Lucy's doorstep, which in actuality was a tall set of wooden stairs constructed from aged timbers to complement the original siding of the tavern. I wondered if the painting had been leaning against the bottom step or actually carried up to the porch and left against the huge oak door that had taken four months to restore to the original wood under layers of paint.

"She went out to call the dog, she said, and there was the picture."

Lucy's dog was big and black, a Lab named "Brutus", as slick and shiny as black plastic. I wondered if he had rubbed against the painting or barked at whoever had delivered it to the tavern.

"Surely she had some explanation. How did it get there? Did she see anybody?"

"She seemed genuinely puzzled, but then her friend did most of the talking. Said the painting was one of her best, that Lucy should never have let it out of her sight. Made me feel like I'd done something wrong taking it down to police headquarters." Mavredes raised his eyebrows, straightened his tie and said, "you know the price tag on that painting?"

I shook my head. If Lila Hunt was setting prices there was no telling how high they would go. Artists joked about the "Lila Hunt Hike" whenever she hung one of their shows.

"Thirty five thousand." He said it like it was a million. "Thirty five thousand bucks. Who's going to pay that kind of money in this city?"

"I would imagine Lila has some place besides Richmond in mind," I said. It occurred to me that the brokerage firm that had purchased its own baker's dozen from me would be delighted to learn their Lucy Moon paintings had just doubled in value. But my major thought was on Michael DeBord and his Japanese employer in Los Angeles. 'Name your price', Michael had said. Never would it have come close to $35,000. But Lila Hunt had the reputation for doubling whatever figure the market would bear, and getting away with it. Sometimes I was almost jealous.

"I asked about her brother, the doctor," said Mavredes. "Like I told you, she was less hostile this time. Said they had a falling-out, a family thing. When I told her Arik claimed David was seeing his uncle, she seemed surprised to learn David hadn't written him out of the family. But it was hard to tell, her friend being there..."

"Stop calling her Lucy's friend," I said. "She's just another art dealer." I reminded myself that's all I was, and it bugged me Lila had stepped so easily into the dual role I used to have as Lucy's friend and the person who sold her paintings. Lost friendship or not, I had come this far. I was determined to prove that David's death had not been suicide, accidental or otherwise. Sometimes when you get a glimpse of the real motivation for a particular action you realize nobody does anything out of pure altruism. I was no exception. If I could prove David had been murdered it wouldn't hurt so much to say 'goodbye' to Lucy.

Mavredes seemed to sense that discussing other art dealers was not my favorite thing at the moment, for he said, "You want to see John Owen Smith?"

When a policeman brought him in, John Owen appeared as angry as ever, a young man on the brink of exploding. Being locked up had done nothing to improve his attitude. A dark scowl created two furrows in the center of his forehead. His hair stood on end as though he had slept upside down and not bothered to use a comb when he awakened. "What are you doing here?" he said when he saw me. He jerked his head in Mavredes' direction, his narrow shoulders flapping. "I don't have to talk to her. She's nothing but trouble, and a two-faced liar, besides. This is a free country. You can't make me do anything I don't want to do. Get me a lawyer."

"Just a few questions," Mavredes said. "She's not going to hurt you." He nodded at me, giving me the go-ahead. Actually, I think it was a test to see if I had more luck than he did getting anything out of our uncooperative prisoner. I hadn't been too successful trying to wrangle a confession out of Jimmy Travers. All I had done was to generate the appellation "bitch". I'd try a little harder with John Owen. Especially since Mavredes seemed to be daring me to succeed.

"I spent the morning with Barbara Barksdale," I said. "We looked at some footage of the movie, including the waltz scene..."

The Crow hunched his shoulders up around his ears. "So?" he said.

I reached into my purse and waved the video tape in his face. "Let's go to the movies," I said. "If Lieutenant Mavredes doesn't mind, I'd like to look at a few minutes of this tape."

"No problem," Mavredes said. "I'm curious about the famous waltz scene myself." He went to the door, growled a few words in the direction of the outer room and in less than two minutes a VCR was wheeled into his office. John Owen said nothing as I slipped the video into the machine. First we watched the now familiar early scenes. Nothing had changed except that the initial sadness I had felt on first reliving that night had almost vanished and I was able to watch the action with objectivity, a quality I always admired and often lacked.

The phone rang before we reached the waltz scene. Mavredes motioned for me to freeze the tape. "Homicide," he said. "Mavredes."

He nodded his head as the person on the other end talked. "Yeah, sure, she's right here." He handed the receiver to me. "Your friend at the newspaper," he said. "She wants to talk to you about a message you left on her voice mail."

Eagerly I took the phone from him. Arabella never called simply to pass the time of day.

"Yes, Arabella, what's up?"

"Got your message," she said on the other end. "Since you told me you were headed for the detective's office I took a chance and called. I've got some information for you about your boxer friend."

"Mayo Johnson." I glanced at John Owen to see if he reacted to Mayo's name. He merely frowned, which was nothing new.

"It seems as though Mayo was headed for the big time," she said, "scheduled to fight Mike Tyson until he got hit the wrong way. He may have lost sight in his eye but he lost a whole lot more—a potential fortune. Painting driftwood animals is hardly the financial equivalent of a Tyson-Johnson match. Had you insured his giraffe? Maybe he was looking for ways to supplement the big bucks he lost because of his accident."

I hung up the phone. Mavredes shifted his body in such a way that I could tell he wanted me to know he was exercising supreme self-control by not asking what Arabella said. I thought about the money Mayo Johnson had not made and what he might have seen as an opportunity to make up for the loss, coke worth a fortune on the street crammed into a giraffe's mouth. I had to do something to make John Owen tell the truth about what had happened.

"Let's see the rest of the movie," I said as I released the pause button on the VCR. I took a chair across the room where I could watch John Owen as the film sped forward to the part showing the governor's Lincoln parked on Cary Street in front of the gallery.

As the car appeared on the screen, I asked Mavredes to stop the tape for a moment. "Look at that," I said to John Owen. "Could it be that one of your friends was in the market for a piece of art from the gallery? A giraffe, maybe? Too bad he missed out. The drugs you stuffed in the animal's mouth waltzed out the door just like the dancers, probably in the pocket of one of your other buddies."

John Owen lunged toward me so quickly that in avoiding being hit I fell sideways over Mavredes' leather chair. Even the detective was taken off guard by the suddenness of the attack. In a matter of seconds he recovered, however, and grabbed John Owen by the shirt, shoving him against the wall.

"What you got against the lady?" Mavredes said. "You already attacked her once. This is getting to be a habit. He turned in my direction without letting go of John Owen. "You all right, Rosemund?"

"Fine," I said, "I always liked this chair." I decided to remain seated where I had landed.

John Owen struggled to get loose but Mavredes held him tight. It didn't keep him from shouting at me. I was definitely not his favorite person.

"I don't know nothing about a Lincoln," he said. "When we couldn't locate the coke I knew it had to be you. You were standing by the fucking giraffe all night, talking to that girl with the butch haircut, looking smug like you owned the world. You took it. You set me up so I couldn't deliver. I could of been killed on account of you." He tried again to twist out of Mavredes' grasp. By this time he was yelling so loudly that two uniformed policemen poked their heads through the door.

"No problem," Mavredes said. Both men withdrew quickly. It was the detective, the Crow and me all alone again. Not my favorite threesome. At this point I would have preferred Harry and Gussie hounding me to reopen the gallery.

"So you deny knowing Jimmy Travers, the man driving the Lincoln?" Mavredes said.

John Owen glowered and rubbed his arm gingerly as though the detective had broken it.

"Then who is we? The Lee sisters?" I said. I was surprised to hear that I sounded calm when my heart was pounding, but Gussie always told me I was actress enough to fool anybody. Come to think of it, the Phantom said the same thing. I had certainly fooled both of us into thinking we had a real marriage long after it had ended. I continued on the same track. "The three of you probably stole the giraffe," I said to John Owen, "even though his mouth was empty. My guess is you thought the drugs were stuffed down lower into the animal's body so you took it to break it open and then were discovered by the neighborhood handy-man. Am I close?" I had a momentary mental glimpse of a courtroom with Tyrone in the witness chair claiming that a girl giraffe had attacked him in the alley. Even though it was all we had, it was not an encouraging picture.

To my surprise John Owen lowered his shoulder blades, affected a sancti-monious expression, glared at Mavredes as though the detective had better watch his step and said, "Connie brought the coke." His voice dropped a decibel. "It was her idea. Got it from a guy patronized her old man's grocery store. She said it would be easy. Nothing to it. The movie shoot was perfect. We'd use the giraffe and nobody would be the wiser." He shrugged, something he did very well. Maybe he liked to feel his shoulders flap. "I just went along with it."

I knew he was lying about his role. But I felt sick to my stomach. Mayo's giraffe. If Connie Lee and John Owen had planned in advance to use the giraffe to plant the coke it meant they also knew Mayo. No wonder Barbara said he looked familiar. His appearance at the gallery the day of the filming had been carefully orchestrated so he might make some of that money he missed by no longer boxing. It had been a plan from the beginning. And I had been taken in.

But I had to hear it for myself. "So we were set up, the movie was just a cover."

"Hell, yeah. Connie was smart. Met that boxer one day at the grocery. He'd come in to buy some milk, *milk*, can you believe it? Guy like that. Anyway, they got to talking and Connie heard about his animals..."

I looked at Mavredes. He was no help. His face was blank. "If Connie and Mayo planned the whole thing," I said, "he was playing a role from the moment he appeared at the gallery." I felt deflated. All the confidence I had in my ability to pick a winner had vanished. I would have bet my life that Mayo Johnson was the real thing.

"No, we used him, man." John Owen almost laughed. "Connie told him all about you. Rosemund Wallace, a sucker for new talent. That's what people say about you in this town. Soft touch with a hard eye. Connie convinced him to come by the gallery the night of the movie shoot with his animals. She was certain you'd buy his stuff."

"Mayo wasn't in on this with you?" I had just been called a sucker and I was feeling better by the minute.

"The hard part was convincing David to use the giraffe in the movie. Connie played up the boxer part real big. David thought you wouldn't go for that sort of art, though, the kind of gallery you had. But it was easier than we thought once he saw the animals. You know how David was, always wanting to do something a little different, be a big shot. And you liked the stuff, too. But somebody took the coke, I still think it was you. And I was left with nothing but a piece of driftwood painted with yellow spots. I reckon you can't hold me on no evidence."

"Two witnesses saw you," I said.

He gave me a blank look and shook his shoulders as though drying the feathers on a pair of wings. "You're shitting me, man."

"Two very honest, very reliable witnesses." I was afraid to look at Mavredes in case he snorted at the mention of Jack and Beverly. He almost succeeded in keeping a straight face. I saw that this was not going to get any easier. "They said you hit my handyman on the head with the animal."

"Well, whoever they were, they were wrong. Nobody can prove I stole anything from your gallery and I sure as hell didn't hit anybody over the head. Just like the drugs, you don't have any proof. You can't hold me without evidence." He folded his arms across his chest as though the argument were closed.

"They described you," I said.

"The hell they did." John Owen jerked his head in Mavredes' direction. "I don't have to listen to this," he said. "I know my rights." He turned back to glare at me again. "I still think you took the stuff."

"Shut up," Mavredes said. "You're in more trouble than you have brains to realize."

"I've said all I have to say. You can't make me talk anymore. I want a lawyer, man. I'm telling you the truth about that giraffe."

"One more question," Mavredes said. "You ever meet David's uncle, Walter McGowan?

John Owen raised one bony shoulder up to his cheek. He wiped the side of his face on the shoulder as if scratching a bothersome itch. "Oh, yeah, the doc," he said, "he and David were screwing the same broad—your little movie companion, Barbara Barksdale."

XXVI

Whether John Owen was telling the truth or not about Mayo's giraffe and Walter McGowan, he was released because I decided not to press charges for assault. Mavredes ranted and raved, telling me that I was making a big mistake, that John Owen should be locked up and Richmond would be safer for it, in particular, I would be safer. But I was not convinced that keeping him off the streets would solve the mystery of David's death. John Owen's drug deal had backfired. Somebody had taken what was sure to be a great source of money for him. Was it Mayo? Or was Mayo cut out of the deal, too? The fact that both of them appeared at my house, one after the other, convinced me they hadn't make the exchange. Unpleasant as the thought was, John Owen wouldn't have attacked me had he gotten his money. I believed he genuinely thought I had taken his stash. And if that was the case, he needed to be free enough to chase his own tail around in circles until we caught the real thief, and David's killer.

Walter McGowan was another matter. I couldn't call Lucy and ask if her own brother was sleeping with her dead son's girl friend. Besides, when I first met Walter in the cafe with Mayo I thought he was gay. Mayo had implied as much when he described the party scene David was part of. And what about Jack and Beverly? They seemed convinced that a man matching John Owen's description had attacked Tyrone in the alley with Mayo's giraffe even though John Owen proclaimed his innocence. Naturally, Carytown's favorite street couple was not to be found when we needed them to testify. Not that I blamed them for making themselves scarce. I had as much told them to run for their lives. Mavredes wasted no time in pointing out that fact.

"You and your street people," he said, "wouldn't surprise me if you preferred their company over the Governor of Virginia."

I gave him a "Gussie look" and left his office. If Arabella had found enough time to check on Mayo, Harry should be able to tell me something about Walter McGowan.

As soon as I got to the gallery I planned to give him another call. I would have to use all my skills to learn more than the bare facts from him. While Arabella was able to read between the lines, getting something out of Harry about a fellow doctor would be a little harder. Harry never gossiped, even about artists. Before his wife had died of cancer he never even discussed medicine. Now he at least was willing to entertain the possibility that all doctors didn't walk on water, and that some even make one or two mistakes in a lifetime.

Mayo and Walter McGowan occupied my thoughts as I walked from the Criminal Building to the parking deck near MCV. Even though they were forever cleaning it up, the area surrounding the medical college hospital always reminded me of a suburbanite's worst nightmare of urban life: streets littered with trash, disheveled men certain to be panhandlers staggering down sidewalks, mumbling to themselves, pathetic old women helped out of ancient Oldsmobiles in the 'no parking' zones in front of the hospital. "The Walking Wounded", Gussie called them. If the Criminal Building didn't get them, the hospital did.

The parking deck was at the end of a block which housed one of the MCV buildings that had been designed in the twenties to resemble an Egyptian temple. Aptly labeled "The Egyptian Building", it was the place where the indigent went for shots, free dental work, cholesterol checks, AIDS testing and other amenities that kept them from dying too soon at the taxpayers' expense.

The usual scruffy crowd was milling about and as I worked my way through the group congregated on the sidewalk someone grabbed my arm. Granted, it was a gentle grab but it scared me half to death. Since John Owen's unwanted intrusion into my house, I was rather touchy. With the most unladylike oath I swung around, ready to protect myself at all costs.

A soft, squeaky voice whispered in my ear. "Miz Wallace, what you doing in this part of town?"

I closed my eyes for a split second, willing her not to vanish. It was Beverly.

"Visiting a friend," I said. "Why are you here, Beverly? Are you sick?"

"Not me," she said, "Jack..." Her voice quivered slightly. I couldn't tell whether it was from anxiety over his health or from the effort it must have taken to walk from Carytown to MCV. She pulled a bottle out of her coat pocket and held it up for me to see. "Pills cost a fortune these days," she said, shaking the bottle. "Good thing I have people looking after me." Then she gave me a sly look as if to say 'and where have you been when I needed you?'

"You want a ride back to Carytown?" I said. "That's where I'm headed."

"You by yourself?"

Just you and me, kid, I thought. "Yes," I said. "It'll give us a chance to talk."

"This ain't your car," she said as we pulled out of the parking deck.

"No, I had a few problems with it. It's in the repair shop."

"I seen that black Lincoln in the repair shop, too," she said, matter-of-factly.

I almost drove over the curb.

"Yes," she continued, "Jack and me, we was looking for another place to stay and was checking out the garages a few blocks over from Carytown..."

"I thought you told me the social worker was moving you into a house on Grace Street?"

She folded her hands over her extended belly and stared straight ahead out the window. "It didn't work out," she said. "You know how it is, you think you're gonna like a place, and something goes wrong, refrigerator on the blink..."

Not knowing the right protocol, I nodded sympathetically. But I was tempted to comment that even the worst house on Grace Street would be warmer than an unheated garage.

"Anyhoo," she continued, "we was looking for just the right location when we passed this open garage door where a guy was working on the car. I knew it was the same one we seen at your place..."

"How did you know, Beverly? All Towncars look the same to me."

She looked at me sideways. "'cause the tall guy driving it that night was standing right there telling the mechanic how to replace the back seat, said it got all scratched up by a drunk passenger who spilled red paint on it."

"Well, let's go," I said and pounded on the gas pedal of the rented car. If only it had been the Jaguar.

Actually we stopped by the house on Grace Street first to deliver Jack's medicine. It was a three-story house with half a dozen metal lawn chairs lined up across the front porch. A white woman and a black woman who looked familiar were sitting in the chairs even though it was cold outside. I waited in the car while Beverly make her way up a steep set of cement steps with no handrail. When she reached the top she wobbled slightly as though she might fall backwards. Then she steadied herself and disappeared through the front door. I looked again at the two women in the porch chairs and remembered where I had seen them. They were Beverly's friends I had talked to at McDonalds.

After what seemed like half an hour Beverly came back out of the house, nodded in the direction of the two women and made her way carefully down the steps.

"Jack says 'hello'," she said after she had settled into the front seat of the car. "He was disappointed that you wasn't driving the Jaguar, though. He wanted to tell folks Beverly had been for a ride in a Jaguar."

"When it's out of the shop, I'll take you both for a ride," I said. I hoped I wasn't being taken for one now. But what I really wanted to know was what had happened in the governor's private car that warranted a new seat? Had David or Jimmy used the car to paint a coil of rope red?

We drove around for ten minutes while Beverly tried to remember the exact location of the garage. Several wrong turns found us in front of locked doors and boarded up buildings. We would sit for a few seconds, motor running, while Beverly pondered and then shook her head and motioned me to drive on. Perhaps it was the fact that we were in an automobile and not on foot that confused her, for she finally asked me to park the car so we could get out and walk.

In the middle of a tree-lined block on North Shepherd Street we found it.

"There," Beverly said, pointing towards a one-story building nestled between an out-of-business furniture repair shop and a beauty parlor with a 'closed' sign in the window. "That's where we saw the car."

At first glance the garage looked like an addition to one of the adjoining buildings. That particular block of Shepherd was a hodgepodge of rambling commercial real estate and small houses turned into apartments with odd angle entrances. Because it was an area lacking clear definition, it would have been easy to overlook if driving by in a car. When I looked more carefully at the garage I saw that it had, in fact, been a house or store at one time, and that the entire front had been removed as if a giant cookie cutter took a hunk out of it. The garage door now filled the space which probably had been a store window or front porch.

"The door's pulled down," Beverly said, "but I'm sure it's the place."

"Well," I said, "I guess we'll knock and see what happens."

What happened next was the sort of do-it-yourself nightmare Gussie and Mavredes warned me about. With Beverly close on my tail I approached the corrugated metal door that covered most of the building's facade. As we got nearer my excitement faded. The door was rusted along the edges and looked as though it hadn't been opened in years. Another dead end, I thought. Patches of weeds poked up through cracked spots in the sidewalk in front of the door. But when I looked more closely I saw black smears of what could have been fresh motor oil on the weeds.

I pounded on the metal door, creating a tinny sound which seemed to echo through the quiet neighborhood.

"Nobody there," said Beverly, tugging on my sleeve. "Let's go."

I shook my head and knocked again, louder this time. Still no answer.

"If no one's there," I said, "it would be great if we could peek inside."

Beverly took a few steps closer to me and stared at the metal door. "Ain't easy to get in," she said, "but them metal doors usually have a hidden latch on the side if you know where to look."

Not having had the experience of living in a garage, I turned the job of getting into one over to an expert, and stepped back so she could take charge. "Be my guest," I said. "I'll be the lookout."

As she moved in front of me I turned towards the street to watch for cars or some nosy neighbor peering out the window. If someone called the police to pick us up for breaking and entering, I could imagine the look on Mavredes' face when we were brought in. I quickly replaced such negativity with a positive attitude and assumed a stance of home-ownership in case anybody was looking.

Behind me I heard a meaningful 'click' and a rusty kind of groan like the gears of an ancient machine. Turning my head slightly I saw the metal door inching upwards.

"Hurry," she said. "Duck inside."

At her command I moved quickly. Working out at the gym paid off in a flexibility I had rarely put to use until now. Beverly had already disappeared beneath the door, crouching down to slip through the opening, more agile than I would have believed possible with the extra weight she carried around. As I followed her lead my main fear was that someone would be standing on the other side of the door.

Instead, there sat the Lincoln with the number one license plate, just as she had described, black and shiny and empty.

"See," she said proudly, "just like I told you."

The car was situated in the center of the space, almost like a prized piece of sculpture. Mechanic's tools were scattered across a long work bench in the back of the building. A blow torch and a pair of goggles lay next to a lug wrench and a box of screws and nails. On the wall above the work bench hung a metal "Drink Coke" sign that would have sold for several hundred dollars in an antique show. A couple of metal folding chairs, streaked with gray paint, sat purposefully beside the powerful automobile as if the two people who had recently occupied them had just left to take a break.

Beverly fingered one of the chairs. I wondered if she was considering it as decorator fodder for her new garage home. Across the room from the chairs a wooden door opened into God knew what. For the moment it was shut and I wasn't ready to check out what was on the other side. I was more interested in the Lincoln and the repair work Beverly indicated its owner had requested.

Carefully I opened one of the car doors. I needn't have worried. A luxury vehicle like that made no noise when you looked inside. The interior was upholstered in dark leather, naturally, and smelled expensive. It was also immaculate except for one tiny infraction. The rich leather which cushioned the back seat was scratched like something rough had been dragged across it. It was also streaked with what could have been dried paint. It was clearly red. As I examined the seat more closely I saw that the abrasions in the leather were not caused by a knife or another sharp object. It was more the sort of surface disturbance you would find when dogs rolled in the dirt, or when two people struggled and something they were wearing rubbed against the grain. How the paint got there was anybody's guess. What was even more interesting was the red silk scarf tossed in the corner of the back seat.

I heard a squeaky sound across the room.

"Miz Wallace..." It was Beverly. Her normal Minnie Mouse voice was more falsetto than usual. I recognized the change was due to fear.

I backed out of the car. "What is it?" I said. "What's the matter?"

She was pointing towards the back door and shaking visibly. "Somebody's coming," she said. "I can hear 'um laughing and talking outside."

Dear God, I thought, what are we going to do? There was no place to hide in the garage. We had pulled down the metal door behind us when we sneaked into the place. If we opened it to escape it would make a terrible noise and they would discover us for sure. I'm not a woman made immobile by anxiety. In fact, being stuck in a challenging predicament brings out the best in me. My brain shifts quickly into gear and I am always able to do something—even if in retrospect, it was foolhardy. It was a skill perfected by having to deal with difficult artists. To support and encourage them but not be overwhelmed by their demanding egos required a large dose of grace under pressure. I had to admit, though, that the present situation was more pressing than an artist questioning why I had hung his best painting in the back of the gallery.

The front door to the Lincoln was still open. For one dramatic second I pictured myself grabbing Beverly, pulling her into the Towncar, then gunning the engine and smashing through the metal door, headed for Petersburg. The only problem with that plan was that while it might get us out of the garage, it wouldn't get us anywhere but in trouble. In a car a mile long with a license plate identifying it as the governor's, we would be a sitting duck on Highway 95. And how would it look when the black and whites pulled us over? The owner of a local art gallery headed towards Atlanta with a bag lady and her eight pound tumor would not endear me to Richmond's cultural elite.

The key was in the ignition, tempting, oh so tempting. I slid across the front seat, gave the key a twist to give the car some power and pushed a button to snap open the trunk.

"Get in, Beverly," I said. "It's our only chance."

She stood paralyzed for a moment and then shuffled across the floor and trailed me around to the rear of the long automobile. I got in first and pulled her in after me. The trunk was very clean and carpeted with a lush rug. What looked like a pile of clothing lay in one corner. At least we'll die comfortable, I thought, and pulled the trunk down. It closed easily and without a sound. Our new surroundings were darker than I would have liked, but we could breathe. I patted Beverly on the shoulder, as much to remind myself that another human being was in the trunk with me as to reassure her. I would have preferred Mavredes, but at that moment I couldn't be picky. We huddled together, creating our own warm cocoon and soon were breathing in harmony.

Though the trunk muffled the noise I heard a door open and voices flooded the garage with sound. It was a man and a woman. The woman sounded vaguely familiar. I tried to place her voice. I had heard it recently but I couldn't decide whether it reminded me of one of my artists or someone else.

"It'll take me a couple of days," the man said. "You gotta order the leather special."

"I'll bring the car back," the woman said. "Jimmy doesn't want to be without it very long. The governor complains if it's not available."

"So when's he gonna pick it up?"

"I'll take it," the woman said, "I know how to drive."

The man laughed. "A little thing like you? You'll never get it around the corner."

At that moment I realized who it was. Connie Lee. Connie Lee who had installed Mayo's giraffe over Lucy's painting the night David Moon shot his movie at the gallery because she liked animals. Connie Lee, who, it appeared, was also a friend of Jimmy Travers.

"You'd be surprised," the woman said. "I have lots of skills."

"Okay," said the man. "You're the boss. I'll let Jimmy know when the leather comes in." There was some additional noise as if someone walked away from the car. Then a grinding sound indicated that the metal door was being raised. A door in the limousine opened and closed. The key turned in the ignition. And we began to move.

"Lord have mercy," Beverly said under her breath, "we're being kidnapped."

A slight bump indicated that we were out of the garage and on our way. The big car maneuvered the streets near Carytown slowly for a while. There were a lot of stop signs and traffic lights. Each time we slowed down I was afraid our driver was going to stop and check the trunk for something. But it didn't happen. The limo proceeded towards its destination for what seemed like a long time, and in reality was probably no more than fifteen or twenty minutes.

At last it pulled over another bump, indicating some sort of barrier or entrance, paused while the driver spoke to someone outside the car, and continued slowly a few hundred yards.

Then it stopped.

Here it comes, I thought. She's going to open the trunk and find us. Beside me, Beverly was breathing hard. Then I realized it was my own breath I heard. Beverly was merely whimpering.

"It's going to be okay," I said. "Nothing's happened yet." Outside I heard footsteps coming around the automobile. I wondered if it were Connie or someone else. Whoever it was stopped beside the back of the car, opened the rear door as though looking for something and then closed it and walked away. In the distance another door slammed. After a while I let out my breath in one long sigh. Beverly took this as a sign that she could stop moaning. Then we were both silent. Relief robbed us of the desire to do anything for a few moments.

"We have to get out of here," I said. Even though it was stating the obvious it sounded like a plan. I slid forward until I was able to run my fingers along the edge where the trunk was shut. I had never been locked in the back of a car before but I had hopes that there would be some sort of latch I could snap that would release us. There wasn't one. Then I remembered that one of the reasons Bernard had bought his Volvo was because he could get to the back seat through the trunk, thereby enabling him to lower the seat and carry some of his larger portraits.

"Let's change places, Beverly," I said. "I want to try something else."

Changing places in the close confines of the trunk was easier said than done but we did it after a few false starts. I shoved with all my strength against the back wall of the trunk, hoping that something would give and that the seat would fold down like Bernard's. It didn't budge. This was getting serious. By now I could smell both Beverly's body and my own and it was not pleasant. In addition, Beverly was moaning again.

"We have to be calm," I said. "Something will happen."

And it did.

Before I could stop her, Beverly began to scream and pound on the trunk of the limousine. Her raspy shrieks were amplified in the small space where we were trapped. Better than suffocating, I thought. Then I joined her in the pounding. Two kids trying to get out of a closet couldn't have generated any more noise.

We were making such a racket that we didn't hear the man enter the place where the limo was parked. When he yanked open the trunk to discover us inside, the look on his face must have matched our own astonishment at being rescued so quickly.

"Who the hell are you?" he said. He was dressed in an official uniform that at first I thought identified him as a policeman. "And what are you doing in the governor's limousine?"

I realized then that he was some sort of guard, and that since he mentioned the governor it was possible that we were parked on state property. Talk about rampant lawlessness.

I climbed out of the car with as much dignity as possible, then reached for Beverly's hand and helped her out. When he recovered from the shock of seeing the two of us, the uniformed man took a few steps backwards and started to speak into the portable phone he was carrying.

"Wait," I said. "I can explain..."

"No, ma'am," he said. "You've broken the law..."

Beverly began to wail. "We was kidnapped," she cried, flailing her arms in his face. "We was kidnapped."

It was enough diversion to make him lose his grip on the portable phone. I grabbed it out of his hand and ran for the door, leaving him to defend himself against Beverly. As I did, I happened to glance in the back seat of the limo. It was empty. The red scarf was gone. That must have been the reason the rear door had been opened and closed. Connie had taken the scarf.

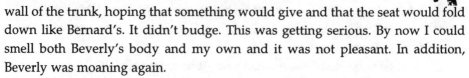

Outside the light was almost blinding after being locked in the dark. It took a moment to get my bearings. The garage I had just exited seemed built into a hill beneath a huge house. Neatly trimmed shrubs and trees surrounded me. On the other side of the tallest row of evergreens was a high wrought iron fence. I struggled up the hill as fast as my slightly numb legs would go only to find myself surrounded by uniformed men like the one who freed us from the trunk of the Lincoln, Capital Police, I assumed. Fortunately, they were either talking to each other or checking someone's identity who was trying to park on the expanse of pavement beneath several bronze statues. When I looked behind me to see where I was, I recognized the Virginia Governor's Mansion. I was in the circular drive in front of the mansion, practically home. I was so happy to be out of the locked car that when I dialed Mavredes' number on the portable phone to tell him that Connie Lee had driven Beverly and me to the State Capital I was able to accept his profane outburst on the other end with no embarrassment whatsoever.

It was embarrassing, however, to be ushered into Governor Brookfield's office without having the opportunity to dress for the occasion. It was some consolation knowing that having an audience with the governor of Virginia would give Beverly something to discuss with her friends. We were led down several long halls adorned with paintings that never would have made it into my gallery. It was not so much the subject matter, which was largely unsmiling white men dressed in uncomfortable-looking clothing, as it was painting style. Not a contemporary look in the entire lot. I considered the freshness with which Bernard painted and wondered when a local politician would have the courage to break out of the old-fashioned portrait mold and commission Bernard to reproduce his image on canvas. A face-lift by Bernard could do a lot to improve politics in the state of Virginia.

We continued up some marble stairs worn in the center from thousands of feet making their way to the center of power in the Commonwealth. The lighting in the building was deplorable, a symbol, I concluded, of the fact that taxpayers' money was not being spent on illuminating any aspect of the present administration's reign. There would be plenty for Beverly to talk about with her friends, however. The looks we got from Brookfield's staff as we were escorted by two guards and Lieutenant Mavredes of the Richmond Police Department were worth a hundred hours of conversation at McDonald's. I'm sure an audience with the governor had never been scheduled with two women who looked like us. Beverly smiled at everyone, nodding "howdy do" in all directions. My only regret was that no photographer was there to capture us on film. I was beginning to think like David Moon, seeing every event as movie potential.

"So you're Rosemund Wallace," the governor said, after Beverly and I were seated in matching blue leather chairs in his large office. "I've certainly heard your name a lot recently. Never been in your gallery, though. Afraid my taste in art doesn't run much towards contemporary." Brookfield was shorter in person than he appeared on television. Good looking in a fleshy sort of way, but still short. Perhaps that was the reason he wore cowboy boots, expensive ones, too, if the amount of hand tooling and silver trim on the tips counted for anything. I made a mental note to tell Harry that he and the governor of Virginia had something in common.

Perched in the leather chair, Beverly resembled a child. Her feet barely touched the surface of the huge oriental carpet covering the floor. Her bare legs stuffed into the high-topped tennis shoes dangled back and forth. She sat quietly with her hands folded over her distended belly and gazed around the room with open curiosity. Probably taking in all the details to tell Jack. As I followed her gaze, I saw that Mayo's driftwood American eagle would have added a real eclectic touch to the decor. The only thing personal in the office was a collection of photographs of Brookfield with such celebrities as the local Sausage King, a U.S. senator who had once been married to a movie star, and an Elvis impersonator. Mavredes stood by the window with an expression on his face resembling a pet cat who has just laid two dead birds at the feet of its owner. The uniformed guards stood on either side of the office door, whether to keep us in or someone out was hard to tell.

Brookfield pressed the tips of his fingers together, a rather dainty gesture for a man wearing cowboy boots. As he spoke, sincerity and concern oozed out his pores. "I thought we had laid to rest your concerns about my aide," he said, "but you seem to have it in for him. Hiding in the back of a state car to spy on him might be a punishable offense."

"It wasn't exactly spying," I said. "I was trying to find out if the damage to the car's upholstery had anything to do with David's death."

"I don't know anything about the car's upholstery," Brookfield said. "And Jimmy certainly has access to the car when it's not being used. Whether or not he overstepped his..."

Mavredes gave me a look which I interpreted as permission to interrupt the governor. "Beverly saw your aide pick up David Moon at my gallery in the state limousine the night he died," I said. "We could be talking about something a little more serious than 'overstepping'."

Brookfield looked at Beverly. "That's you?" he said. "You're the one who claims to have seen my personal aide with the boy who committed suicide?"

"Yes," Beverly said in a clear, squeaky voice, "but it wasn't suicide." She glanced at me for approval. Her skinny legs were swinging wildly back and forth. I winked. We were definitely a team and headed down the winning stretch.

The governor leaned across his massive mahogany desk, focused his brilliant blue eyes on Beverly and said, "Why didn't you go to the police?"

Beverly stopped swinging her legs and turned towards Mavredes, uncertain as to whether he was friend or foe. After all, she had witnessed the detective bursting into the ladies' room at McDonald's, waving a gun and frightening the customers. "I was scared," she said. "Too many people getting hurt, that boy dying, that colored man getting beat up with the giraffe...who would listen to Jack and me?"

Brookfield's eyes widened slightly. "Giraffe?"

At the window Mavredes shifted uncomfortably. "It appears to be the same giraffe, Governor, that matches the head you received in the mail, and was stolen from Rosemund's gallery. Why you got the damn thing is anybody's guess. It appears as though the giraffe was being used as a pickup for a drug deal that may conceivably have involved Jimmy Travers."

"Ridiculous," Brookfield said. "How did we get from a hideout in my Lincoln to accusing my top aide of drug dealing?" He waved his hand in Beverly's direction as though she had already been dismissed. "And who's to trust a thing this woman says?"

Mavredes straightened his tie. It was already perfect. He ran his hand down the back of his neck. It was clean shaven. Not a hair was out of place. "Well, Sir," he said. "It's not only her word that raises some questions about your aide. We've got a video shot in front of Rosemund's gallery the night David Moon died that shows a vehicle resembling your private automobile parked outside. That photo, coupled with testimony by two eye-witnesses, is troubling." The detective took a few steps closer to the governor, glanced once at his expensive cowboy boots, and then into his sincere face.

"The worse thing, Sir, is the fact that Miz Wallace here thinks the woman who drove the Lincoln back to the governor's mansion was the person one of the suspects identified as involved with the drug plant. I'm afraid we're going to have to take Jimmy Travers in for questioning."

XXVII

When I called the West Coast from the gallery later that day I recited everything that had happened and told Michael it was beginning to feel a bit like round-up time. "Not that Jimmy admits to anything yet," I said, "but with a shot of the limousine on film in front of the gallery he's going to have a tough time proving he wasn't there. Even the governor did a bit of side-stepping when Mavredes started acting like he believed Beverly when she said she could identify Jimmy. I was really proud of her, she didn't back down at all. When Jack is well enough to be the second witness, Jimmy may be forced to tell us what really happened."

I neglected telling Michael that although Jimmy was in jail, John Owen was out, sort of like murder suspects playing musical chairs, a potentially dangerous game that I probably shouldn't be part of. But there were some things only John Owen seemed to hold the key to and I wanted to discover what they were without everybody telling me I was making a mistake. With Jimmy in and John Owen out, the tables were reversed and pressure might be brought to bear on the right person.

Besides, Michael was several thousand miles away. What difference could it make to him if I had contributed to the release of a murder suspect?

"You could have suffocated in the trunk of that car," Michael said. I smiled to myself as I heard the concern in his voice. The other side of the continent didn't seem so far away, after all.

"Well, I'm still alive," I said, "and ready to hear what you discovered about Lucy's slides."

He shifted into his professional mode, all business now. I could almost visualize him sitting back in his chair, his handsome forehead furrowed from concentrating so hard. It was the first time I had considered a man's forehead 'handsome' and I grinned into the telephone as he talked. The man was probably handsome all over.

"It didn't hit me at first," he said. "I kept projecting the slides onto a screen to study them enlarged. Finally I loaded three projectors at once and had the images flow in chronological order, faster and faster. It was kind of like watching a movie in fast-forward. Probably the tenth time around something clicked."

"What was it?"

I attempted unsuccessfully to imagine what he might have discovered. Lucy's paintings were certainly familiar to me, but perhaps that familiarity was part of the reason I hadn't been able to see as clearly as a stranger might see. If you've lived with something, or someone, long enough, after a while you get accustomed to their quirks and oddities. It was a bit like living with the Phantom. I hadn't realized how peculiar he really was until I had been divorced from him for almost two years. I thought about the Lucy Moon painting I had owned for a longer time than I had been divorced and how differently I looked at it after David died.

"According to the slides," Michael said, "over the years Lucy painted a few people, sort of ambiguous figures, hard to tell whether they were male or female, but they were definitely major images in a handful of paintings."

"It's not what she's famous for," I said. "Trees and surreal flowers are more her thing."

"That's just it," Michael said. "Because she's done several hundred pictures, it makes the few figures she's painted even more significant. As I flashed her slides on the screen over and over, because they were so rare, the people really began to stand out."

"Yes?" I wondered what was coming.

"They varied in age," he said. "They started young, almost like children..."

Instantly I recalled the painting of the child beside a window with the curtain drawn to one side and tied with a red cord.

"...and gradually they got older. It was almost like Lucy was watching, or observing, a child growing up. Once I saw that, I pulled all the slides of people out of the collection and projected them onto the screen in chronological order."

"I'm listening," I said.

"Every painting that contained a person also contained something else."

I sat very still, cradling the telephone in one hand, wanting him to go on but not wanting to hear what was coming. "Don't tell me," I said. "It was a red cord."

"Yes," he said. "Sometimes it was only a short piece of rope, you had to look hard to see it. But one way or another, red rope was in every painting containing a person and not in any of the others."

I thought about the painting hanging over my fireplace and how many years I had looked at it, loved it, in fact, but never saw the red cord in the hand of the figure in the picture until after David died. If I had overlooked something I had lived with for years it was no wonder I had overlooked what Michael was describing. My perception of myself as a sensitive, perceptive art dealer just dropped a few notches. "I can't remember all her paintings," I said. "How was the cord used?"

"Oh," he said, "lots of different ways. In some cases it was tying a curtain or a hand, do you recall the painting of the pair of hands resting on the back of a chair?"

"Vaguely," I said. "There was rope in that one?"

"Just a piece, almost threads really, beneath the chair on the floor as though it had been dropped. If you used your imagination you could believe it was dropped as the hands grabbed the chair. There was another one with hands tying the rope around the trunk of a tree. Odd, when you view them all together without the softening influence of her other images."

I swallowed hard. "What do you think it means, Michael?"

"This is only a guess," he said, "but the paintings containing people may be Lucy's life story, from childhood to adulthood. Much art is autobiographical, as you well know. And I can only surmise that the red rope plays a major role in Lucy's life, either symbolically or literally."

"Michael, this is really terrible. If what you're saying is true, and her son died with a red rope around his neck, what must be going on in her mind?"

"I suppose it depends on what the rope represents," he said. "And that's a mystery we may have a hard time solving."

I called Gussie as soon as I hung up with Michael.

"Thought you'd left town," she said. "You haven't been at the gym for ages."

"I've been busy," I said. "I'll explain later. I want to ask you to do something for me."

"If it concerns David Moon, forget it," she said.

"Gussie, please. It's very important. Jimmy Travers is in jail. Beverly and Jack are witnesses who will swear he was driving the car they saw at the gallery, the one that picked David up after the movie shoot. They're in protective custody, they won't run away again. And John Owen Smith, one of the guys filming the movie with David, claims there was a drug deal going down that night. We were right about the giraffe, too. The stuff was crammed in its mouth waiting to be picked up."

"So that's why John Owen stole the animal?"

"It's more complicated than that," I said. "The wrong person took the drugs. John Owen didn't get his money. Nobody seems to know what happened, but John Owen's mad at the world." And especially me, I reminded myself.

"I suppose he's in jail, too," Gussie said.

I had no choice but to lie. She would never have helped me if I told her he had attacked me twice and that I hadn't pressed charges because I wanted to see what he would do when he was released.

"Sure," I said, "all locked up. There's just a couple of missing pieces, or people, rather."

There was a long silence on the other end of the line. "What do you want me to do?"

"I want you to go over to Church Hill, to a grocery store. Pretend like you're a friend of those two Korean girls who were filming the movie with David. Say you went to school with them, that you were in a class together. Their parents own the store. Say you have a message for them, whatever. You'll think of something. It's important that we find out where they are, one of them, in particular.

Connie, Connie Lee."

"I suppose now you think she murdered David Moon."

"No, at least not by herself. But I think she helped steal Mayo's giraffe and maybe took the drugs she had planted in its mouth instead of letting the pickup person get them."

"Rosemund, back up. You've lost me. Exactly why are we looking for Connie Lee?"

As briefly as possible I told her about John Owen's claim that Connie had brought drugs to the gallery and that Barbara Barksdale, David's ex-girlfriend, had insisted that John Owen was the one making the delivery. No money had exchanged hands, however, because someone had taken the drugs before John Owen could hand over the giraffe. I told her about the giraffe head, about finding the Lincoln in a garage near the gallery and the trip to the governor's mansion with Beverly. I also said that Connie had taken a red silk scarf from the back seat of the car, a scarf that might match the silk threads around the sculpture that had propped up the bathroom window the night the giraffe was stolen from the gallery.

To her credit, Gussie listened quietly. Perhaps it was only because she was convinced I had lost my mind and was humoring me. Or maybe because she had been the one who discovered the red strands of silk in the bathroom window that night at the gallery.

Whatever her motivation, when I completed my recitation, she said, "I'll go to this Korean market for you because you are my friend. I will inquire into the whereabouts of Connie Lee because you are my friend. I will report back to you what I find out because you are my friend, but I will also say, because you are my friend, that you are wrong about David's death. Nobody killed him. He did away with himself, accidentally or on purpose. Maybe because he was involved in this drug deal you're talking about or maybe because he was a sex freak. But you are an art dealer, Rosemund, used to be a damn good one. You are wasting precious energy and valuable time when you could be selling ten thousand dollar paintings, hell, you could be selling my furniture..."

"Thank you, Gussie. I'll never forget this. Now, the grocery store is just a few blocks from the Hill Cafe..."

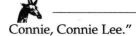

It was getting late in the day. The gallery was still filled with Mayo's sculptures, minus the giraffe. I went downstairs from my office and turned on all the gallery lights, including the spot lights outside. I even unlocked the door just in case a gallery client saw the lights and had to come in to see if I really had some art on display. There, I thought as I blew some dust off one of the pedestals displaying Mayo's animals, open for business. If Harry drives by, he'll be so excited he'll wet his pants.

The moment I thought about Harry I remembered Walter McGowan. Harry was supposed to let me know if he found out anything interesting about his medical colleague. Whether Harry and I would define "interesting" in the same way remained to be seen. I trudged back upstairs to my office to call him. I've got to get a portable phone, I said to myself. All this going up and down stairs was a poor substitute for my regular workout at the RAC.

I was about to dial Harry's office number to see if he was still at work when I heard the front door to the gallery open. Even though I had made a great show of turning on all the lights downstairs and issuing a silent invitation to the world to appear at my doorstep, I was surprised that someone was actually coming in.

"Be right down," I called over the balcony. I couldn't see who it was. Probably examining Mayo's sculptures, I thought. Maybe I'll make a sale. It would certainly give me an excuse to call Mayo, ask him some pointed questions, perhaps. I finished dialing Harry's number and let it ring until his service picked it up.

"Dr. Brown is gone for the day," the voice said. "Is this an emergency?"

For an instant I considered saying 'yes', just to see what would happen. There were footsteps on the metal stairs. An over-eager customer, I thought. I'd better give them some attention. I hung up the phone without leaving my name, put my art dealer's smile on my face and walked out of the office.

A young black man was standing at the top of the stairs. His hair was cut close to his head. It was a perfect match for his pencil thin moustache. In one ear lobe a gold earring glistened. He was also wearing dark glasses. Hard to see the art, I thought, if you're wearing glasses.

"Good evening," I said. "I'm Rosemund Wallace, the director of the gallery. We just reopened for business this afternoon." The dry cleaners at the corner had been robbed twice in the middle of the day by a black male with prominent jewelry. Oh well, I thought, it won't make my day any worse than it's already been.

"I know who you are," he said, taking off the glasses. "I met you and that cop at the video studio. I'm Arik Lawson. Don't you recognize me?"

I peered closely at his face, wondering if he was telling the truth. He looked friendly as well as vaguely familiar. The Arik Lawson we had encountered at the studio had been noticeably unfriendly. He had also sported a beard.

"We weren't exactly on intimate terms when Lieutenant Mavredes and I left the video studio," I said. "You come to talk or to look at the art?" My mind was racing. What possible reason could have brought him to the gallery?

"I thought you'd be glad to see me," he said. "I even shaved for the occasion." He rubbed his bare chin. The absence of whiskers had changed his appearance decidedly. I never thought much of a man with a beard, anyway, perhaps because the Phantom grew a beard at least once a year and then would shave it off just when it was beginning to look good.

"Our previous get-together had all the warmth of a bunch of barracudas meeting for lunch," I said. "You'll have to pardon me if I don't lay out the red carpet." His unexpected presence made me uneasy in spite of the change in his manner. I took a few steps closer to the stairs, just in case.

He laughed. "I was a little tense," he said. "It's not everyday you lose a friend. And then to have the police breathing down your neck like you'd done something wrong." I couldn't tell whether his regret was genuine or not. But perhaps this was as close to an apology as he could come.

"You didn't show us all the film, Arik. You left out the waltz scene but I got a look at it anyway. I saw it on the copy of the movie you gave Barbara."

He put his glasses back on and leaned carelessly against the edge of the balcony. "I guess I made a mistake," he said. "It was that cop made me nervous. If you had come by yourself..." He glanced over the balcony at the driftwood animals on display below. "These belong to that boxer?"

"Yes," I said, "the one who carved the giraffe." I didn't have to say which giraffe. Arik removed his glasses again and stared at me.

"I thought so," he said. "Giraffe was something else." With exaggerated deliberation he leaned way over the balcony. "Don't see it though, you find a buyer?"

"Did you know what was going on with that giraffe?"

He laughed. "Besides sales?"

"If you were really David's friend you must have known he was involved in something he should have left to the big boys," I said. "Barbara seems to believe that's the reason you didn't show us all the movie footage, that you knew the waltz scene contained a shot of Jimmy Travers' limousine, or maybe I should say the governor's limo, in front of the gallery."

Arik blew on the lenses of his dark glasses. As quickly as they steamed up he wiped them down the front of his shirt. Then he carefully placed them on the ledge of the balcony, adjusting them so they hung precariously over the edge. "What would you say if I told you I was the last person to talk to David alive?"

I tried to match him cool for cool. I was sorry I didn't have a cigarette to light so I could blow smoke rings in his face. "I'd say you were either lying or had some reason to protect yourself by not telling the police."

"Well, you're wrong on both counts," he said. "I know I was the last person David spoke to before he died because he called me from the gallery. I've been trying to figure out a few things in my head. At first I thought he couldn't get the money to finish the film and decided to check out, but if he was going to do away with himself, the phone call just didn't add up."

Oh boy, I thought, let's see where this goes.

"He called on that phone in your office. He told me he was sitting on your desk like he owned the place, you know how David talked, said maybe he could afford a desk like that when the movie stirred up attention in the right places."

"Sounds like he planned to finish the movie whether he had the money or not."

Arik lifted himself onto the edge of the balcony next to his dark glasses. His feet dangled against the low balcony wall in a way that reminded me of Beverly perched in the governor's blue leather chair. "Well, he hoped to finish it. That was the deal with Jimmy Travers. David could finish the movie because Travers was supposed to make sure some state money came his way through the Virginia Film Office or something like that. Travers made like he had the clout to see it happen. Told David the Film Office had a reputation nationally, that a bunch of big shots working for the governor would promote any film made in Virginia."

"So what happened?" I said. "According to my witnesses, Jimmy was hanging around the gallery that night and David went off with him in the Lincoln. Maybe Jimmy raised the ante, put up conditions David didn't like."

"I came to the same conclusion," Arik said, "but I didn't tell anybody about the phone call until now."

"Why me?" I said. "Why tell me?"

"'Cause you don't let up about David," he said. "Plus the fact that you seem to be the only person who doesn't believe he killed himself. That counts for a lot. After his phone call, I don't know what to believe. I knew you went to Barbara's. She called me right after you left, blabbed on and on about the car like I should of erased the tape, that kind of crap. But I knew what I was doing leaving it on the film. Why should I protect Jimmy Travers? What did he ever do for anybody? Including David. He wasn't just lining up David with the Film Office out of the goodness of his heart..."

Now it was coming. I sucked in my breath in anticipation. I could hardly wait to tell Gussie she was wrong about my most outstanding quality, it was really that I never let up.

"It was like this," Arik said. He looked very uncomfortable on the edge of the balcony. I kept thinking that he might lose his balance and tumble over backwards into the wooden jungle waiting below. "David called me when he got back to the gallery, said he had been for a ride with Travers to get things straightened out."

"What sort of things?" The missing drugs, I was certain. But what about the scratched leather and the red paint?

"Hey, don't be in such a hurry. We got all night. Anyway, like you guessed, he said things with Jimmy didn't go exactly like he planned. Uh, there was supposed to be...a...an exchange of...of merchandise." I was surprised that Arik seemed embarrassed telling me what had been planned. It occurred to me that it might have been because he was making up the story as he went along. His earnestness was compelling, however. I listened carefully as he continued.

"David guaranteed a certain quality of goods," he said. "Travers would make sure David got what he wanted in return. But when he called from your place, he said there were a few problems. Then he put me on hold..."

"My phone doesn't have a 'hold' button," I said.

"Figure of speech," Arik said. "He told me to wait a minute, that somebody was coming in the door, that he'd be right back..."

"And?"

"Well, that's where the shit hits the fan, he never came back. I waited for a while, then hung up in disgust. Somebody else must of gotten his attention."

"That can't be all," I said, taking a few steps towards him. I must have startled him or he hadn't expected me to move, for he jerked backwards as if I were about to hit him. I hadn't meant to throw him off balance, but something about my manner must have been disconcerting. He grabbed for the edge of the balcony to regain his balance but it was too late. With an expression of panic on his face he wobbled from side to side. And then he lost all control and started to fall backwards as both hands flailed the air. I was close enough to grab his hand and to give him a good pull up right. He was very heavy. It felt like my arm was being yanked out of its socket. I pulled again, thankful that I had been working out at the gym for the past four years. Like a couple in a passionate embrace, we fell sideways onto the top of the circular stairs at the edge of the balcony. We ended up in a heap on the metal stairs, legs and arms everywhere, just as the front door of the gallery opened.

We must have been an interesting sight: a middle aged white woman in the arms of a twenty-year old black male, writhing at the top of the stairs of the Rosemund Wallace art gallery. Living art, one might say. The couple framed in the doorway was young, I think, though I'll never know for certain. They stared at us, gasped audibly and slammed the door in their haste to get out of the place.

So much for integration in Richmond, I thought, as I tried to disentangle myself from Arik.

Arik smoothed all his parts back in place with as much dignity as possible, got to his feet and pulled me up after him. For a moment our complexions must have been pretty similar in color: he was very pale and I felt very dark with embarrassment.

"Maybe I'd better lock the front door," I said. Without another word I eased past him down the stairs as fast as I could go, turned the key in the door, ran my fingers through my hair and grabbed one of Mayo's pedestals to steady myself. My pulse was racing, from shock as much as fear. I wondered if the potential art buyers who had fled from my front door had called the police.

By this time Arik had regained his composure, picked up the dark glasses, which, miraculously had not been knocked off the balcony ledge, placed them over his eyes and made his way down the steps. His legs wobbled a little but I pretended not to notice. He placed himself behind one of the other pedestals, the one displaying the American eagle. For protection, I guessed. There was no telling when this white woman might leap at him again.

"You are something else," he said from behind the pedestal. "I guess I'll have to tell you everything."

I wondered what I might have learned if we had tumbled all the way down the stairs wrapped in each other's arms.

"There's more?" I said cooly, as though the thought had never entered my mind.

"David told me since the deal had gone bad he had to do a lot of sweet-talking to Travers while they were riding around in the Lincoln. Really played up to him, leading him on. They had some kind of tussle in the back seat when Travers wanted a little more than David was willing to put out. Scratched the leather, too, with the zipper on his leather jacket. It really pissed Travers off, so he brought David back to the gallery and sort of dumped him."

That explains the scratches on the leather seat, I thought, but not the red paint. One down, only a hundred more questions to go.

"Barbara told me John Owen was arranging the switch, I assume with Jimmy Travers, that David wasn't involved."

"David was trying to play both ends," Arik said. "He promised to get the drugs for Travers. He was sort of the go-between. I tried to talk him out of it, that he was headed for nothing but trouble. I told him anybody who worked for the governor was protected. But I guess if the drugs were missing, he owed Jimmy some sort of explanation. The funny thing is, he told me Jimmy brought over some props from the Fire Station Theater. The two of them were playing a trick on somebody, David said. But Jimmy got pissed off and backed out.

"He say what kind of props?"

"Something they had painted, I think. Beats me what it could of been."

Later when I reflected back on it, I should have realized that Arik and I were illuminated in the center of the gallery like some prized piece of art. The lights I had turned on earlier to show off Mayo's animals showered us with a brilliance which could easily be seen from the outside. People eating at McDonalds could see the entire contents of the gallery through the large expanse of glass in the front window. And anyone driving down Cary Street could see us plainly, too, from a block away. Although it had cost a lot of money, Harry and I had planned it that way when we renovated the building for the gallery. It was important to see the contents of the Wallace Gallery coming or going through Carytown.

The glass crackled sharply when the first shot hit the front of the building. For a second it reminded me of the hail stones that had descended suddenly on the gallery one night during an opening in the summer when a freak storm knocked out the power in Richmond. There was another sharp noise and the glass shattered. It clearly was not hail. Arik grabbed his shoulder and fell forward across the pedestal where he had been standing. Blood splattered Mayo's American eagle with brilliant crimson drops. Another shot and the eagle shattered into several dozen pieces, exploding in my face. Whoever was shooting was trying to hit me, too.

I dropped to the floor and crawled forward along the carpet towards Arik. He was lying on his side, clutching his bleeding shoulder and moaning. At least he wasn't dead.

"Get the lights," he said. "Turn...off...the...lights."

Again a shot cracked more of the glass, splintering another of Mayo's animal sculptures, a horse, this time.

Ridiculous, I thought, nobody shoots an art dealer. Then I remembered Arabella telling me about the artist whose show she had panned, who appeared at her front door with a child in his arms and threatened to wreck her car, smash the sculpture in her front yard and blow up her house. There was another shot. I wondered if any glass would be left in the front of the gallery.

Arik moaned louder. I wondered how badly he was hurt and whether he knew who was playing 'Shootout at the OK Corral' on Cary Street. Either someone followed him to the gallery or they were watching the place to see who came in and decided Arik was as good a target as any.

"The lights," he cried again.

Changing directions, I began to crawl towards the back of the exhibition space to the light switch, weaving my way in and out of the group of pedestals holding what remained of Mayo's sculptures. It was going to be difficult explaining to him that art galleries were usually safer than boxing rings. Had the sculptures and the pedestals not been there, the gallery would have been like an open bowling alley and I might be bleeding on the floor, too. And I wasn't even an athlete.

When I finally reached the light switch in the back of the building and plunged the gallery into darkness I realized I was shaking. I sat on the floor in the shadows and shivered. The good news was that the sound of a siren pierced the silence. Although it seemed to take them forever, someone had heard the gunshots and called the police.

I cried out to Arik. "Are you okay?"

"I'm covered with fucking wood chips," he called back. "If we ever get out of here, I'm gonna suggest that boxer use a better grade of wood for his animals."

Flashing lights lit up Cary Street in front of the gallery. It sounded like several people were running up the sidewalk. I wondered if the owner of the fancy new 'Emerson's Apparel" next door would put a 'for sale' sign in her window tomorrow.

XXVIII

I was getting to be a familiar face at Police Headquarters. Several people in uniform greeted me by name when we walked in. Since they were friendlier than the crowd at McDonald's I didn't mind seeing them again, even though they didn't offer coffee. The only problem was that every time I had cause to be in Mavredes' office it was because someone was trying to do away with me. It wasn't my favorite reason for spending so much time in the detective's company. If Gussie had been there, with a little imagination it would have been a bit like double-dating. I had enough sense not to tell him I had sent her into Church Hill to look for the owner of a red silk scarf.

"Don't take it personally," Mavredes said to me. "You just got mixed up with the wrong crowd." The wrong crowd, increasingly, appeared to be David Moon's friends. At the moment I couldn't decide into which category I should place Arik Lawson. The story he told me about David was wild enough to be true or self-serving enough to be false.

He seemed just as unhappy as I was to be there, especially since he was the one with the bullet hole in his shoulder. We had made a stop at MCV where the female doctor on duty had patched him up with the comment that art sounded like a dangerous business.

Mavredes had questions, too. "Okay, Lawson," he said, "what's the real reason you went to Rosemund's gallery? She's been roughed up by enough of David Moon's friends already without you threatening her."

Arik lowered himself into a chair without an invitation. My guess was that he was in more pain than he indicated. He kept touching his shoulder and wincing imperceptibly. The doctor at the hospital had given him a shot for the pain but warned him that it wouldn't last long.

"I had no reason to threaten her," Arik said. "It's like I told you. I'd been thinking about David's phone call the night he died, and decided I would tell her what he said. It was her gallery, you know." As though that explained everything.

"So, what's the connection between the phone call and you being the subject of somebody's target practice?"

"Maybe they weren't shooting at me," Arik said. "Maybe she was the target." He rubbed his freshly shaven face as though getting used to the feel of a clean chin was a new experience for him. I wondered when telling the truth would be a new experience for him.

"We got a couple people at McDonalds who say they got a look at the guy who took a shot at you," Mavredes said. "Tall white male, wearing a cap over his head, funny shaped shoulders. Sounds like a friend of yours from the movie shoot. Now, why would a friend try to pick you off unless you had done something to make him mad?"

I felt like I should raise my hand to get Mavredes' attention. When he finally looked in my direction, I said, "I told you it was important to release John Owen." I wondered if I'd be saying the same thing if it was my shoulder wrapped in bandages. "He couldn't have been after me. He's already tried that once and it didn't get him anywhere. Arik had to be the one he wanted. After you let him go he probably was watching Arik and followed him to the gallery."

Mavredes' good manners came into play. He merely smiled grimly at my comment and continued to focus his attention on Arik. "If one of David's camera crew was after another one of the guys at the film shoot," he said, "might it possibly have something to do with the giraffe?"

I watched Arik's expression change from earnest detachment to serious concentration as though the detective had just asked a question he had never considered. He pulled on the ear with the gold earring. He looked at his watch. He crossed one leg and stared at his jeans as though they would supply him with the answer. "You probably won't believe me if I tell you," he said at last.

"Try me," Mavredes said. "I've had sensitivity training and know how to be a sympathetic listener. We don't beat suspects with rubber hoses around here anymore." He removed his jacket and made himself comfortable. I looked around the office for a coffee pot and then remembered the machine down the hall. The stuff was bad enough to make only a desperation run if we went on too long with Arik.

"David was a serious artist," Arik said. "His photography was not bad. He had a good chance at making it. He was also good at doing things he shouldn't do." He began to clinch and unclench his free hand. "I was the one who was always rescuing him when he got in too deep. I warned him to stay away from that flipping fairy in the governor's office." The more relaxed Mavredes seemed to get, the more tense Arik became.

"Now, now," Mavredes said, "we only use politically correct language in this office." He looked very comfortable, like he was actually enjoying himself. Maybe his interest in art was sincere. "I told you I've been to workshops on these issues."

Arik looked at me for guidance. I was beginning to enjoy myself, too. I smiled sweetly, trying to mimic Gussie. "Travers, the Republican homosexual, had something David wanted," he said.

"Let me guess," I said. "Access to money to finish his movie was his number one priority. So David was willing to set up a drug deal the night of the movie shoot. Connie and John Owen would bring the drugs. Jimmy would bring the money. David would get his grant from the Virginia Film Office—Jimmy would get his drugs. A simple, four-step plan, guaranteed to get you in big trouble."

"Supposing you're right," Mavredes said, "what happened to the drugs?" He looked first at Arik and then at me. "Sometime during the night of the movie shoot the drugs were removed from the giraffe's mouth. Travers never took delivery and John Owen has turned into a gun slinger because he lost both the drugs and his money. The two of you could of gotten your heads blown off, and just when I was growing very fond of you both."

Arik stuffed his free hand in his jeans pockets and began to pace the floor. For the moment, he seemed to have forgotten his shoulder wound. "You won't believe me," he said. "I may have been David's best friend, but you probably won't even believe that."

As I watched him pace, I suddenly understood what he was trying to say. From the first time I met Arik I had considered him an easy read. It was true now. The same second sense that provided me with information about an artist or a piece of art kicked in. At that instant I knew what he had done. I only wished I had that much certainly about who killed David Moon. Especially since it appeared that even his friends didn't believe he had been murdered.

"You took the drugs," I said. "You're the one who cleaned out the giraffe's mouth. John Owen must have figured it out. That's why he followed you to the gallery. He probably decided I was a lost cause and Connie probably didn't do it or she wouldn't be on such good terms with Jimmy Travers. But you were operating a camera that night. How did you pull it off?"

Arik's mouth opened a little wider. His eyes glistened. I took it as a compliment. His shoulders sagged as though a great weight had been lifted. He dropped into one of Mavredes' chairs. "David thought you were something else," he said. "He kept reminding his mother how lucky she was to have you selling her work, but she kept insisting nobody owned her. I guess the next thing you'll be telling your friend here what I did with the stuff."

I was good but not that good. I had no idea what Arik might have done with several thousand dollars worth of cocaine.

By this point, however, he seemed willing to show us. Maybe it was because someone had taken a shot at him, someone who had figured out he was the one who had screwed up the exchange at the gallery, John Owen Smith, who was roaming free in Richmond with a gun. And who undoubtedly knew exactly where we were at the present moment. It was not a particularly pleasant thought, but I figured as long as we were sheltered in Mavredes' office we were safe.

"I hid it on Brown's Island," Arik said. "I'll take you."

The three of us left Mavredes' office, ensconced ourselves cozily into his car and took off for Brown's Island, the place where Mayo Johnson liked to salvage driftwood from the banks of the James River. I wondered how much of a coincidence that was, but decided it was not the time to ask Arik any questions about Mayo. So far, he had said nothing to implicate the ex-boxer. Yet, there was no mistaking the look on Mayo's face in the film. He had seen something. At the moment I was more concerned with the possibility that John Owen was following us than I was trying to figure out whether Mayo was involved.

In the weeks that had passed since I went scavaging for wood with Mayo and his wife, Brown's Island had begun to look like it was preparing for winter. Perhaps it was because the island was surrounded by water and the ravages that attacked its banks when storms blew down the river forced it to reflect the seasons faster than the streets of the city. Even in the darkness, as we crossed the bridge leading to the island, we could see that most of the trees on the island had lost their leaves. They stood like dark sentinels guarding gray outcroppings of rocks scattered throughout. The lights of the city not far away seemed to ring the island like a glittering necklace of diamonds.

The bridge itself was brightly lit, an inviting stretch of cable and metal that curved from urban Richmond onto the island. In the summer young couples strolled across the bridge and picnicked on the island long into the evening. Summer festivals were held almost every weekend, causing traffic jams as people lined up to take the walk across the bridge. The festivals were one of the few things the city dreamed up to attract suburbanites into town after working hours. They were hugely successful bashes with music and food, causing urban entrepreneurs to claim people would move back into the city if only offered more family entertainment. Another of the "if onlys" that dropped regularly from the lips of our noble leaders.

Since it was dark, Arik had borrowed a flashlight from the Police Department. Mavredes seemed to have his own flashlight ready for any occasion which he pulled out of a desk drawer and stuck in his coat pocket. It made an untidy bulge marring the line of his fashionable jacket. Nobody offered me a light, but they didn't insist I stay home, either. I was glad I had worn flat shoes and jeans. Arik said we had to do some walking. The gates at both ends of the bridge were shut in the fall and winter. A "Keep Out" sign on the first gate didn't faze Mavredes, who vaulted over it easily.

"Come on," he said when we hesitated. "You've got the law on your side."

Since my legs were the shortest in the group, Arik took one quick look at me as I contemplated the gate, then picked me up and deposited me on the bridge on the other side of the gate with Mavredes. He leapt over the gate to join us.

When we reached the opposite end of the bridge, Mavredes stepped aside and motioned for Arik to lead the way. He stood there for a few moments as though trying to remember which way to go. It was a little eerie once we reached the ground and were several hundred feet lower than the highest point of the bridge. Because they were magnified in the evening lights, the buildings of the financial district seemed much bigger than usual, almost as if they had grown in the night air. Arik took the lead, with Mavredes and me not far behind. I wondered if we resembled three black bugs to anyone staring out a window of one of the closest high rise buildings.

"It looks different at night," Arik said. "I'm not sure of the landmarks."

Beside me Mavredes sighed. "We've got all the time in the world," he said. I noticed it was the third time he had looked over his shoulder towards the bridge behind us. It made me slightly edgy, but then I couldn't believe anyone would bother us. If a watchman from one of the neighboring buildings was bold enough to check on a couple of flashlights weaving across Brown's Island, we'd see him coming. All Mavredes had to do is flash his badge or something and we'd be fine.

We were midway across the island when Arik stopped. "We gotta backtrack," he said. "I know I didn't go this far." We made a 60 degree turn and headed in another direction.

I caught up with him and touched his arm. "How did you get the stuff out of the giraffe's mouth," I said, "without anybody noticing?"

"It was while David was talking to everybody about the waltz scene," Arik said. "Remember how he was so specific about directions? The waltz scene was supposed to represent taking your place in life, you know, going through the door and out into the world, that kind of crap."

"Does anybody actually know how to waltz these days?" Mavredes said.

Harry did a pretty good job, I thought, but he wasn't as light on his feet as Mayo. I guess if you dance around a boxing ring long enough you learn all the right moves.

"I hid the stuff in a camera case," Arik continued. "Nobody saw a thing."

I wondered if that were true. The expression on Mayo's face when I saw him on the film looking in the direction of the giraffe may have indicated he saw more than he let on.

"Why'd you do it?" Mavredes said. "You plan to sell it yourself?"

"David was my friend. I hadn't decided what I would do with the stuff, throw it in the river, maybe. I was just trying to keep him out of trouble."

"Yeah," Mavredes said, "and the governor of Virginia is an avid collector of contemporary art."

Arik stopped and turned to face the detective. "I knew you wouldn't believe me. Friendship don't mean shit to anybody these days. David could have gotten himself killed if..." Abruptly he stopped as he realized what he had just said. "Shit," he mumbled, "shit."

"Who do you think was at the door the night he called you?" I said. "Whoever it was probably killed David."

"Are you on that kick again?" Mavredes said. "Still convinced that somebody came into the gallery to commit murder?"

"Yes," I said. "I'm sure of it."

"Well, you're the only one," Mavredes said. "It was simply a drug deal gone bad. We've got all the evidence here. At least we will, when Lawson shows us where he hid the stuff. By stealing the coke, Lawson here may have inadvertently contributed to David's demise. If Travers was deprived of the drugs he was expecting, David had no more bargaining power. No power, no film. People kill themselves for a lot less these days."

I remembered the scratched leather and the red paint in the back of the limousine. I remembered what Gussie had said about the intoxication of border line sex. I thought about David's sense of the dramatic, how he was always interested in performance. It was uncomfortable trying to imagine how far he might have been willing to go. Maybe he had invited Jimmy back to the gallery to put on a show for him. I tried to picture David draping himself with black plastic, but my mind refused to go any further than that. Maybe everybody was right, maybe it had been accidental suicide, with or without an audience.

"If I made a mistake," Arik said, "I'm the one who has to live with it. The last thing I need is a preachy cop." He stopped near an outcropping of rock that glistened in the damp air and held up a warning hand. Mavredes and I both became very quiet. Arik gestured towards the bridge. "A car's been sitting at the other end of the bridge since we got here," he said. "And he just turned on his lights, maybe to see us better."

"Yes," Mavredes said. "He drove up not long after we arrived. I've been aware he hasn't moved."

"Well, you could have mentioned it earlier," I said, looking in the direction where they had pointed, "so I could have been worrying. All this time I've been enjoying the scenery."

Arik ignored me and turned, instead, to Mavredes. "What do we do next? I don't want anybody shooting at me again."

"Do you suppose it's John Owen?" I said. In the back of my mind another name appeared, Mayo Johnson. If Mayo had seen Arik hide the drugs he could have been following him as easily as John Owen.

"Don't move," Mavredes said. "Both of you just stand where you are." He opened his jacket slightly to reveal the revolver strapped beneath his arm. The lights from the parked car shining relentlessly on us made me feel extremely vulnerable. Any minute I expected gun shots to ricochet off the gray rocks. "Looks like we have to wait this out," Mavredes said. "That, or one of us has to walk over to the car and ask them politely to douse their lights."

"Just out of curiosity," I said to Arik. "Did you bring us down here to show us what you did with the drugs or is this your idea of fun and games?"

"Don't turn around," he said, "but a couple dozen feet from where we're standing is a tree bending out over the water like it's ready to break."

I attempted to look at the tree without turning my head. I saw that

Mavredes didn't budge. Nerves of steel, I thought.

The roots of the tree were partially visible as if a giant hand had given the tree a good yank and then changed its mind and left the thing to die. The exposed roots, which were twisted and gnarled in imaginative ways, might have provided endless possibilities for the kind of animals Mayo brought to life. To take my mind off the parked car with its headlights trained on us, I attempted to see a horse in the closest twisted root.

"Tied to a branch in that tree," Arik said, "is a plastic bag submerged in the water a few feet. Around Brown's Island the water's not as deep as it is below Richmond. It's what I promised to show you. I put a rock in the bag to hold it down. Nobody would ever find it. With that spotlight trained on us, though, nothing in the world could make me pull it up."

"We'll create a diversion," Mavredes said. He turned to me. "Are you game, Rosemund? It could be dangerous."

Dangerous, I thought. How would he describe what had been going on up to this point?

"Sure," I said. "You want me to run across Brown's Island naked and see if he shoots at me?"

Arik laughed. Leave it to me to discover a way to break the tension.

"No, it won't come to that," Mavredes said. "Arik and I will try to divert his attention from this spot by doing the running. As soon as we take off, I want you to crawl over to that tree and pull up the bag Arik says is submerged under water."

"I don't want nobody shooting at me," Arik said. "Once is enough."

"You don't have any choice," Mavredes said. "When I give the word, you take off like you're trying to escape. I'll shoot a few rounds in the air and yell for you to stop."

David would have loved it, I thought.

"Okay," Mavredes said, giving Arik a shove in the back. "Get going."

"Wait," Arik said. "If I'm going to die I want to confess something."

"This is not a fucking confessional," Mavredes said.

"It's about the giraffe."

"Forget it," Mavredes said. "We know all we need to know about the giraffe."

"No," I said. "Let him talk."

"A lady after my own heart," Arik said. He grinned broadly in the dim light that clothed us in the safe shadows. "The governor of the Commonwealth of Virginia received the giraffe head in the mail, didn't he? Well, I was the postman. I sent it to him after I dug it out of the trash behind the gallery. It was a warning to Travers. He was in and out of Brookfield's office often enough to know what came to the honorable man's attention. Shit, he may have opened the package himself. As soon as he saw it, he must of known somebody was on to him."

"In other words 'back off'," I said.

"Better than a telegram," Arik said.

"You're a fucking genius," Mavredes said. "Now let's see if you're creative enough to save your ass."

Arik hesitated for a moment, and then took off. Whether it was out of fear or not, he seemed to really get into the act. He waved both arms in the air and began to yell, not words, but sounds resembling Navajo war whoops. His shrieks echoed wildly across Brown's Island, bouncing from rock to rock as though amplified by some hidden sound system. He was smart enough not to run in a straight line, but to weave in and out among the rocks and shrubs that dotted the island.

"Stop!" Mavredes cried. "Stop!" He glanced once in the direction of the car lights, then waved his pistol in the air so it couldn't be missed, and pulled the trigger. The gun shots coupled with Arik's war whoops created a cacophony of weird sounds that were mesmerizing. As I watched, Mavredes began to run after Arik, but much more slowly than I would have predicted. Then I realized it was part of the dramatic scenario both men were playing out. Altered illusions, just like Lucy Moon's paintings. If someone in the parked automobile really thought a criminal was being chased by a police officer, he or she might be more interested in the chase than in watching me.

After the second round of shots I dropped down behind a rock and began to slide across the damp ground on all fours. I was glad it was dark so that any crawly creatures I might encounter would get out of my way before I saw them. Clumps of rough grass beneath my hands soon gave way to slippery patches of mud as I inched closer to the water's edge. A couple of times I slid forward onto my elbows in the mud. By this time I was near enough to the water to smell its fishy sourness and to hear it rolling rhythmically against the bank. It was a peaceful sound, a lullaby rocking a bag of cocaine to sleep in the deep.

Arik's cries and Mavredes' gun shots seemed very far away. I rolled sideways to try to see if the noise had done anything to affect the parked car. I could still see the lights, but it seemed that the car had moved to a different location. It was impossible to hear whether the motor was running. At this point my job was one of retrieval. As long as nobody shot at me I was willing to grovel in the mud as long as necessary.

Arik had indicated that a fishing line was attached to the longest branch which extended out over the water. Once I reached the exposed root system I could see the branch easily. A closer look revealed the line. Like a transparent spider web, it glistened in the damp air. To the uninformed it could have been another piece of river trash that became entangled in all the trees that grew on the bank. The only problem was that I couldn't reach it as long as I was lying flat on my stomach. And if I stood up to grab it I would expose myself to the glare of the headlights. I lay still for several moments trying to decide what to do. When I looked over my shoulder across the island where Arik and Mavredes had taken off I couldn't see either one of them. Since I assumed the detective hadn't actually shot Arik, I had to trust they were following some sort of plan that would see all of us safely on the other side of the bridge before the night was over.

Several long sticks lay on the ground beside the tree roots. I picked up the closest one and stuck it out over the water to see how far it would reach. Too short. I dropped it into the water and reached for a second one. If I crawled a little closer to the river and leaned out over the water I might be able to reach the line. There was a slithering noise as something near me slid down the embankment and landed in the water. Snakes were not supposed to be out in the cold weather, I reminded myself. The dirt was very soggy beneath my body. I could feel it oozing through my fingers like wet clay, penetrating the clothing covering my chest and stomach.

I dangled the second stick out over the water. After a couple of misses it caught the fishing line. I twisted it round and round the line. So far so good, I thought, but what do I do next? I had no choice but to get up off the ground a few feet and try to pull both the stick and the line closer to the bank. This meant stepping into the water beneath the exposed roots. I prayed it was not too deep near the bank. After taking hold of the biggest root and tugging on it to make sure it wouldn't break, I eased my feet into the water. It was very cold. The mud was slippery and I almost lost my balance. Terrific, I thought, I'll drown and nobody will hear me go under.

I made a mighty lunge and pulled hard on the stick. To my amazement it responded to my movement and did not break. In fact, the branch that held the fishing line bent slightly from the pressure of my effort. I pulled again. This time the line was almost within my reach. If I could get a few inches closer I could touch it. Of course, this meant moving deeper into the murky water. I took a deep breath and slid forward. The water came up to my waist. I grabbed at the branch, pulled it towards me and touched the fishing line. By this time I was shaking from the cold but I was almost there. Gingerly I pulled the line tighter and tighter with one hand while retaining a grip on the big tree root with the other. At last both the line and the stick were mine. As I reined in the line I had one bad moment when I imagined Arik had either lied to us or someone had beaten us to the treasure and the line would be empty.

The plastic bag broke through the surface of the water like a miniature white whale. My feeling of exaltation was almost as great as if it had been a rare sea creature instead of an illegal substance whose existence may have led to David Moon's death. It dangled in the air at the end of the line, tormenting me until I was able to pull it in. As it swung in my direction, the rock used as the weight almost hit me in the head. A fine way to die, I said to myself. But scooting back up the muddy bank with the bag in my hand was easier than I had expected. As I lay panting on the cold ground I realized how quiet the island was. And dark. No cries. No gun shots. No car lights.

Only two men standing over me, telling me I was a heroine. What I really wanted was a good cup of coffee.

XXIX

The next day the *TIMES DISPATCH* ran a photograph of the gallery on the front page of its *Metro* section. It featured Harry and me standing on the sidewalk pointing towards the remains of the glass facade which was now in the process of being boarded up. Bernard was in the picture, too, concern spread all over his face. The business writer for the paper, not Arabella, wrote a sympathetic article explaining that a patron of the gallery had been mistaken for a drug dealer while talking with the gallery director and had been shot at by an unknown assailant. Although no drugs had been found, the police were investigating, the article said. It was more bad luck, according to the writer, for the gallery which had recently been the scene of the suicide of a young artist. Mitzi Emerson, the new owner of the clothing boutique, was quoted, too. "I wouldn't have moved to this neighborhood," she said, "if I had known it was frequented by a criminal element."

In the photograph Harry and I looked appropriately sad. The Rosemund Wallace Gallery might not be open for business but it was generating more publicity through its extra-curricular activities than any solo art exhibition might have attracted. This kind of publicity had not been part of my marketing plan.

The article and the photograph were all part of Mavredes' plan, however. Even though he had recovered the missing drugs, thanks to me, he wanted to keep that information confidential for a while, hoping we could force the suppliers to surface again. Arik had been instructed to keep a low profile and to contact Mavredes the first time anything suspicious happened. I hoped it wouldn't be as suspicious as getting his head blown off. The driver of the car at Brown's Island had finally sped off into the night after trying to follow Arik's and Mavredes' mad chase in his headlights. Mavredes had gotten close enough to the car to see that a woman was driving. But not close enough to recognize her. I was convinced it was Connie Lee.

I hadn't heard a word from Gussie since I asked her to try to find the whereabouts of Connie Lee. Every time I called I got her answering machine. It was not like Gussie to be unavailable. Most of the time she was locked up in her studio working. She had so many orders to fill she had hired an assistant. I was beginning to worry that maybe I had asked her to do something that might endanger her life—especially since the encounter with the automobile at Brown's Island. Meanwhile, I had nothing better to do than try to see a certain local physician who specialized in eye surgery.

"Your good doctor seems to have a lot of money he shares with the community," Harry told me while we were posing for pictures in front of the gallery. I had not discussed with him how I had spent the previous evening. That was a secret between Arik, Mavredes and me. "He likes charity cases, but only ones with artistic roots. Evidently he's supported half a dozen young artists who would have starved in an unheated studio had it not been for Dr. Walter McGowan. I couldn't find out much more. McGowan is unmarried, lives in a renovated house in Church Hill, on the national historic register and all that."

"How 'bout his taste in partners?" I said. I remembered that John Owen had told us Walter may have been involved with Barbara Barksdale, and not in a fatherly way. "Does he like girls or boys?"

Harry blushed. "Now how would I know?" he said. "I'm not much of a social animal."

"Gossip," I said. "Gossip is the oil that keeps the wheels of society running." Even though Harry had started going out since his wife died, I realized he still had a ways to go. He would be no help at all to the gallery unless he learned whose back needed scratching and why.

Harry rubbed the side of his head. "I'll see what I can find out," he said. I knew he wouldn't have a clue as to how to begin. I would have to go directly to the source: Barbara Barksdale, herself.

When she heard my voice on the phone she sounded surprisingly friendly. "I'm trying to get my life together," she said. "Sorry you've having so much trouble at the gallery. I saw the picture in the paper. Somebody sure did a number on you. I hope they catch whoever did it. Carytown is becoming right dangerous."

I waited for her to ask a question or to suggest who might have shot up the place but she moved smoothly back to her favorite topic, herself. "Yes," she said, "I'm trying to line up some photography shows of my own work. David always told me I could make something of myself." She paused. "You know the guy you asked me about, that ex-boxer who painted the animals?"

"Yes?"

"Well, I remembered why he was familiar. I was going through my photographs like I said, selecting the best ones to submit to some galleries, I found a picture of him." Her southern drawl was heavier than ever. I wondered what she would sound like if she made a conscious effort to be herself.

"With David?" If it was a photograph of Mayo with David, we were back to square one.

"No, not David, bless his heart. It was a picture of Mayo and a friend of his, somebody I wasn't supposed to talk about." There was a long silence on the other end. "It doesn't make any difference any more, does it, now that David's dead."

"If it can help David, you should tell me," I said.

"I'll meet you somewhere," she said. "I'll bring the picture and we can talk. I might even show you some of my work. You have a gallery, after all."

Not to exhibit photographs by you, honey, I said to myself.

"How 'bout the Hill Cafe in Church Hill?" I said. "Know where it is?"

"Sure, it was one of David's favorite spots. Name a time, I'll be there."

She kept me waiting a mere forty-five minutes. And she was not alone. The man who walked through the door of the cafe with her looked exactly like he did when I met him weeks earlier with Mayo Johnson. Same wrinkled suit, same bow tie slightly askew, same gentlemanly manner mixed with bemused detachment. They made quite a pair, Walter McGowan and Barbara Barksdale. Were they lovers as John Owen had claimed? Or was it an uncle comforting the girl friend of his deceased nephew? I tried to figure out their relationship as they approached the booth where I had camped out for almost an hour and consumed enough coffee to allow Juan Valdez to replace his donkey with a tractor.

Barbara was wearing vintage black crepe trousers, a man's tie and a 1940's rabbit jacket that resembled the fur Tyrone had tried to sell me a couple of times. Her lips were bright red and painted wide across her mouth in a Joan Crawford smear. There was no sign of the combat boots. She was downright glamorous. I could hardly believe she was the same woman who was part of David's film crew at the gallery. Her jacket almost made me homesick for Tyrone. Since his dismissal from the hospital, Tyrone had orchestrated a first-rate performance to show how disabled he was as a result of his head wounds. The Carytown merchants rallied around him nobly. Just as he must have known they would. The giraffe attack was probably netting him more money than all his mowing, raking and weeding put together.

Barbara slid into the booth opposite me, flung her jacket across the back of the seat and plopped a thick art portfolio on the table. "I'll have a Bloody," she said in the direction of the bar. Then she leaned across the table and whispered in her Scarlett O'Hara voice. "Hope you don't mind that I brought David's uncle along. I understand the two of you have already met."

Walter slid into the seat beside her. "Nice to see you again," he said. "You're looking lovely as ever—none the worse for wear, considering what you've been through." He gazed around the restaurant. Different art covered the walls since we were there with Mayo, nudes again, but this time painted with a steadier hand. "Yes, indeed," he said, "one of David's favorite places."

I couldn't get over the fact that Barbara and Walter were together. Were they flaunting their relationship or were they here out of mutual concern for David?

Barbara fluttered a little in the booth. It was hard to tell whether her exaggerated southern mannerisms were for my benefit or for Walter's. The waiter delivered her Bloody Mary and took Walter's order for one, as well. I asked for a coffee refill and waited for Walter to explain why he was there.

Instead, he smiled at Barbara as she took a long sip of her drink and puckered her lips. "Whew! Enough hot sauce!" She took another sip, batted her eyes, and slid the portfolio across the table at me. "Take a look," she said. "Tell me what you think. Be honest about my abilities, now. I can take it."

Since it appeared that the subject of Walter's presence was not first on the agenda, I opened the portfolio and pulled out a couple of photographs. I found myself staring into Austin Meyerson's face. He had an artist's beret tilted over one eye and a glass of whiskey in one hand. A cloud of smoke swirled around his head, to simulate a smoke-filled club, I decided. Cliche-ridden or not, Austin was more interested in looking like an artist than I would have expected.

"Curious," I said. "I didn't know Austin was into playing games."

"Thought you'd like that one," Barbara said. "Since he works for you at the gallery I threw it in. We were playing around in the photography class at VCU I told you about, the one I took with David. We were all into games. Austin was in the class, remember? I had forgotten he did a bunch of shots with us."

Politely I laid the photograph aside. "I know what Austin looks like," I said. "I'm interested in the picture of the boxer."

"I thought you wanted to see samples of my work." Barbara seemed genuinely hurt.

Maybe I've been an art dealer too long, but every time an artist wants to show me their work I find it impossible to say 'no'. Even someone like Barbara. It also occurred to me how I treated her might have some effect on Walter. There were a million questions I wanted to ask him. I wondered whether it had been his idea to come along, or whether Barbara had suggested it.

"Okay," I said. "Show me what you've got."

One at a time Barbara placed black and white photographs in front of me. From the size of the portfolio it looked like she had brought nearly a hundred pictures, mostly people dressed in strange costumes and staring at the camera with odd expressions on their faces. Actually, they weren't bad photos, several were rather interesting. The shot of Austin was one of the more pedantic images.

Periodically Walter tapped a particular photograph with one of his perfectly manicured fingers and made a favorable comment. I wondered if there really was a picture of Mayo or if the whole thing had been a ruse to get me to look at Barbara's work.

After several minutes Barbara laid out a handful of photos of David. In particular, David with the baseball cap and a camera. In some of the pictures he had the camera aimed at the photographer: a picture of a picture. In one photograph he was standing on his head shooting a shot of a reproduction of Michaelangelo's sculpture 'David'."

"David was something of a ham," I said.

"Of course he was," Barbara said. "Why do you think he wanted to make a movie?" She glanced towards the bar again. "I believe I'll have another Bloody. Anything for either of you?"

Wistfully I recalled the Scotch, and Mavredes. "No thanks," I said. "I'll stick with coffee."

"I'll get the drinks," Walter said. He left us for a moment. I wondered if it had been planned. As soon as he got up from the booth Barbara placed a photo in my hand of David in an army officer's uniform.

"What's this?" I said.

"There was another side of David," she said. "I tried to tell you but you wouldn't listen. Take that picture you're holding, the uniform."

"Okay, what about it?"

"He posed for that shot in silk boxer shorts and a pair of high heeled pumps. Got a big kick out of it. 'My other half', he said. Not many people saw that side of him."

"But you did."

"A few others. Some of the guys in the photography class. They were more self-conscious about it than David, though. He always poked fun at them. 'Loosen up', he'd say. 'A few lost inhibitions never hurt anybody.'" She took the photograph out of my hand and placed it face down on the table.

"May I call you 'Rosemund'," she said.

"Of course." I had thought we were already on a first name basis.

"Rosemund, that's why I believe you are wrong about David's death. David played games with images on film I would never show you or anybody. In front of it or behind it, the camera was part of his game. He was always arguing with his mother about the superiority of the camera over a paintbrush."

"What are you trying to say, Barbara?"

"I think David was into another one of his games the night he died, that he dressed up in that black plastic and was playing around with the rope. It was red, you know, nothing plain and ordinary for David. It had to be red. And then, whack! The game turned sour." She looked over at the bar where Walter stood watching us.

"Are you suggesting someone was there with a camera?"

She looked at me over the top of an empty glass, almost as if she were using the glass as a shield. "David would never dress up like that without a camera to capture his latest image on film."

I picked up another photograph. It was a naked man seen from the rear. He was wearing a Halloween mask on the back of his head, which created the impression that his head was turned all the way around backwards. The mask grinned at the camera.

"David," she said. "See what I mean?"

The certainty I felt about David's death slipped a bit as I reexamined the photographs. I seemed to be the only person who thought he had been murdered.

"I came to see the picture of Mayo Johnson," I said. "Where is it?"

Without another word she flipped quickly through the remaining photographs and placed the picture in my hand. It was definitely Mayo. He was dressed in his boxing shorts. His hands, encased in boxing gloves, were drawn up close to his chest in what I assumed was a pugilistic pose. Displayed behind him was a banner reading "Virginia Heavyweight Champion". What was most interesting, however, was the man standing beside him. It was not David Moon. It was a middle aged man in a wrinkled suit and bow tie.

I tapped the photograph with my finger. "Walter," I said.

Almost on cue he returned to the booth with two Bloody Marys in his hand. "The waiter's bringing your coffee," he said. "I couldn't carry all three. I took the liberty of ordering a plate of barbecued shrimp. Thought we might need a bite to eat." He took his place beside Barbara again and pointed to the photo of Mayo and himself. "Not bad, huh?"

"It isn't exactly public knowledge that the doctor who saved Mayo Johnson's eye is David's uncle," Barbara said. "When you started asking me all those questions about Mayo I didn't know what to do."

"The first time we talked you told me David had an uncle everybody treated like shit," I said. "At the time I didn't know you were referring to Walter. Now it appears you two knew each other quite well."

The barbecued shrimp arrived. Daintily Barbara picked up one with her fingers. I decided to follow her example even though the sauce ran down my hand.

"What do you mean?" She gave her mouth a wipe swipe with a napkin and the lipstick smeared. A couple of barbecued shrimp and her glamorous image had gone down the tube. Walter didn't seem to mind. He offered her his napkin.

"John Owen Smith made some accusations about the two of you," I said bluntly. There was no reason to be subtle. "Suggested that you enjoyed more than a friend-of-the-family relationship."

"Well, John Owen is a son of a bitch," Barbara said, glancing quickly at Walter. He gave her a pat. I assumed it was on the knee. "I told you I warned David about him."

"If David was playing games with black plastic," I said, "could John Owen have been on the other side of the camera recording the game for posterity?"

"John Owen didn't know his ass from a hole in the ground...but, yes, he could use a camera." Barbara stuck a whole shrimp her mouth. It was hot. Sauce dripped down her chin. Walter speared a shrimp with his fork. They chewed simultaneously. Neither one of them seemed particularly interested in the direction I was taking them.

Walter retrieved his napkin from Barbara and dabbed the edge of his mouth where a drop of sauce had lodged. "What did your cameraman tell you about me?" he said. He seemed amused there was anything to tell.

"That you were sleeping with David's girlfriend."

I expected a denial. To my surprise Walter merely stabbed another shrimp and chewed on it delicately.

"Let me tell you about Walter," Barbara said. "He's a very sweet man. He helped that boxer. You already know he was the doctor that fixed his eye. He introduced David to Jimmy Travers, too. It was supposed to be a way to help David get state money to finish his movie..."

I kept my mouth shut. And waited. The loosening power of two Bloody Marys could not be diminished by one cup of black coffee and a handful of shrimp.

"Anyway..." Barbara searched for the words, casting glances at Walter as she talked, almost as though she needed his permission to continue. "Walter offered to put up the money for David, but David wouldn't hear of it. He said Lucy would kill him if he accepted a nickel from his uncle."

I looked at Walter. It was time he did some explaining.

"Why does Lucy hate you? What happened between the two of you?"

"Ah, my dear sister, Lucy, what can I say? That Lucy has an over-active imagination. It's one of the things that makes her a fine artist, of course. But imagination can get out of hand. It can become a filter that alters the way you see life. Lucy embellishes reality, so to speak. She changes things, makes a situation fit her image of how it should be, people as well as circumstances, so you never quite know where truth stops and fantasy begins."

"That still doesn't explain why she hates you."

Barbara touched Walter on the arm tenderly. I saw the quick pressure her fingers applied to his skin. The gesture told me more about their relationship than either of them needed to put into words. Where David fit in was becoming more and more unclear.

"Lucy believes I did something to her when she was young," Walter said. "She's convinced I'm the cause of her nightmares. She also thinks I led her son down the road to damnation." Barbara dropped her hand from his arm and reached for his hand. I saw her give him a tight squeeze. It might have been to comfort him or simply to encourage him to keep talking. I remembered what Barbara had told me about Lucy's nightmares the first time we talked. "Lucy paints her dreams," she had said. It could have as easily been Walter as David who told her.

"And are you the cause of her nightmares?"

Walter gave me one of his courtly smiles. He sighed and suddenly seemed very tired. "I would have done anything for David," he said. "He was family and I loved him...but..."

I finished the statement for him. "Introducing Jimmy to David was your way of trying to alter Lucy's view of reality."

"Something like that," Walter said. "Ironic, isn't it?"

"What? That Jimmy may have killed him?"

"David may have wrapped himself in the plastic and tied the red rope around himself, pretending he was gift-wrapped to make fun of his mother's paintings. Or Jimmy may be the one who got him into the black plastic. It was the kind of thing Jimmy preferred. Not my taste at all, but each of us has our own little secrets. So, in a way Jimmy might have killed him, but not like you think. He might have helped him die in a 'David Moon sort of way'."

"I don't understand."

"Don't you get it, Rosemund?" Barbara said. She shook her head and frowned. Every time she let go of the Southern Belle routine she became more attractive. At the moment she was almost pretty. Her next words were delivered matter-of-factly and free of all traces of an accent. She leaned forward so that her face was a few inches from mine. "David didn't go for girls," she said, emphasizing the word 'girls'. "It's something Walter knew for a long time, I knew, we both wanted to protect him. I loved David but I was never his girlfriend or his lover. I was his cover, his front, his faghag, his altered illusion."

David Moon's secret.

It seemed so insignificant now that I heard it. I wondered if Lucy knew. She was an open-minded woman, it shouldn't matter to her. He was her son, nothing should have mattered to her as long as he was alive. But sometimes when someone is dead we insist on retaining illusions that might eventually be dissolved in the course of a lifetime. I knew death might be the most altered illusion of all. I couldn't think of anything to say. It seemed intrusive at the moment to ask if David had a lover, even if the answer might have provided a key to his death. Maybe later, or maybe never. I wasn't sure I even wanted to know. Barbara's love life seemed incidental, too. Any questions I had about Walter McGowan no longer concerned me. I took a drink of lukewarm coffee.

"So now you know everything," Barbara said.

If only she had been right.

When we left the Hill Cafe we went in opposite directions. I was grateful to have the Jaguar back from the repair shop and slouched comfortably in its low belly for several moments before turning on the ignition. So now I understood David better. But understanding him still didn't explain his death, if he was murdered. Too many questions kept going round and round in my head. It was more than the fact that I wanted to be right and that everybody else needed to be wrong. It was too easy to say David's death was suicide, even accidental suicide. David was too complicated for that, too much of a showman for it to end that way. A set up, maybe, a scene for a photo shoot like Barbara and Walter suggested. But an ending without credits.

There was also something else about my meeting with Barbara and Walter that didn't sit right. I couldn't quite put my finger on what it was. Mentally I reviewed what they had told me, David, Jimmy Travers, Mayo Johnson, John Owen, no, it didn't concern them.

And then I remembered.

Austin Meyerson. It was not so much the actual photograph of Austin in Barbara's portfolio. It was that he had never mentioned he knew David or Barbara, that he had taken a class with them, that he had shot a number of photographs with them, and he never thought it important enough to mention to me. Even after David died.

I was so deep in thought the tap on the window on my side of the car made me jump. My first response was John Owen had tracked me to Church Hill and had a gun aimed at my head. I turned the key in the ignition, ready to flee, and took a quick glance at the window.

It was Gussie. She was grinning. I rolled down the window and laughed with relief.

"Scared me to death, knocking like that."

"I'd recognize the Beast anywhere," she said. "I'm parked around the corner where I've been hanging out with Connie Lee. You want to hear about it?"

"What do you think?" I said. "Climb in. We'll drive around. I've been drinking coffee with Barbara Barksdale and Walter McGowan for the past hour and couldn't stand the inside of another restaurant."

We took off as soon as she lowered herself into the passenger side of the car. I knew there was no love lost between Gussie and the Jaguar, but I hoped it would behave itself as long as she was in the car. We drove a few blocks to Chimborazo Park which overlooked the city and the James River. Most of the leaves were off the trees. We could see for miles. A wide, gray expanse of river front development spread out before us. A few joggers were circling the park. I parked the Jag in a spot where we could enjoy the view and leaned back in my seat to listen.

"If I hang around with you long enough," Gussie said, "I may get good at this stuff."

"You going to tell me how you found her?"

Gussie gave me one of her looks and then grinned shamelessly. "I could lie and tell you I followed her parents down a dark alley, but the truth is that Connie was in the grocery store minding the cash register when I came in. There was nothing to it. If she's guilty of something, she doesn't act like it. Her father told me she'd be at the store this week. I've stopped by every day since you called me to check her out. I was about ready to give up, but today I hit the jackpot."

"She's guilty of something, all right. The evidence is yellow with black spots. Did she try to run away when she saw you?"

"She didn't recognize me from the movie shoot at first. Looked at me kind of funny when I came in, though, like she knew me, but didn't."

"And...?"

"I said I had come to warn her that John Owen Smith was out of jail and was looking for her, that he was convinced she and Jimmy Travers had cheated him out of his money and he was going to kill both of them."

I stared at Gussie in amazement. "You said all that?"

"Sure, I'm a creative artist, remember?" She couldn't stop grinning. "Connie said she didn't know what I was talking about, of course."

"Of course."

"And then I pulled my ace. I told her you had been in the trunk of the car she drove back to the Governor's Mansion for Jimmy. You should have seen her face. She turned colors I could use on my furniture. I suggested that if she tried to get hold of Jimmy she'd discover he was in jail. She got real quiet at that, probably because she's tried to reach him and nobody will tell her where he is."

"You are good, Gussie, really good."

"What really cinched it was the scarf. I told her the police had found strands of red silk at your gallery the night the painting and the giraffe were stolen and you had seen a red scarf in the back seat of the Lincoln. Since it was gone when you got out of the trunk, you figured it was probably hers. She broke down, Rosemund, and started crying, said they took the giraffe and climbed out the window like we suspected. She and her sister and John Owen thought the drugs had slipped down into the giraffe's neck so they had to get it out of the gallery to give it a good once over. But it was empty. They panicked. They thought Tyrone was the police so they hit him over the head."

"Tyrone? The police?"

"Undercover, or something. Anyway, her parents have convinced her she's in deep trouble. I think she's really scared. She's waiting for you at the store. The funny thing is, she insists they threw the giraffe's head in a dumpster behind the gallery and they didn't take Lucy's painting."

That explained how Arik got hold of the giraffe head to send to Governor Brookfield. But if the Lee sisters and John Owen didn't take the painting, how did it find its way out of the gallery?

XXX

Connie Lee was not the only one waiting for us at her parents' grocery store. We parked the Jaguar and walked into the store and into John Owen Smith holding a gun. Connie and her parents were standing in the back of the store in front of a row of canned vegetables, looking scared. I didn't blame them. When I saw John Owen, his shoulders drawn up almost to his chin, I was scared, too.

"I didn't know you were having a party," Gussie said, looking around, "I would have brought a present." No one laughed. No one else seemed to be in the store. It felt very empty.

"Shut up!" John Owen said.

Gussie and I joined the Lees against the wall of vegetables. For one fleeting moment I wondered what would happen if each of us grabbed a tin can and hurled it at John Owen. The expression on the faces of the three Lees indicated they wouldn't be receptive to the idea.

"I want the coke or the money," John Owen said, to no one in particular, "or both."

"Greedy," Gussie muttered under her breath. I was glad I was the only one who heard her.

Connie started to wail. "I didn't do it, John Owen, I swear I didn't. I was just trying to keep Jimmy on the leash until you could find out what happened to the drugs. That's why I was with him. I did it for you." Mrs. Lee looked like she was going to pass out. Her eyes were rolling around in her head. She clutched her husband's arm and swayed gently from side to side.

John Owen frowned. His face twisted in confusion. He seemed not to know what to think. "Some fucking bastard took the stuff!" He waved the gun wildly. "It was gone! I'm a dead man if I can't produce the money!" He aimed the gun at me. "I know you're involved. Arik came back to your place, didn't he? He's no art lover. You and Arik had a plan, didn't you? Tell me where you hid it." He pointed the gun at Connie again. "You heard me," he said. "She could of taken the stuff and hidden it at her place."

Her? I felt indignant. I had a name.

"Rosemund Wallace," I said. "Please don't refer to me in the third person."

"Nobody shoots up an art gallery in Richmond, Virginia, and gets away with it," Gussie said.

It was a mistake. John Owen lunged at her, hitting her across the face with the gun barrel. Probably because he needed to hit somebody and she had the misfortune of opening her mouth last. She staggered, and grabbed Mr. Lee's free arm for support. Now he had two fainting women to hold up. For one terrible moment I thought John Owen would shoot her. He might have shot somebody had the front door to the grocery not opened.

A black woman entered. An attractive, very familiar woman wearing an African head wrap. I sucked in my breath and looked at John Owen. He shoved Mr. Lee towards the front of the store.

"Get rid of her," he said. "Get her out of here fast or I'll shoot your daughter. We'll be behind this shelf watching what you say."

Tight lipped, Mr. Lee pushed both his wife and Gussie in my direction and headed for the front of the store as fast as he could go. The two women staggered against me and then righted themselves as John Owen dragged us behind another shelf. The side of Gussie's head was bleeding. Mrs. Lee noticed the blood and quietly reached into an apron pocket for a handkerchief touching Gussie's wound. John Owen kept the gun aimed at Connie's back.

"I'm looking for some fresh turnip greens," the woman at the counter said. Her voice carried all the way to the back of the store. When Gussie heard her she seemed to lose some of her dizziness. Recognition filled her eyes. She glanced at me for conformation. Silently I nodded my head.

It was Billie Johnson, Mayo's wife.

That old art dealer's sense of timing warned me to be very still, to wait and watch. A true artist brought out their best work at the very end of a presentation. Even though she lived in Church Hill, Billie wouldn't have come to the store at this particular moment by accident. What was she up to? What really gave her away was the request for turnip greens. Mayo had told me they never ate the stuff.

"Yes," Mr. Lee was saying, "we have nice greens. How much you want?"

"Oh," said Billie, "several pounds. But I'd like to pick them out myself."

"Oh no, ma'am," Mr. Lee said. "Not to bother yourself, ma'am. I'll pick the best for you."

"I insist," Billie said. "My husband always wants me to pick out his greens. He's a very fussy man." She walked across the front of the store towards the fresh produce. John Owen closed in tighter on Connie and gestured for all of us to move further back, closer to the meat counter behind the canned goods. Mrs. Lee shut her eyes and swayed towards Gussie, took a good look at her bruised head and said what sounded like something motherly in Korean.

"Damn," Gussie muttered, looking at the handkerchief. "I'm bleeding again."

John Owen waved the gun at her. "Shut up," he mouthed. "Shut up."

It was cold standing near the meat counter. It was also closer to the back door. I peeked around the canned goods and watched Billie sort through the greens amidst the other produce.

"Some of these greens look tired," she said. "What do you have in the back? Some fresh greens, maybe, that you haven't put out yet? Or maybe I'll just take these and get a good ham hock for flavor. My husband likes a nice hunk of fatback in his greens." She began to walk towards the rear of the store where we were huddled in front of the meat counter. I was tempted to yell out her name as a warning, but that same sense that helped me in the past urged me to stand very still until the right moment.

What the right moment would be was unclear, just that there would be a right moment.

And there was.

Mayo burst through the back door of the store while our attention was focused on Billie as she marched towards the meat counter with the hapless Mr. Lee in tow.

He tackled John Owen before he realized he'd been hit. This makes it twice, I thought; the third time he's out. John Owen fell against the meat counter, swinging his arm wildly. To my horror he didn't let go of the gun. It fired once. But before he could pull the trigger again Mrs. Lee grabbed a hunk of meat from inside the counter and threw it at him. The gun clattered to the floor. Mayo grabbed it and pointed it at John Owen. I bent down to pick up the packaged meat.

It was a hamhock.

"Billie was in the car at Brown's Island," Mayo explained later as we waited for the police. "She was keeping an eye on you while I was busy. I knew the camera guy had taken something out of the giraffe's mouth. I saw him take it just as we were getting ready to shoot the waltz scene at the gallery. I didn't know what it was."

"Arik," I said. "Arik Lawson. When I saw your face on the film I thought you had seen something. You were looking towards the corner where the giraffe and Lucy's painting were hanging."

"Yeah," Mayo said. "I found out he worked at that video company and followed him for several days. I was right behind him when he stopped by the gallery that night. I was trying to keep an eye on you and the gallery when all hell broke loose. I thought he was trouble, messing with the giraffe, you know—when all along it was this other guy. Shows that appearances can fool you." He waved the gun at John Owen, who had been tied to the front counter near the cash register with a piece of rope Mr. Lee salvaged from a packing crate in the back. "So, naturally, I followed him here."

I was relieved to see the rope wasn't red.

"You were watching when John Owen took a shot through the window of the gallery?" Gussie said.

"Yeah," Mayo said, "I figured I'd be more help if I followed the guy who fired the gun than if I ran in to see who was hurt."

"What if Rosemund had been hit?" Gussie said.

Mayo smiled broadly. "Even if she was wounded," he said, "Rosemund Wallace wouldn't die. Richmond needs her. What would this town do without her gallery?"

"Yes," Billie said with a laugh. "Where would Mayo show his art?"

"If you were following John Owen," I said, "how did Billie know Arik took Mavredes and me to Brown's Island?"

Mayo gestured towards his wife. "She was with me," he said. "She stayed at the gallery and watched until that detective came while I went after this guy." He gave John Owen a nudge with the revolver. "Then she drove along behind you while I followed this guy on foot. She saw you stop at MCV..."

"I must say that worried me a bit," Billie said.

"Then you went to the detective's office and the next thing you know, you were off to Brown's Island, my old stomping ground. Billie tells me you weren't looking for driftwood, though."

I shook my head in amazement and grabbed Billie's hands in gratitude. "So that was you in the car, flashing your lights at us while Mavredes and Arik played games with each other all over the island?"

"Running around like crazy men," Billie said. "Just what were they doing? I could never figure it out. I was so busy watching them that I lost you. Where did you disappear to?"

"Fishing," I said. "I went fishing." Then I turned to John Owen.

"In a sense, you were right about me," I said. "For almost five minutes I had your drugs in my cold little hands."

John Owen stared. "What, what you talking about?"

When I explained, everybody laughed. Even Mr. and Mrs. Lee. I think their laughter was out of relief, however. If they tried hard enough, they might be able to convince themselves their daughter hadn't been involved in anything more than the theft of a giraffe.

XXXI

We all had our war wounds to display. Gussie's generated lots of sympathy at the gym. The gash on her face was more dramatic than the bruises I had sustained when John Owen attacked me in the front hall of my house. A crowd gathered around her shortly after we arrived for our workout. Since I had a lot of lost time to make up for, I was busy with the new, long-slung bicycles the athletic club had installed in my absence. While I pedaled away, Gussie drank coffee with some of the jocks at the front desk. I was glad for the solitude. A little voice inside me asked if I wanted to reopen the gallery. I wasn't ready to answer that question.

Everybody who was guilty of almost anything had confessed, John Owen Smith and the Lee sisters for planning a drug deal and attacking Tyrone. John Owen had even been willing to identify the big guns who were after both the money and his head. They were locked up for as long as Mavredes could keep them in jail. Since Jimmy Travers admitted his role in the whole nasty business, Governor Brookfield had almost apologized for obstructing justice. Mavredes never told him that Arik had sent him the giraffe head as a warning to Jimmy.

Mavredes had promised to try to get the head back. If he did, I would be in the awkward position of trying to decide whether to keep it for myself or to return it to Mayo. Leave it to Arik to complicate things. Since the drugs had been recovered and no drug deal had materialized, Arik Lawson didn't seem to be guilty of anything except shaving his beard. Walter McGowan and Barbara Barksdale had come close to confessing the real meaning of their relationship. I probably would never know whether Walter had been telling me the truth about Lucy.

Mayo Johnson was trying to make up his mind whether to try to get the boxing commissioner to let him schedule a rematch with Mike Tyson. Beverly and Jack had been moved by the Department of Social Services into a small apartment that had once been a garage behind a house on Idlewood Avenue. It had heat and indoor plumbing and was only a few blocks from the gallery.

Everything was falling into place, except for the fact that nobody seemed guilty of killing David Moon.

And nobody but me still thought he had been murdered.

I pedaled harder on the new bicycle machine. I could feel the burn around my thighs. Good, I thought. If I keep this up I'll be ahead of Gussie.

She joined me all too soon. "So the new glass is being installed in the gallery window today," she said.

I could only manage a grunt. Sweat was unclogging my pores. It felt good.

"I guess that means you'll be reopening soon," Gussie said. She settled into the adjoining bicycle.

"Maybe," I said, panting, "and maybe not. I can't complain about the number of artists who want to exhibit at the Rosemund Wallace Gallery, though. I've been inundated with slides and resumes. I should be flattered and it should be fun. But I'm not, and it isn't. Maybe Richmond doesn't need me any more."

"Who would sell my furniture?"

"There's always Lila Hunt."

Gussie took a swing at me. "I'll move back to Texas first," she said.

I stared at the zig-zag lines on the bicycle's computer. I was surprised to see that I had gone up and down more hills and at a faster pace than I had imagined. Maybe I was on an upswing and didn't know it.

"As soon as I shed five more pounds," I said, "I'm on my way to the gallery. I promised Harry I'd make a decision this week."

Gussie reached out for my hand as I stepped off the bicycle. "Rosemund," she said gently, "there's life after David..."

An hour later, when the phone rang at the gallery, I answered it mechanically, expecting another question about reopening or the date of our next show.

"Wallace Gallery," I said. "This is Rosemund Wallace."

"It's me," the nearly breathless voice said, "Arabella, I'm on my car phone. Call your detective friend and get out here fast! I think Lucy's in trouble." Arabella usually spoke quickly, but this time her words came like bullets.

"Hey, wait a minute," I said. "Slow down. What's going on? Where are you?"

"In Goochland," she said. "I drove out to work on an article with Lucy, the one I told you about earlier, the one about David. We didn't have a lot of time because she was waiting for some guy to arrive to help her wrap paintings to ship out of state. She had half a dozen standing against her studio wall and kind of shooed me out of the place."

"What's the problem? Seems like a good idea to let people help her. She could just hole up in that huge house and never see anybody."

"Listen to me," Arabella said. "This is no time to discuss Lucy's personal habits. Something's wrong."

"All right," I said. "I'm listening...but I don't think Mavredes will take too kindly to a call from me. The case is closed, as far as he's concerned."

"It's the guy, he arrived while I was still there, so I left after a few minutes. It was obvious she wanted to get to work. But as I went to my car I happened to glance in his van..."

"And?" Ever the reporter, I thought. Nosy, even. Never overlook possibilities for a story.

"There was a big roll of black plastic on the front seat."

Oh, I thought. A chill rippled down my arms. My hand holding the telephone felt cold. "A coincidence," I said. The response was as much for myself as for Arabella. "Black plastic is going to spook us all for a while. Don't get so excited."

"There's more. I drove my car out her driveway so they'd think I left, parked it on the road, slipped back and hid behind some bushes."

Visualizing Arabella in her leather jacket crouching behind a bush was almost funny. But then, the newspaper business had never really appealed to me.

"It's over, Arabella," I said. "Bringing a roll of black plastic out to Lucy's studio is nothing to get alarmed about."

"I watched him go back to his van to get it..."

"Sounds innocent enough, to help her wrap some paintings. Black plastic is always what Lucy uses to cover her canvases." If that was all there was to it, why was I feeling more and more uneasy?

"Rosemund! Will you shut up and listen to me?" Arabella was yelling over the car phone in earnest now. I took a few deep breaths and willed my heart to stop pounding as I tried to concentrate on what she was saying.

"He had something else with him! Something he took into Lucy's house along with the black plastic. I saw it tucked under his arm. You've got to call the police."

My throat was suddenly so dry that I could barely get out the question. "What? What was it?"

"Red rope, oh my God, Rosemund, he was carrying a coil of red rope."

Had Mavredes not been in his office when I telephoned him a moment later I would have sped out to Goochland by myself. But he answered his own phone, ordered me not to leave the premises until he got there, and pulled up in front of the gallery in less than ten minutes. A police car was right behind him. Inside were three officers, two white men and a tall black woman I wanted on my side if it got down to choices. Bernard came to the door of his studio to watch as I ran out of the gallery and jumped into Mavredes' car. I wondered how often he wished for a more sedate neighbor. In a few moments we swerved onto the expressway a couple of blocks from Carytown, zipped through two toll booths and sped up Highway 64, blue lights flashing, headed west towards Charlottesville, which was the quickest route to the Goochland turnoff where Lucy's tavern was located.

On the way I repeated to Mavredes what Arabella had said over the phone. He simply shook his head, indicating neither disbelief nor dismay. Then he asked the question I had not thought to ask. "Who is the guy? Anybody we know?"

"She didn't say, someone Lucy hired, I guess."

"...and instructed to bring black plastic and red rope? I don't think it's a stranger off the street, Rosemund. It's either somebody we know or a comedian with a sick sense of humor."

"But it wouldn't be John Owen or Jimmy. They barely escaped with their ass intact. They wouldn't pull anything as bizarre as showing up at Lucy's with a hunk of red rope."

"And who does that leave? The other cameraman, Arik Lawson, your boxer friend, Mayo Johnson, Lucy's brother..."

"Oh, come on," I said. I folded my arms across my chest and sank lower into the seat, aware that it was uncomfortably familiar. But if not the men Mavredes just listed, who would have driven to Lucy's with black plastic and a red rope? We could eliminate her brother. Considering the family deep freeze into which Lucy had placed Walter McGowan, she would hardly have allowed him into her house, let alone ask him to help her wrap some paintings. And Arabella had met Mayo Johnson at the movie shoot so she knew who he was and would have identified him as Lucy's guest. In fact, Arabella would have stayed and visited with him, another artist to interview, another story to write.

That left Arik.

What if Arik's theft of the drugs had not been to protect David but to sell himself? What if his claim of striking fear into the heart of Jimmy Travers by sending the giraffe head to the governor had been a sham? Maybe he wanted to scare Jimmy, all right, but so that he could keep the drugs by making certain Jimmy didn't cause any fuss. The warning to Jimmy may have been real, all right, but as a threat to expose him, not simply to scare him off. And all along, I had thought Arik was truly David's friend.

But as much as I wanted to believe he was capable of murder, it didn't make any sense to kill David. When he claimed David called him on the gallery phone, had somebody really been at the door? Had he made up the whole story because he had killed David? The phone had been off the hook on my desk when Bernard and I found David. The one person who could have told us the truth was no longer with us.

And whether or not Arik murdered David, why would he be after Lucy?

Whatever the answer, I wondered if we would make it to Goochland in time.

When I consider how far police cars push the speed limit it amazes me there are so few accidents. During most of the trip up 64 I looked out the side window at the trees flying past instead of out the front to see how many cars we nearly hit. By some miracle we managed to pass every car on the road safely, the trucks, too. The police car led the way, its siren screaming. When we reached the turnoff to Lucy's place, Mavredes picked up his transmitter and told them to cool it. We wanted to go in unannounced. As we eased our way onto the edge of the property, Arabella popped out from behind some trees, flagged us down, yanked open the car door and jumped in before we had a chance to stop. Her hair was sticking out in all directions. She looked afraid.

"Took you long enough," she said. "Lucy could be dead by now."

"We got here as soon as we could," I said. Actually, we got there sooner than anybody had a right to, given the distance from Carytown to Goochland County. Normally it would take forty-five minutes. We made it in half an hour. We parked in the trees at the foot of the paved driveway so no one would see us from the house. Lucy's property was thickly wooded to maintain the kind of privacy she preferred. The trees had turned brown but most of the leaves were still on the branches. Goochland was always behind Richmond city in its change of seasons. I was grateful; the leaves provided a lacy wall of dull gray camouflage.

With Mavredes leading the way, we edged forward from tree to tree in single file. I brought up the end. I wondered what homicidal fury Mavredes would unleash if we arrived to discover a dozen paintings neatly wrapped in black plastic standing on the front porch awaiting the UPS man. But as we came in sight of the tavern only the van Arabella had described was visible. I was relieved to see it was still there.

Until I realized whose it was.

Odd how we seem to move in slow motion when a fact we want to resist invades our brain. I pointed at the van and opened my mouth to speak. But my vocal cords seemed to freeze. No words came out. I pointed again, in hopes that moving my arm would cause my tongue to generate a sound. Arabella, Mavredes and the Richmond police force had moved on ahead of me, intent on their mission and unaware of my sudden distress. I leaned against the side of the van, fighting nausea. No, I thought, no. I peered in the window of the van. There was the owner's familiar stuff, his jacket, his tools, the plastic coffee container he carried wherever he went.

Arabella turned back and motioned me to hurry.

I nodded numbly and stumbled after them, repeating his name again and again in my mind. The name of the young man with the black plastic and the red rope. The young man who had loved Lucy's paintings so much they made him cry. The same young man who had been in the photography class with David Moon and Barbara Barksdale. The person I trusted to install all my shows at the gallery. The person who loved art almost as much as I did. But it was not Arik...

It was Austin Meyerson.

"We need to exercise a little care," Mavredes said. "Lucy may be in danger, but she may not. It would be embarrassing to burst in the front door, guns drawn, to discover Lucy and her guest on their hands and knees taping plastic over some picture of daffodils."

"Sure," Arabella said, "and tying it with red rope like a birthday present." She was almost jumping from one foot to the other in agitation. "What are we waiting for? Lucy could be dead, knock down the door."

"No," Mavredes said. "If we storm the place it could push Lawson, or whoever is in there with her, over the edge. It's easy to lose a life that way."

"Let me..." I said. My voice broke. "I'll knock at the door and pretend that I came to patch things up with Lucy. If everything's on the up-and-up, we haven't broken any law and we'll all go home. If she's in trouble, I'll, I'll scream."

I was glad to see that Mavredes was considering my suggestion. I needed to be the one who confronted Austin first. I needed to see his face, to discover for myself if he had it in him to kill someone. No, not just "someone", David Moon. I had to know if Austin murdered David. No assurances from a homicide detective would provide that guarantee. I would know when I saw him. Had it been Austin all along? Austin, who didn't have to climb a ladder to steal a painting because he had a key to the gallery and knew the alarm system code? It had never been about drugs or giraffes or politics. All this time it had been about art.

How could I have been so blind?

Mavredes looked towards the house, back at me and then nodded his approval. If, however, I had told him that Austin, not Arik, was in the house with Lucy, and that I was convinced Austin was the one who took the painting from the gallery and secretly deposited it on Lucy's doorstep and maybe killed David, I wondered if he would have been so willing to let me go in first.

"Either way we do it, it's risky," he said. "For one, we don't have a warrant, so we're in trouble if we barge in and there's no problem. And if we don't act like storm troopers, we could place her in greater danger. If we make a mistake and don't go in..." He let his words trail off.

"Let me go," Arabella said. "You don't look like you feel too good, Rosemund."

I shook my head and drew myself up to my full height. "I need to do this," I said. "He won't suspect anything from me. If you appear at the door, he'll wonder why you came back. If Lieutenant Mavredes backs me up, I'll be fine. The rest of you can go around by the creek and enter the house through Lucy's studio. The studio door is always open."

Mavredes motioned the three police officers to go around the back of the tavern as I had suggested. They disappeared into the trees without a word. I knew if they were careful they could slip all the way around the building without being seen. The woods continued down the back embankment to the edge of the creek. Arabella started to ask a question and Mavredes motioned her in the same direction. She flashed me a "thumbs-up" and obediently hurried after the police.

And then Mavredes and I were alone. He smiled at me, the kind of clean, fresh grin that had made me want to pair him off with Gussie shortly after I met him. "Scared?" he said.

"Yes," I said, "but she used to be my friend."

"You got guts, girl," he said. "Just don't be polite if you need to yell. I'll be right under the porch awaiting your call." I started up the steps, grateful he didn't insist the police enter first and grateful he didn't pat me on the head. Harry would have given me a fatherly pat. Actually, Harry would never have let me get this close to the house.

Maybe Mavredes knew.

I almost tripped on the second step. Damn these old taverns, I thought. The risers were a little too high, making it slightly awkward to take the stairs in a smooth gait. Once on the porch I stared at the door, remembering how many times I had given that door a light tap and opened it, announcing my arrival with a laughing call into the front hall.

I looked through the narrow glass panel beside the front door and raised my hand to knock. Then something made me pause. Directly in my view was the painting that had caused so much trouble. Lucy had hung it so that it would greet visitors as they entered the hallway just as Arabella and Mavredes had both said. There was the same androgynous figure wrapped in black plastic standing at the edge of the woods, almost like an old friend, and bound forever with the ubiquitous red rope. The picture was hanging askew, however, as if someone had knocked it as they passed or had removed it to look at it and replaced it to hang crooked. On the floor under the painting I could see a knife and a hunk of red cord, dropped perhaps in a struggle, or worse.

At that moment the thought struck me that Lucy would not be dead, yet. That just as David's death had been choreographed to resemble suicide, his killer had meant it as an art form. Austin loved art and artists. If he had something deadly in mind for Lucy, he would make certain it was staged as an art form, too. And art could never be rushed. A true artist took his time. Care and deliberation ensured that a masterpiece resulted from his efforts. It must have been Austin entering the gallery when David was on the phone upstairs with Arik. All he had to do was use his key and walk right through the front door.

I could imagine the perverse artistic pleasure David's death must have given him. Art with a capital "A". Sophisticated composition, the right background, perfect props: black plastic, red rope, death in an art gallery where the victim's own mother's paintings were hanging on the walls. Hanging, just like David.

Austin had achieved his goal for the son. What did he have in store for the mother?

Beneath the porch Mavredes was probably wondering what was taking me so long. I heard a noise somewhere inside the house, down the hallway, perhaps, or in the living room that adjoined the hall. Instead of knocking, I tiptoed across the porch floor so that I could peer in the living room window. Sensing movement below me, I glanced down towards the ground to see Mavredes slip to the other side of the steps, his pistol shining in the light. He was definitely sticking close to me. While the rope and the knife alone didn't indicate anything ominous, I was afraid of what I might see through the living room window.

But I had to look.

The window was undraped. Lucy didn't like to cover any of her windows because the view to the woods would be blocked. The living room was filled with shadows. She never turned on the lights unless she had guests who wanted to look at her paintings. She always displayed half a dozen recent paintings in the room like a mini-gallery. I did a quick survey of the cluttered space as my eyes grew accustomed to the dim shapes. In the center of the room was a kitchen chair, one of the same chairs which Mavredes and I sat in to drink coffee with Lucy when we brought her the news about her son. This time it was Lucy who was sitting in the chair. Or at least I assumed it was Lucy. I couldn't see the person's face because it was loosely covered with a plastic hood. The person in the chair was, in fact, totally wrapped in black plastic, tied with red rope and rendered immobile. It had to be Lucy. No one else was in the house except Lucy and her visitor.

The visitor was standing beside the chair. It definitely was Austin. His attention was focused entirely on the plastic covered still life he had created, or contrived. It was a scene fit for only for the most bizarre painting or photograph. I couldn't look away. Mesmerized, I stared at Austin as if he were a serpent, ready to strike. He didn't move. Neither did the figure in the chair, who, by this time, I was certain was Lucy. For one terrible moment I thought maybe I was wrong, that she was dead, truly stilled in life, that he had killed her and tied her upright in the chair. However, as I watched, her foot moved slightly as if she were waking up or coming to life. It occurred to me that perhaps Austin had drugged her or knocked her out before tying her up.

The movement seemed to activate something in Austin that had been frozen until that moment. He took a few steps towards the plastic bound figure and pushed her shoulder beneath the plastic as though his carefully contrived setup was coming apart. His mouth began to move as though he was saying something to her. I couldn't hear anything through the wall, though, so I had no idea what was going on. She began to struggle. The chair rocked back and forth from her movements to get free. At the same time Austin reached over to another chair and picked up something. In the shadowy room it was hard to see what it was. There was a flash, then another and another. Austin had a camera. He was taking pictures of Lucy in the chair. At least it meant she wasn't in immediate danger. I recalled the knife used to cut the rope was still lying in the hallway beneath the painting. But the plastic could suffocate her if pulled too tightly. As I watched, I saw Austin reach down into Lucy's lap and pick up a loose piece of red rope I hadn't noticed before. He looped one end of it around Lucy's neck and the other end around his own neck. He gave the rope a slight yank, and shot a few more photographs of Lucy while he swayed back and forth. Then he aimed the camera at himself. The flash must have blinded him for a second as the swaying stopped. He took another photo and started again. The swaying movement pulled the rope tighter around both their necks. Lucy and Austin were bound together in a dance of death.

At that moment Lucy began to scream. It was muffled by the black plastic and the rope tightening around her neck but it was loud enough to hear through the living room wall. It was a horrible scream, the scream of a wounded, terrified child, not the scream of an adult woman. I remembered the image of the child in Lucy's earliest paintings. I pictured the image of hands typing rope into loops in several paintings. I recalled what Michael had said about the sequence of paintings telling the story of her life. Something long repressed was being activated in front of me. Mavredes must have heard Lucy screaming. He bounded up the front steps, ran across the porch to where I was standing, took one look over my shoulder and broke the window glass with the butt of his revolver.

"Don't move or I'll shoot," Mavredes shouted. With his left hand he shoved me towards the front door. "Get in there," he said. "Get in there and help her."

Austin looked in our direction slowly as though his reflexes had been tampered with. He grinned and yanked tighter on the red rope linking him with Lucy as I raced for the front door. It was the last thing I saw before I pushed open the door. Lucy never locked it. I don't think she even knew the location of a key. I heard a gun shot. Mavredes pounded across the wooden floor behind me. I had been right when I imagined how fast the man could move if he had to. I was barely through the door when he rushed past me. Without thinking, I grabbed the knife off the floor and ran after him into the living room. There seemed to be too much noise in the house and I realized the three police officers and Arabella were running up the stairs from the studio where they must have been when they heard the gun shot. .

Mavredes was holding both Lucy and Austin like a circus performer managing a two-headed freak. Austin was bleeding and he had slumped forward. But the weight of his body was pulling the rope tighter around both his and Lucy's necks, strangling them simultaneously.

Mavredes was doing his best to keep that from happening but if he let Austin fall, the noose around Lucy's neck would be yanked so hard it would cut off her breathing. Because of the rope binding her to the chair she was paralyzed.

"The knife!" Mavredes yelled. "Use the fucking knife!"

I lunged across the floor towards the tangle of bodies and sliced the rope linking Austin with Lucy's shrouded figure. Austin fell to the floor with a heavy thud and Lucy slumped sideways in the chair. The blood from the gunshot wound made a vivid stain on Austin's white body, a long stream of red which mimicked the frayed rope. The three police officers had arrived by now and yanked at the black plastic covering Lucy's still form. When her face was free I was startled to see how pale she looked.

Arabella asked the question I was afraid to put into words. "Is she, is she all right?"

The black policewoman gathered Lucy in her arms and carried her to the sofa. Lucy moaned softly, more like a whimper than a sound resembling the horrible shriek I had heard though the living room window. Arabella sat down beside her and placed a pillow beneath her head. She began to cry in earnest now, an infantile wail children might emit if separated from their parents in the middle of the night.

"He did it," she cried. "He hurt me, he always hurt me, tying me up in the dark, leaving me alone..."

Mavredes bent down beside her. "Austin?"

Lucy seemed to look right through him. "Walty," she said. The wail intensified. "Walty hurt me. He hurt me..."

At first I didn't understand. Walty?

And then I knew. Walter McGowan. The brother she never wanted to discuss. The brother she pretended didn't exist. The brother she never wanted David to know. The brother who told me Lucy always imagined things that weren't there. The brother who insisted Lucy hated him for his life-style, that she was convinced he had led David down the road to perdition. My head was spinning. Who to believe? Oh God, who to believe?

"I'll get a quilt," I said. "I know where she keeps them." I ran through the living room to Lucy's bedroom upstairs over the kitchen, but not merely to get something to cover her up. I had to get out of the room. It was too close. A young man I thought I knew lay bleeding on the living room floor of an old tavern in Goochland County, where paintings by the famous Lucy Moon stared down at him. Had he planned to kill her? Or was he trying to duplicate something that had happened with David? Something that had gone terribly wrong? And at this moment David's mother was sobbing her heart out on the sofa because of something that had been done to her long ago by a boy called "Walty", her brother, Walter McGowan.

I grabbed a quilt off the foot of Lucy's bed and clutched it tightly for a long time.

Finally I took several deep breaths and returned to the living room with the quilt. By this time Austin was handcuffed and sitting in a chair flanked by the two male police officers. The wound in his shoulder where Mavredes shot him had been cleaned up and was covered with a white bandage. Neither he nor Lucy looked at me as I handed the quilt to the policewoman. Mavredes stood to the left of the sofa, writing in his little notebook as the policewoman wrapped Lucy in the quilt.

I stopped directly in front of Austin. "Why?" I said. "Why did it happen?"

He looked up at me and for a moment it was like it had been between us when we worked together on a show at the gallery. I saw a flash of the warmth and humor we had shared monthly. Harry and Rosemund and Austin, an unbeatable team, always installing the best exhibit in town. And then his eyes dulled and he was someone I didn't know.

"If the great Lucy Moon's son had played along," he said, "it never would have ended the way it did. I let myself in the gallery with the key, just like I always did when there was a show to hang. I thought maybe he'd like to celebrate, but he was down, feeling really bad. Filming the movie was really getting to him, that, and he had run out of money, used up his inheritance, didn't know if he could get any more out of the state. Jimmy Travers was supposed to help, but David said the whole thing was screwed up. I talked him into letting me take some pictures. It cheered him up. We started playing around with the black plastic that had been wrapped around Lucy's paintings. He started making fun of me, saying I didn't have it in me to push the edge. I think he was waiting for somebody else to turn up, but since I was there, he made do with me. It was a new game, he said, he even had the props. It was crazy. He had covered a couple of feet of rope with red house paint...red rope over the beam, the black plastic, standing on a box with a noose around his neck, it was his idea. Making fun of me and his mother's paintings. I didn't want to go along, but he insisted, called me a girl for not trying. 'Pull tighter', he said, and laughed. I had the camera set up when I pulled the box out from under him. And then, and then he wasn't laughing, he was just hanging there and, and, he never came back." Austin's voice broke and he began to sob.

Across the room Lucy was sobbing, too, real tears, as if her heart would break.

Thirty minutes later Mavredes and I pulled out of Lucy's driveway in tandem with the police car. Behind us Lucy stood on her front porch with Arabella and the black police woman. I wondered what Lucy was thinking. The two male police officers had headed back to Richmond with Austin. Mavredes said it would be difficult to know whether to press charges or not. At the end of the long drive I turned to look back. The three women were still outlined against the doorway, one tall figure and two smaller ones. My chest felt like someone had twisted my heart into a pretzel. I wished I had been the one remaining behind to comfort Lucy instead of driving back to Richmond with a homicide detective. But I was the last person she was willing to let help her. A stranger was easier to deal with than me. I had seen her at her absolute worst, when she had broken down. She never allowed anyone to witness any vulnerability on her part, even when David died. It was difficult to admit that our friendship had been so one-sided she would hardly know I was gone.

To disguise my sense of loss I turned to Mavredes and said matter-of-factly, "What do you think her brother really did to her as a child?"

"We'll probably never know," Mavredes said. He did not look at me but kept his eyes on the road. "She'll certainly never tell us."

I settled back into the comfort of the seat, grateful he hadn't noticed my eyes had filled with tears. There were some things about David I would never tell anyone, either. It was a bit disquieting to realize I was getting used to the inside of Mavredes' car. "Maybe it was all in her mind," I said. "Maybe nothing actually happened. Or perhaps it was a game like David was playing and she got scared and made it into something more than it really was."

"Well, Austin may have done her a favor."

I gave him a Gussie look, raised eyebrows and all. It was wasted, however; his eyes never wavered from the road. It occurred to me the whole thing was bothering him more than he wanted to admit.

"I think the shrinks call it 'catharsis' or something," he said, clearing his throat. "you heard her yelling. It was like a..."

"...primal scream," I said, "sort of back-to-basics therapy."

"Yeah, that's what I was getting at. Austin may have given her some kind of emotional release."

"He almost killed her," I said.

"Yeah, well..."

"Thanks to Arabella we got there in time. It's just too bad Lucy will never speak to me again. "

"She'll get over it." He reached over to pat my hand. I was suddenly so tired I didn't even feel surprised by this gesture of compassion. "She's had a lot to deal with, more than most people could handle. Give her a little time."

I nodded silently. What else was there to say? We drove back to the city in silence...

XXXII

Three months later Lila Hunt launched a retrospective of Lucy Moon's paintings at her gallery. *THE RICHMOND TIMES DISPATCH* went all out and gave her a full page spread in the big weekend Entertainment section prior to the opening. Arabella wrote the feature article, replete with color photographs of several paintings, including the black plastic covered figure standing on the edge of the forest. I had a hard time looking at it. Too many emotions were stirred up by the image. I wondered why Lucy allowed it to be in the article in the first place, she always said it was like a bad penny. But then, maybe having it on display for the whole world to see did her a world of good. Part of the catharsis Mavredes suggested. In the story Arabella called it one of her finest paintings, quoting Lila, of course, adding it had been acquired by a private collector for an undisclosed amount of money. I was grateful Arabella omitted Lila Hunt was the dealer who had arranged the transaction. It was embarrassing enough that everybody in town knew I was no longer handling Lucy's work without it being broadcast in print.

The article referred briefly to the tragic death of Lucy's son, David Moon, without going into the gory details about my gallery. Arabella had also been careful not to mention that Austin Meyerson had almost done away with Lucy, too. It was a family secret we all wanted to preserve. This was an art show, after all. Some sort of decency had to be maintained. *THE TIMES DISPATCH* was not the *THE NATIONAL INQUIRER*. The art community wanted to help Lucy put her troubles behind her. Her retrospective was the major art event of the year. Since the art community also wanted to be part of the action, gossip and sympathy took second place.

I went to the opening with Gussie and Bernard. When Bernard insisted on driving, I managed not to display my hurt feelings, reminding myself that while the Jaguar was fine for one person, it was a little cozy for three. And besides, it might rain and then where would we be? Gussie wore black as usual, looking like the genuine article, and causing a minor stir. I had been tempted to invite Mavredes to come along, but at the last minute decided against it. Since he had not yet shown me his paintings, I was reserving judgment about him and Gussie as a potential couple.

Bernard, who somehow had wrangled a portrait commission of Governor Brookfield out of the dregs of our dealings with Jimmy Travers, wore a new cashmere jacket, wingtips and a conservative tie. "If I have to hang around Republicans," he said, "I might as well look like one." I was wearing a red dress that had required recent alterations in the hips and waist thanks to extra hours at the athletic club, and which fit me in such a way to elicit a comment from my mother had she been around to voice an opinion.

"Wow!" Bernard said as I climbed into the back seat of his Volvo. "You trying to steal the spotlight from Lucy?"

"It's all theater," I said, remembering David had been trying to make a statement about performance, too. "If I look like a successful art dealer who used to sell Lucy Moon paintings, maybe I won't feel like such a failure."

Gussie and Bernard voiced all the proper demurs, reminding me I had solved Richmond's first art-related murder and I was a heroine, not a failure. I tucked my skirt under my legs, crossed my ankles demurely in the darkened car and thought about Michael DeBord. Lucy's painting might have been his. Or, at least, an acquisition for his Japanese company. We almost did it. I guess we accomplished the next best thing, though, by saving Lucy's life. Maybe 'failure' wasn't the right word, after all.

It was almost impossible to find a parking place anywhere near Lila's gallery. After cruising the block half a dozen times, we finally gave up, parked in a lot and walked six blocks. The sidewalk in front of the gallery was crammed with people trying to get inside. The dress ranged from black tie to vintage and blue jeans. Every Richmond female who had gotten her picture in the newspaper over the past decade was there. And smiling, of course, while searching for the photographers. From the slow movement in and out the door it was obvious the crowd who had come to see twenty years of Lucy's work had no intention of taking a quick peek and running. They had come to stay.

And why not? I thought. I would want the same crowd at my gallery if I were hosting a retrospective of Lucy's work.

We milled around outside for a while, talking to people we knew, which, frankly, was every other face. Between Bernard and me, we could put together an impressive mailing list. I could tell Gussie was uncomfortable. She never liked openings in the first place, even openings at my gallery. She warmed up after a bit when a couple of her clients spotted her and pushed their way through the crowd to rave about a piece of furniture she had designed for them. Bernard worked the crowd, letting people know that in spite of his roster of Republicans, he still had a few spots on his calendar to book a portrait commission. At one point, I thought I spotted Barbara Barksdale and Walter McGowan, but I couldn't be certain. To tell the truth, I wasn't sure what I would say to them if they came up beside me.

Several loyal souls asked me how I was feeling about Lucy and Lila. Smiling, I put on a good front. "I wish her only the best," I said, chin in the air. David Moon would have been proud. "She deserves it."

And then we were inside with all the glittering people. Lila knew how to draw Richmond's moneyed crowd. Wine was flowing. A table was loaded with heavy hors d'oeuvres. A flutist elbowed his way through the rooms, fingers flying lightly over his flute although his music was drowned out by the din. In spite of the crush of people in front of them, as usual, Lucy's paintings dominated the gallery. I found myself staring at them like a naive undergraduate who wandered by mistake into a graduate level seminar. The paintings were spectacular. I was as awestruck as ever. Twenty years of viewing Lucy's work had done nothing to dim my appreciation. Someone stuck a wine glass in my hand and I wandered around the gallery trying to examine each canvas as closely as possible.

The early work was as strong as the most recent paintings. Seeing them all together as an expression of a lifetime of painting was an emotional experience. Much of the work I was familiar with, although some images I knew only from slides. Their owners had loaned them to Lucy for the retrospective and in a couple of cases hovered over them like a proud mother with a new infant. The colors were the same, the recognizable images all there, brilliant reds, greens from the Forest Series, turquoise ocean waves.

But something was missing. I stood against one wall and in spite of the people blocking my vision, I was able to see a portion of most of the paintings in the gallery. Only one contained a piece of red cord, and it was the one in the movie which now belonged to the unidentified collector who had put $35,000 in Lila Hunt's bank account. Why had Lucy selected no work containing the red rope? Michael had considered those paintings the story of her life.

"Hello, Rosemund." The familiar voice came over my right shoulder.

Clutching my wine glass and hoping I hadn't spilled a drop on my red dress, I turned slowly, not quite certain what expression should be on my face.

"Hello, Lucy," I said. "You must be very proud tonight. It's a powerful show."

She moved a few steps closer so we were face to face. She was wearing a rust colored pants suit, her jade necklace and the hat with the pointed feather. She looked terrific.

"This is very awkward," she said, "but I want to thank you. You know I was never very good with words."

Not knowing how to respond, I took a long sip of wine.

"It's been the worst year of my life," she said, "and I've treated you like crap. But the worst is over now. At least I've gotten rid of what haunted me all my life. I want to give you something to make up for the way I've behaved." By this time she was whispering. People had gathered around us almost like they were circling the wagons, watching, listening. Everyone in the gallery knew Lucy and most of them knew who I was. In particular, they knew I was her former art dealer. I could sense they were hanging on our every gesture, waiting to see what would happen. I searched the room for Bernard or Gussie but instead of spotting either one, my eyes seemed to rest directly on Lila Hunt not ten feet away. Her beautiful face was flushed above her black silk blouse and pearls. It was impossible to tell whether it was from the excitement of the event or from anger that I was having a tete-a-tete with Lucy. My red dress suddenly felt too tight, but my stomach muscles refused to tighten up and I was certain I resembled a pot-bellied old broad in her daughter's clothes.

"You don't have to give me anything," I said, wondering if Lila would have said the same thing had the tables been reversed. "I'm just thankful we found out the truth about David's death." I shifted the wine glass from one hand to the other as Lucy moved in a little closer. Our faces were now only inches apart.

"I owe you everything," she said, "and I've acted like a first class bitch."

This was becoming very uncomfortable. "Oh, cut it out, Lucy," I said. "We know each other too well for that. It's okay, look, a lot of people are waiting to talk to you. I'll catch up with you later." At last I spotted Gussie. She was watching me with a funny expression on her face.

"No, no, wait," Lucy said. She touched my arm lightly. "I want you to have the painting."

Painting? What painting?

"What are you talking about?" I said.

"The black plastic, the forest scene. It's yours. It belongs to you."

She could have told me I lost my underpants in the middle of the gallery and I would not have been any more stunned. "The paper said an undisclosed collector bought it," I said.

She smiled. Her green eyes glistened. The feather on her hat dipped slightly in approval. "Do what you want with it," she said. "I was the undisclosed collector. It's yours. Now let me get back to the wolf pack before they eat both of us alive." Instantly she was absorbed by the crowd.

"So," Bernard said in a loud whisper, "you going to sell out to the Japanese?" I turned around to see him standing near a potted plant.

"You heard."

"Every word. Quite a scene. An art to art talk. Should have been in a movie." He took me by the elbow and edged me towards the front door where Gussie was waiting, trying to look as inconspicuous as possible. It didn't succeed. Every man who walked by turned to give her the once over. Actually, a couple of them glanced at me, too. Bernard glared back at them. I felt safe and secure. As we pushed our way through the crowd pouring into Lila Hunt's gallery I caught a reflection of myself in Lila's front window. My stomach didn't stick out at all. I grinned at my reflection and wondered how difficult it would be to learn Japanese.

THE END